Also by Constance Laux

Diamond Rain
Devil's Diamond

LORDS OF DESIRE

Diamonds and Desire

∞

Constance Laux

A SIGNET BOOK

SIGNET
Published by New American Library, a division of
Penguin Putnam Inc., 375 Hudson Street,
New York, New York 10014, U.S.A.
Penguin Books Ltd, 27 Wrights Lane,
London W8 5TZ, England
Penguin Books Australia Ltd, Ringwood,
Victoria, Australia
Penguin Books Canada Ltd, 10 Alcorn Avenue,
Toronto, Ontario, Canada M4V 3B2
Penguin Books (N.Z.) Ltd, 182–190 Wairau Road,
Auckland 10, New Zealand

Penguin Books Ltd, Registered Offices:
Harmondsworth, Middlesex, England

First published by Signet, an imprint of New American Library,
a division of Penguin Putnam Inc.

First Printing, August 2000

10 9 8 7 6 5 4 3 2 1

Copyright © Connie Laux, 2000
All rights reserved

PUBLISHER'S NOTE
This is a work of fiction. Names, characters, places, and incidents either
are the product of the author's imagination or are used fictitiously,
and any resemblance to actual persons, living or dead, business
establishments, events, or locales is entirely coincidental.

Another one for David

Chapter 1

London, 1897

Aggie O'Day's shapely backside had always been more of an asset to her than was her keen mind. It was a sad fact—but sadly, true—and once she'd reconciled herself to it, she'd learned to use it to full and devastating advantage.

A shapely backside, a smile that was known to melt male hearts at twenty paces, a face as sweet as a Botticelli maiden's. Fleeting attributes at best, Aggie knew, but for now they served her well. It was, after all, not her intellect that had first earned her access to the offices of Horace Wallingstamp, the publisher of the *London Daily Enquirer and Illustrated News Chronicle*. The Smile had gotten her through the *Chronicle*'s front door. The Smile and a wink bought her way past the clerk who sat guarding Mr. Wallingstamp's office like an avenging angel.

In a perfect world, Aggie's ambition, along with her razor-sharp intelligence, would have been sufficient to convince Mr. Wallingstamp that she had what it took to be a newspaper reporter. But this wasn't a perfect world. Aggie was practical enough to admit that. And honest enough to recognize that Wallingstamp's final decision to hire her was influenced not by brains, or attitude, or even initiative, but by the Smile.

She was enough of a realist to know that a shapely backside didn't hurt, either. At least not usually.

"Oh, hell!" Grumbling under her breath, Aggie held her skirt up under to her chin while she tugged hard at the front of the trousers she was trying to squeeze into. Though she and her brother, Bert, were of a size, the cut of his trousers told her beyond the shadow of a doubt that the two of them were not of a shape.

With a final and definitive effort, Aggie fastened the top button. She held her breath, then slowly let it out. The trousers didn't burst. Heartened, if not completely comfortable, she proceeded to do up the rest of the buttons and managed a smile nearly as tight as the trousers.

Moving slowly so as not to disturb the rhododendrons that hid her from view of the residential neighborhood just on the other side of the bushes, Aggie slipped off her skirt. She got rid of her jacket, too, and her high-collared white blouse. She'd worn one of Bert's black wool jerseys beneath it, and once the blouse was discarded, she smoothed the sweater into place and felt through the darkness for the sack she'd brought along to stow her clothes. That done, she lifted Bert's broad-brimmed fedora from the grass at her feet, wound her long red hair into a tight knot atop her head, and shoved the hat down on it.

"There," Aggie whispered. "How do I look?"

In the faint light of the gas lamp that glowed beyond the shelter of thick rhododendron leaves, Aggie saw her brother open one eye, then the other. He looked relieved to see her finally and fully dressed, or at least more relieved than he'd looked all the while she was struggling with her clothing and he'd kept his eyes squeezed shut. Now he peered through the darkness in her direction.

"Cor!" Bert breathed the single word with a mixture of amazement and reverence. "Our own mum wouldn't know you! Crikey, Aggie, but if you don't look like a bloke. Leastways what I can see of you. In all them black clothes, bless me if you don't blend right into the night!"

Aggie smiled. "That," she told him, "is precisely the idea. Now . . ." She brushed her hands together and took a step toward the high brick wall that separated them from the grounds of Raleigh House. From beyond the wall, the sounds of music and laughter cascaded out of the house, rolling toward them in muffled waves over the well-manicured lawn. "Give me a hand, Bert. It's up and over the wall!"

"Aggie—" Bert stepped forward, but he didn't offer a hand. He looked from Aggie to the wall and back at Aggie. For a lad of twenty, Bert O'Day could be remarkably mature when he had a mind to be.

Aggie groaned. Something told her this was one of those times.

"It ain't smart," Bert said, and though he tried his best to sound as self-assured as he could to a sister who was six years older and a good deal more worldly-wise, he didn't quite meet her eyes. "I've said it afore and I'll say it again. It ain't smart you goin' in there, Aggie. And it ain't right."

"Right? Piffle!" Aggie brushed off the comment with a quick flick of her hand. "Since when does right have anything to do with the newspaper business?"

"Well, it may be as that's how you folks at the *Chronicle* see things, but it ain't the way the rest of

the world works. There's such a thing as scruples,
Aggie. And chivalry."

Scruples were not something Aggie liked to think
about. Especially when it came to her work. She
skirted the issue completely, focusing instead on what
she knew to be Bert's biggest weakness—his soft
heart.

"Chivalry! That's what this is all about, isn't it,
Bert? You don't want me to go in there"—she tipped
her head in the direction of the wall and the ostenta-
tious town house she knew lay beyond it— "because
you want to do it!"

Even in the dark, Aggie could see her brother
blush to the roots of his carroty hair. It should have
been enough to endear him to her. Instead, it simply
confirmed everything she knew about the way the
world worked. And about a woman's lack of place
in it. Everything she knew about men.

With a grunt of disgust, Aggie turned back to the
wall. "Give me a hand up," she said. "I'll show you
soon enough what I'm able to do."

Bert's voice was pleading. "But if you're caught,
Aggie . . . if you're found out . . ."

It was hard to argue with Bert when he was being
so damned sincere.

Aggie let go a long sigh, half of it made up of
surrender, the other half of frustration. "I'm not
going to be found out," she told him. "Not if I'm
quick and careful. I've explained it all to you before,
Bert. What with all the guests, everyone in the household is bound to be busy. Too busy to notice me.
Besides, it's not as if I'm going in to steal anything.
I just want to have a look."

"Right. A look. Around the home of Maxwell Barclay. While he's hostin' a party for every nob in Lon-

don." Bert shook his head in disgust. "It's as daft a plan as you've ever had. And you've had daft plans aplenty. He's one of the richest men in the world, Aggie. And from the look of the carriages that have been goin' in and out all evening—" Bert glanced over his shoulder. As if on cue, another dashing coach passed through the gates thirty feet to their left. After stopping briefly so that the coachman might announce his passengers to the servants who waited at the gate, the carriage rolled down the winding drive that led to the front of the house.

"It looks as if anyone who's anyone is here tonight. If you go marchin' in there"—Bert poked a finger in the general direction of the house—"chances are you'll come marchin' out on the arm of a constable."

"Not if I don't get caught!" Aggie growled the words between clenched teeth and looked toward the drive and the uniformed servants, who were even then moving forward to welcome another carriage. She signaled Bert to keep his voice down and stepped closer, her own voice a harsh whisper. "We've been over this a thousand times. I've got to get a look at Arthur's Crown before Barclay puts it on display. You know that well enough. Every newspaper in the city is talking about the crown and not one person has seen it yet. If I'm the first—"

"If you're the first, you may be the last."

"The last? What are you saying? You mean—" A sound somewhere between a laugh and a sob choked out of her. It was sweet of Bert. Really. But he didn't really think . . . ? "Is that why you want to be the one to take the chance of going in there? You're afraid for me? And it isn't because of the police, is it? You're thinking of the curse!"

The words of the curse had been printed in the

Chronicle dozens of times since the crown had been unearthed in Wales by one of Barclay's crack archaeological teams. His voice low and mysterious, Bert repeated them: " 'All hail the monarch of the Britons who possesses this crown. Woe be to whoever does dare to defile it. Death and destruction shall follow its path. And glorious praise to the rightful sovereign who is its owner.' " With a shiver, Bert shook off the spell of the ancient curse and was himself again.

"That's the curse, and you know that well enough yourself," he said. "You've written all about that there blinkin' crown time and again since it's been found."

For a long moment Aggie couldn't bring herself to respond. Bert was a trusting soul, and for that, she supposed, she should be grateful. Without thousands of trusting souls who spent thousands of their pennies every day for stories such as the one about Arthur's Crown, the *Chronicle* would be out of business and Aggie out of a job. Still, he was her brother, and he obviously cared enough about her to sacrifice himself on her behalf. For that, if for nothing else, she owed him the truth.

"Bert . . ." Aggie gathered her thoughts and the courage to destroy his illusions. "Bert, when I wrote that story about the headless ghost in that church in Croydon—"

Just thinking about it made Bert's eyes grow round as saucers. "Cor! You must have been frightened, and that's for certain. Goin' into that haunted church all by yourself where that weepin', wailin' ghost was—"

Aggie interrupted before he could go any farther. "What about the story I wrote about the monster in the Thames? You remember. There was a man on the docks who swore he'd seen it."

"A cousin of that beastie up in Loch Ness. Yes, of course I remember, Aggie. It was the talk of the town for days on end. But—"

"And the cabinet minister who is really the emperor of Ethiopia in disguise? And the beings from other planets who some say live right here in London?" She looked at her brother long and hard. "I have no doubt you remember those stories, too. But think about them. Are you sensing something here, Bert? Are you seeing a pattern?"

"You're right. Yes. Of course." Bert accepted the ugly truth far more stoically than she had expected. "I understand exactly what you're sayin'. You are bold, there's no doubt of that. If you are brave enough to face such horrors as headless ghosts and people from other planets, you are certainly capable of nippin' into Maxwell Barclay's and—"

Had they been anywhere else, Aggie would have screeched with irritation. Instead, she curled her fingers into her palms, holding in her annoyance. "I am not brave," she insisted in no uncertain terms. "And I'm not bold. At least not in the way you're thinking. What I am is a liar, Bert. A practiced, artful, accomplished liar. You don't think any of that is true, do you? The monster in the Thames? The headless ghost?" Aggie couldn't help herself, she had to laugh. "Damned if you're not as gullible as the rest of the world!"

Was it Aggie's imagination or did Bert seem to deflate before her eyes? He blinked at her in silence for a few long seconds, and when he found his voice, it broke over the question he was obviously reluctant to ask. "Then the story . . . about Arthur's Crown . . . it's . . ."

"Oh, there's a crown right enough." According to Aggie's sources, that much was true, and she refused to let Bert worry over it. "And if the reports are to be believed, it's a crown like no other. Ancient as the Round Table. Gold encrusted with diamonds."

"And the curse?"

"Doom and pestilence! Death and suffering!" Aggie caught herself before she burst into laughter again. She stifled the sound, one hand over her mouth. "It's gammon and spinach, Bert," she said once she was able to control herself. "All smoke and pickles. Curses sell newspapers! And I daresay Barclay doesn't mind one bit. The more interest I stir up in the thing, the more people he's likely to get to pay their pennies when he finally puts it on display."

The truth dawned and Bert nodded, but where Aggie expected him to be disappointed, a new kind of admiration glowed in his eyes. He joined in the game readily enough. "Then you think you can create a sensation? With the stories about Arthur's Crown? If folks think as how there's a curse on the blinkin' thing—"

"Now you're getting it, Bert!" Aggie clapped him on the shoulder. She turned to the wall, ready to scale it. "The more exciting a thing is, the more likely it is that people will want to read about it."

"Like that there Shadow fellow?"

Bert's words stopped her in her tracks. In spite of her resolve not to let her annoyance show, Aggie gave a quiet harrumph. It seemed there were only three topics of interest in London that spring: The celebration of the queen's sixtieth year on the throne, which was scheduled for June. The curse on Arthur's Crown. And the Shadow.

The subject of the Shadow was an especially sensitive one, and Bert knew it. That, of course, was exactly why he'd mentioned it.

For the better part of three years, the man known only as the Shadow had baffled Scotland Yard and bewildered London Society. He was the boldest of jewel thieves, a man known only by the calling card he left at the scene of every robbery. He targeted the rich and the well-connected and had been involved in a string of celebrated burglaries, including one particularly baffling caper in which he'd managed to carry off an ancient, and priceless, Greek artifact from the British Museum. Thanks to a stream of melodramatic and sensational newspaper accounts, the Shadow had become something of a legend. To Aggie's endless chagrin, not one of those newspaper articles had been written by her.

"There you ago, Aggie, my girl. Don't look so upset." Bert's smile was tipped with just enough sarcasm to let her know he was evening the score. As much as he tried to pretend it didn't bother him, it was obvious he didn't like his illusions destroyed, whether they were about curses or beasties in the Thames. "You'll have your chance at the Shadow one of these fine days."

"And do a better job of it." This time when Aggie harrumphed she didn't even try to keep her displeasure in check. "Wallingstamp doesn't know what he's missing," she hissed. "That's as certain as certain can be. He sends me out looking for headless ghosts and humbug sea monsters and gives every lead about the Shadow to Peter Askew." She tossed her head, a vigorous movement that did little else but

knock her hat awry. Straightening it again, she set
her jaw. "They'll learn a lesson this time, won't they?
Wallingstamp won't dare ignore me any longer. Not
after I'm the first outside Barclay's circle to see Arthur's Crown. Bright and early tomorrow morning,
I'm going to present Wallingstamp with a sketch of
the thing." She touched the pocket of her trousers
and the small leather-bound drawing book she'd
tucked away there. "He'll know my true value then."

"Cor, and if you ain't the smartest woman in London." The fact, of course, was undeniable, but Aggie
was grateful that Bert had finally realized it. "Only,
you'll be careful, won't you, Aggie?"

It was too late to worry about being careful. Aggie
knew it. But Bert didn't have to. "Of course I will,"
she told him. "And you stay put and be quiet. Those
servants at the gate won't have much to do after the
last carriage is in. They'll be lounging about looking
for a little excitement. Make sure you're not the one
who gives it to them. I'll be back as fast as I can."
Aggie gave her brother a smile and a wink. "With a
drawing of Arthur's Crown."

Convinced at last, Bert cupped his hands, and
when Aggie stepped into them, he boosted her to the
top of the wall.

Crouching low, Aggie reached for the bull's-eye
lantern he handed up to her and waited for the next
carriage to approach the gate. It was the safest time
to make a dash across the lawn, she'd decided, when
the servants at the gate would be far too busy to
notice her.

With the shadow of an oak tree cloaking her, Aggie
watched silhouettes glide past the brightly lit windows of Maxwell Barclay's glittering ballroom and
listened to the captivating melody of a waltz. Outside

the tall French windows, guests were scattered on the wide veranda. Women walked arm in arm, their evening gowns ghostly white in the darkness. Men talked together in small groups. Here and there, a couple left the crowd and headed into the privacy of the garden.

The whinny of horses drew Aggie's attention away from the house and back to the matter at hand. She tensed, waiting for the carriage to pull up, and when it did, she gulped down a breath for courage, grasped the bull's-eye lantern in shaky fingers, and hopped down off the wall, heading toward Raleigh House and the elusive treasure that lay inside.

"Lord Stewart! Fancy seeing you here!"

It was not the first time that evening that Stewart Marsh had endured much the same comment. Ever since he'd arrived at Maxwell Barclay's, he'd found himself in the uncomfortable position of socializing with all the people he usually did his damnedest to avoid. This was at least the sixth time in the last hour he'd bumped into some crusty old warhorse friend of the family. Like all the others, this old fellow delivered the statement with all the huffing and puffing that made it unnecessary for him to add, "And about time you got yourself out into public, too."

As he had done the five times before, Stewart replied with the vague sort of smile everyone expected from the Marsh who was more famous for his scholarly pursuits than for his social skills. Right before he offered some mumbled excuse and disappeared back into the crowd, he heard it again:

"Lord Stewart! Fancy seeing you here!"

There were times that evening when he'd heard the statement spoken with all the astonishment

Moses must have felt when he saw the burning bush. Other times he'd heard much the same words whispered person to person behind his back. There were two times—no, three, he corrected himself—when he'd encountered women of his acquaintance. Each time, the woman's eyes had widened. Each time, the statement had been delivered in a breathless sort of whisper, filled not so much with surprise as with anticipation.

And each time, he'd acted exactly the way he was supposed to act. As if his mind was preoccupied with more important things and he didn't have the slightest idea what the lady might be hinting at.

Stewart sighed. He wasn't really disappointed. From what he'd seen of this year's crop of Society darlings, there was little to choose from and even less of interest. Still, it was one thing to be a genius. It was another to always be expected to act like one.

Even so, Stewart played his part and, if he did say so himself, he played it especially well. He was appropriately ill at ease when it came to making small talk, singularly erudite when someone asked his opinion about the newest scientific discovery.

Yet even that, it seemed, was not enough. Society was filled with perils for any man, brilliant or not. Especially a man who was young, wealthy, and—if the remarks he occasionally overheard were accepted as true—particularly handsome, even if he was obliged to wear spectacles.

It was no wonder he usually did his level best to avoid these dreadful galas! Not four hours into the evening and already he'd had to rise to several challenges. He'd been adroit enough to keep from being dragged out on the dance floor. He'd been clever enough to keep from becoming entangled in what looked to turn into an ugly altercation between the women who sat on either side of him at dinner. He'd been quick enough to escape his Aunt Winifred, an ancient old bird with a reputation as a formidable matchmaker and a girl in tow whose face could stop the most dependable eight-day clock.

The effort had soured his mood considerably. And generated a fierce thirst. As eager to quench it as he was to avoid any further entanglements with elderly aunts or women with hope in their eyes and lust in their hearts, Stewart hurried toward the only place where he knew the drink would be stronger than champagne and the company exclusively male—the cardroom. He threaded his way through the throngs of men who lounged about watching the games at various tables and headed for the whisky bottle and soda siphon that had been set upon a rosewood table on the far side of the room.

No sooner had he poured himself a generous drink than he felt a friendly whack on the back. "Stewart!" someone called above the general buzz of voices that filled the room. "Fancy seeing you here!"

Ready to make his excuses and escape as quickly as he could, Stewart turned. He was much relieved to see the Earl of Longstock, his eldest brother, beaming at him from behind a newly grown and quite lavish moustache.

"Charles!" Stewart pumped his brother's hand and smiled, genuinely relieved. "You're looking well. How are Susannah and the children?"

Much to Stewart's dismay, Charles ignored the question, focusing instead on the same subject everyone else seemed to be obsessed with: the fact that Stewart—as famous for his love of privacy as he was for his aversion to the London social scene—had actually accepted an invitation to a dinner party.

Charles stood back and took stock of his youngest brother. "I don't believe it! Ned said you were here." He nodded toward their brother Edward, who was watching a nearby game and who, when he saw them together, made his way in their direction. "I told him he must be out of his mind. Stewart? Hobnobbing with Society? I told him he was mad!"

"I might be mad, but I know my own brother when I see him." Edward joined them, resplendent in the uniform of the Queen's Horse Guards. He clapped Stewart on the back in greeting before he poured himself a drink. "I told you he was here, Charlie," Edward said. "I'd know this Long Shanks anywhere! He's at least a head taller than the rest of the crowd. Easy to spot, eh?" Edward poked Stewart in the ribs. "Especially for old Aunt Winnie."

"I hear Aunt Winnie isn't the only one looking for him."

Where he came from, Stewart had no idea, but they were joined by their brother Matthew, who might have looked every inch the archdeacon of the church that he was if not for the hint of devilment in his eyes. "I hear there is more than one young lady hereabouts who's ecstatic at the prospect of finally sinking her claws into the delicious young Lord Marsh! What say you?" Matthew gave Stewart a broad, theatrical wink. "You wouldn't want to disappoint the ladies, would you?"

"I hear they are already disappointed." Like magic, the other two Marsh brothers appeared, George from one direction, Lowell from the other. George was for all intents and purposes a respectable banker, but he fancied himself something of a ladies' man. Considering the subject, it was no surprise he would join in the fun. "They flirt with him like mad, you know, and—"

"And he prefers his dusty books and his musty library!" Lowell was a barrister and not about to let anyone else have the last word. Though he was the smallest and the slightest of the six sons of the Viscount of Chilbury, he jumped into the fray in much the same way he always had when they were all younger and tumbling through the halls of Chilbury Manor.

Stewart was taller than the lot of them and broader than all but Edward. He was a better horseman than George, and faster by far, both mentally and physically, than Lowell. Though he was not nearly as spiritual, he was far brighter than Matthew, and though Charles would make a perfect viscount once their father was gone, there was no doubt that if Stewart put his mind and his considerable talents to it, he would be just as able an administrator and a damned sight better orator than either the present or the future viscount.

Yet even at thirty years old, he knew none of that was enough to compensate for being the youngest of six. Not of these six.

Stewart sipped his drink, feeling much the same as he had back when he was a boy and his brothers joined forces to torment him. He'd learned long before that there was only one way to retaliate. Only one way to stand his ground and keep his pride, and prove his worth both to them and to himself. He simply had to be quicker, and more clever, and a good sight more cagey than the rest of them.

Casually, he glanced around the closed circle his brothers had made around him. Except for George,

who'd had the unfortunate luck to inherit both their
mother's mousy coloring and her considerable over-
bite, the others all shared the famous Marsh good
looks and coloring—hair that was chestnut-dark and
eyes that some compared to sapphires and others, to
ice. "I might ask what the rest of you are doing
here," Stewart said, his gaze traveling from his brothers to the red-velvet-covered walls and the gilt trim
that seemed to have been painted on anything that
didn't move. "I thought we Marshes lived in the
ether, far above the nouveaux-riche."

"At least we have a good excuse." George tossed
down what was left of the whisky in his glass and
handed the empty tumbler to a nearby servant. "The
real social season won't start for another six weeks
yet, and there hasn't been much to do. The ladies
are frightfully bored." He rolled his eyes, no doubt
recalling some recent conversation with his wife, a
woman who was known to be nothing less than difficult. "When this invitation came, my Margaret went
rabid. 'We must meet this Barclay fellow,' she claimed.
'He is all the talk of London!' "

"Him and that crown of his everyone is nattering
about."

Matthew's comment was innocence itself, but it hit
far closer to the mark than Stewart would have liked.
Hoping to let the subject die a natural death, he made
a great show of pouring himself another drink. He
might have known his brothers would not let so obvious a comment slip by. They were all over it in
an instant.

"That's it, of course!" Lowell fairly crowed. "That
explains everything. It's why Stewart is here. If the
newspapers are to be believed, this Barclay fellow
has a veritable treasure trove of antiquities. He's col-

lected them from all over the world. But odds are it's the crown you're after, eh, Stewart? You're hoping for a look at the thing."

Stewart turned to find his brothers looking damnably pleased with themselves.

"I hardly want to take a look at the crown," he said and comforted himself with the thought that for once he was actually telling the truth. He removed his wire-rimmed spectacles and wiped the lenses with his silk handkerchief. "What I mean, of course, is that a gold crown encrusted with diamonds seems an impossibility given the historical context," he told them. He replaced his spectacles carefully. "The real Arthur wasn't some medieval monarch with stacks of gold and jewels. He was, more than likely, a Dark Age Celt. One with Roman sensibilities. If you consult Bede or Geoffrey of Monmouth you'll undoubtedly see what I mean. And as for a curse . . ." This time Stewart didn't even try to disguise his skepticism. "Now if the crown were Sumerian, or even—"

"Don't get him started!" Edward led the laughter that greeted Stewart's impromptu lecture. "You have been squirreled away in that library of yours for too long! We're talking gold, man! And diamonds! Enough to pay a king's ransom! You must be interested! The newspapers certainly are. News of the crown and its curse has eclipsed even that of the Queen's Diamond Jubilee. Everyone in the entire empire is interested!"

"I'm sure that Shadow fellow is."

Again it was Matthew who seemed, whether he knew it or not, to get right to the heart of the matter.

"They say he's made two attempts on it already." Lowell repeated information he must have picked up in one of the more bourgeois of London's newspa-

pers. It wasn't true, of course. Stewart knew that for
a fact. But he wasn't about to add his opinion to the
lively discussion of crime and burglary that followed.
Stewart listened as his brothers examined and discarded every theory that had been paraded through
the popular press.

"Man's a menace," George said with a bark of
righteous indignation.

"A reprobate," Lowell remarked.

"There are those who say he must be a magician,"
Matthew chimed in. "Or an accomplished actor."

"Or a madman," Charles offered.

"Still . . ." Edward swirled the whisky in his glass.
"Whoever he is, you've got to give the fellow credit.
He must have nerves of steel."

"I'd say, rather . . ." Stewart had been waiting for
the right moment to put an end to their speculations.
He'd found it, and as if pronouncing some especially
learned theory, he cleared his throat and blinked at
his brothers from behind his spectacles. "I'd say,
rather, that other portions of the man's anatomy are
built of solid brass."

The strategy worked, just as he'd planned. In the
bellow of laughter that followed his remark, he took
his leave, and while his brothers were still chuckling
and wondering that the brother they thought to be
the least cosmopolitan had made the most pithy comment of the night, Stewart left the room.

Outside the doorway, he quickly studied the faces
of the guests who laughed and talked and moved
toward the ballroom, and when he was satisfied that
no one there would detain him, he eased himself
through the crowd and on toward the front of the
house.

In the deserted foyer, he paused long enough to

remove his spectacles and tuck them carefully into his pocket. He took a deep breath, looked around one last time to make certain he was alone, and satisfied, slipped like a shadow up the winding staircase that led to the third floor.

And Arthur's Crown.

Chapter 2

With utmost care and with great and incalculable risk to life and limb, the intrepid reporter, representing the highest and, indeed, the most noble aspirations of the great profession and the best interests of that most excellent example of journalistic integrity and masterful news reporting, the London Daily Enquirer and Illustrated News Chronicle, and its most estimable, enlightened, and discerning readers, crept into the room where Arthur's Crown must surely be concealed.

It was as dark as the inside of a cow, and from all sides, glass-fronted cases gleamed, repositories of those fabulous and priceless treasures unearthed around the world by Maxwell Barclay, tycoon and adventurer. In the thin beam of light emanating from the reporter's own humble bull's-eye lantern, the coins of ancient civilizations sparkled. The jeweled eyes of heathen gods, their faces rendered in masks of gold and silver, twinkled like the glory of a million stars. The curved and diabolic blade of a Saracen scimitar sparkled . . .

"Oh, hell. Not 'sparkled' again. I've used 'sparkled' once already." Her lips thinned with the effort of concentration, Aggie grumbled to herself. As if the artifacts displayed in Maxwell Barclay's gallery of treasures might provide the inspiration she so obviously needed, she stared at the display case directly in front of her. "The curved and diabolic blade of a Saracen scimitar . . . Flashed? Sparked? Burned? Yes.

Of course. That's it." She repeated the recast sentence quickly, committing it to memory. "The curved and diabolic blade of a Saracen scimitar burned through the darkness." Aggie smiled, satisfied.

As soon as she was able, she would record the sentence in her journal, along with the rest of the story she'd been composing in her head, but for now, she would have to satisfy herself with memorizing the words. It was just as well. Working to remember the story she hoped to see blazoned across the front page of the *Chronicle* someday soon helped her forget that her hands were trembling enough to make the light of her bull's-eye lantern waver.

Not that she was afraid.

The very thought made Aggie's jaw tighten with outrage. Fear was not a legitimate emotion. Not for a journalist. Still, she had to admit that creeping through a ground-floor window at the back of the home of one of the world's wealthiest men had a way of making one a bit tense. And scurrying quietly up the servants' staircase and through darkened hallways to a room filled with treasures the likes of which even she'd never imagined did make a girl feel all jitterish.

That would surely account for the fact that her palms were damp and her stomach was dancing like a drunken guest at an Irish wedding. The solution to her discomfort was clear: sketch Arthur's Crown and leave as quickly and as quietly as she'd arrived. Simple, she told herself. If only she could find the bloody crown.

Grumbling with frustration, Aggie swept the light of her lantern over the glass-fronted cases one more time. It was getting late, and she didn't need to remind herself that Barclay's guests wouldn't stay forever. If she was going to find the crown, she had to find it soon.

The thin beam arced around the room, its light touching the tapestries on the walls and the gilded stucco ceiling, the priceless paintings and an assortment of antiquities, both beautiful and bizarre. Finally, it glanced across the door of an elaborately carved mahogany wardrobe that stood against the wall on the far side of the room. A prickle of excitement skipped over Aggie's shoulders. She centered her light on the wardrobe and took a good, long look, tallying its features. "Thick sides. Stout doors. A fine hiding place if ever I saw one," she told herself, and she hurried closer.

It was an excellent place to store a treasure, right enough. Besides its thick sides and stout doors, the wardrobe had a shiny brass lock. Aggie's excitement faded, and she sighed. Even before she yanked on the door, she knew there was no chance it would budge.

Tapping one finger against her top lip, she assessed the lock from either side and cursed herself as she did. For some time, she had been meaning to learn the fine art of lock picking. It was, after all, the kind of skill that could prove useful to a reporter whose talents far outweighed her opportunities, and she always suspected that someday it would come in handy. Now it appeared as if someday was here. And she was ill prepared.

"Oh, hell!" Aggie drummed her fingers against the wardrobe. She considered her options, but only for a moment. "All in the name of journalism," she told herself. She reached into the pocket of Bert's black jacket and pulled out a slim metal letter opener at the same time she promised herself—and Maxwell

Barclay, in absentia—that she would try her best not to do too much damage.

> *As cool as a cucumber, as bold as a miller's shirt, the dauntless and determined reporter began work on what was to be the most extraordinary revelation in a career brimming with astonishing finds. Even against incredible odds and with the ever-present and ominous threat of the curse that hangs over the crown always at the fore, the reporter was not deterred in the all-important pursuit of the truth. Faithful readers of the* Chronicle *deserve nothing less. They deserve to be among the first who will see, albeit vicariously, the fabulous treasure that lay just on the other side of the stout mahogany doors. With steady fingers and a firm and noble resolve, the reporter used such means as were necessary to gain access to the treasure, a means so secret and so marvelous it cannot be explained in these pages, but the effectiveness of which was certain.*

"No bloody chance of that!" Aggie backed away from the wardrobe and the lock that, in spite of her best efforts, refused to give way. She hated to have her thoughts interrupted when she was in the midst of composing deathless prose, yet this time she could hardly help it. Her narrative would be for naught if she didn't find the crown.

Setting her shoulders and adjusting the letter opener in her grip, she made ready to attack the recalcitrant lock again. She had just inserted the letter opener behind the faceplate of the lock when she heard a sound out in the passageway.

The short hairs on the back of Aggie's neck stood on end, and she held her breath. She heard the beating of her own heart and the rush of silence against her ears. Beyond that came the muffled sounds of music and laughter from the party. And nothing else.

Slowly, Aggie let go the breath she'd been holding.

"It's your imagination, my girl," she told herself. She might actually have believed it if the door to the room hadn't swung open.

With the flick of her thumb, Aggie extinguished the flame in her lantern and scrambled for a place to hide. There were French doors on the same wall as the wardrobe, but she had no idea where they led. Something told her this wasn't the time to find out. The closest place of concealment was behind the sofa that stood at a right angle to the wardrobe. On her hands and knees, Aggie scurried around an elaborately carved table, praying she had been quick enough and quiet enough to escape detection.

Her heart slamming against her ribs, she crouched behind the sofa and waited for the person who had come into the room to flick on the switch that would light the electric chandelier that hung at the center of the ceiling. But there was no burst of light. There was no sound other than that of the door whispering closed.

For the space of a dozen heartbeats, the room remained in complete blackness. Then a thin beam of light shone from the direction of the door. Curious, Aggie carefully peered over the back of the sofa. She was just in time to see a shadow detach itself from the doorway and glide silently across the room.

Maxwell Barclay's display room was blessedly quiet, appropriately dark, and, most important of all, just as deserted as Stewart had hoped it would be. This far above the din of laughter and music, the sounds of the dinner party were nothing more than muffled memories. Up here and all alone, he needn't worry about well-meaning brothers or matchmaking aunties or old friends of the family who were eager to catch him up on the latest news. He heaved a sigh of relief. After hours of chitchat that was as tedious as it was uninspiring, he could finally get down to business.

Stewart closed the door behind him and paused, both hands on the crystal knob, his back to the door. He pulled in a long breath, steadying and centering himself, enjoying—as he always did—the tingle that charged through his bloodstream like the recoil that comes from downing a glass of expensive whisky. The sensation was as familiar as it was exhilarating, but he knew better than to take it for granted. Or to stop too long to enjoy it. It wasn't excitement he felt. The thrumming in his veins and the drumming in his heart were alarms, nothing more, warning signals that reminded him he needed to be quiet. And clever. And very, very careful.

In his profession, he could afford to do little else.

It was a sobering thought. Not that Stewart needed it. He was a cautious man and always had been, a man who was deliberate, and determined, and me-thodical. And because of that, he was always success-ful. He asked no more of himself. He expected no less.

Turning the thought over in his head, he pulled a dark lantern half the height of a pencil from a hidden pocket inside his dinner jacket, lit it, and slid the beam of light around the room. With the ease of long practice, he glanced around, quickly and efficiently assessing the room and its contents. Just as he had expected, the walls were lined with glass-fronted cases that contained shelf after shelf of artifacts. Stewart cursed under his breath. What he wouldn't give to take a closer look!

He pushed the temptation away. For now, he had no time to give in to it. The party wouldn't last much longer, and even if it did, there was always the chance Barclay might decide to parade his treasures before one or more of his guests. That would be inconvenient and a damned sight awkward. As if it were a talisman against the possibility, Stewart fingered the Webley's No. 2 pistol he kept in his pocket.

When he saw the mahogany wardrobe that stood against the same wall as the French doors leading onto the balcony, he smiled to himself. If his information was correct—and it had better be, considering the twenty pounds he'd paid one of Barclay's servants—the crown was hidden inside.

Barclay had had the wardrobe designed by a man named Jagger, in Limehouse near the East India Docks, who was remarkably clever when it came to cabinetry work. For a good deal more than twenty pounds (and the promise not to let the authorities know about the devilishly clever folding ladders that Jagger manufactured for a certain less-than-honest clientele, who used them to gain access to upper-story windows), Stewart had managed to persuade the man to describe the wardrobe. In addition to the outer lock, he found out, there was an inner door as well, one with a combination lock.

Eager to get to work, he made his way carefully through the maze of furniture and bric-a-brac that clogged the room, sidestepping what looked to be a fine example of a sixteenth-century Turkish table inlaid with tiles. The lock on the outside door was a stout little thing, solid brass and as sturdy as a spinster's corset. A man who was strong and ambitious enough might use a nickel-plated jemmy to force it, but it would take considerable time, demand considerable effort, and cause considerable noise.

Instead, Stewart set his lantern down on the Turkish table and turned it so that its light shone directly on the lock. Like a skilled surgeon preparing for a particularly difficult incision, he drew a deep, calming breath and pulled a small but useful set of lock-picking tools from his pocket. He had nearly inserted the pick into the lock when he noticed the scratches.

Straightening, Stewart took a careful look at the long, thin indentations that marred the surface of the wardrobe all around the lock. His lips thinned with contempt. Someone had already had a go at the lock, and it wasn't someone who knew what he was doing.

For one moment he actually thought about turning around and leaving. After all, his reputation was at stake. Once the crown was in his possession and he left the calling card that told the world he was the one who'd taken it, he hated to think that anyone—police, journalists, even Maxwell Barclay—might think he had been the one who made a mess of what should have been nothing more than a simple, efficient, and elegant burglary.

But there were more important things to consider than his reputation. Stewart didn't need to remind himself of that. For now, he had no choice but to swallow his pride and damn his reputation. And that was exactly what he did. Right before he inserted his pick into the lock and got down to work.

From her hiding place behind the sofa, Aggie watched as a dark figure crossed the room and stopped directly in front of the mahogany wardrobe. The mystery man moved with all the sleek elegance of a panther, slipping through the room as if he were one with the shadows. He was so quick and so quiet, she might have thought she was dreaming if not for the fact that her heart pounded painfully against her ribs and her breaths came so fast, she had to fight to control them.

Aggie curled her fingers into fists and pressed her nails into her palms, forcing herself to bridle the blind panic that threatened to send her running willy-nilly from the room. She couldn't afford to move a muscle. She knew that well enough. To calm her mind and soothe her spirits, she reminded herself that in her time with the *Chronicle,* she'd faced perils aplenty. Narrow squeaks all, yet she'd managed to find her way out of each and every one of them.

But there never had been one as narrow as this. She gauged the all-too-short distance between herself and the man. It was too far to the door to make a run. Too dark to look around for another avenue of escape. She had no choice but to keep quiet and control her fear.

If only it was as simple to control her curiosity.

Before she could stop herself, Aggie leaned forward to get an even closer look at the man. In the thin light of his own lantern, she could just make out his silhouette, and she took her time cataloging his features, the better to remember them.

He had a well-shaped, if slightly aristocratic, nose. His square jaw spoke of character and breeding. His hair looked to be dark. It was thick, and even while he was standing there, a lock of it drooped over his forehead. Absently, he pushed it back with one hand, and she noted that his fingers were long and slender. Like a musician's. Or an artist's.

His shoulders were broad, his legs long, the build of a man who spent his days in the saddle hunting and his nights in pursuit of pleasure no more strenuous than fine food and gracious company. He must have been a guest of the house, for he was wearing evening clothes: dark trousers and jacket, snowy white waistcoat and shirt. But while the cut of his clothes certainly proclaimed him to be a gentleman, there was something about him that Aggie thought more roguish than genteel. Perhaps it was the way he stood before the wardrobe, his head tipped to one side, his chin just high enough to proclaim an arrogance that was nearly palpable.

Or perhaps it was the lock picks that made her suspicious.

A sizzle of excitement raced through Aggie's bloodstream, and suddenly she found herself far more fascinated than fearful. Her eyes went wide and before she could stop herself, she was fully on her knees, straining for a better look.

She heard a faint *click* and the satisfying sound of the wardrobe door opening. In spite of herself, she knelt a little straighter. But while she hoped to see the glory of Arthur's Crown sparkling back at her from the wardrobe, all she saw was yet another door. One that looked to be made of solid steel.

"Blimey!" Aggie whispered the single word under her breath. Fortunately for her, the man was too busy to take notice. As if he wasn't the least bit surprised by the formidable-looking inner door, he glided his hands over it, apparently checking for weaknesses. When he'd determined there were none, he flexed his hands, rubbed his thumbs over the tips of his fingers, and went to work on the combination lock.

The stranger was dark and dangerous, surely and most thankfully not the kind of man the respectable readers of the Chronicle *are ever likely to encounter. It is just as well, for one look at him confirmed the most unfortunate*

*truth: he was of that pitiable and most lamentable class,
those without conscience or morality, who choose, for their
own twisted and unaccountable reasons, to prey upon the
good fortune of others. The man's eyes were like diamonds,
hard and cold, sparkling now and again with the fires of
greed and the flames of unquenchable avarice. His shoulders rippled with muscularity, every inch of which spoke
of a raw, uncontrollable power that he would, no doubt,
employ without hesitation if he deemed it expedient. In the
light of the lantern he used to ease him through his dastardly task, the tendons in his hands shone, each as knotted
as a rope, bespeaking the kind of strength that is so often
and so deplorably the gift of the unprincipled, the ruthless,
the criminal.*

Though she itched to get at her notebook and record what surely must rank with the finest of her
writing, Aggie held her breath and kept her place.
She watched the man twirl the combination lock
anticlockwise once, then again. As he did, he bent
his ear toward the door. He shifted slightly, angling
his body to get at the lock more easily, and for the
first time Aggie had a good look at his face.

She had been absolutely right about the aristocratic nose and the strong, square jaw, and she congratulated herself, glad to see that her reporter's
instincts were as accurate as ever. But from that
point, she was sorry to say, her imagination had
completely failed her. This was hardly a man of the
criminal classes. He had neither the beetled brow
nor the dark, close-set eyes she expected of a common burglar. He was not misshapen, or unkempt,
or foul, nor did he look unintelligent. He looked
rather like one of the dashing heroes in the novels
that Aggie so enjoyed, and for a moment it was all
she could do to keep from sighing her approval and
her appreciation.

He was devilishly handsome, with fine, clear eyes of a shade that some call Chinese blue and others liken to one of those incomparable spring skies that so often spread their beauteous light above the heads of all Britons. His hair was neither black nor that muddy brown which is seen so commonly and so regrettably, but a color more like oak leaves in autumn, deep and rich. This man could not possibly be of the criminal classes. He was far too handsome, far too fine, far too noble to be—

Rubbish! It wasn't often that Aggie discarded her own well-written prose, but this time even she couldn't bring herself to believe it. One look at the arrogant tilt of the man's chin was all she needed to reframe her opinion of him. He was not the type who was destined to be a hero, for the heroes she swooned over in penny dreadfuls were tried and true, courageous and virtuous, dauntless yet humble. And this man was anything but.

He was far too cocksure. Though he was engaged in an endeavor the likes of which would lead to certain incarceration if he were to be discovered, his shoulders were rock steady, his hands firm against the tumbler. He was supremely confident, as bold as brass buttons and as nervy as they come.

He was also as handsome as sin and twice as tempting. And right now, Aggie reminded herself, he was far more dangerous.

The thought caused a shiver of apprehension to tingle across the back of her neck, and that was enough to bring her to her senses. She slid back behind the sofa. Her palms were moist and her hands felt icy. She tugged the sleeves of Bert's jacket down over them and did her best not to give in to the tendency to get all trembly.

There are few times in a reporter's life when fear over-rides all other emotions. As is so often true, fear must be set aside, even in the face of the most formidable odds. Discovering the truth is all that matters, even though it may mean sacrifice and the demonstration of incredible courage. Yet this reporter felt fear. Very real fear. Here was a man of that type which it is far better to avoid, and here was the Chronicle's *stouthearted reporter, no more than a few feet away, witness to his perfidy. If the reporter were discovered . . . If the reporter were found to be there, to, so to speak, shine the good, true light of journalistic integrity on his dark purpose and record his devious deeds for all the world to read and revile, there was no telling what might happen. Was he a violent man? It seemed a distinct and disturbing possibility, for those who are unscrupulous are often vicious as well. Yet the dauntless reporter did not leave. Could not leave. For the* Chronicle *(and all who work under its noble banner) strongly believes its duty to the truth is a most sacred trust. To run would be to deny our most valued and esteemed readers the singular opportunity of watching a felon at work and thus of gaining some insight into his illicit methods, a look behind the face of a criminal and into the pure evil of his mind and his soul.*

At the same time Aggie nodded, satisfied with the progress of her story, she knew her own words were true. As much as she would have liked nothing better than to stay hidden behind the sofa, she knew that if she was to turn this experience into a story—and what a story it would be!—she would have to learn all she could about the man and his methods. She would have to chance another look.

Drawing in a breath for courage and holding it deep in her lungs, Aggie carefully raised herself to her knees and peeked over the back of the sofa.

The man was gone.

It took a full second for Aggie to register the information, but in that second a gamut of emotions rocketed through her—amazement and relief, astonishment and, mostly, confusion. She sank back down to the floor to think through the puzzle. She was barely there when she heard a metallic click very close by. The next thing she knew, the cold barrel of a pistol was pressed against her head.

Chapter 3

"Move a muscle . . . make a sound . . . and I shall splatter your brains all over this very expensive collection of curiosities."

The man's voice was a purr in Aggie's ear, its softness in startling contrast to the hard barrel of the gun against the side of her head. Wide-eyed, she swallowed around the knot of panic lodged in her throat. It wasn't difficult to follow the man's directions. She couldn't have moved if she'd tried. Her body was frozen with fear at the same time her mind raced.

At the moment it hardly mattered that she'd been right about the stranger all along. His public school accent proved he was a gentleman. But the fact that his enunciation was impeccable was not nearly enough to outweigh the facts that he carried a gun and that she'd seen him in action. The man was a professional thief. No doubt of that. He was also brazen, cocky, and as sharp as the business end of a tin tack. Which meant, she very much feared, that he wouldn't hesitate to shoot.

"How long have you been here?" The fellow punctuated his question with a nudge of the gun barrel. "How long have you been watching?"

Though she was sorely tempted, Aggie reminded herself this was not the time to mention that he'd told her not to make a sound. Stalling for time, considering her options—which appeared to be woefully limited—she hunched further into the folds of Bert's jacket and tried her best not to sound as terror-stricken as she felt. "Don't want no trouble, guv." Aggie's voice was no more than a croak from a mouth that was suddenly as dry as her palms were damp. "Just got lost, is all. There I was, looking for the back door, and—"

"And if you expect me to believe that, my good chap, you can go hopping to hell and pump thunder." The man's voice was no more than a whisper, and all the more sinister because of it. He slid the gun away from Aggie's forehead and jabbed it into her shoulder blade. "On your feet," he said. "And don't try and move too quickly. I have rather an extraordinary range of talents, you see. I'm a crack shot, but I have a tender regard for antiquities." His voice dipped until it was no more than a growl. "I'd sooner shoot you straight through the heart than damage any of these marvelous treasures."

Aggie had no choice but to obey. Her knees feeling like India rubber, she rose to her feet. She didn't need to look to know that the man had the gun—and his gaze—trained full on her, even when he crossed the room to retrieve his lantern. She could feel the intensity of his eyes as he tried to get a better look at her, and she instinctively tugged Bert's fedora down further to hide her face.

He was without pity, this man who was one with the night. He was ruthless and depraved, surely not a man who would show kindness to any person, much less one who had discovered him at his nefarious trade. He was callous and cruel, dastardly and debased. He was a crimi-

nal of the lowest order, coldhearted and malicious, hateful
and barbaric and monstrous and—

Aggie stopped before she could frighten herself
further. Her story would have to wait. For once, there
were more important things to consider. Like how
she was going to get out of this situation alive.

She hardly had time to think through the problem
before the man shone the lantern full on her. After
the darkness, the light was blinding. Aggie squinted
and turned her head away, but not quickly enough.
The man grumbled an oath.

"You're no more than a boy!" His surprise was as
evident as his annoyance, but he was, after all, a
gentleman. Thinking he was dealing with a child, he
lowered his gun, and Aggie breathed a sigh of relief.

Clearly bedeviled, the man shook his head. "What
were you thinking, lad? That you could nip into a
place such as this, find a few stray shillings, and nip
out again before anyone noticed? Here's a fine mess
and no doubt."

"Yes, sir." Aggie pulled at the brim of her hat the
way she'd seen so many street urchins do. In the
process, she managed to hide her face a bit more. So,
he thought she was a boy? There was no harm in
that. At least for now. She lowered her voice as much
as she was able. "Does that mean, sir, that you ain't
gonna shoot me?"

"Oh, I'll shoot you, all right. If I have to." He
raised the gun to prove his point, then lowered it
again just as quickly. "But, damn it, I'd really rather
not. You're too young to die, and I do find violence
rather a waste of time and energy. Besides, I'd really
rather not cause a stir. It would bring the fine folks
belowstairs running up to see what had happened,

and I don't think that would be good for either one of us."

"If I'd be shot, I can't see what difference it would make to me, sir."

"You're right. Of course." The man laughed quietly and tipped his head, acknowledging that she'd gotten the best of him. "So, that brings us to the crux of the matter." He set his lantern down on the nearest table and perched himself on the arm of the sofa, tucking the pistol into his pocket. His voice was as sober as his expression. "What are we to do with you?"

"I could go the way I comed." Aggie took a step toward the door at the same time she slid her gaze to the man, noting the details she would need once she began the arduous task of turning this experience into a story—if she lived long enough to tell it. Carefully, she cataloged each and every one of his features: the unexpected hint of laugh lines at the corners of his eyes; the tiny wedge-shaped scar on his chin; the very telling fact that his evening clothes were as fine as she had supposed them to be and had cost far more, no doubt, than a reporter for the *Chronicle* made in donkey's years.

He had the kind of face that could make even the most levelheaded woman swoon. That alone was enough to make the story enticing, at least to the *Chronicle*'s female readers. They liked nothing better than a hint of romance thrown in with their blood and thunder, and unless Aggie was very much mistaken, here was a man who could give it to them in full measure.

Even in repose, his aristocratic bearing was unmistakable, as was his raw, animal strength. Except for a nose that sat slightly askew, as if it had been broken a time or two, his features were even and his chin so strong and steady, it looked to be carved from the noble stone cliffs of this great island. There was more than a hint of danger about the man, a savage, primitive quality that any woman who was wise would recognize and any woman who was decent would do her best to avoid. Yet at the same time, oh, how he tempted! His were eyes that beckoned and lips that might whisper promises too sweet to be spoken aloud. His was a face that would haunt a woman's dreams. His was a heart that could not be taken, but one that, if a woman gave herself to him body and soul, would surely break her heart in return.

"Oh, dear!" Aggie whispered the words, a warning to herself that she was headed in a direction where it was neither safe nor advisable to go. She ignored the tiny thread of warmth that gathered inside her and forced herself to erase from her mind her latest efforts at prose, lest the man see that she was blushing.

She directed herself back to the matter at hand. "Like what I was saying, sir . . ." She took another step toward the door, talking with her chin pressed down into the folds of Bert's jacket, the better to disguise her voice. "I could go the way I comed. Through that there passageway what's outside the door and down the back stairs."

"The stairs? Really?" Was it her imagination or was there a note of genuine admiration in his voice? The man folded his arms across his chest and settled himself more comfortably. "Let me guess how it all came about. You were clever enough to hide somewhere until the servants at the gate were busy. Then you hopped over the wall. Am I right?"

Aggie nodded.

"After which you ran hell for leather across the lawn. Correct?"

Again she nodded, and this time she couldn't help but smile as well.

"The party was going on at the front of the house, and the servants were all busy. That meant the back of the house was fairly quiet, at least away from the kitchen. You must have come in that way. The window of the conservatory?"

"That's right, guv." Finally someone recognized the brilliance of her plan.

"You've got more guts than brains, lad." The man gave a sharp snort of derision. "That's the most unoriginal plan I've ever heard. And the most dangerous. What the hell is wrong with everyone, anyway?" Apparently too exasperated to keep still, he rose and paced the length of the sofa and back again. "Why does everyone think it's so damned easy to be a burglar? It isn't, you know. There's more to it than simply slipping in a window and slipping out again with the family silver. It isn't some kind of sport. It can be devilishly dangerous, which is why you"—he poked a finger in Aggie's direction—"must promise you will never do it again."

"But I—"

"No. That isn't good enough." The man cut off her protest with a sharp movement of one hand. "Did you hear me say it was dangerous? You're far too young to waste your life rotting in jail, and that's exactly where you'll end up, you know. If you're not killed by some outraged homeowner with a blunderbuss. Besides"—he looked over his shoulder at the mahogany wardrobe—"you'll give the professionals a bad name, mucking about that way. Doing damage and leaving behind a mess. You'll never open a lock like that."

"Yes, sir." Aggie took another step toward the door. She had a clear shot at it now. She could run, and she doubted he could stop her, not without causing a ruckus. Still . . .

Her gaze slipped over to the wardrobe. It was a shame to give up so easily. After all she'd been through, it would be an honest, crying shame to leave before she'd even had a look at Arthur's Crown.

Logic warred with her reporter's instincts. The caution suggested by her common sense was just as quickly replaced by visions of the sensation she would create when she showed Horace Wallingstamp her story about the crown, the one that would prove she was his best reporter, even if she was a woman.

It didn't take her long to make up her mind.

Smoothly, she moved toward the wardrobe. "Ain't no wonder you don't think much of the likes of me," she told him. "I ain't never even been in a grand 'ome such as this, what with all these fripperies and such. I ain't much of a burglar, guv, but I suppose as how you know that, you being a professional yourself."

The comment was supposed to put the man more at ease. Instead, his suspicious glare was back in an instant. He pulled himself up to his full, impressive height, and for a second Aggie thought he might strike her. She tensed, waiting for the blow, and was very much surprised when he burst into a muffled laugh.

"Is that what you think? That I'm a burglar?" Bemused, he shook his head. "Now, lad, you may be young, but you are, apparently, not completely addlepated." He stared hard at Aggie. "Do I look like a burglar?"

She had no choice but to answer. Cautiously, she looked up at the same time she prayed the shadows were deep enough to hide those attributes she knew might reveal her gender—the sweep of color in her cheeks and the soft bow of her lips that, as she'd been told by many a man, looked sweet enough to kiss. She bit her lower lip, the better to hide its shape.

Once he had her attention, the man tipped his head, as if daring her to dispute what was so painfully obvious. "Do I?" he asked, briefly pointing to himself. "Do you suppose a burglar dresses like this?"

"No, sir." Aggie shook her head. She looked away as quickly as she could.

"And do you suppose a burglar—a real burglar, not one playing at burglary as you are—would be foolish enough to attempt a robbery while the house is full of people?"

"No, sir."

"There." Satisfied, the man nodded. "That wasn't so difficult to figure, was it? You see what a terrible mistake you've made. I don't suppose there's any reason not to introduce myself. My name is Barclay," he said. "Maxwell Barclay. I am the owner of this house."

"You ain't Barclay!" The second the words left her lips, Aggie knew they were a mistake. She stumbled over them, as if she could call them back. But it was too late for that. The man's eyes narrowed, and he looked at her carefully, suddenly wary.

Aggie turned her head away and scrambled to explain. "What I mean, sir, is I've seen that there Barclay fellow. Comin' and goin', that is, in that fancy carriage what he drives. And you, you ain't him, sir. Beggin' your pardon and all, but he ain't nearly as tall as what you are, sir, or as fine made. He's as ugly as a mud fence, which you isn't, and he's got big ears besides, and—" Aggie gulped down the panic that rose with every word and sidled toward the door. "And I wouldn't 'a thought nothing of it at all, sir, except when you didn't turn on the lights when you comed in, and I suppose as how that don't necessarily mean you don't have any more business here than I do, sir, except that's what I was thinking, is all. And then I was thinkin' as how you was looking for that there wardrobe, sir, and I thought you might be interested in having a look at the crown and—"

"Crown?"

The single word turned Aggie's blood to ice. She froze along with it, and too late, she realized she'd made a colossal blunder. As if to underscore the fact, she heard the faint *click* of a pistol being cocked. In the glint of the lantern light, she saw that the man again had the gun in his hand.

"What do you know about the crown?"

"Know? About a crown?" She managed a laugh that didn't sound the least bit convincing, not even to her. "Why, nothing, sir, I—" Even Aggie wasn't a good enough liar to continue the charade. For once, she'd run out of words. Her shoulders drooped and her insides trembled. She stuffed her hands into her pockets so he wouldn't see how badly they were shaking, and she stared silently into the barrel of the gun that was trained full on her.

"A petty thief, eh? Here by chance and looking for pennies. I think not." As sleek as a shadow, the man slid between Aggie and the door, and if she'd thought him menacing before, there was no doubt she had to think again. She'd aroused his suspicions, that was for certain, and a suspicious man was a dangerous man, especially when he had a gun in his hand.

"Back to my original question. What to do with you?" He reached in the direction of the bellpull that hung against one wall. "We could rouse the house. Since you don't think it's possible that I'm Maxwell Barclay, perhaps you'd get to meet him in the flesh. And perhaps one of his fine, strapping servants could call the police. Then again . . ." He took his hand away from the bellpull. "It would be a pity to interrupt a perfectly lovely party." Step by step, he closed in on her. "The world will hardly miss one less guttersnipe. I suppose it's easier just to shoot you and have done with it. I—"

Aggie didn't wait to hear any more. Where before her options were wretchedly lacking, now they were wretchedly apparent. She had a choice: jail or the grave. She wasn't sure which she was choosing when she snatched the letter opener out of her pocket and chucked it at the man.

Under the best of conditions, Aggie was a poor hurler. In the dark and with her hands all trembly, she missed her mark completely. The letter opener hit three feet to the man's left, shattering one of the glass display cases. The man swung around, his face registering a range of emotions: surprise, annoyance, and finally complete exasperation. It was the last thing Aggie saw before she turned and headed toward the French doors and whatever lay in the darkness beyond them.

She might have gotten there if not for the table

that stood squarely in her path. By the time she saw the low, square shape, it was too late. She tumbled over the table, sending it flying with a crash into another of the display cases. The man let out a curse that was nearly as deafening.

Aggie hit the floor at the same time the table hit a third display case. Glass rained down on her, and she squealed and covered her head. A marble statue next to where she lay toppled, and the head of the thing rolled across the floor and settled next to Aggie's nose. A shield that had been propped on a stand banged to the floor, a large porcelain vase overturned, and a bronze pot bounced past. Aggie dared to look up just in time to see the man with the gun heading out the door.

"Oh, hell!" she grumbled and called after him, "You can't leave me here like this. It ain't fittin'. It ain't proper. It ain't—"

She didn't have a chance to get the rest of her tirade out. The sound of ripping fabric filled her ears, and Aggie covered her head and pressed her nose to the floor just as a large tapestry slid off the wall and landed directly on top of her.

Out in the passageway, Stewart straightened his tie and smoothed his dinner jacket, patting the inner pocket to make sure his pistol was tucked neatly away. He knew it wouldn't hurt to buy himself some time, so he removed the key from the lock of the display room door, clicked the door closed behind him, and locked it. On his way to stand in the shadows along the opposite wall, he deposited the key in the potted aspidistra that took up most of one corner. Silently, he counted to ten, at the same time taking a few calming breaths. After a lifetime of living with a large and exceedingly loyal retinue of Marsh retainers, he knew servants well enough to realize it wouldn't take Barclay's staff long to respond to the commotion. If he played his cards right and paid attention to his timing, he'd be ready for them.

Just as he'd expected, the hue and cry had already begun belowstairs. From the direction of the ballroom, he heard voices raised in alarm, and much as he'd anticipated, the cries were followed by the sound of pounding footsteps. In a matter of moments, the relative quiet of the third-floor passageway was shattered. The man he recognized as Barclay's butler bolted up the steps two at a time. In his wake was an entourage of male servants, including the footman, the wine steward, and a brawny fellow who carried a stout cudgel the likes of which made Stewart grateful he was not the one they would find amid the chaos of the treasure room.

A pang of guilt assailed him, but only for a moment. The lad knew about the crown, and that meant he was anything but an amateur. He'd been sent by someone to try and steal it. If only he'd had the chance, Steward would have liked to question him. He would have liked to find out who that someone was, right before he used his persuasive personality—and the threat of his pistol—to put the fear of God into the boy and send him scuttling on his way.

From the shadows, Stewart watched Barclay's servants arrive at the door of the display room at the same time a gaggle of dinner guests surged to the top of the stairs. By then, it wasn't difficult for Stewart to blend into the crowd. Pasting his most bemused look on his face, he slipped his spectacles on and fell into step beside a heavyset woman who was huffing and puffing from the exertion of taking the stairs. It just happened to be his Aunt Winifred.

"Terrible. Terrible, that's what it is." Aunt Winnie's cheeks were red. Her brow was rimmed with sweat. "There's someone been murdered and no doubt. That must be what the noise was all about. Things tumbling with a terrible thump! Broken glass! Good heavens! I believe I shall faint!" She twined her arm through Stewart's and leaned against him. "It's a good thing you're here, my dear," she said, and in spite of her professions of weakness and her continued heavy breathing, she proceeded to elbow her way through the crowd, dragging Stewart along with her.

They were just in time to watch one of the burlier servants put his shoulder to the door. With each try, a murmur rippled through the crowd, and when the door finally gave way, a titter of excitement went up along with a smattering of applause. The crowd surged forward, then fell back as Maxwell Barclay made his way up the stairs.

It was the first time Stewart had seen their host since before dinner, and not surprisingly, Barclay looked much the worse for wear. No doubt the strain of hearing the noise of broken glass in a room where each object was more precious than the next was enough to put any man's nerves on end. Barclay's face was colorless. His jaw was so tight, Stewart could fairly hear his teeth grinding together. Barclay excused himself through the crowd, and when he approached the doorway his servants moved away to give him room and allow him to be the one to push open what was left of the splintered door. Barclay reached inside and touched a finger to the switch on the wall, the overhead electric light sprang to life, and Stewart, along with the rest of the crowd, strained for a look inside.

The chaos was even more extensive than he had imagined. Three of the display cases were smashed beyond repair, and a fourth was badly cracked, its glass marred by a spiderweb of veins. A suit of Moorish armor lay in shambles of the floor, what was left of an ivory and gold Egyptian obelisk square on top of it.

In the middle of the devastation lay a tapestry with a telltale bulge beneath it. The servants hurried forward and pulled the would-be burglar out from under the tapestry and to his feet. For a boy who was strong enough to hurl a letter opener across a room that landed with a wallop, he was smaller than Stewart had imagined, and from what he could see of the lad's face beneath the bent brim of his hat, even younger than Stewart had expected.

By this time, the crowd further back in the hallway was impatient. They surged forward, and Aunt Winnie, much to her delight, was swept into the room. Stewart had no choice but to go along with her. Her eyes bright with the prospect of more excitement, Aunt Winnie dropped onto the nearest sofa, and Stewart moved to stand near the mahogany wardrobe, cursing under his breath. What a pity to be so close to the crown and not be able to get his hands on it! He contented himself with leaning against the wardrobe. It was as inconspicuous a spot as any, and he crossed his arms over his chest and settled back to watch, curious as to what might happen next. As he expected, Barclay didn't waste any time taking control of the situation.

"You!" His voice shaking, Barclay looked at the servant who stood nearest the door. "Go around and fetch a constable. It looks as if we've caught ourselves a burglar."

"No!" surprisingly, the objection came from the burglar himself. Straining against the grip of the servants who had hold of his arms, the boy struggled to break free. "Wasn't me, guv," he said. "I didn't touch a thing. There was this other bloke and—"

The boy's objection was cut short by Barclay's cynical laugh. "Innocent, are you?" He stepped forward and eyed the boy up and down. "Then explain what you're doing here. And what the hell—" Aware that there were ladies present, Barclay remembered himself. He swallowed back whatever else he might have said and righted the Turkish table.

The lad tried again. Like a trapped animal, he glanced all around the room and, seeing no hope of escape, scrambled to save himself. "But it weren't me, sir. It was another chap. One of your guests, it was."

At the same time a buzz of outrage and incredulity swept through the crowd, Stewart's insides went cold. It wasn't like one of these street urchins to mount a defense, especially not in the face of a roomful of his betters. The boy had spunk, that was for certain, and that meant he could be dangerous.

As unobtrusively as possible, Stewart glanced around, looking for a way to the door and the oblivion of the crowd, but by that time it was too late. The room was packed cheek by jowl with curious dinner guests. He couldn't leave without looking conspicuous, and looking conspicuous was something he tried never to do. Instead, he forced himself to look only mildly interested in the proceedings and watched as the burglar looked all around the crowd. His gaze glanced over Stewart, then dismissed him instantly. It was the spectacles, of course. They were enough to change the look of any man's face, as was the light, and Stewart breathed a small sigh of relief. The lad might be daring, but that didn't mean he was smart.

Just as Stewart congratulated himself for out-witting the boy, the lad's gaze slid across the crowd and back to him. "That's him," the lad said, pointing directly at Stewart. "That's the fellow. Him what's standing over there!"

All eyes turned to Stewart. So did their host. Over the years, Stewart and Barclay had played a game of cat and mouse, outbidding each other at auctions, outsmarting each other when it came to dealing with those shadowy characters who ran the country's illegal antiquities trade. Time and again, Barclay had prevented Stewart from getting his hands on some antiquity he sorely wanted. Time and again, Stewart had been only too happy to return the favor. There was no doubt in Stewart's mind that Barclay suspected he was the one who'd outbid him for the Damascus Emerald, and unless Barclay was completely oblivious, he also suspected—and rightly so—that Stewart was the one who'd bought the Mask of Kali out from under him.

Stewart wondered what else Barclay suspected. Did he question why a man of Stewart's notoriously reclusive habits had accepted this, of all invitations? He'd be a fool not to, and Stewart knew one thing for certain. Maxwell Barclay was anything but a fool.

Looking appropriately confused and bewildered, Stewart watched as Barclay came toward him. He stopped three feet in front of Stewart and looked back over his shoulder toward the burglar. "Is this the fellow you mean?" Barclay asked.

"That's him, right enough." The burglar leaned forward, trying for a better look. "Leastways, I think it is. He looks different, you see. If I could hear his voice, I'd know then for certain. You see, the lights was out and—"

"And this is an outrage!"

With an outcry worthy of his station in life, Charles pushed through the crowd and insinuated himself into the scene, looking every inch the viscount he would someday be. He gave Stewart a look of quiet confidence, but his moustache quivered. For three hundred years, the Marshes had held positions of power and influence within the country, and the breeding of every one of those years was evidenced in the ring of Charles's voice. "What the devil is going on here, Barclay?" he demanded. "Put an end to this nonsense at once. It isn't proper. You can't have some guttersnipe from the streets accusing—"

"Unhealthy, that's what it is." George was right behind Charles, acting, as always, as if the fate of the empire itself depended on his every move.

"Not only unhealthy—illegal," Lowell chimed in. He craned his neck, trying to see past the woman who stood between him and Barclay, and when Ned strode through the crowd to join in the fray, he fell in step behind him. Without a word, Ned took stock of the situation, looking from Stewart, to Barclay, to the burglar, to the devastation that surrounded them all. Slowly, his eyebrows rose, and when he glanced back at Stewart, there was a question in his eyes, one Stewart was grateful he didn't have to answer.

It was Matthew, as always, who put things into perspective. No sooner had he huffed and puffed his way into the room than he burst into laughter. "My brother? A burglar?" Matthew gave Stewart a friendly slap on the back. "That is the most preposterous thing I've ever heard!"

There was no way Barclay could stand up to the Marshes. Not all six of them. A frosty smile on his face, he spoke to Steward from between clenched teeth. "Yes, of course it's preposterous. A man of your standing . . . a man of your position . . . it hardly seems likely that you would spend your time . . ." Reluctant to make an accusation outright, he dismissed the rest of whatever he might have said with a casual wave of one hand. "Yet . . ." He shrugged, the gesture deprecating enough to keep the other Marsh brothers at bay and just defiant enough to challenge Stewart further. "Yet, of all people, why you?" Barclay asked. "Why not that fellow?" He pointed toward one of the other dinner guests, who immediately blustered his innocence. "Or that fellow?" he asked, pointing to another. He poked his thumb into his own chest. "Why not me?"

"Interesting that." Stewart scratched one hand through his hair, mussing it at the same time he managed to shield his face a bit from the burglar's keen gaze. "There is a theory . . ." he said. "A certain doctor Freud in Vienna who believes that a person's motives are not always—"

"Good Gad! Now you've done it, Barclay!" With a groan, Ned dropped onto the sofa next to Aunt Winnie. "Prepare yourself for a lecture."

"An interminable lecture!" George joined Ned and Aunt Winnie.

"An interminable, boring lecture!" Lowell concurred.

"He'll talk forever," Matthew said to no one in particular. "You may as well make yourselves comfortable." Following his own advice, he pulled up a chair, brushed glass off the seat, and settled down.

Before Stewart knew it, all five of his brothers were turned to him, looking if not rapt, at least politely amused. He wondered if they realized how much of a favor they'd done him. Each minute he could stall meant another minute closer to the arrival of the police. And the ignominious and quite timely exit of this burglar who didn't know how to keep is mouth shut.

"Yes . . . Freud . . . Yes . . ." Stewart searched his mind for everything he knew about the subject. "The man is a genius, of course. He believes—"

"Oh, hell!" It was the burglar who interrupted. "Don't you see what he's doing? He's distracting you, is what."

"Now, see here, young fellow . . ." Lowell began.

"Respect your betters, my lad," George chimed in.

". . . in a thing called psychoanalysis," Stewart went right on, easily falling into the part his brothers had so expertly—and so inadvertently—offered to him. Uncrossing his arms, he gestured toward the burglar. "A boy like this—"

Stewart stopped in midsentence. There was a cut on his hand. It wasn't serious, but it was obviously fresh. Anyone with half a brain and even a quarter of the imagination God gave a goose could put two and two together and see that it had been made by flying glass. In all the excitement, Stewart hadn't noticed it—until now. Thankfully, neither had anyone else. Quickly, he tucked his hand into his pocket. But not before the burglar got a look at it.

"Here. Wait a mo'." The burglar wiggled out of the grasp of the servants who had hold of him. "Did you see that, guv?" he asked Barclay. "Did you see the way that there chap has—"

Stewart couldn't wait to hear any more. He had to

do something, and he had to do it fast. Inside his pocket, his fingers brushed the calling card he'd meant to leave on the wardrobe when he left with Arthur's Crown. Calling on a store of sleight-of-hand tricks he'd practiced since he was a boy trying to outwit his brothers, Stewart expertly palmed the card, and with an actor's skill he pretended to see something on the floor beneath the wardrobe. He stooped and came up brandishing the card.

"Here! What's this, then?" Blinking at the crowd from behind his spectacles, Stewart held the card aloft in two fingers. "It looks like . . . It is! A calling card. Here, Barclay." He handed it to their host at the same time he glared at the burglar over Barclay's head. "Read it to us. What does it say?"

Barclay accepted the card, and his eyes popped. "The Shadow!" His voice rose with an excitement that was instantly echoed around the room.

Stewart stepped forward and clamped a hand onto the burglar's shoulder. "That's right, Barclay. You've caught yourself the Shadow."

The room erupted with the sensation, and under the cover of the noise, the burglar grumbled, "I'm damned if I'll let you get away with this." As quick as a cat, the boy sank his teeth into Stewart's hand. The attack was enough of a surprise to catch Stewart off guard. He flinched and pulled his hand away, and the boy took off.

After that, chaos reigned. Stewart made to go after the burglar and ran into George, who had decided to make a dash after the boy himself. It took some doing to calm him down and get him out of the way, and by that time the burglar had already dodged two servants who tried to intercept him and headed toward the French doors. Barclay tried to go after the boy, but that didn't work either. He slipped on broken glass and went down on both knees, cursing all the way. Ned sprang up from the sofa, but Stewart waved him off. Before anyone else had the presence of mind or the quickness of wit to follow, the boy threw open the doors and headed out to the balcony.

Though the burglar couldn't possibly have known what lay beyond, Stewart did. Once he'd learned that Arthur's Crown was being kept at Raleigh House, he'd walked by dozens of times, checking for the entrances and exits he might use to gain quick access and just as quick an escape. Because the house was built on a slight rise, it was not as far a jump from the balcony to the lawn below as might be expected, but the burglar couldn't have known that. Still, by the time Stewart pushed his way through the frantic crowd and onto the balcony, the boy was already going over the rail.

He dropped over the side into the darkness, and Stewart heard a thump and a muffled oath. Cursing himself, his luck, and the circumstances that had turned what should have been a simple burglary into a farce worthy of the most flamboyant London music hall, Stewart followed.

Keeping his knees bent and his muscles relaxed, he dropped over the railing, and when he landed in the soft grass, he rolled and instantly came to his feet. He was just in time to see the boy pull himself upright not a yard away. The lad didn't stop, not even to look around. He took off toward the brick wall that surrounded the property, intent upon reaching the freedom that lay beyond.

Stewart had the advantage. He'd seen the lay of the land. He was larger and stronger than the boy.

But each of the young burglar's steps was fueled by fear, and that made him very swift indeed. They zigzagged across the lawn and through the rose garden and around a series of topiaries that had been planted outside the ballroom doors, with Stewart always just a few steps behind. By the time they neared the wall, each breath felt like fire in Stewart's lungs.

Finally, the boy slowed to gauge the best way over the wall, and Stewart saw his chance. He made a grab for the boy and managed to catch hold of his hat. It came off with enough force to snap the boy's head back. Stewart saw his opportunity. He paused, ready to pounce.

And stopped dead still, too astounded to move.

When the boy's hat came loose, so did the coil of hair that had been wound around his head. A cascade of curls caught the moonlight and tumbled around the burglar's shoulders.

"A woman!" Stewart stared in wonder. Her ruse uncovered, the woman stopped too, but only long enough for Stewart to register a quick impression of her. In the thin light of a half-moon, her hair was the color of a copper penny. Her skin was clear and smooth, like porcelain. Her mouth was open in alarm, her lips full.

She didn't hold still for long. Taking advantage of his surprise, the woman whirled and jumped. She caught the top of the wall and with a grunt, hauled herself to the top, and if Stewart had any doubts as to the burglar's sex, they were erased instantly.

She had a nicely rounded backside, and in spite of the fact that he told himself he should continue the chase, he was, after all, only human. And a male human at that. He couldn't help but appreciate the sight, especially when, once she got to the top of the wall, her trousers split from end to end.

The last thing Stewart saw of the burglar as she disappeared over the wall was a hint of lacy—and very unburglarlike—bloomers.

Chapter 4

"Stuff and nonsense!" Too irate to keep quiet, too incensed to keep still, Aggie slammed her hand against the table with enough force to rattle the crockery. "Listen to this," she said, and when Bert went right on eating the kippers and eggs he'd cooked for tea, she assumed he was listening and read the article on the front page of the day's *Chronicle*.

" 'An attempted burglary last night at the home of prominent businessman Maxwell Barclay has given police a vital clue as to the identity of the Shadow, the infamous thief who has terrorized London for the past three years.' "

"Can't see how that might upset you." Bert shoveled a forkful of kippers into his mouth. He craned his neck to try to see the newspaper lying on the table between them, and when Aggie refused to give it up or turn it so he might have a better look, he pointed to the article with his fork. "It's a fact, ain't it?" he asked. "The police do have their first clue."

"Thanks to me." Aggie drummed her fingers on the table. "And who is it writing the article? Peter Askew, that's who. A man who doesn't have one crumb of my talent. 'An attempted burglary last night at the home of prominent businessman Maxwell Barclay'!" She repeated the opening of the article with a sneer. "Imagine using words as bland as that to tell of something so exciting." In exasperation, she shoved the paper away, then pulled it back again when she realized Bert might try to snatch it.

"Askew wrote the article, and he's got it all wrong. Listen. It says here . . ." She skimmed her finger over the columns of type. " 'Scotland Yard Inspector Stanley Greenfield, who is in charge of the investigation, is now convinced the Shadow is a young man of less than average height with fair skin. The Yard, he says, has Maxwell Barclay to thank for this valuable information, for without his assistance and his very real bravery in facing down the scoundrel, the police would not be this close to identifying the suspect.' "

Aggie snorted. "Hah! They've identified *me*. That's who they've identified. They're looking for a young- ish man, short and fair, when they should be looking for a tall fellow, a very tall fellow with an elegant accent and hair all thick and chestnut brown and eyes . . ." Before she could stop herself, Aggie sighed. "Eyes like—"

"Like the glittering stars that sparkle in the midnight sky!" Bert clapped both his hands to his heart and spoke in a falsetto voice, then dissolved into laughter. "You sound as if you're describing some hero from one of them romantic stories."

"Romantic? Hardly." With a shrug of her shoulders, Aggie sloughed off the memory of the man's blue eyes, his strong chin, and broad shoulders—and the way the sight of him had sent a tingle up her spine. She trailed a finger across the newspaper page and refused to meet Bert's eyes. He had an uncanny way of knowing what she was thinking, and this was one thought she wasn't about to share.

"He's a common thief," she reminded her brother and herself. "Though not so common, if you take my meaning. Bert, I was this far from the Shadow." She held her hands apart only as much as the length of a pistol barrel. "I stared right into his eyes. I talked to the man. And damn!" She brought her hand down on the table again, this time with enough force to knock the toast out of its rack. "No one believed me. They believed him instead. Some nob with spectacles from some hoity-toity family. You should have seen the way he blushed and stammered his way through his explanations as if he were afraid of . . . well, of his own shadow! Still, they believed him."

"And no wonder!" Bert picked up a piece of toast from the table and chomped into it. "First, he's a gentleman. You said so yourself. He was dressed like a gentleman and he spoke like a gentleman and you said as how when the commotion started, those other gentlemen came to his defense. In a house filled with swells, who do you suppose they would believe, him or you dressed up in my frazzled old clothes? Then . . . well . . . there is something else." Bert ripped off a chunk of the toast and took rather too long to chew it. He also refused to meet Aggie's eyes, and it was that more than anything that told her he was going to say something she didn't like. Aggie tensed, waiting to see what it might be.

"It occurred to me," Bert said, "that maybe that there spectacled fellow was right all along. Maybe he wasn't the one you saw trying to pinch the crown. Not that I'm saying as how you're wrong," he added quickly when he saw Aggie's eyes narrow. "But per'-aps, just per'aps, it's as how when the lights came

on, you got confused. You said as how once everyone
crowded into Barclay's treasure room and all the
shouting started, you couldn't be certain. Per'aps the
man you saw going after the crown wasn't the same
fellow that chased you."

Though it was the first time Bert put voice to the
question, it was not the first time Aggie had considered it. It had tumbled around in her head throughout the long, sleepless night. She hated being unsure
of anything, almost as much as she hated admitting
it. Still, it was difficult to escape the feeling, or the
confusion that gnawed at the edges of her confidence.
The pictures flashed through her mind, the same
ones that tickled her imagination in ways that
wreaked havoc with both her single-minded determination and her heartbeat.

One second she pictured the handsome, dashing,
dizzyingly dangerous thief, and her blood heated
and her skin tingled and her pulse thrummed like
the engine of one of those sleek motorcars she'd seen
about town. He was a man with a heart of flint and
eyes of fire, one whose every move was elegant and
whose every look forewarned that there were perils
ahead, both to a woman's heart and to her virtue.

The next second the picture melted and re-formed,
and in spite of herself, Aggie couldn't help but feel
puzzled and sorely disappointed. Could her bold and
handsome thief really be one and the same as the
man who'd chased her through the gardens of Raleigh House?

Even now, it seemed an impossibility. The thief
who'd meant to steal the crown was brave and reckless. And the man who had tried to catch her when
she made her headlong dash to freedom? The tall,
rather ungainly fellow who seemed too often at a

loss for words and too ill at ease in company had little in common with a master criminal. He was reserved and diffident. From behind his spectacles, he blinked at the world at large like a slightly flustered owl, amused at the same time he was baffled. He was handsome enough, surely, in a boyish sort of way, but there was no air of danger about the man, no arrogance, no swagger. Had it not been for one thing, and one alone, Aggie might have convinced herself that they could not be one and the same man.

"He had the Shadow's calling card," she said to Bert. As if he'd been able to follow along in her thought processes and knew how she'd come to the conclusion, he nodded his agreement and his understanding. "It wasn't simply lying there on the floor. He didn't simply find it. And we know I didn't leave it there." The very thought, and all it meant, caused a sizzle of excitement to snake its way clear through to Aggie's bones.

"It's the biggest story of my life!" Aggie leaped out of her chair and paced the modest dimensions of the parlor. She trailed a finger along the back of a threadbare sofa and went to stand near the mantel. "It's the most amazing story old Wallingstamp has ever even imagined. Arthur's Crown is nothing compared to this. And the most marvelous part of it is that for once I don't have to invent any of it! No ghosts or sea monsters. No chasing after government ministers, asking them questions they have no intention of answering. The Shadow's real, and the story's true, and it will sell newspapers by the barrowful. I've seen the Shadow with my own eyes, Bert. I've practically been killed by him, too, though I won't go into how heroic and brave I was about the whole thing. I know what sort of pistol he carries, and what kind of dark lantern he uses. I even know what he looks like, with and without his spectacles. Now, if only I can find out his name!"

Bert nodded, apparently in agreement, but even before he spoke, Aggie knew he would bring up some objection to her plan. He didn't disappoint her. "And what are you going to do when he sees you and recognizes you?" he asked. "It's a known fact that the man is some sort of genius. How else could he have deceived everyone for so long? He's bound to have figured that you're a danger to him, Aggie. And bless me but I'm sure you'll pretend that it isn't true and that it doesn't frighten you in the least and that it doesn't matter, but that means he's a very real danger to you."

It was not the first time the same thought had crossed Aggie's mind. Like the last time, and the time before, she discarded it with a twitch of her shoulders that, had she been being truthful with either Bert or herself, she would have admitted contained just the least bit of trepidation. "He won't recognize me. Not if I'm very clever. And if there's one thing I am, Bert, my boy—"

"It's very clever. Yes, I know." Bert rolled his eyes, but he did it in too good-natured a way for Aggie to take offense. "Does that mean you have a plan?"

"Indeed I do." Aggie hurried back to the table and flipped through the pages of the newspaper. When she found the Society news, she pointed to an item in one of the columns. "Tea party," she said.

"Tea party." Though his enthusiasm hardly matched hers, Bert repeated the words. "You're going to invite the Shadow fellow to tea?"

For an instant, the image was too appealing to discard. Aggie and the stranger. A steaming silver teapot. A bouquet of flowers between them. He would reach across the table and touch her hand and—

Aggie reined in her errant imagination. "No, I'm not going to invite him to tea. But according to this article, there's going to be a tea party at Maxwell Barclay's in one week's time. You see what that means, don't you?"

Aggie didn't wait to find out if he did. Too proud of her plan to wait another moment to reveal it, she plumped down in the chair across from her brother. "He's bound to be there. It's the same modus operandi, as we say in the reporting business. A house full of guests. People coming and going. The kind of well-heeled crowd that is hardly suspect when it comes to burglary. It's the perfect opportunity for him to have another go at the crown, and I'll wager a side of beef to a dozen of claret that he'll manage another invitation. He'll be there right enough." At the very thought, Aggie's heartbeat quickened. It had nothing at all to do with the handsome thief, she told herself, and everything to do with the excitement that came from having such a clever plan. "I'm going to be there, too."

Bert snickered. "Got an invitation, do you? Nice of Barclay to invite you back after all the damage you done."

There were times when Aggie appreciated Bert's sense of humor. This wasn't one of them. She gave him as forbearing a look as she could manage. "I am going to work at the tea party," she explained. "There's bound to be a servant girl at Barclay's who wouldn't mind an afternoon out. I'll pay her. Borrow her frock. Do her job for her. Society folk never bother to look at servants, so even when I find the Shadow, he won't notice me. I'll be just another

64   *Constance Laux*

housemaid. Like the dozens of others who will be
hard at work at the party."

"Yet a man might take a second look at you." It
was not a compliment coming from Bert, simply a
statement of fact. "You've got a way about you that's
hard for a man not to notice, Aggie. And if that particular man does notice, and if he takes a gander,
and if he realizes—"

"He won't." In spite of herself, Aggie remembered
the cold feel of the gun barrel against her forehead.
She shivered. "He can't," she said, refusing to give
the thought further consideration. "I simply won't
allow it. Besides, I'm not planning on getting close
enough for him to see me. Once I find him, I'll just
keep my eye on him. Then I'll fabricate some excuse
to ask one of the other guests who he is. And
that . . ." She brushed her hands together as if the
scheme were already accomplished. "That will be
that. And I'll have a bit of information no other reporter in the empire has. Not even Peter Askew."
Aggie glared down at the *Chronicle*.

"I'll know the name of the Shadow." She had to
smile in response to Bert's look of unabashed admiration. "After all, all I'll need do is follow him, catch
him at his nefarious acts, and the rest will make publishing history!" She shivered, picturing the stir she
would cause and how it would change her life. "The
next time Maxwell Barclay has one of his parties,
Bert, I'll be arriving through the front gate. Guest of
honor, don't you know! The woman who unmasked
the Shadow. It's all very simple, really."

"If you ain't discovered and tossed out on your
arse."

"Discovered? I'm too clever by half for that."
Aggie laughed. "I'll blend in so perfectly, they won't

know I don't belong. And once I have the information I need . . ." She sighed, content. " 'The woman who unmasked the Shadow.' I like the sound of that, don't you?"

"I don't know, Aggie." Finished with his meal, Bert collected the dishes. "It seems a risk, and not just from that Barclay fellow. If this Shadow is everything everyone says he is, he might be a wrong 'un to cross. Is it worth it? For a newspaper story?"

Aggie didn't bother to answer. Worth it? Of course it was worth it.

Bert would not be so easily put off. A plate in each hand, he stopped outside the door that led into the passageway. "We don't need the money that bad, Aggie. Not enough for you to risk your life. I make a good salary over at the printing press. We've got the house free and clear from Mother's will, and with the allowance Papa left us—"

"This has nothing to do with money." But of course it did. Though Bert was younger than Aggie, he had the absurd notion, as did so many others of his gender, that he was responsible for providing for all the family's needs. And like so many other men, he was too proud to accept help. Aggie allowed him his pride. She didn't bother to bring up that though they had the house free and clear, it was sorely in need of repairs. She didn't bother to point out that though they had an allowance from their late father, it was barely enough to keep them alive. She didn't bother to mention—because she wouldn't for the world have hurt Bert's feelings—that though the money he made setting type at a printing house was helpful, it was simply not enough.

But if Bert was allowed his pride, surely she was, too. "This is a matter of principle," she told him, and it was true. "There are women marching in the streets, demanding their rights. Don't you realize it, Bert? Proving myself an equal to any of the men reporters is my way of supporting everything those women march for. It's my way of proving that a woman can have as much talent as a man and can use it just as well. Why should Peter Askew get to write every story about the Shadow? Is he a better writer than I am just because he has a—"

Bert didn't wait to hear any more. His face went pale, then suddenly flushed, and he hurried out the door and into the kitchen before Aggie could finish.

"All I ask is that you be careful, Aggie," he called back to her.

"Oh, I'll be careful, all right." Smiling at her brilliance and at her boldness and at the very fact that her plan could not fail, she closed the newspaper and folded it neatly. "Careful to close the net," she purred. "Right over the Shadow."

There was something about returning to the site of a past humiliation that didn't sit well with Stewart. He wasn't used to being made to look a fool, even if it was only to himself. He stood beneath a billowing tea tent in Maxwell Barclay's garden and he didn't need to remind himself that the last time he'd set foot on the property, he'd been outmaneuvered, outfoxed, outrun, and nearly unmasked.

All by a woman who, by even the most charitable definition, was a rank amateur when it came to the art of burglary. She was without a doubt one of those irrational females who acted long before they thought and managed to create one cock-up after another because of it. She was obviously devious, and shrewd enough to fool them all with her disguise. He would give her that much. Just as he would admit, if only to himself, that she had her share and more of daring. But she was a menace, both to Stewart's freedom and to his mission. He knew that well enough.

And, damn him, but he couldn't get her out of his head.

It was maddening, and, Stewart reminded himself, not at all like him. He was hardly inclined to the poetic, yet today, like every day since he'd stumbled across the woman burglar, he looked at the sun and thought of hair the color of flame. He glanced at the new green of the lawn and was reminded of eyes that sparkled like emeralds in the moonlight. From across the expanse of the tea tent, he heard a woman laugh. It was one of those brittle, desperate laughs a woman uses when she's trying very hard to win a suitor, and Stewart couldn't help but think it pitiful, just as he couldn't help but think of another, very different kind of woman. One who had the temerity to break into the home of one of the richest men in the world. And the neck to stand up to a man with a gun. And the ingenuity to manage an escape when it looked as if all was lost.

He glanced around at the elegant women in their terribly expensive tea dresses and thought instead of the hint of cheap lace he'd glimpsed through the tear in the burglar's trousers and of the nicely shaped and very appealing backside that had occupied far too many of his thoughts and far too much of his time since that night. His temperature soared at the same time his mood plummeted.

"Damn it," Stewart mumbled.

"Talking to yourself again, old man?" As seemed usual these days, Stewart's brothers appeared out of nowhere. Charles grinned at him from behind his moustache. George and Lowell beamed at him over their teacups. There was no sign of Edward or Matthew, but he had little doubt they would materialize soon enough.

"Not talking." Stewart offered his brothers a tight smile. He might have known they'd be here, and it wasn't as if he wasn't happy to see them. If only they stayed out of the way. "Grumbling. I'm grumbling to myself."

"Not a good thing to do," George offered. "You're probably hungry. Here." He thrust his plate toward Stewart. It was heaped with creamed herring, and it smelled awful. Stewart declined the offer with a polite shake of his head.

"Doesn't have anything to do with that ugliness last time we were here, does it?" Lowell asked. "The grumbling, I mean. I for one didn't think you'd accept this invitation. Didn't I say that, George? Didn't I say we wouldn't see Stewart? He would never accept another invitation from Barclay. That's what I said. Surprised to see you, boy. What with Barclay nearly coming right out and—"

"Barclay's a fool." As expected, Edward appeared, and over his shoulder, Stewart saw Matthew bringing up the rear, carrying what looked to be a week's supply of sweets from the buffet table.

"The man insulted the entire family. That's what he did." How Matthew knew exactly what they were talking about was beyond Stewart. He didn't even try to figure his way through the thing. He let his brothers carry on. They would, whether he tried to stop them or not, and the distraction gave Stewart time to look beyond the tea tent, toward the house. From here, he had a good view of the back of the house, and he carefully noted which windows had

been left open and which might offer him the best—
and the least noticeable—access.

"Imagine, thinking Stewart was a burglar!" George
could barely contain his laughter. "No offense, old
boy," he told Stewart. "But you have to admit—"

"It is preposterous," Lowell concluded. "You? A
burglar? I could see Ned as a burglar." He nodded
toward Edward. "He's just the type, don't you think?
All that dash and daring. It's his army training, don't
you know. And Charles would make a splendid burglar. He'd simply browbeat anyone who challenged
him. Why, even Matthew—"

"Certainly not!" Matthew's mouth was full of Ma-
diera cake, but he made as much of a protest as he
could. "I am, after all, a man of the cloth and—"

"And why not?" Charles glanced around at the
circle of Marsh brothers. "I'd venture to guess that
we could all of us be burglars if we were clever
enough. Don't you remember the night of the dinner
party? Not an hour earlier we stood in the cardroom
speculating about the Shadow. Which of us expected
the Shadow to be a young boy? When you think
about it, that's just as preposterous as Stewart being
a burglar."

It was even more preposterous than that, but Stewart wasn't about to tell them so. In lieu of offering
an opinion, he nodded as if he was following the
conversation very carefully and took another look at
the house. From here, he could just see the French
doors that led into the treasure room, and much to
his annoyance, it looked as if Barclay had spent the
last week taking precautions. The windows had been
reinforced with a mesh of steel, and if Stewart wasn't
mistaken, the servant who stood on the balcony outside the French doors was no servant at all but what

the lower classes called a split, a private detective who'd been hired, no doubt, to make sure there wasn't a repeat of the dinner party fiasco.

"Damn." It wasn't until he found his brothers staring at him that Stewart realized he'd been muttering again. "Damned clever," he added quickly. "I was thinking that Shadow fellow must be damned clever. So young and with such a reputation."

"I say, I wonder if the police are any closer to finding him." Matthew popped a piece of seedcake into his mouth and chewed it thoughtfully. "Have they contacted you, Stewart? You were the only one who had a good look at the fellow."

"And there's something preposterous in itself," George noted. "Imagine, all of us there and Stewart the one who had the sense to go after the fellow. Pity he outran you, old boy."

"Pity, indeed." Stewart removed his spectacles and carefully cleaned the lenses with his silk handkerchief. "But you see"—He slipped his spectacles back on—"I didn't have a good look at the fellow, and I've told the police as much. He was too fast for me."

"You got ahold of his hat," Matthew reminded him.

"I found his hat," Stewart corrected him and, with a look, dared them all to challenge the statement. "After he was already over the wall. I found his hat on the ground. Never did have a chance to see the fellow's face. No better than any of us did up in Barclay's treasure room."

"Pity," George observed. Lowell nodded his agreement.

"Pity," Matthew concurred.

"Pity." Another voice joined in the chorus of laments, and Stewart turned to see Maxwell Barclay coming their way with another man in tow.

Stewart needed no introduction to Inspector Stanley Greenfield. Though hardly older than Stewart himself, the inspector was something of a legend in London, a Scotland Yard detective who had risen through the ranks through sheer dogged determination and the force of a personality he'd heard some compare to that of a terrier with the scent of game in its nose. Those qualities, along with his razor-sharp mind and unerring instincts, had allowed Greenfield to crack any number of cases that had come to be known, before his involvement, as unsolvable. Two years earlier, after another of the Shadow's spectacular burglaries (an exquisite scepter set with amber and rubies that had once belonged to Casimir the Great of Poland), Greenfield had vowed to the government, to his superiors, and to the public through a series of dramatic newspaper articles, that someday he would see the Shadow in the dock.

Though he was decidedly out of his element and definitely conspicuous in his brown tweed suit and utilitarian bowler, Greenfield prowled through the fashionable crowd, his gaze assessing and curious. He glanced over the other Marshes with only slightly more than the interest ordinarily afforded them, but when he came to Stewart, his eyes brightened just enough for Stewart to know he had been the topic of some recent conversation.

There was no reason to panic, at least not yet, and reminding himself of the fact, Stewart stood his ground while Barclay introduced Greenfield all around. When the formalities were finished, Barclay turned toward Stewart. "It is a pity, isn't it?" he asked. "Just what I was telling Greenfield here. Pity you were so close, yet never had a chance to see the Shadow's face."

Was it Stewart's imagination, or was there a note of sarcasm in Barclay's voice?

He shrugged off the question and the uneasy feeling that skittered across his broad shoulders. It hardly mattered what Barclay knew, or what Greenfield might suspect. They had no proof, and never would.

"We were just discussing the fact that it was damned high-minded of Stewart to accept your invitation to tea, Barclay." Always the crusader, Matthew broached the subject. Stewart would have preferred that they discuss anything else, but on second thought, he knew he was lucky it was Matthew who'd taken up his cause. Given the chance and the least bit of provocation, the others wouldn't have been nearly as polite. Or as subtle.

Matthew pulled back his shoulders, mustering as much outrage as was possible for a man whose chin was spotted with icing sugar. "You didn't treat him well the last time he was here, Barclay."

"That's right," Lowell added. He looked toward Greenfield, ready to explain, and it was clear, at least to Stewart, that his brothers did not think the inspector's opportune appearance and the fact that he'd chosen the Marshes to converse with, anything more than sheer coincidence.

But perhaps it *was* only that.

The thought crossed Stewart's mind, but only for a moment. In his experience, there was no such thing as coincidence.

"Barclay here nearly came right out and accused Stewart of being a burglar," Lowell told Greenfield.

"And made things damned uncomfortable for him," George agreed.

"And for the whole family," Charles reminded him.

"Which is why . . ." For the first time, Greenfield joined in the conversation. He glanced from brother to brother, his expression not nearly as apologetic as might have been expected from a man of his class. His gaze rested, finally, on Stewart. "Which is why, naturally, I can't help but wonder why you accepted Mr. Barclay's invitation to join him this afternoon."

From behind his spectacles, Stewart blinked at the policeman and mumbled something that may or may not have been an explanation. "I'm here, of course . . . That is, Barclay here was kind enough to invite me, and . . . Of course, it isn't as if I don't understand what happened . . . And I'm upset about it, but really, a man can't . . ."

Stewart went on, delaying at the same time he was hoping to make them all as ill at ease as he, apparently, was. The tactic worked, at least on his brothers. By the time Stewart was done stammering, Charles was looking up at the tent, Edward was shaking his head in wonder, George was examining the tips of his boots, Matthew was well into another slice of Madeira cake, and Lowell was leaning forward as if to help Stewart find the words he was so obviously lacking. Even Barclay looked embarrassed. Only Inspector Greenfield continued to stare, waiting for an answer.

With a sigh, Stewart gave it to him. He shuffled his feet and looked down at the ground. "If you must know," he said, "I was hoping to see someone. Someone I . . . I first met . . . that is, someone whose acquaintance I made the night of the dinner party."

He cleared his throat and looked up again, over the heads of his brothers. There was little comfort in the realization that he didn't have to try hard to look embarrassed. As much as he hated to admit it, even to himself, he knew there was a grain of truth in what he was about to tell them. "I was hoping . . . That is . . . er . . . I thought I might . . . run into a . . . a certain woman."

"I knew it!" Matthew smiled, inordinately pleased, though Stewart did not like to think why. Charles nodded knowingly. George and Lowell grinned. Edward nodded.

Inspector Greenfield had the good grace, or at least the good manners, to accept the statement at its face value. "Then I wish you good luck," he said, and with a look that urged Barclay to come along with him, he backed away into the crowd.

"A woman!" Matthew beamed. "That's wonderful news, boy. Tell us about her."

"Not that little squit Aunt Winnie was towing about," George said, rolling his eyes to the heavens.

"Or those two who were practically drooling over you over the dinner table," Charles added.

"I . . ." Stewart scrambled to provide enough of an explanation to keep them all at bay. He might have succeeded if his attention hadn't been distracted. From across the tent, he heard the sound of merry laugher. He looked over just in time to see a woman on the arm of a distinguished-looking gentleman. The couple had apparently just arrived. Nodding and talking, they worked their way through the crowd. Stewart couldn't see much of the woman. Her back was to him. But he took one look and his excuses to his brothers died on his lips.

The woman's waist was slender. Her shoulders

were creamy. Her hair was adorned with flowers and piled on top of her head. It was the color of flame.

Before he even had a chance to think where he was going or what he might do when he got there, Stewart made his way through the crowd. By the time he got to where the woman stood, his heart was pounding like one of the brass bands that played in Hyde Park on Sunday afternoons, and his knees felt much as they had the night he'd chased after the burglar—as if he'd run too far too fast, with a great deal too much at stake. It was an awkward feeling, especially for a man who prided himself on restraint, yet he could hardly help it. He watched as the woman threw back her head and laughed.

And stood stock-still when she turned around and he had a good look at her. The woman's face was pleasant, not pretty. Her eyes were mediocre, not matchless. Her lips were thin, not full and not at all sensuous. Not the kind of lips that invited kissing.

She was not his burglar.

For some reason he didn't even want to attempt to explain, the realization sent a stab of disappointment through him. It was ridiculous, he told himself. Ridiculous and illogical and absurd to feel so crestfallen when all he should have felt was relieved. He skirted the woman and her companion and headed for the buffet table, hoping to look as if he had some logical destination in mind when he made his impetuous dash across the tent.

Stopping in front of the table, Stewart glanced over his shoulder at the woman. Not that he needed to reassure himself. One look had told him she was not the woman he'd met in Maxwell Barclay's treasure room. That was a very good thing, Stewart reminded himself.

The thought was sobering, and Stewart held on to it with all the determination of a man who knows what's best for him, even if he isn't inclined to acknowledge it. Lost in his own thoughts and not paying the least bit of attention to what was going on around him, he waited patiently while some apparently minor household problem distracted the servants. Once it was resolved, he accepted a plate from a waiting servant.

It was just as well that the red-haired burglar was nothing more than a common thief, he reminded himself, absently instructing a servant to pile his plate with potted shrimps. It was just as well that common thieves didn't mingle with those above their social class. It was just as well that the woman with the dazzling eyes and the face of an angel and the audacity, it seemed, of the devil himself was a piece of his past and would never become part of his present. Or his future.

He was determined to steal the crown, and he wouldn't allow any interference, no more than he would tolerate the distraction of a woman whose face continued to drift through his dreams, no matter how often he forbade himself to think about her. There was little consolation in the thought. And none at all in a plate full of potted shrimps.

Stewart handed his dish back to the astonished servant who'd just given it to him and stalked out of the tent. There was one consolation and one alone in all of this, he told himself. He would never have to worry about it again. Not about the woman burglar. Or the havoc she had caused his usually sound sleep. Or the fact that, as he had already proven once today, just the sight of red hair left him breathless and wondering and not sure if he was afraid it might be her. Or afraid it might not.

With any luck at all, he would never see the woman burglar again. He knew it was true. His head, his logic, his considerable intellect told him as much. Just to reassure himself and prove how pleased he was with his own reasoning, he tried for a smile that, judging from the fact that the crowd parted before him, must have been more of a scowl.

The realization only made the scowl deepen, nearly as much as the thought that while his head might tell him one thing, other portions of his anatomy conveyed a different message. One that had nothing to do with logic. Or reasoning. Or intellect. And everything to do with hair like flame. And cheeks as smooth as porcelain. And as shapely a backside as he'd ever seen.

How a dribble of Devonshire cream no bigger than her fingernail could slide off its spoon and make such a mess across the front of Aggie's borrowed black dress was a mystery to her. A mystery, but not surprising. By this time in the afternoon, she didn't expect anything else. It had been much the same all day.

The tea she splashed while pouring for an elderly and quite impatient gentleman with muttonchop whiskers had landed in a series of brown dots across Aggie's crisp white apron. The jam she spilled on the damask table linen left a purple blot that she was able to hide with a serving tray and a series of spots on her white cuffs that were all too evident. The tea cakes that she piled by the dozens onto the silver dishes set upon Maxwell Barclay's table made her fingers sticky and left a residue of tacky streaks across the skirt of her dress that seemed to multiply each time she looked at them.

It was late. She was tired. Even to Aggie, it was becoming more evident with each passing moment that she wasn't much of a servant. And the others were beginning to take notice.

Out of the corner of her eye, Aggie glanced up and down the serving side of the buffet table. The bright-as-a-new-penny girl to her right doled out Madeira cake as if she'd been born to the task, and she probably had been. She took a look at Aggie's cuffs and her top lip curled. The impeccable fellow to Aggie's left gave every guest a nod and a bow along with each piece of seedcake he served them. He took one look at Aggie's apron, and his gaze turned positively wintry.

As if to underscore what he was no doubt already thinking, Aggie dropped the tea cake she was about to put on a plate. The cake landed with a splat. Icing side down. On Aggie's skirt.

"Oh, hell," she grumbled. Too late, she reminded herself that servants did not use such language. But by that time, there was no taking the words back.

The girl to Aggie's right gasped. So did the elderly lady to whom Aggie was supposed to be serving the cake. The servant on her left made a small gesture toward the footman who stood at the head of the table, directing the queue. The footman nodded his understanding, and had Aggie been writing about the incident instead of trying to get through it with her disguise—and her pride—intact, she might have called the look he gave her as black as the Earl of Hell's riding boots. The footman gestured to the steward. The steward signaled for the butler, a distinguished-looking fellow who stood directly outside the entrance to the tea tent, coordinating the efforts of the staff with all the earnest fervor of a general leading his troops toward certain death. The butler started toward Aggie, and there was no doubt in her mind that she was about to be found out.

Quick thinking was in order. So was fast action. Grabbing one of the half-full tubs in which the Devonshire cream had been brought out from the kitchen, Aggie hoisted it into her arms and headed toward the house. In the press of the crowd, it wouldn't be hard for the footman, the butler, and the steward to lose sight of her—or so she fervently hoped. Just to make certain, she took the long way around, through the garden and on toward the far side of the house. She stopped in the shade of a lilac bush, set down the tub, and wiped her sticky hands on the skirt of her gown.

"Bloody hell," she mumbled. "It ain't easy being a servant." And hardly worth the effort, she reminded herself, if she didn't find the man she was looking for. As mindful of her purpose as she was annoyed that it had yet to be achieved, she peeked around the corner of the house and back toward the tea tent. "I was certain he'd be here," she grumbled to herself. "Hell and damnation! How can I be the woman who unmasks the Shadow when I can't even find him?" The very thought was enough to send Aggie's temper soaring. She leaned back against the wall of the house and thought through the problem, but even as she did, the thought—and the words—captured her imagination.

"The woman who unmasked the Shadow." She purred the words under her breath, liking the sound of them very much indeed. Someday, she would have a chance to tell the world her story. Someday,

Horace Wallingstamp would realize her talents and allow her to be the one who would write about the Shadow. Someday, after she unmasked the Shadow, Wallingstamp would come crawling to her, begging to publish her story.

Would she snub him? Aggie couldn't say. She thought not, not if he admitted she was more talented than Peter Askew. Not if he promised her as much pay as the men reporters received. Not if he realized that what she'd accomplished would go down in the annals of journalistic history. She could picture the words she hoped would someday be emblazoned on the front page of the *Chronicle*.

The Shadow was close, very close. Close to the acme of his questionable career. Close to the height of achievement, the apex of success, the zenith of victory, as least in the way victory is defined in a mind warped by avarice and inclined toward criminal tendencies. Close, so close, to the prize he had so long sought, the one for which he risked all. He stood still and silent, his tall, lean body silhouetted in the light of his own dark lantern, and he stared at the wardrobe where Arthur's Crown was secured.

No other, except this humble reporter (whose exploits of that harrowing night are brilliantly documented elsewhere and who will, therefore, not recount them at this particular time but who humbly suggests that readers who are interested in a narration of the earlier Drama and all that resulted from it can purchase reprints of the stories concerning it at the offices of the London Daily Enquirer and Illustrated News Chronicle *in that same city), had ever been clever enough to discover the actual whereabouts of the crown. Even had they been so astute, or so fortunate, no other thief in this or any other country had the cunning or possessed the brazen audacity and inherent dishonesty to pose as a friend, to act as a guest, and to enter the home of Maxwell Barclay for the purpose of stealing the crown. No one had the daring, the very real daring, of this man, a man who would flaunt his place in Society and trade his reputation, his life and—dare the words be written?—his very honor for a chance to possess a crown that had graced the head of so fabled a monarch.*

The only one brazen enough to attempt such larceny was the Shadow, a man whose brilliance might have, in some happier time, been turned to good, but one who had chosen instead, a life of Evil.

That fateful night, the Shadow thought he was alone. He was not. One intrepid reporter stood between the man and his mission. One intrepid reporter had been brave enough to dog his steps, and clever enough to penetrate the myth to find the man behind it.

One reporter—

"One reporter . . ." Thinking, Aggie lifted the tub and headed on toward the kitchen. She had to get the words right. If the story was ever printed—when it was printed, she corrected herself—it was far too important not to get right. She braced the half-filled tub against one hip and went over the words in her head. It wasn't easy to concentrate. Just thinking about how exciting it would be to reveal the Shadow's identity to all the world was enough to make her anxious to get back to the task at hand. She reminded herself that she had only come to the house to avoid the butler, and when she looked around and made sure the man was nowhere to be seen, she headed back in the direction of the tea party. And the Shadow.

Only one reporter waited now in the darkness, listening, watching, with hopes high and breath bated for the Shadow to make his move.

He was there in the darkness. Even if this reporter had not been able to see him in the wan light of the lantern, there was no doubt of his presence. It vibrated in the air like the rumble of distant thunder. It hummed through the atmosphere like the oncoming of rain some say they feel

*long before it falls from the skies. It brushed every inch of
the reporter's skin, like the tingle of charged atmosphere
that presages a lightning strike, skimming over arms and
legs, grazing neck and hair, reaching to that soft, secret
place where—*

Suddenly struggling for breath, Aggie nipped the
sentence—and the thought—in the proverbial bud.
"Enough of such as that," she told herself in no uncertain terms. She firmly reminded herself that there
was no room in her story, or in her dealings with
the Shadow, for such flights of fancy, and she got
back to her composing.

*He stood before the wardrobe where Arthur's Crown
was kept secure inside an iron safe, and he thought his
dream was about to come true. How fortunate for the
people of London, for the country and the empire and the
world at large, that he had not figured on the courage of
one reporter, or on those masses of Chronicle readers who
were noble enough, and law-abiding enough, and moral
enough to cry out, "No more!"*

*No more would they tolerate his fiendish endeavors. No
more would they allow him to take for himself all that was
beautiful, all that was precious, all that was priceless and
rare. No more would each man in this great city sleep
uneasy, and each woman wonder how she might protect
herself against an intensity of purpose so potent, it might
be deemed—we dare to say for fear of offending the sensibilities of our more decorous readers—ardent.*

*Carefully, using those means too secret and too criminal
to report in these pages, the Shadow opened the safe and
moved nearer to it. When he moved back again, something
sparkled in his hands, something the likes of which even
the readers of the Chronicle, who are used to great won-
ders, have never seen.*

Arthur's Crown.

*It dazzled the eyes, a ring of jewels too precious to assay,
a circlet of gold beyond compare. The Shadow raised the
crown before his eyes and he smiled a smile as cold as a*

cooper's duck and then turned to leave, his prize finally
and completely in his possession.

That is when this reporter, at no small risk to life and
limb, rose from a handy place of concealment and blew on
the whistle that had been provided for the express purpose
by those marvelous fellows at Scotland Yard who knew
the reporter's value and allowed for the brilliance of the
reporter's plan.

Surprised, the thief froze and mumbled a word that
might be reported if not for the fact that the Chronicle
values the morals of its most esteemed and Christian
readers.

The lights came on. And for the first time, this reporter
was face-to-face with the man the world knew as the
Shadow.

"Brilliant!" Aggie was still congratulating herself
when she rounded another corner and crashed head-
on into a man coming from the other direction.

The tub flew out of Aggie's arms, and a great spray
of Devonshire cream went up all around. A good bit
of it landed on Aggie, right before she tumbled to
the ground. She had the fleeting impression that a
great deal more of it spilled on the pathway, and
that might have been all for the better, if not for the
fact that the man slid on the wet flagstones and
landed smack in it.

It was some moments before Aggie caught her
breath and came to her senses. When she did, it was
to the sound of the man's hearty curses. She closed
her eyes against a wave of embarrassment and a dol-
lop of cream that dripped from the streamers of her
cap onto her cheeks. Her backside ached from the
fall. Her borrowed maid's dress was covered with
cream. Her hair was in her eyes. She pushed it away
with one hand just in time to see the man splayed

in the pathway opposite her wipe a smear of cream from his spectacles.

As suddenly as Aggie's breath had returned, it was gone again, blocked by a ball of panic wedged in her throat. Her mouth open, she sat as still as stone.

And stared at the Shadow.

Chapter 5

Stewart lay in the middle of the garden pathway, propped on his elbows. The air had been knocked out of him, and for a long moment he wondered if the fall had dislodged his senses as well as his breath, or if he'd struck his head and was in the middle of an all-out, full-scale, injury-induced hallucination.

It was the only thing that might account for the woman who was sprawled just to the other side of the stone walk. Her skirts were above her knees, her dress was spattered with cream, her hair was in her eyes. Still, he would know her anywhere. As well he should. This past week, his memories of her had wound through his dreams like a wraith and preoccupied his thoughts, his imagination, and his desires, in ways that were as intriguing as they were really quite alarming.

Both Stewart and the woman were still too stunned to speak, too surprised and too shaken, and he took the opportunity to see if his memories of her matched the reality.

In his daydreams, he had pictured a woman of classical beauty. Venus rising out of the sea, her red hair loose and glorious around her, hiding all her most interesting attributes at the same time it hinted at the treasures that might be discovered by a man who was daring enough to seek them and lucky enough to be given even half the chance. He had pictured her nose as straight and slim, her skin as clear and as pale as the finest porcelain. Her eyes, he was sure, were an especially vibrant shade of emerald.

But it seemed that dreams were one thing, and reality something else all together. He saw now that the woman's nose wasn't the least bit like those of classical beauties. It was small and turned up slightly at the end. It was a good deal too perky for Stewart's liking, yet he found it appealing in a perplexing sort of way. He had been wrong about her eyes, too, if his own weren't playing him false from behind the spots of cream that had splashed onto his spectacles. In the light of day, her eyes were the color of the leaves on the ancient oaks that bordered the garden path, a fresh green, flecked with just a hint of blue and sparked with a touch of gold that might have been ascribed to surprise, or embarrassment.

Her skin was just as smooth as he remembered. At least he'd been right about that. But the moonlight under which he'd first seen her had played tricks on his eyes. Her cheeks were not porcelain-fine, but sprinkled with freckles, hundreds of them. They reminded Stewart of the mix of cinnamon and sugar that Cook used to blend for the Marsh boys' bread when they were young.

He had imagined her as one of the sylphlike beauties who adorned the walls of ancient murals, and he saw now how wrong he'd been. She was petite and dainty-looking enough, but when last he'd seen her, she was wearing a man's trousers and jacket. Now, swathed in layers of lace-edged crinolines that tangled with the skirts of her black dress, she looked to be all woman, as voluptuous as a goddess in a Roman painting, with a small waist and nicely curved hips. Stewart didn't need to remind himself—not here, not now—that the part of her that was flat against the pavement was just as rounded and shapely. Instead, he skimmed a look over her slim ankles encased in their sturdy black boots and her slender legs enclosed in their heavy black stockings, and wondered how long he might be able to make it seem as if he was still stunned, not staring.

Not long, he supposed, not when his gaze wandered farther, from the jumble of skirts around her knees to the white apron that had twisted about her waist, to the steady rise and fall of her bosom as she fought to catch her breath.

There was no way he could make his appraisal of that portion of her seem casual. There was no use even trying. Stewart forced his gaze to move on, to the woman's face. It was smeared with cream and her hair was a fright. It was not about to be contained by the pins that, no doubt, were supposed to hold it in a knot beneath her white cloth cap. One carroty curl hung in her eyes. Another skimmed one shoulder. A mass of streamers were attached to her small white cap. They were stuck to her cheeks and forehead by a coating of Devonshire cream, and she brushed them back with one small-boned hand, succeeding only in smearing more cream onto more places.

The very sight was enough to make Stewart smile, and something about smiling brought him back to his senses. Sitting up a little straighter, he looked again from the black dress, to the white apron, to the cloth cap.

"You're a housemaid!"

It was not the most original thing he had ever said, and certainly not the least bit clever. But it was concise. He would give himself that. With a grunt, he pulled himself to his feet. If smiling had brought Stewart back to his senses, something about finally shaking himself out of a daze made him positively rational.

He stood staring down at his redheaded burglar and reminded himself that she was neither a vision nor a dream. She was a very real woman, and the fact that they'd encountered each other as if by accident was, far too clearly, no accident at all.

The realization sobered Stewart. He knew he had to be as cagey and as cautious as he'd hoped to be when he made his first attempt to steal Arthur's Crown. More so, he reminded himself. For in this instance he couldn't afford to fail as he had then. He needed to play his part, and play it for all it was worth.

"A housemaid . . . that is to say . . . what I mean, of course, is . . ." As if suddenly remembering his manners, Stewart wiped one hand clean against the leg of his trousers and offered it to the woman. "I didn't see you coming at all and . . . You will forgive me, I hope. We've made a terrible mess, it seems, and—"

Even if he hadn't been doing his best to dissemble his way through the situation, Stewart realized words might have failed him the moment the woman put her hand in his. Hers was small and warm, the skin smooth and soft. It fit quite nicely inside his. Before he could lose himself in the feel of her, or thoughts of where the touch of her skin against his might lead, Stewart helped the woman to her feet.

Out of the corner of her eye, she eyed him as

warily as he studied her, and it was that, even more
than the look of her or the memories that jostled
Stewart's imagination, that convinced him he'd made
no mistake. The housemaid in the spattered dress
was the lady in the midnight garden. And the lady
in the midnight garden was the burglar who had
stumbled onto Stewart's attempt at the crown.

There was no doubt she recognized him as surely
as he did her. In that one moment of awareness, her
eyes went wide and her cheeks flushed with color.
She was enough of an actress to hide her reaction.
She brushed her skirts down into place. She scraped
a finger over her face to rid it of at least some of the
cream that was smeared there. She picked her ribbons away from where they were stuck to her cheeks
and smoothed them back against her cloth cap.

It wasn't until she was done that Stewart felt ready
to play the first card in his hand. He stepped back
and looked the woman up and down. "Don't I know
you?" he asked.

Her cheeks went from pink to ashen and her
mouth dropped open, and when she spoke it was
with an Irish brogue thick enough to be nearly be-
lievable. "Know you? Faith, and I don't see as that's
a possible thing. You said it yourself, sir, and no
mistake. You said I was a housemaid, which I am.
And you being a gentleman . . . Well, sir, you can
see as how the likes of you don't seem likely to know
the likes of me."

"Yet . . . Well, I may be mistaken, of course . . .
though I hardly ever am, as you would most certainly know if you knew me better, but . . . Well, I
digress. What I mean to say is, yes. Yes, I'm sure of
it. I do believe I know you." Stewart stepped back.
He cocked his head to one side and took a long, slow

look at the woman. He might actually have enjoyed himself but for the uneasy feeling that he wasn't so much admiring her as he was sizing her up as an adversary. "You do look deucedly familiar," he said. "The eyes. The hair. The mouth. I know!" He brightened considerably. "The last dinner party. Last week."

The woman may have been a skilled actress, but she wasn't quick enough to disguise the catch in her voice. "I don't know what you mean, sir. I don't remember no dinner party and—"

With two steps, Stewart narrowed the space that separated them. "Of course you do. Or at least you should. I . . . I certainly remember you." He had never intended to betray the fact that he did remember, all too clearly, yet he couldn't help but wonder that his own voce sounded suddenly so breathless.

The woman noticed. He was a fool to think she wouldn't. She looked up at him and for the first time, he realized she was not as nervous, or as discomfited, as he'd thought her to be. She was biding her time, waiting for her moment, just as he had done. Now that it had come, she saw her advantage and allowed herself a smile that might have charmed the birds out of the trees.

"Oh, no, sir!" the woman purred, and though she tried for a look that was innocence itself, even she was not a good enough actress to conceal the spark of sensuality he suspected was as much a part of her as was her flaming hair. "It could not have been me. For when last Master Barclay hosted a dinner party, I had my day out. I was home, don't you know, sitting at the side of my sickly white-haired mother that whole night through."

As quickly as he could, Stewart struggled to salvage what was left of his advantage. And his dignity.

He gave a smile to match hers. "Did I say *at* the dinner party. I am sorry. I do sometimes get ahead of myself. I didn't mean to say *at* the dinner party. I meant to say *after*. In the garden. Under the moonlight."

Again, she flashed him a look of innocence, and Stewart realized that whatever else the woman might be, she was an expert at trifling with a man's emotions. She batted eyelashes the color of a ginger cat. "You can't think I'm that sort of girl, sir. Meeting a gentleman in the garden. In the moonlight!" She gave a little shiver. The motion jiggled her shoulders and her breasts, wreaking havoc with her ribbons and nearly doing the same to Stewart's self-control.

He reined it in, or at least he might have if a drop of Devonshire cream hadn't trickled off the woman's ribbons and onto her nose. Before he could stop himself, Stewart retrieved his handkerchief and wiped the drop away. There was more cream on her cheeks, and when he made to brush it away, her eyes drifted closed.

Was it part of her game, or was she as disconcerted by his touch as he was by hers?

Stewart didn't like to consider either option. He only knew that two could play the game as easily as one. He skimmed the handkerchief over her cheek, then brushed at the long streak of cream that caked her neck from the high collar of her gown all the way to her left ear.

By the time he was done, his breath was coming a bit too fast for his liking. Still, he congratulated himself. He seemed to have the upper hand. The woman held her breath, her eyes closed, every inch of her poised as if to see what might happen next.

"There." He paused, his hand lingering just above

her skin. "I think that's helped a bit. I can . . . I can see . . . your face somewhat better, or at least as well as I'm able. You really are a frightful mess, don't you know. But . . ." He bent down for a better look. "But I'm sure I've seen you before. I have a memory that is quite prodigious, you know. Photographic, some call it. There's no mistake. No mistake at all."

Was it Aggie's imagination, or was there just enough of a murmur to the man's voice to make it sound as if he might be as nonplussed as she was? It was impossible, of course. Impossible that he might feel the same vibrations that tingled over her skin each and every place he touched her. Impossible that so simple a thing might make his head spin, as hers was spinning, or his heart beat the same furious rhythm as hers.

He was, after all, the Shadow, and not a man who could be so easily distracted or amused. He was the epitome of elegance. The embodiment of reckless-ness. The essence of romance.

> *His was a heart not easily ensnared nor one that be-stowed its affections easily. But when it found itself entan-gled, it was the truest and the most stalwart, the loyalest and the most devoted, worshipping at the altar of that most sacred of all affections, that most impassioned of all sentiments, that most cherished of all the emotions.*
> *Love.*

Aggie's breath caught on a small hiccup of exhila-ration. She controlled her runaway imagination and reminded herself that she had more important things to think about than the fact that the Shadow's touch was as tantalizing as a whisper, as full of promise as a June morning, as irresistible as—

"Cor!" The single word escaped her on the end of

a sigh. It was enough to make Aggie remember herself. In an effort to preserve what was left of her integrity, she took a small, quick step back, away from the man's disturbing nearness. Her eyes snapped open and she found herself staring.

It seemed that the epitome of elegance, the embodiment of recklessness, and the essence of romance did not look at all elegant, reckless, or romantic. Not when he was covered with Devonshire cream.

The man she knew as the Shadow was, in the glaring light of day, not nearly as heroic-looking as she remembered, and in spite of the fact that she told herself it was foolish, she couldn't help but feel the bite of disappointment.

Elegant?

He was tall and slim, certainly, just as she remembered him to be. But it was difficult to think of any man as elegant when his tie was askew and his face adorned with cream. His clothes were expensive enough, and he wore them rather well, but he was not, by any means—or by any stretch of Aggie's considerable imagination—the debonair rogue whose face had insinuated itself into so many of her daydreams of late. Without the benefit of darkness, the glamour of danger, and the trappings of a criminal genius, he reminded her more of the standard Oxford don presented in so many West End theatrical productions: well dressed, well groomed, well bred, yet apparently so unconcerned about things as trivial as fashion and as unimportant as appearance as to make it all look like something of an accident.

Reckless?

Thanks to a string of extraordinary robberies that took the cunning of a genius to plan and the daredeviltry of a madman to carry off, the Shadow's very name was synonymous with adventure. But the longer Aggie stared at the man, the more she wondered.

The hair she'd thought of as a sinister shade like ancient leather was, in reality, very ordinary brown, and smeared with cream besides. The eyes she remembered so well as fierce and piercing were hidden behind a pair of cream-dappled spectacles that made him look like a boiled owl. And as for carrying a pistol . . .

Aggie shook her head, not so much baffled by the transformation as she was simply amazed by it. He didn't look the type who would know how to hold a pistol, much less hold it to anyone's head.

Romantic?

Hardly. A twinge of some emotion that felt, inexplicably, very much like regret nipped at Aggie's insides. As the Shadow, the man had excitement emanating from every pore. Romance seethed in the air around him. Passion pulsed in his every breath.

In reality, the man—whoever he was—was quite unassuming, more than a little unsure of himself, and so busy tripping over his own words as to make any resemblance to the Shadow not only improbable but absolutely unthinkable. Just the way he was in Barclay's treasure room after all the lights came on and he found himself facing an audience.

Was it an act? Aggie had no doubt. She was, after all, herself an expert at fabrication. She knew a deception when she saw one. Even one this good. The only question now was, Which was the lie? Was the Shadow really a bookish gentleman who sputtered his way through life? Or was the bookish gentleman really the incredibly dashing Shadow?

Still staring at the man, Aggie shook her head. She

didn't have any answers. But she intended to find them. Her fame and her fortune depended on it. So did her reputation as a clinking good reporter. Her job was no different now than it had ever been. She needed to get past the facade that this man had so skillfully built around himself, to shine the light of truth upon his dark deeds. To expose him to the world as the Shadow. No matter what.

The thought emboldened Aggie. It reminded her that she was very close to finding out what she'd come to Raleigh House to discover. It reassured her, and thus reassured, she redoubled her efforts.

"Oh, sir, you do have a way with trying to turn a girl's head." She turned up her smile a notch and beamed at the man. It was not the Smile. Not yet. The Smile was something she didn't use lightly. She saved it for the most critical moments, the way an unscrupulous gambler kept an ace in his sleeve for those times when all seemed lost. "Imagine! The two of us together in a moonlit garden." Aggie herself could well imagine. All too well. She rid herself of the thought with a shake of her shoulders and gave the man a knowing look. "I would'a thought more that we might have met inside the house."

He didn't rise to the bait. Not as she'd hoped. He simply raised one cream-gilded eyebrow. "Pleading guilty?"

"Did I say as much?" Aggie tossed her head. It was a well-practiced move and any other time she knew it would have made her curls bounce. Men liked bouncing curls. This time, however, the maneuver simply caused one sticky ribbon to drop into her eyes. She swiped it back and dared a step closer to the man. "What I was meaning, of course, is that a gentleman such as yourself looks more the type who wouldn't enjoy dallying with a housemaid nearly as much as he would enjoy . . . say . . . havin' a look at Master Barclay's treasure room."

If she expected him to throw up his hands and admit to her that he was the Shadow, she was sorely disappointed. The man didn't look anywhere near close to surrender. He nodded and spoke slowly, looking more than ever like a don explaining a very simple concept to a roomful of students too dense to understand.

"No doubt," he said, "you are thinking of Barclay's treasure room because that is the room in which we first met. Well, I suppose met is not exactly the right word. But it is the room in which I first saw you. I was in the throng, you see. One among that great herd of dinner guests who galloped up the stairs to see what the commotion was all about. And you—" He scratched a hand through his hair and though his look was innocence itself, Aggie couldn't help but notice the glint of challenge in his eyes. "Damn me if I'm wrong," he said, "but I swear you were the one who caused the commotion."

"Only because I had to. You might have shot me if I didn't!"

Too late, Aggie realized she'd completely forgotten to use her Irish brogue. Annoyed, at him and at herself, she pulled a face.

Pleased to have gotten a rise out of her, the man smiled. "Then you admit it. It was you."

"And if it was?" Aggie folded her arms across her chest. "What will you do? Call the police?" She laughed and hoped she sounded as indifferent as she intended and not as anxious as she felt. "Pardon me for asking, but who in their bloody right mind would believe that a housemaid could possibly be a burglar?"

The man clicked his tongue. "Please! Wherever do you servant girls learn such language?" He allowed himself another smile, but this one was not at all as pleasant as the last. This one was hard around the edges, as cold as the look that turned his eyes from smoky blue to a color as icy as diamonds. "You're right, of course. No one would believe a housemaid could possibly be a burglar." He paused long enough to make his point. "No more than they'd believe a gentleman could be a thief."

"Unless there was proof, of course."

"Of course." He gave her a nod, acknowledging the logic of her argument. "But, I think it safe to say, there never will be."

"Do you think so?" Aggie tilted her head from one side to the other, sizing up the man who stood before her, dragging out the silence, waiting for him to show even the smallest sign of discomfort.

He didn't seem to care. He assessed her as openly as she studied him, and when he grew tired of the game, he turned and walked casually down the path and away from her, removing his spectacles and cleaning the lenses with his silk handkerchief. He took rather longer than he should, so completely absorbed in what he was doing and so obviously ignoring her, that Aggie couldn't help but become annoyed. When she cleared her throat to remind him of her presence, he stopped, replaced his spectacles, turned, and looked at her as if he'd completely forgotten she was there.

"Oh . . . yes." He looked at her expectantly. "You were saying?"

It was enough of a rebuff to cause Aggie's annoyance to turn instantly to anger. She glared at the man, biting off her words. "I was saying that a person who is clever enough and persistent enough might find the proof."

"Really?" He glanced at her as if she were nothing more than an afterthought. "And who," he asked, "might that person be?"

There was nothing Aggie liked more than a direct challenge. And this was as direct as any challenge could get. She squared her shoulders and raised her chin. "Me," she told him.

"Really?" He looked at her as if she'd told him the sun was not truly the center of the solar system. Or the earth was not actually round. A moment of bewilderment melted into a chuckle of incredulity. "You? Really? Well, that's a . . . that's a splendid sort of fantasy, though I'm not at all sure what you're trying to accomplish. What, exactly, do you hope to prove?"

They had both laid their cards on the table, and Aggie couldn't see that there was anything to be gained by continuing the game. She looked at him levelly. "That you are the Shadow."

The man's smile faded, but he didn't look away. He kept his gaze full on hers, waiting for her to back down, and when she didn't, his expression went as hard as stone. "Do you know who I am?" he asked.

"No," Aggie told him. "But I intend to find out."

"And when you do?"

"When I do . . . then you'll see." Like a trained actress, Aggie had a perfect sense of timing. She knew when it was time to go. She whirled away from the man.

"Brave words from a little housemaid," he said, and in spite of all they'd said and all the more they'd hinted at, it wasn't clear whether the words were a simple statement of fact. Or a threat. "But I'm quite afraid, really, that it will all be a terrible waste of time. You've confused me with someone else, I think. I'm not the man you're looking for."

"Is that so?" Aggie glanced at him over her shoulder. "Then I suppose I will find that out for myself, won't I?"

"You will." He gave her the smallest of smiles. "I guarantee it."

"And I—" Aggie never had time to finish. Before she could, the butler came around the corner, and with one look at the man, the maid, and the mess of Devonshire cream all around, stopped in his tracks.

The butler's mouth dropped open. His face went pale. "Good heavens, sir, what's happened?"

"It's nothing. Really." In spite of the fact that the man waved away any concern, the butler was not about to be put off. He turned on Aggie, his face grim.

"You, miss! What sort of mess have you caused? And what is the meaning of involving Lord Stewart—"

"Lord? Stewart?" A thrill of excitement tingled through Aggie's body. She looked beyond the butler to the man, a man who finally had a name. One familiar enough to anyone with even a passing knowledge of the aristocracy. There was only one Lord Stewart she could think of. "Lord Stewart? Marsh?"

As if they'd just been introduced at some glittering soiree, Stewart gave her a nod and a brief bow.

It was an exchange that might have interested the butler had he been paying the least bit of attention. Instead, he was so intent on the embarrassment of inconveniencing a person of such importance that he went right on scolding Aggie.

"You are to report to Mrs. Briscoe, the house-keeper, right now, young lady. We cannot tolerate—" The butler stopped and took a hard look at Aggie. "That is, we cannot allow—" He leaned nearer for a better look. "We cannot—"

Finally, the butler backed away. His composure dissolved in the same instant that astonishment over-came him. "I say! Who in the name of the holy mar-tyrs are you?"

It was time for Aggie to go. Before the butler had a chance to recover from his surprise or Stewart had a chance to think through all of what had just hap-pened, she turned and ran down the pathway.

This time Stewart didn't bother to run after her. Better to let her disappear than to risk a scene. He listened to the butler sputter apology after apology, and it wasn't until after the fellow had got it out of his system that Stewart dared to interrupt.

"Are you telling me you don't know that woman?" he asked.

"Heavens, no! I am so sorry, sir. But I know the staff, of course. There is no mistake. The woman was— She was—"

"An imposter!"

Stewart wasn't sure if he should laugh or curse. Instead, he stared at the spot where only minutes ago, the woman with hair of flame and eyes as fresh as springtime had stood staring at him, measuring him as openly as he was measuring her, questioning him as surely as he was questioning her, issuing a challenge, and not backing down in the least, even when he did his best to throw her off the scent.

"Damn!" Stewart mumbled the word, half in amazement, half in awe, and when the butler thought his comment was aimed at the operation of the household, Stewart waved away the man's fears and sent him for a wet towel so that he might clean up.

It was only after the butler had gone and Stewart was all alone that he allowed himself the luxury of thinking through all that had happened. "Interesting," he mumbled. She was certainly a determined little thing, he knew that much about her. And feisty as well. In spite of her obvious attributes, it was clear she could also be a formidable opponent. There was no use tempting such fates, or leaving a track of Devonshire cream across Barclay's rugs.

Arthur's Crown would have to wait. At least for now. For now, Stewart had other things to worry about.

If the housemaid was no housemaid at all, who was she? What did she want?

And just how dangerous could she be?

Chapter 6

In the Footsteps of the Shadow
by
A. O'Day

As had been proven time and again under the most trying of circumstances and at great endangerment of life and limb, this reporter has risked all for the sake of bringing the most exalted and commendable Light of Truth to our most estimable readers. It is a well-known fact that this reporter has stood firm against adversity. It is a well-documented actuality that this reporter has stared into the terrifying face of death and has braved horrors too chilling to recount, even in these pages.

But never before has this—or any other—representative of the press encountered perils so fierce, dangers so deadly, fear so real, and a criminal so devious and so very sinister as what will be related here in the pages of The London Daily Enquirer and Illustrated News Chronicle *over the next weeks. It would be wise not to allow this sequence of articles to be read by the elderly, whose hearts might not be strong enough to withstand its alarming revelations. Nor should it be read by, or even discussed in the presence of, the very young, for children are, by nature, Innocence itself, and it would be irresponsible, nay, it would be immorality of the worst sort if they were to be exposed to such shocking accounts of such sordid and depraved activities.*

This is not a journey for the faint of heart, or for those who are panic-prone or cowering. This is a look into the very essence of Evil, one that will surely make blood race and pulses pound. One that will leave each and every person who reads it breathless.

Join me, faithful Readers, as we travel the highways and byways of this great City, from wretched alleys to the glittering homes of the privileged. Draw near and read, as we explore the criminal mind, hoping to find there some understanding of its workings at the same time we find in ourselves (as in our Christian duty if not our wiser impulse) some glimmer of Compassion. Be there as together, we follow a fiend and study his habits. Watch as we unmask the man who lives in darkness, as we reveal his true identity to all the world. Join in a mighty anthem of thanksgiving as we end his vile Reign of Terror and bring him, finally and most fittingly, to Justice.

Come along in the Footsteps of the Shadow.

Reading through the words again, pleased with their rhythm, sure that the tone and message were just what she wanted, a little thrill of excitement ran over Aggie's shoulders. It was the best opening to what would surely be her best story ever. The best opening story to what would certainly be the best series of articles ever to run in any newspaper, anywhere. She knew that unequivocally. Her articles would attract attention. They would cause a stir. They would make people everywhere eager to read the next installment of her narrative, and the next installment after that, until they waited in queue outside the offices of *The Chronicle*, anxious for every last detail of the story, hanging on every word.

Too excited by the prospect to keep still, she tapped her pencil against her chin and smiled down at the leather-bound journal opened on her lap. She was so pleased with what she'd written, she nearly hummed a little tune. She would have, if not for the fact that she was seated outside the office of Horace

Wallingstamp, publisher of the *London Daily Enquirer and Illustrated News Chronicle,* and Mr. Wallingstamp was, as he liked to remind the reporters who worked for him, a Serious Journalist.

Aggie wiped the satisfied smile from her face and glanced over at Bill Bickles, the clerk stationed outside Wallingstamp's office. When she'd come in some minutes earlier, Bickles had, as he always did, ogled her. Aggie somehow managed, as she always did, to control her irritation at such blatant boorishness and give Bickles a subdued version of the Smile. It was enough to secure fifteen minutes' time with Wallingstamp but not enough to encourage Bickles, who, despite his spotty complexion, his receding hairline, and a body that might charitably be described as cadaverous, thought of himself as quite the blade.

Fortunately, Bickles was busy entering figures in a ledger and had not seen Aggie's slip of journalistic aplomb. She was just as glad. Bickles was a notorious gossip, and she didn't like to think he might spread word to Peter Askew or any of the other reporters that she was looking especially pleased with herself. No use alerting the competition to the fact that her journalistic star was about to eclipse theirs, that their paltry careers would soon be all but forgotten. As soon as she convinced Wallingstamp to let her write about the Shadow.

Even as Aggie had the thought, Wallingstamp's door snapped open. At the same time Bickles ducked inside, Peter Askew stepped out. He was a middle-aged man, heavyset and thick-jowled, who favored plaid suits in garish colors. When he saw Aggie obviously waiting for a chance to talk to Wallingstamp, he clamped down harder on the unlit cigar between his teeth and his face turned a shade darker than his maroon coat and trousers.

"Why, if it isn't little Miss O'Day." Askew stopped short of clapping his hat on his head and instead gave Aggie a brassy salute with it. He glanced at the journal on her lap, and Aggie instinctively closed it. "Working on another ghost story, are you, girl? Bet the chief can't wait to hear about that!" Askew chuckled. He carried a newspaper under one arm, and he flicked it open and pointed to an article that took up a goodly portion of the front page.

"Have you seen the latest?" he asked, and when he saw from the icy expression on Aggie's face that she had, indeed, seen the day's news, his grin widened. "Police Close In on the Shadow." Reading the headline that marched across the page in bold letters, Askew heaved a sigh of satisfaction. "Looks good right there above my name, don't it? Only right, of course, I'm sure you'll agree. It's a man's world, Miss O'Day, and a man's right to be there on the scene when things of import happen. I'll be there, right on the scene, when they put the cuffs on that Shadow fellow, and won't that make a story and a half! And you?" With a practiced spin, Askew twirled his hat, thumped it onto his head, and strode to the door. "I suspect a little girl like you will still be writing about ghosties and ghoulies!"

Aggie didn't bother to reply. Not that she didn't want to. She had a string of words ready on her lips, words that included "mistaken, misguided, and misinformed." She might have been tempted to hurl each and every one of them at Askew if Bickles hadn't appeared and told her Mr. Wallingstamp would see her.

Aggie stood and tucked her journal into the pocket

of her navy blue skirt. She tugged at her matching jacket, straightened the straw boater perched on top of her head, and took a deep breath.

"Mr. Wallingstamp . . ." Even before the door to Wallingstamp's office closed behind her, she launched into the words she'd been practicing since she'd decided to approach him. "I have information that will benefit the *Chronicle*, and I am prepared to share it with you and with our readers if you will only give me the chance."

"What's that you say?" Wallingstamp, as Aggie should have expected, hadn't been listening. He was seated behind his desk, paging through a sheaf of newly printed pages, and without even looking up, he stubbed a cigarette out on the pitted surface of the desk, lit a fresh one, and used it to point somewhere in the general direction of the room's only other chair. "Sit down, O'Day," he said. "What is it you want?"

Aggie went over to the chair, but she didn't sit. She clutched her hands together at her waist. "I have information," she said. She waited for the publisher to look up, and when he didn't, she cleared her throat. "I have information," she said again, louder this time, just to be sure he could hear. "Information about the Shadow."

This time Wallingstamp did look up. His chubby cheeks quivering, his chubby fingers working nervously over the cigarette, he stared at Aggie, obviously waiting for more.

"The accounts you published about the Shadow . . ." Aggie glanced at the accumulation of newspapers strewn about Wallingstamp's office. "The information you've been provided . . . short man, young, fair-skinned . . . they aren't exactly accurate."

"What's that you say?" Wallingstamp sat up straight. "Are you telling me you know something Peter Askew doesn't?"

The truth was too delicious to deny. Smiling and finally able to relax now that Wallingstamp recognized her value and her brilliance, Aggie sat down, shoulders back, chin high. "That's exactly what I'm telling you. You see, Mr. Wallingstamp"—she leaned forward in the chair, sharing the confidence, "I know who the Shadow is."

Aggie was not sure what sort of reaction she had expected to the statement. Wild excitement would have been nice. Warm enthusiasm, though not nearly as exhilarating, might at least have been welcomed. Complete silence was not something she'd counted on.

"Did you hear me, Mr. Wallingstamp?" she asked. "I know the identity of the Shadow. I've seen the fellow at work. I've talked to him and practically been killed by him, too, though I won't go into how heroic and brave and . . . Never mind." She excused her impetuosity with a quick smile and launched into an explanation of the plan she'd so cleverly concocted and the words she'd so carefully rehearsed.

"If you let me write about him, I could set the record straight. I know enough to start right now, but if I'm allowed to continue . . . if I can follow him long enough, I'll even be able to catch him at his thievery. Wouldn't that make a fine conclusion to a series of stories! They'd be lined up from one end of London to the other, just to buy copies of the *Chronicle*. Can't you see it now? It's as good an opportunity as we'll ever get. Better than good, for I know something even the police don't know. They're looking for the wrong man, don't you see. They're looking for a short fellow when they should be looking for a tall fellow, and though they don't know it, they're not really looking for a fellow at all, and they should be looking for a fellow. What I mean, of course, is that, of course, he is a fellow. The Shadow, I mean. Mr. Wallingstamp? Mr. Wallingstamp, have you heard a word I've said?''

In response to the sound of his name, Wallingstamp blinked. A long ash fell from the end of his cigarette and landed in a heap on the pile of papers he'd been reading. He brushed it away and ended up with more ash on his shirt cuffs than on the floor.

"Are you telling me . . ." Like a man waking from a long sleep, Wallingstamp shook his head. "Are you telling me—"

"That I can deliver the Shadow. Yes." Aggie beamed her satisfaction. "It's as good as done, Mr. Wallingstamp, sir, but I hope you realize I am the only one who can do it."

"You." Wallingstamp looked Aggie over quickly, as if gauging her sincerity. "You know who the Shadow is?"

"Yes, sir." Aggie saw the fluttering smile that rippled the corners of Wallingstamp's mouth, and she couldn't help herself, she had to smile in return. "I am more than willing to reveal all, of course. If I am allowed to write the articles."

"Miss O'Day, you can write the whole damn newspaper if you like!" Wallingstamp leaped from his chair and came around to stand in front of Aggie. He grabbed her right hand and pumped it in his. "The Shadow? You say you can deliver the Shadow?" His cheeks bright with excitement, Wallingstamp grinned. "How soon can you get started?"

It was just what she had been waiting for. Carefully extracting her hand from his, Aggie stood. "Today. Now. I can get started right away."

"Excellent!" Wallingstamp rubbed his hands together. "Can you have an article ready for tomorrow's newspaper?"

Aggie touched a hand to the journal in her pocket. *In the Footsteps of the Shadow, by A. O'Day.* The words floated through her mind like the sense of euphoria that filled her spirit. "I will have it ready," she assured Wallingstamp. She hurried toward the door. "And you won't be disappointed, sir. It's as fine a story as ever there was, and that's for certain. This story has everything: mystery, romance, intrigue. Why, there's even a bit of glamour, for once I hint at the fact that the man's a member of the upper class—"

"What's that you say?" Wallingstamp's surprise could not have been more complete. His mouth dropped open. His face went pale. "He's a . . . the Shadow's a gentleman?"

It was just the kind of reaction Aggie had expected, and it cheered her no end. The reading public in general would be just as surprised as old Wallingstamp. "Just so." She nodded. "And not only a gentleman, but a well-connected one as well." She gave Wallingstamp a knowing wink. "There is nobility in the Shadow's bloodlines."

Wallingstamp's face went from pale to paler. When Aggie made to leave the office, he grabbed her arm and refused to let go. "Nobility?" The word was no more than a squeak from the publisher's mouth. "Now listen here, O'Day, you're not actually expecting me to believe that this Shadow fellow is—"

"Won't it make a sensation!" Aggie grinned at the

very thought. "I'll write it so as it comes as a surprise. Just like it did to you. I'll write it so as to draw out every ounce of the drama, and the scandal! Won't it be grand!" A thrill of excitement ran through her. "I'll write it so as—"

"You'll do no such thing!" The dazzle of excitement in Wallingstamp's eyes turned to cold fear. "You can't go accusing a member of the gentry—"

Aggie laughed off his apprehension. "I'm not accusing," she assured him. "It's a known fact. I've seen the man with my own eyes. I've spoken to him."

"No." Wallingstamp shook his head. "There's no way on this good green earth we could publish a story like that. Not without proof."

"Proof?" The single word was like a pin pricking the balloon of Aggie's hopes. As quickly as her prospects faded, her anger surged. "You never needed proof about that ghost in Croydon," she reminded Wallingstamp. "You never asked for proof about the beastie in the river."

"Ghosts and beasties don't threaten libel."

"And that's what it comes to?" Aggie couldn't believe her ears. "It's the story of a lifetime," she reminded Wallingstamp. "The most sensational thing ever. You can't not print it, just because you say you don't have—"

"Proof." Wallingstamp folded his arms over his chubby belly. "I'll not go up against the likes of some swell from the aristocracy without ironclad proof. It would be lunacy to do otherwise. Let me remind you, it would be the end of your career and the ruin of me."

"But—"

"No buts, O'Day." Wallingstamp opened the door

and nudged her outside, and it was clear to Aggie that the interview was over. "Proof. Conclusive, absolute, irrefutable proof. Without it, I won't print the story."

"But—"

It was the last thing Aggie had a chance to say before Wallingstamp's door swung closed in her face.

"Proof!" Standing before the parlor mirror, Aggie *harrumphed* the word under her breath. "Well," she grumbled, pulling at the bow tie she couldn't manage to do up correctly, "if it's proof Wallingstamp wants, damn him, it's proof he'll get."

"Aggie? Who are you talking to?" Bert had spent the afternoon tidying up the garden shed, and now that he was clean and ready for dinner, he tramped down the stairs and peeked into the parlor. At the sight of the mustachioed young man who stood before the mirror fumbling with his tie, Bert's eyes popped open wide. "Sorry," he blurted out. "I didn't know we had visitors. I was looking for Aggie and—"

The rest of Bert's words were lost in a gulp of astonishment. He scrambled into the room, pointing at what he'd thought for a moment was a stranger. "Aggie?" Bert's surprise was complete enough to make Aggie laugh. "Aggie, is that you behind that great bushy mustache?"

"That it is." Aggie lowered her voice, trying to sound like a man. "What do you think, my boy? Do you like it?"

Bert stepped back for a better look. His gaze skimmed the sturdy brown boots Aggie wore to match a brown lounge suit. He looked over her white shirt with its stiff collar and cuffs, and her brown bowler hat, and the fuzzy brown moustache she'd pasted under her nose. When he glanced at her untied bow tie, he shook his head and moved forward.

"Would you mind telling me what in the name of all the saints and angels this is about?" he asked. He tied the tie for her, and when he was finished, he turned her toward the mirror so she could take a look at his handiwork. "Are you on your way to a masquerade?"

Aggie smiled her approval, both of the way Bert had managed to take care of the tie and the fact that for a moment she had fooled him completely. If her disguise was good enough to fool her own brother, it would certainly do for what she had in mind. "No masquerade," she told him. "At least not in the way you're thinking. I'm going after the proof Wallingstamp demands, and the way I see it, there's only one way to get it."

"Dressed as a man?" Bert scratched a finger through his hair. "Can't see how that's going to help."

"Can't you?" Aggie didn't like the way a bit of her hair poked out from under the edge of the hat. She removed the hat, pinned her hair tighter to the top of her head, and plopped the hat back over it. "What better way could there possibly be for me to go about town without being noticed?" she asked. "If I was dressed as myself . . ." She shook her head, as dissatisfied with the idea now as she had been when she'd first thought of it. "Well, it would be conspicuous, wouldn't it? A woman following after a man, perhaps even after dark. He'd be sure to notice me then."

"He?" Now that he was finished helping with Aggie's tie, Bert took a look around the room. It must have been the first time he noticed the mound of clothes piled on the sofa, because his ginger-colored eyebrows rose nearly to his hairline. He went over to the clothes and poked through them.

Bert held up a black nun's habit and a white wimple, and his cheeks went ashen. "Aggie, you're not actually thinking about—"

"It's a stroke of genius, Bert." Aggie snatched the habit out of his hands. She might have returned it to the pile if Bert hadn't been busy pulling other garments out. He found a butcher's apron and leather cap, a dark suit like the one worn by the jarveys who drove hansom cabs, and a red dress with short, puffed sleeves and a scandalously low-cut bodice.

Bert's face went from pale to pink, and he dropped the scarlet dress as if it were on fire. "Where did you get all this?" he asked.

Aggie grinned. "From John Harcourt. You remember him—the gangly lad with the bad eye and the limp. He works over at the Adelphi Theater with the costumes and—"

"And you tricked him into helping you. Really, Aggie, that's hardly fair."

"Hardly unfair," she corrected him. "It isn't my fault John finds me attractive. It was a fair trade. He told me he'd get me some costumes if I would promise him a kiss."

"And did you?"

"I promised," Aggie said. She smiled at her own cleverness. "I didn't deliver. I told him his reward depends on the success of my little venture."

"But you haven't explained to me what that venture is."

Aggie shook her head, amazed that her own brother could be so slow witted. "It's the Shadow, of course," she explained. "Or at least it's the man who is the Shadow and says he isn't."

"Lord Stewart, you mean?"

"Yes. Lord Stewart." Aggie turned away from her brother. She didn't like to think why, but when she thought about Stewart Marsh, nobleman and thief, her cheeks were inclined to get hot and her heartbeat tended to speed up. It was a reaction brought on, no doubt, by the exciting prospect of ending the man's notorious career, but there was no use letting Bert get other ideas. She fiddled with the bristling moustache, smoothing it into place and trying not to sneeze when it tickled her nose.

"I've been able to observe the man enough to know that he leaves the house most evenings, but I haven't been able to follow him. Not without fearing detection. Now that I have these disguises, things will be different." She gave the tie one last tug. "From now on, I'll be able to slip in and out of the shadows, trailing him every step of the way. Tonight . . ." She straightened the bowler hat on her head. "Tonight, I shall be a proper young business-man. Tomorrow night . . ." She glanced at the clothing piled on the sofa. "Tomorrow night perhaps I shall be a nun. I rather fancy myself as looking quite holy in a habit. And after that . . ." Aggie fingered the red dress.

"After that, perhaps I shall be a lady of the night. What do you think, Bert? With my hair piled high enough and my gown pulled low enough across my shoulders . . ." She laughed at the look of utter as-tonishment that crossed Bert's face, and she was still laughing when she headed for the door.

"Perhaps I may yet surprise Lord Stewart Marsh,"

she said. "Enough to steam up those spectacles of his!"

Outside the main entrance of the Royal Opera House, Stewart stopped long enough to fasten his cloak around his neck and glance at the throngs hurrying away from the theater. Sometime while he and his brothers had been inside watching the production of *Aïda*, it had started to rain. Now the fashionable crowd scurried around the old theater on Bow Street, calling for cabs and vying for positions under the portico at the front of the theater, one of the few places in the vicinity that provided protection from the downpour. Though he found it damnably inconvenient most of the time, this was one instance when Stewart didn't mind being recognized as one of the fabled Marsh brothers. He and his brothers found a dry spot beyond the commotion at one corner of the portico, and no one dared challenge them for it.

Unfortunately, just as they got there, Charles met an old friend, Matthew ran into a former parishioner, Lowell was detained by a client, Edward met a fellow officer, and George came across a woman of his acquaintance who seemed quite enchanted to see him again. Waiting for them to finish with their socializing, Stewart kept well out of the way. He drew in a lungful of damp air and let it out slowly, surprised that, for the first time in a week, he'd been able to relax. The opera was not his favorite of pastimes, and when Charles had suggested it, Stewart's initial reaction had been to reject the invitation out of hand.

But it had been an uneasy week, and his unease had caused him to suspend his pursuit of the crown. At least for now. The thought caused a sensation like cold fingers on Stewart's neck. He twitched it away and took a quick look around. For the first time in the last few days, he didn't feel as if he were being watched; if nothing else, he supposed he had the opera to thank for that. A few hours' musical diversion was apparently as good for a man's soul as it was for his conscience. Or perhaps a seat at the opera was just too expensive for the police to afford.

Uneasy with the thought, Stewart glanced around again, more carefully this time. Though the police might not be willing to send someone to watch him inside the opera house, they might have someone waiting outside. It was exactly what had happened a few days earlier when he was followed to a bookshop by a fellow in a cheap suit and a bushy moustache. Exactly what had happened again just two days later when a fellow who looked to be a hansom driver just happened to be waiting outside his home when Stewart left it, and outside the library when he visited it later in the day. Coincidence? Stewart thought not. He wasn't a man who believed in coincidence, just as he wasn't a man who believed in chance.

A squeal of voices raised in a mixture of giggles and curses interrupted Stewart's thoughts, and he watched as a group of courtesans who normally plied their trade both inside and outside the theater ran toward the shelter of the portico, skirts flying. The seven of them huddled as close to the overhang of the portico as they could, fearing, no doubt, that if they got too close or took up too much of their betters' precious dry space, they would be unceremoniously escorted away.

One of the girls, a brassy blonde with crooked teeth, gave Stewart a knowing look and, as amused as he was glad of the diversion, he nodded to acknowledge her. She knew a wealthy gentleman when she saw one, and she elbowed one of her companions, who elbowed another in turn, and before Stewart knew it, six pairs of eyes and six saucy smiles were trained his way. The seventh woman, a petite thing in an ill-fitting red gown, with inky hair piled up under a theatrical-looking hat, kept her back firmly to him.

It was just as well, Stewart decided. One less woman to disappoint. He had no intention of doing anything more strenuous that night than going home and reading the last chapter of a fascinating dissertation on the life of Caradoc of Llancarfan.

"Lot of rot, that, don't you think?" Finished with his client, Lowell came over, apparently commenting on the production, the singing, and the story line of the opera. He saw the courtesans, smiled briefly, and got back to the matter at hand. "Imagine all that to-do over one woman! Wars and treachery and being buried alive. What man in his right mind would consider such a thing?"

"Well, that fellow in the opera certainly did," Matthew said, joining them. "That tenor fellow. He was enough of a romantic to betray his country for the love of a woman."

"Enough of a fool!" Stewart hadn't even realized he'd spoken until he heard his own voice, and by then it was too late to take the words back. All his brothers had gathered, and each of them stared at him.

"There's a telling statement." Charles stepped back, his arms crossed over his chest, his head to one side, his eyes just bright enough with mischief to make Stewart wish he'd kept his mouth shut. "Chafing from some shattered love affair?"

As was to be expected, the others pounced on the opportunity to torment their youngest brother. They were joined by the courtesans, who laughed and threw out a ribald comment or two.

"Brokenhearted after being scorned by your lady love?" George asked with a melodramatic sigh.

"Disheartened at finding out that woman you'd hoped to see again at the tea party was not all you expected her to be?" Matthew said, giving Stewart an encouraging pat on the back.

Stewart dismissed them all with a frown that was enough to cause one of the courtesans who looked to be more forward than the rest and more eager to earn her night's rent, to back away in alarm. "You are all quite mad," he told his brothers.

"Not as mad as that fellow in the opera," George said. "He was mad for the love of Aïda. Willing to die for the girl. And you—"

"You said he was a fool," Lowell finished for him.

"Do you really think so?" It was Edward who asked the question, and because Stewart knew he was the only one with enough sense to actually listen rather than badger and bedevil him, he answered.

"I didn't say he was a fool to be in love with her." It seemed a strange topic to be discussing with his brothers in so public a place, especially with a group of harlots listening, eager to hear the rest of whatever Stewart might have to say. But even that was no stranger than the fact that the entire time Steward had been watching the opera singers in their black Egyptian wigs, he had been thinking instead of a woman with hair the color of a desert sunset. Too baffled by the thought to consider it further, he removed his spectacles and carefully cleaned them.

"What I meant, of course," he told his brothers,

replacing his spectacles and firmly ignoring the welcoming smiles on the faces of the courtesans, "is that he was a fool to betray his country. Certainly you understand that, Edward. As do the rest of you." He glanced quickly at his brothers and wondered how an opera that was intended to be no more than a pleasant diversion had led to a topic more important to him than any of them could even imagine. "Though love might be an interesting enticement, it can certainly never take the place of a man's honor. Or his duty."

"True enough," Edward agreed. He straightened the jacket of his dashing uniform. "Yet there must be some portion of even you, Stewart, old man, that recognizes the romantic pull of the whole story. Here's a fellow willing to give up everything he owns—"

"Everything he believes in," Matthew interjected.

"Everything he holds dear," Charles joined in.

"For the love of a woman." Edward was not himself a romantic fellow, yet even his eyes took on a dreamy look. "The perfect woman! Admit it, Stewart." Edward glanced over his shoulder toward the prostitutes. Six of them continued to hang on every word. The seventh, her back still firmly to Stewart, had sidled away from the crowd a bit, and he had the distinct feeling that if not for the steady downpour, she would have walked away. "Even you must consider the possibility sometime," Edward said, drawing Stewart's attention. "You can't spend all your days bent over your dusty books."

"And your musty antiquities," Charles added.

"And your fusty old library," George concluded.

There was no use trying to put off the whole lot of them. In spite of himself, Stewart smiled. "I can't believe you don't have better things to do than worry about me," he told them.

"We don't." The statement came from Charles, and there was a rumbling of agreement all around.

"Well, you should." Stewart clapped his top hat on his head. The rain hadn't lessened a bit, but there was something about standing outside the theater that made him feel conspicuous and vulnerable. Again, he glanced around, and again, there was no sign of the poorly disguised policemen who had been following him all week. No one was paying the least bit of attention to him. Except for the prostitutes.

"I can take care of myself," Stewart told his brothers. "I don't need your advice or your meddling. Especially when it comes to women. You know me well enough to know there's no cause to worry. I'm not the type who goes running off—"

Stewart happened to glance toward the group of prostitutes just as the one who'd kept her back to him looked over her shoulder. There was something familiar about the woman's profile, though he could not for the life of him imagine what it might be. He dashed the thought aside and continued.

"I'm not the type who goes running off—"

The woman turned around again, and when she realized Stewart was looking right at her, she flinched and took off into the rain.

Stewart was convinced his eyes were playing tricks on him. It was the only thing that would explain the fact that he'd imagined the woman to have an upturned nose, and a sprinkling of freckles on her cheeks that even a heavy coating of rouge could not hide. He dismissed the thought with a shake of his shoulders and watched the woman disappear behind the curtain of rain that surrounded them. She rounded a corner and was gone.

Even as Stewart started in on his statement to his brothers one more time, "I'm not the type who goes running off—" he knew he'd never finish it. Consigning his better judgment and his wiser instincts to perdition, he took off running after the woman.

His brothers were too startled to object and much too wise to risk getting wet to follow. The harlots called out to him, but what they said he didn't even want to imagine. Stewart splashed his way through a puddle and around the corner. Twenty yards ahead of him, he saw the woman.

"Wait!" The moment he called out to her, Stewart knew it was a mistake.

The woman glanced over her shoulder, saw him, and tried to dash away. She tripped over her sodden skirts and nearly went down in the gutter. "Oh, hell!" he heard her grumble, and as he watched, she hoisted her skirts up above her knees and bounded off.

Stewart supposed he should have followed. He might even have done it if he hadn't been soaked to the skin and suddenly chilled to the bone. Instead, he watched the woman make her escape, and if there had been any doubt in his mind as to who she was, it was erased when she ran past a streetlamp and he saw the black dye from her hair washing away in rivulets down her back.

Chapter 7

Trailing after Stewart Marsh was nearly as exciting as watching candle wax harden.

The thought occurred to Aggie after only one evening of following him. After two, she feared it was true, and after three, she was certain of it. The man she had suspected was the most daring, the most romantic, and the most brazen thief in all the empire was, in his everyday life, as dull as graves, as ordinary as porridge, and more boring than boring was ever meant to be.

Except for the small excitement outside the Royal Opera House, the rest of the week had been, as she explained to Bert just that morning, an exercise in futility. In spite of the fact that her feet hurt where the borrowed boots had pinched her toes, her neck chafed where an assortment of stiff collars had rubbed it, and she had, thankfully, just seen the last of the rash on her upper lip caused by the glue she'd used to stick on her false moustache, Aggie had nothing to show for her efforts. No proof of anything—conclusive, absolute, irrefutable, or otherwise—except that Stewart Marsh was as predictable as Big Ben, as studious as a schoolmaster, and as bland as blancmange.

Which is why she'd decided to take matters into her own hands and confront him.

Determination tingling through her like the heat that came from drinking a glass of brandy, Aggie touched a hand to the journal tucked in her pocket. She would find her proof in the footsteps of the Shadow, she vowed, and a whacking good story besides. And she would beat everyone to it, Askew and Wallingstamp, Maxwell Barclay, even Stanley Greenfield.

Watching from a bench along the wall, Aggie saw Stewart walk into the British Museum. She was hardly surprised. After a week of dogging his every step, from bookshops to museums and from libraries to even more bookshops, she'd learned enough to know that he was a man of habit. It was Wednesday. It was half past ten in the morning. And on Mondays, Wednesdays, and Fridays at half past ten in the morning, Stewart Marsh always went to the reading room of the British Museum.

Today, with his spectacles sliding down his nose, his hair falling into his eyes, and a sheaf of papers under one arm that looked as if it would spill to the floor at any moment, the Essence of Evil looked more like a garden-variety schoolmaster than a criminal genius.

Aggie sighed, feeling disappointed, and not for the first time, she wondered why. Was it because Stewart was hardly the stuff of which rousing good newspaper stories were made? She liked to think so. After all, her interest in the man was purely professional. It had nothing to do with the Shadow who drifted through her dreams, the dashing scoundrel whose heart was pure passion and whose every look was as inviting as sin. It had everything to do with the fact that the more she saw of Stewart, the more she questioned herself.

Could a man who spent his days hunched over dusty volumes of Greek and Latin really spend his nights slipping into the homes of the wealthy and slipping out again with the family treasures? It seemed unlikely, yet that night at Barclay's she'd been so sure.

Aggie twitched her shoulders, ridding herself of the thought. If there was one thing she knew, it was that indecision could prove fatal. Both to her story and to her career. Perhaps Wallingstamp was right, she told herself, popping off the bench where she'd been seated and falling into step behind Stewart. All she needed was a little proof.

By the time Stewart nodded his greetings to the guards who stood nearby and stopped to say a few words to the earnest-looking fellow sitting behind a desk outside the museum's reading room, she was ready. She walked up behind Stewart, and when the man at the desk raised his eyebrows as if to ask what she was doing there and what she might want, Aggie gave him her brightest smile. "I am with Lord Stewart," she said.

She might have known she was in trouble when Stewart did not respond instantly, or even turn to see who had spoken. For what seemed far too long a time, he stood very still, his back to her, his shoulders uncommonly steady. Eventually he would have no choice but to turn around, of course. To do anything else would be unspeakably rude, and she knew enough about the gentry to know they would never risk being rude. At least not in front of an audience. It was, after all, the reason she'd chosen this very public place to confront him.

When he finally did turn to her, Stewart was enough of a gentleman to offer Aggie a quick bow, but not enough of one to even try to pretend to look pleased.

In the dim light of the museum passageway, his eyes were the color of smoke. His lips were set in a thin line that made it look as if he was holding in some great emotion which might have been anger, or exasperation, or something else altogether. There was no mistaking his expression. It was forbearance itself, as vaguely disinterested as the quick appraisal he gave Aggie.

His gaze skimmed her straight dark skirt and jacket. It touched her white blouse with its high collar and lace edging. It wandered over the smart straw boater she wore tilted rakishly atop her head. It rested on her face.

"Ah!" he said. "My shadow!" His gaze flicked over her again, and for a second his eyes brightened. "How good of you to remember to wear sensible clothing. The staff here at the museum does so frown upon scarlet women in scarlet dresses. I wondered when you might decide to show yourself again."

Aggie clicked her tongue and tossed her head, at the same time hoping she'd gotten all the black dye out of her hair. "Show myself? I don't know what you're talking about," she told him, sounding nearly as imperturbable as she'd hoped she would. "And I do believe you are confused. I am not your shadow, Lord Stewart. But you are surely mine."

"Really?" With one finger Stewart pushed his spectacles up the bridge of his nose. He stared at her a moment longer, his expression growing puzzled. "I'm afraid, actually, that I don't have the slightest idea what you're talking about." He stepped away from her and toward the door of the reading room, adjusting the papers under his arm. "Now, if you'll excuse me . . ."

Aggie had not thought to so quickly lose her opportunity to speak to him. Spurred on by the memory of Horace Wallingstamp, her own curiosity, and that one word "proof," she took a step to follow Stewart. "But I won't excuse you," she said. "Not yet." She blurted out the words before she could stop herself and was surprised when Stewart actually listened. He stopped and stared at her, waiting for more.

"You do remember me, don't you?" she asked, and though she was certain he did, Stewart didn't reply. He blinked at her from behind his spectacles. "Of course you do," Aggie said. "Remember? The garden?"

He didn't respond, but turned to leave.

"And before that!" Without even thinking, Aggie reached out for him and grasped his sleeve. "At Maxwell Barclay's." She glanced from the man behind the desk, who was pretending not to be listening, to the guards, who were leaning forward, trying to catch every word, and she saw that she might yet gain some advantage. She flattened her hand against Stewart's sleeve and slid it as far as his elbow. "You remember," she said, adding enough of a seductive purr to her voice to make the man behind the desk blush. "Upstairs. After dinner. It was dark, surely, but just as surely, I remember you."

Stewart went noticeably pale. He coughed. Cleared his throat. Ignoring both the man behind the desk, who was, in spite of his best efforts, smirking, and the two guards who were both, coincidentally, looking up at the ceiling, he muttered something under his breath that Aggie couldn't quite hear. If the look that flashed through his eyes meant anything, she was just as glad. He grabbed her arm and pulled her to the far side of the corridor. "Look here, young lady," he said in a harsh whisper, "what's this all about?"

It was an easy enough question to answer. Or it might have been, if he hadn't still been holding on to her arm. The heat of Stewart's hand went straight through the sleeve of Aggie's jacket, straight through the blouse she wore beneath it. It went even deeper than that, Aggie realized, heating blood and bone, curling through her like warm honey.

The awareness did little for her composure. Her face heating, her cheeks, she was sure, as red as bricks, Aggie didn't dare look into Stewart's eyes. She looked, instead, to his hand against her sleeve, half expecting to see a plume of smoke rising from beneath his fingers.

He took the look for a message. Quickly he pulled his hand back to his side. "I . . . I asked you a question," he said, adjusting and readjusting the bundle of papers beneath his arm. "I asked you who you are and what you want."

"I might be able to answer that question for you, Lord Stewart."

From behind her, Aggie heard the sound of a man's voice. She turned and gasped in surprise. In her search for newsworthy stories, she had haunted the environs of the government seat of power at Whitehall long enough to recognize one of the most influential and trusted of Queen Victoria's advisers on sight.

From his shock of white hair to his face filled with wrinkles and wisdom, Sir Digby Talbot looked exactly as he had the last time Aggie had come this

close to him. The way she remembered it, that was
the very day her story about the Ethiopian royal family appeared on the front page of the *Chronicle*. Sir
Digby had read it, it seemed. He had taken great
pains to tell her exactly what he thought of it. It
might have been grand to report his reaction, if his
assessment hadn't included a good many words
Aggie knew would never see their way into print.

Aggie swallowed hard and managed a smile that
might charitably have been termed wan. "Sir Digby."
She offered her hand and was not at all surprised
when Sir Digby didn't take it. "How good to see
you again."

It wasn't, of course, at all good. But it was interesting. Interesting that so important a man should arrive
at such an out-of-the-ordinary place at exactly the
time Stewart was always there. Her nose twitching
at the smell of a story, Aggie perked up. "Do you
and Lord Stewart have an appointment?" she asked.

"None of your business." Sir Digby was not the
sort of gentleman who ever growled or grumbled,
but in this instance he found an opportunity to do
both. He glared at Aggie and turned a look that was
only a little less hostile on Stewart. "Do you know
who this is?" he asked. He didn't wait for Stewart
to answer. Sir Digby grunted. "Of course you don't
know who it is. If you did, you wouldn't be standing
here talking to her. Name's O'Day. Known as 'A.
O'Day.' Writes for that gossipmongering, talebearing,
rag-mannered . . . that *Illustrated . . . Daily . . .*
whatever!"

Now that her anonymity was spoiled, there really
seemed to be no point in continuing the charade.
"The *London Daily Enquirer and Illustrated News Chronicle*," Aggie corrected him. She whisked her journal

out of her pocket, flipped it open, and grabbed her pencil. "Lord Stewart," she said, turning to him, "I'd like to ask you a few questions."

If Stewart was surprised by the revelation, he didn't show it. He looked at Aggie rather as if she were pinned in place under glass, and when he was done dismissing her as a specimen without interest, he rolled his eyes. "Really, Miss O'Day, if you are some Society reporter intent on finding out if I am engaged to be married this Season—"

"Are you?" It was the last question she would have asked. The last thing she should have been worried about. But once the words were spoken, it was impossible to take them back. Aggie lifted her chin and waited for Stewart's answer, making it look for all the world as if it was the most natural thing in the world to ask, a polite question rather than an instinctive reaction to a topic that, unaccountably, caused her a quick, sharp stab of panic.

"No." Stewart seemed as surprised to be answering the question as she was asking it. He recovered his aplomb in less than a heartbeat. "No," he said again, more firmly this time. "You can tell your readers—"

"She will tell her readers anything she likes." Sir Digby's assessment was not too far from the mark. Not that Aggie would ever admit it or show the least bit of remorse. She watched color rise in the old statesman's cheeks. "Not to worry about that, my boy. If it pleases her, Miss O'Day will tell her readers that you are marrying Queen Cleopatra reincarnated into the vicar's daughter. Or perhaps she'd prefer a story that links you with a woman from Mars. That's about the size of it, isn't it, girl? You'll make up whatever suits your needs."

"That A. O'Day?" Stewart looked over Aggie's head toward Sir Digby, and damn them if they didn't talk as if she wasn't even there. "The A. O'Day who writes that asinine nonsense about—"

There was no use letting him get carried away. Aggie interrupted without a qualm. "As I was just about to ask . . . Sir Digby, you are obviously here at the museum to meet with Lord Stewart. Can you tell me if this appointment has anything to do with the Sha—"

"Do give my regards to your parents, Lord Stewart." With a nod toward Stewart and an icy look in Aggie's direction, Sir Digby backed away. "I would love to stay and speak to you about the family, but I am on my way to see Mr. Rowlings, the director of the museum. We have had this appointment for quite some time, and I would hate to be late." He paused long enough to make certain that Aggie seized his meaning, and when he was sure she had, he turned and walked away.

"Not the A. O'Day who writes that gammon and pickles about sea monsters and ghosts?"

Aggie gave Stewart a sour smile. She had hoped that when he finally learned her identity, he might say something more in keeping with the respect her talents deserved, or at least something a bit more civil.

"Yes," she told him. "A. O'Day. Aggie O'Day." She managed to control the acid in her voice, but just barely. "I'd like to ask you a few questions about—"

"The same A. O'Day. . . ." Still stunned, Stewart gaped at her and fought to control the rise of disbelief in his voce. "The same A. O'Day who managed to write all that twaddle about a curse on Arthur's Crown?"

Instinctively, Aggie defended herself. "It isn't twaddle," she told him, even as she reminded herself that, of course, it was. "It is a known fact that—"

"Holy jumping mother of Moses!" Stewart's exclamation had more to do with annoyance than with surprise. He spun away from her and stalked into the reading room.

Aggie followed right along. "You cannot dismiss the possibility of a curse," she told him, keeping her head and sounding, she thought, far more reasonable than he was acting. "There are, after all, many mysterious things in this world. Things that most people cannot even fathom. There are—"

"Wailing ghosts and monsters the size of houses who slink in and out of the shadows along the river?" He slapped his papers down on a nearby table and visibly fought to control the exasperation that seethed through his every word, at the same time struggling to keep his voice to a whisper. Even so, the people seated at the tables around them were less than appreciative. More than a few glanced up and frowned and some others, less patient, reminded them that this was a reading library and not a schoolyard or a rugby field.

Aggie hardly cared, and Stewart apparently did not notice. He turned and marched toward the aisles of bookshelves that surrounded the central section of the room. "How can anyone be so mindless as to repeat that sort of irresponsible nonsense? Or worse yet, invent it. Which is, I suppose, what you must have done. Invented the curse, I mean. Am I right?" He pulled to a stop long enough to glare at her, as if that might cow her into admitting the truth, and when it didn't, he turned on his heels and kept walking.

"A curse," he mumbled. "A curse on the crown of a fifth-century warlord. It isn't mentioned in Geoffrey. Bede and Nennius never say a word about it. And you . . ." He whirled to confront her, and Aggie nearly slammed into his chest. She pulled up at the last second, avoiding a collision, and looked up into eyes that shot blue fire. "You, Miss Aggie O'Day, you who don't know a fig about the fifth century or crowns or King Arthur—"

"Of course I know about King Arthur." Aggie dismissed his criticism with a shrug. "I've read Tennyson, the same as has everyone else. I know all about—"

"You know all about nothing. And now you're telling the world. You've got everyone in town talking about your damned fool curse and anxious to see the crown and—" Whatever else he was going to say, Stewart thought better of it. He clamped his lips into a tight line and turned toward the bookshelves again, and for the next few minutes he said nothing at all. He looked through title after title, obviously in search of something in particular, or perhaps in search of nothing at all.

Aggie watched as he lifted one especially large book from the shelf, paged through it, then put it back again. He did the same with a second book. A third. A fourth. The silence grew as close around them as the shelves of books to Aggie's left and right. The aisle between the shelves was narrow, and though the entire center of the room was illuminated by the windows that lined the huge domed roof, in the stacks it was dull and gray. The smell of old leather pressed in upon Aggie from every side. Warm air, heavy with the scent of musty paper, filled her lungs. It was an atmosphere that invited confidences and hinted at intimacy.

For some reason she didn't even want to think about, the very thought caused a shiver to tingle its way up Aggie's spine. She stilled it with another thought. This was also a location that afforded her a unique opportunity. She stood between Stewart and the only exit out of the stacks. It was time for her to get to work.

"You know," she said, her voice walking the fine line between suggestion and compromise, "you don't need to sort through all these books yourself. You can tell them what you're looking for, and they'll bring the right books to you at your table."

Noting her change of mood, he glanced at her out of the corner of his eye. "Yes, I realize that." He chose another book and opened it. "They know me well enough here. They allow me to find my own books."

"You come here often, then?"

In spite of himself, Stewart gave her a wry smile. He shook his head in wonder. "You know I do," he said, turning to her. "You've been following me like a dog after a butcher's wagon. What is it you want, Miss O'Day? If not a story for your Society pages, then what?"

Aggie had a reply ready for him. It might even have been a clever one, had she found the breath to give it. She looked up into eyes that were impossibly blue and wondered how she'd found herself here in the warm half darkness with a man who, despite the fact that he did his best to appear terribly stuffy and just as terribly dull, still somehow made her heart beat double time and her pulse pound hard.

Stewart looked down into eyes that were impossibly green and reminded himself that this was not the time or the place to allow his imagination free rein. If it were, he might have been tempted to think about the soft bow of Aggie's lips, or the way her man-tailored jacket stopped at just the right place to emphasize hips that were femininity itself. He might have let himself wax poetic about the way her hair was swept up, exposing a neck as pale as ivory, or even allowed his gaze to dip from the determined tilt of her chin all the way down to where her lace-edged collar brushed the hollow at the base of her throat.

If he placed a finger there, would he feel her heart beating? Would it be as unsteady as his?

With a noise that echoed like rifle shot through the stillness, Stewart slammed shut the book he was holding and rammed it back into place on the shelf, scattering his errant thoughts and bringing himself back to reality.

He recalled that at Maxwell Barclay's tea party, he'd wondered about the mysterious redhead who sometimes played the burglar, sometimes the maid. He reminded himself that in the time since, he'd used his considerable talents and a variety of sources that were wide-ranging and capable, to try to discover the identity of the mysterious woman who dogged his steps and haunted his dreams. Much to his annoyance, he'd found out nothing, and that had made him nervous.

Was she with the police? The thought had crossed Stewart's mind more than once, and for a while he'd assumed she was working with Inspector Stanley Greenfield. Aggie had reinforced the notion when, after the opera, he realized she was the one in the suit and silly moustache who had followed him on a book-buying outing. She'd enhanced it further when, dressed as a jarvey, she'd waited for him outside this very museum. And as for the night outside the opera house . . .

Stewart discarded the thought before it could distract him from the subject at hand. There was no use remembering the way Aggie looked in the scarlet dress. No use thinking about her creamy shoulders, or her slender neck, or the fact that the dress was cut low enough to spark a man's imagination in ways that were neither right nor proper.

He reminded himself that he had a mission to accomplish, and no matter now attractive the woman, no matter how tempting the eyes and the lips and the hollow at the base of her throat, he knew now that Aggie was a threat to that mission. She was neither thief nor servant nor detective. She was a newspaper reporter, one who was apparently ready to stop playing games and start getting down to business. And that made her all the more dangerous.

He held on to the thought, or at least he tried. It might have been infinitely easier if Aggie O'Day—bungling burglar, incompetent housemaid, and a journalist on a crusade that could expose him to the world and compromise a mission that he held more dearly than his life—hadn't been so damned kissable.

The situation might have been easier to tolerate, and a good deal less bothersome, if Aggie hadn't acted as if she knew exactly what he was thinking. It was as if she could read every wayward thought that steamed through his head at flank speed. And she wasn't surprised by any of them.

She wasn't the least bit reluctant to take advantage of the temporary madness that robbed him of his reason, either. Her pencil poised above a kind of journal that looked to have been put together from poorly tanned leather and inexpensive foolscap, she flicked her tongue across her lips, then gnawed her lower lip between her teeth. It was an innocent and unconscious action, surely. Or it might have been, coming from any other woman. Coming from Aggie, Stewart had serious doubts about it being unconscious. Or innocent. He had no doubts whatsoever about it being provocative.

"Hell in a handcart." The sound of his own voice was enough to startle Stewart, but it wasn't until he heard the words that he knew how appropriate they were. It was exactly where he was headed. Hell in a handcart. One pushed by a calculating redhead.

"I beg your pardon?" It was just as well that Aggie didn't wait for him to repeat himself. Obviously deciding that whatever he'd said wasn't at all what she wanted to hear, she made ready to write. "I want to ask you some questions," she said. "About your criminal tendencies."

It was all Stewart needed to bring him back to his senses. Forcing himself to remember who he was, and who he was supposed to be, he picked up another volume and pretended to be engrossed in it. If there was one thing he'd learned about Aggie in their short acquaintance, it was that she had only a small store of patience. There was something about annoying a woman who could herself be so annoying that was, in its own perverse way, quite enjoyable.

Stewart ran his finger down the page that fell open in front of him. Force of habit, he supposed. He could never really pretend to be reading a book. There was always something that captured his attention, whether he wanted it to or not. This time, it was quite a cogent discussion on the actual site of a Dark

Age battle designated in history books only as Cerdicesleag. It wasn't until he heard the incessant tapping of Aggie's toe that he realized he actually *had* become quite engrossed.

"Oh!" Stewart looked up, pleased to see that his campaign of trying to vex her had worked. There were dark stains of color in Aggie's cheeks, and her lips were pressed together as if it was all she could do to contain her anger. As eager to escalate the battle as he was to see what she was made of and how far he could goad her before she retreated, he cleared his throat. "You know," he said, "there are eighty-four thousand books here in the reading room. Eighty-four thousand that you can see, that is." He closed the book he was holding and, deciding it needed closer scrutiny, he did not reshelve it. "There are more than four million all together. Four million books, that is. They are stored on forty-eight miles worth of iron shelving."

"Yes, that's lovely." Aggie offered a tight smile. "But while that is truly fascinating, what I'd really like to know about is—"

"The building was designed by Panizzi in 1854." Without even looking through it, Stewart picked up another book and another after that. They were thick and heavy, and he held them in the crook of his arm, stacking one atop the other. The irony did not escape him. He was building a wall between himself and Aggie, one he hoped would be strong enough to keep her questions out. And his secrets in. He looked down at her from over the pile of books. "The dome in the reading room is really quite spectacular, don't you think?"

"I think," Aggie replied, "that you are avoiding my questions. If you'd only—"

"The names of nineteen great authors are inscribed there near the dome, high up on the walls." It wasn't easy to pretend to be oblivious to Aggie's spluttered protests, not when they caused her lips to pucker into a most delectable pout. Nor was it easy to ignore the sensation like electricity that shot through his body when he reached for another book and his arm brushed hers.

Time for a hasty retreat of his own.

It was the best advice he'd given himself in quite some time, and Stewart followed it as quickly as he could, before he could change his mind. He shouldered his way past Aggie and headed down the aisle, picking up book after book and adding them to his stack without even looking at the titles. "Chaucer, Shakespeare, Bacon, Milton, Addison, Swift, Pope . . ." He didn't have to look up to the dome that dominated the center of the room. He knew by rote the names of the authors inscribed there, and he repeated them, a sort of litany intended to dispel his fantasies and keep him from succumbing to temptations he had not, until that every moment, ever thought could be so tantalizing.

"Chaucer, Shakespeare, Bacon, Milton, Addison, Swift, Pope . . ." He paused long enough to glance over his shoulder at Aggie, who was scrambling to keep up. "I say, Miss O'Day, you're not writing any of this down. I thought you were interested in the reading room."

"I am interested in you."

The enormity of the statement struck as soon as the words were out of Aggie's mouth. She stopped dead and squeezed her eyes shut, and it was evident she had not meant to say as much, at least not in so many words. She reddened from the base of her neck all the way to the roots of her already fiery hair.

There was some small pleasure in hearing her say the words, some puzzling warmth that found its way to his heart along with them, and Stewart decided right then and there that it was just as well her eyes were closed. Otherwise she might have seen the smile that threatened to betray him.

Fortunately for both his self-control and his pride, he did not have time to think it through and figure out what it all meant. In a show of pluck as impressive as any he'd ever seen, Aggie opened her eyes, swallowed her chagrin, and forced herself to keep her gaze levelly on his. "That did not sound at all as I meant it to," she said. "What I mean, of course, is—"

"What you mean is that you are in the throes of creating some elaborate and far-fetched fiction, and for some reason I cannot fathom and do not want to examine more closely, you have decided to place me at the center of it." Stewart's words crackled like gunfire. It was not, he told himself, too harsh a response. Not for a woman who had hounded him and harried him and followed him from one end of London to the other, hoping to find Lord-knew-what and, in the process, keeping him from the work he should have been doing. He refused to feel guilty.

It might have been easier to follow his own advice if Aggie hadn't acted as if she'd been shot through the heart. Her eyes widened just enough to make her look a bit like a startled deer. Her right hand went to her breast, pressed there as if to ward off his angry words.

Stewart told himself she hadn't earned his sympathy and she didn't deserve it. Still, he found himself speaking with a little less anger, and a little more patience. "Look . . ." He sighed. "There are, perhaps, any number of publishers who might be interested in romantic fiction of the sort you are obviously trying to write. But I do fear the public as a whole will not accept it. It is far too fanciful and far-fetched. I'm really terribly sorry, but I . . ." He shook his head, not the least bit sorry.

"Don't you think I wouldn't love to be this Shadow fellow you're after?" he asked. He walked toward the table where he'd left his papers, deposited his books, and looked up toward the dome, lost in reverie. "There's a thought! Dashing. Handsome. Bold as brass! And rich as Midas, no doubt. At least he must be, with all the gold and jewels he's carried off." He twitched his shoulders, getting rid of the daydream and gave Aggie what he hoped looked enough like a wistful smile to pass muster. "It is every little boy's dream to be a romantic hero, and believe it or not, those dreams don't change much when the boy grows into a man. There's some appeal there. I will admit that much. Slinking through alleyways and slipping through upper-story widows. But I . . ." Stewart patted the stack of books on the table.

"I am a scholar, Miss O'Day. Nothing more. The fact that you've been following me makes me think you've got me mixed up with someone else. It's because of that damned silly burglary of yours, of course. What were you trying to do? Have a look at Arthur's Crown?" She didn't need to answer. He could see the truth there in her eyes. He had to give her credit, she had nerve enough for a dozen newspaper reporters. It was that, more than anything, that put the fear of God into him.

Not that he would ever let her know it. The

Shadow hadn't been able to keep his identity and his real purpose a secret all these years by running at the first sign of trouble. Or by being easily intimidated. This time, it was more important than ever that he keep his composure, hold tight to his secrets, and complete his mission. Stewart didn't have to remind himself of that. This time, there was nothing he wouldn't risk. He would have to play his part with Aggie O'Day, and play it for all it was worth.

Hoping the gesture was decisive enough to send a clear message, Stewart gave Aggie a curt nod. He turned, sat down, and pulled the top book off the pile and opened it. He adjusted his spectacles, focusing on the small, cramped type. "I'm really terribly sorry," he said, almost as an afterthought, "but I am not your man."

Aggie clutched her pencil so tightly that her knuckles were white, and the silence stretched taut. The very thought that he could dismiss her as nothing more than a woman with an imagination too fanciful for her own good was enough to send a burst of anger through her. As usual, her anger only made her more determined than ever to prove her point.

" 'I am really terribly sorry, but I am not your man.' " Aggie repeated the words under her breath at the same time she scribbled them into her notebook. It was just as well Stewart was busy over his books. Otherwise, he might have seen the way her fingers trembled and her letters wobbled, and she'd be damned if she'd let that happen. She stood behind him, shoulders so tight she could feel her muscles straining, and waited for him to make the next move.

She might have known it would be cheeky.

"I beg your pardon?" Stewart turned, and his eyebrows shot up, almost as if he'd forgotten she was there. "What was that you said?"

"I said . . ." Aggie made a great show of looking at her journal. She read the words back to him very carefully. " 'I am really terribly sorry, but I am not your man.' "

His head cocked to one side, Stewart considered her response. "That's what I thought you said. But why—"

"It's really quite good." Aggie brightened. "I can picture using it as the beginning to one of my articles. 'I am really terribly sorry, but I am not your man.' " She repeated the words, giving them a dramatic and somewhat ominous reading. " 'So said the man who was really the Shadow,' " she said, saying the words aloud as they came to her. Before they could escape her, she jotted them down. " 'Yet, gentle reader, you will see in these pages that the man who so boldly proclaimed those words is—' "

"The man who so boldly proclaimed those words is quite exasperated." Stewart looked at her over the wire rims of his spectacles. "You do seem the ambitious type, and while I find that quite commendable—"

" 'Dazzled by ambition.' " Aggie made a quick note of it. "That's good. Very good. It gives the reader a keen insight into the warped mind of a criminal. What was it you said? That night at Barclay's? You said something about that Freud fellow and about how he believes that a person's motives are not always—"

"Are you analyzing me?" Stewart bristled. "See here, young lady, I will not sit here and have you tell me what I'm thinking. Or what it means. I am a man of infinite patience, but—"

"Patience," Aggie made a note of that, too. "I could see as much. That night at Barclay's. The way you assessed the situation before you ventured too far into the room . . . the way you took your time about having a go at that lock on the wardrobe. Patience, yes! I can see that would be a very valuable asset in a profession such as yours."

Stewart stared at her. For a good long while. He blinked. Pushed his spectacles back up where they belonged. Blinked again. Finally and very slowly, he rose from his chair. He gave the stack of books what could only be described as a look of longing, and glared at Aggie.

"You're insane," he said, right before he turned and left the room.

In a scene fraught with dramatic possibilities, it was not the rousing finale for which Aggie had hoped. No matter. She would find her drama soon enough.

With a satisfied smile Aggie watched Stewart leave. She closed her journal, tucked it away, and headed out of the reading room, being sure to keep well behind him. She would find her drama, sure enough. Just as she would find the proof that Horace Wallingstamp demanded. And she knew exactly how she would do it.

It was time to employ the Smile.

Chapter 8

Flirting with men was second nature to Aggie.

It wasn't something she was ashamed to admit, nor was it something she had any misgivings about doing. She was enough of a realist to know a woman would never make her way in a man's world without some unfair advantage, and she had learned early on that a pretty face, a silvery laugh, and, of course, the Smile were her own special advantages. Unfair or not, it hardly concerned her. What mattered was that by using these assets she generally got her way. And tonight more than ever, her way was exactly what she wanted.

Reminding herself of the fact, Aggie watched the dour-looking servant at Sir Digby Talbot's front door take hold of the single sheet of heavy vellum paper she handed him. In elegant script, the card proclaimed to all the world that the honor of Miss Aggie O'Day's presence was requested at this gathering hosted by Sir Digby, who was heading the queen's Diamonds Jubilee festivities, in honor of those organizing the celebration. The servant glanced from Aggie to the invitation. He looked back up, and curse him if he didn't look the tiniest bit skeptical.

The forgery was a good one, or at least it better have been; Aggie had paid for it twice. One payment was made to a servant right there at Sir Digby's who had pinched a legitimate invitation at her behest. Another went to have the invitation copied by a counterfeiter. If the look the servant was giving both Aggie and the invitation meant anything, the forger was not as skilled as his prices were reasonable.

She decided not to hedge her bets. Aggie sidled a bit closer to the servant—and to the front door— and batted her eyelashes, leaning toward the man just enough for her ivory wrap to fall away from her bare shoulders. "There isn't a problem, is there?" she asked.

The poor man never stood a chance. Try as he might, he couldn't keep his gaze from sliding down. From Aggie's lips curved into a pretty pout. To Aggie's neck and the string of almost-real-looking pearls she'd bought from a pawnbroker in Limehouse. To the gown Aggie had borrowed from her friend Rosie, a chorus girl at the Adelphi Theater who was mistress to a man who could afford such things. The gown was a confection the likes of which Aggie had never worn before. The sleeves were short and gathered above her elbows. The skirt was cut close against her hips. The neckline of the gown was square and low, and it left no doubt that Rosie was not nearly so well endowed as Aggie. In spite of the fact that she'd tugged her corset tight enough to make breathing nearly impossible, there was no containing the swell of her breasts. They showed just enough over the top of the plunging neckline to make the servant's ears turn red.

"No problem. No, miss." The man dragged his gaze back to Aggie's face. "You have a nice time, miss," he said.

Before he could come to his senses and change his

mind, Aggie snatched the invitation out of his fingers and hurried into the party. She deposited her wrap with another waiting servant and congratulated herself. Her womanly wiles worked every time.

But if all that was true, why did the very thought of using them to pry information out of Stewart Marsh set her stomach fluttering and make her heart feel as if it would pound a hole right through her ribs?

Her throat was suddenly as dry as her palms were wet inside her satin, elbow-length gloves. Aggie scolded herself. She'd promised herself she wouldn't think about it. She'd told herself—more times than she cared to admit—that the only thing that mattered was her story, and the fame and fortune that would trail in its wake like the sweeping train of Rosie's gown. She vowed she wouldn't give a second thought to the disarming way Stewart stammered around a subject when he was unnerved. Or the fact that, time and again, his bluster was considerable, but his touch was gentle. She swore she wouldn't allow herself to be the least bit affected by the man. Not by the way he talked, or the way he laughed, or the almost convincing way he pretended to be something she knew he definitely was not. And certainly not by the fact that her blood heated every time he looked at her.

Aggie pressed a hand to her heart, fighting against the panic bunching inside her. Tonight, she reminded herself, it was Stewart's turn to be unnerved. And distracted. And dazzled.

Just as she'd been since the night she met him.

He might be as smart as be damned, and easy on the eyes, and enough of a rogue to tempt a girl to forget herself, but Stewart Marsh was, after all, only a man. And men could be charmed.

He was also the Shadow, Aggie reminded herself, raising her chin and sailing toward the ballroom, and it was time to stop dillydallying. Time to start getting her proof.

She had hoped for a reprieve, or at least enough time to take a turn around the room and get the lay of the land, but there was a pause in the music and most of the dancers had left the room for refreshment. The moment Aggie excused herself around an elderly matron blocking nearly all of the double doorway and nodded a greeting to a young buck who nodded back with obvious approval, she saw Stewart at the far side of the dance floor.

He stood with his back to her, facing the French doors that had been thrown open in deference to the mild evening, deep in conversation with the same circle of men she'd seen him with at the opera. She had done enough research to know his family inside and out. By the look of them, the men must surely be Stewart's brothers. All but one of them had the same color hair, acorn brown sparked with mahogany highlights under the blaze of the electric chandeliers. Except for a rather astonishingly handsome brother in the uniform of the Queen's Horse Guard who was nearly as tall, Stewart was at least a head higher than the rest. His shoulders were broader by far, which on thought of it, seemed an odd thing for a scholar but not at all odd for a man who made his living prowling into and out of upper-story windows.

The familiar rat-a-tat-tat of an unsteady heartbeat started against Aggie's ribs. She paused, gathering her courage, doing her best to convince herself she was as ready as she would ever be. Throwing caution to the wind at the same time she tugged the bodice of her dress just a little higher over her breasts, she called upon the Smile and headed straight for Stewart.

"There you are. I've looked all over for you." Aggie placed one hand on Stewart's sleeve, the gesture conspicuously intimate, especially in so public a place. "In this crush of people I thought never to find you."

The silence that descended over the little group was no less than absolute. The brother she knew must be Matthew, the cleric, froze with his champagne flute partway to his mouth. Another brother, the one who must certainly have been Lowell, had the unfortunate bad manners to let his mouth drop open. The handsome brother in uniform stepped back and took the measure of the situation, a smile lighting his face. The other two simply stared. And Stewart . . .

Using her best and brightest version of the Smile, Aggie looked up into an expression that, had she been recording the occasion for posterity, she might have described as one of total and complete flabbergastation.

He recovered in less than a heartbeat—she'd known he would—and by the time he did, Aggie was ready for him. She slipped her arm through Stewart's and glanced from brother to brother. "You might have told me you'd be here with your family," she said, her voice tinged with the tiniest shade of disappointment. "I thought we were to have some time alone."

"That's it!" The brother who looked to be the oldest, so therefore must have been Charles, gave Stewart a playful punch on the arm. "That explains everything. Now we know why you're here tonight."

"You devil!" Matthew didn't sound at all the way

a man of the cloth might be expected to sound when he mentioned that particular personage. He lifted his champagne glass in salute. "You cheeky devil! You never told us—"

"And I can see why." The brother who must surely have been George, the banker, closed in, a smile in his eyes. He took Aggie's hand and raised it to his lips. "Keeping this delicious little secret to yourself, were you, boy?" he asked Stewart over Aggie's fingers. "I can see why. She's absolutely— "

"A stunner!" Lowell blinked in astonishment, but whether it was at Aggie or at the realization that he'd let slip with a sentiment that was probably best left unspoken in mixed company, she didn't know.

The brother in uniform intervened. "You might introduce us," he suggested. "Or is the young lady's name as much of a secret as your obvious friendship with her?"

In spite of the fact that he did his best to look as dispassionate as he sounded, Aggie couldn't help but notice Stewart's gaze slide the length of her body. It rested on the plunging neckline of her gown just long enough to assure her that borrowing the dress had been worthwhile. "The young lady . . ." Stewart uncoiled his arm from Aggie's and deftly spun her back in the direction she came. "The young lady is just leaving."

"Not so fast!" Charles intercepted her and putting one hand politely on her elbow, turned her back the other way. "If you think you're going to keep this a secret from us, Stewart, think again."

Buoyed at having found support where she least expected it, Aggie ran one gloved finger from the snowy cuffs of Stewart's shirt that showed beneath his jacket sleeve all the way up to his elbow. "You heard them, Stewart. You can't keep me a secret. Not any longer. They were sure to find out sooner or later."

"Find out what? You're not engaged, are you?" Matthew's cheeks turned as red as pomegranates. "Mother will be ecstatic!"

"She always said you locked yourself away with those dusty books of yours far too much, you know." Charles added.

"And that you'd never find a woman that way," George reminded him.

"But he seems to have done quite nicely for himself." Edward topped off the conversation by offering Aggie a soft smile. "Are you and Stewart old friends?" he asked.

"She and Stewart are not friends at all!" It must have taken all the breeding of a dozen generations of blue-blooded Marshes for Stewart to keep his voice down to a reasonable grumble. He sent his brothers a look that silenced them instantly, then turned the full measure of his fury on Aggie. "If you must know," he said, "this is Aggie O'Day. She's a newspaper reporter."

He said the words as if he expected the skies to open and a lightning bolt to punctuate them. He was nearly persuasive enough to convince Aggie. When nothing happened, she was happy, and happier still when it looked as if Stewart's brothers didn't care about her profession in the least.

"Mother will be a bit disappointed," Lowell commented. "But she'll get over it."

"And Father, of course . . ." Matthew shook his head. "Father will question your judgment. But once he meets Miss O'Day . . . once he sees how absolutely charming she is . . ."

"And once he realizes she's from a good family . . ."
George glanced at Aggie, sizing her up. "You are
from a good family, aren't you?"

"Of course she's from a good family." It was Edward who came to Aggie's rescue. "Stewart wouldn't
dream of marrying a girl who wasn't."

This time even Stewart did not have the fortitude
to bear the torrent of his brothers' enthusiasm. The
sound that escaped him could be described only as
a growl. "Miss O'Day isn't here to marry me," he
said between clenched teeth. "She is here because
she's writing a newspaper article. She's got it into
her head that I am someone I am not. She's following
me, hounding me, badgering me—" he glared down
at her—"because she believes I am the Shadow."

If Aggie thought the silence that had welcomed
her entrance was complete, she was surely wrong.
This time the silence was as deep as, apparently, the
Marsh brothers' surprise was unequivocal.

But only for a moment.

George burst into laughter. Charles wiped tears of
amusement from his eyes. Lowell clutched his sides
and nearly spilled his drink. Edward shook his head
as if to say that someone—Stewart or Aggie, he
wasn't sure which—must surely be insane, and Matthew puffed out his cheeks and grinned like the
Cheshire cat eating cheese.

"You see?" Stewart turned an eye on Aggie. "Even
my family thinks it a preposterous idea."

"A preposterous plan, more likely." Still smiling,
Charles gave Stewart a broad smile and with a quick
bow to Aggie, moved away. "Surely you can come
up with a better story than that, old boy. If you want
to be alone with the woman—"

"Just tell us." Edward gave Stewart a wink and

followed Charles. "You don't have to pretend at some clandestine interview for some inconceivable newspaper story."

The others moved away as well.

"The Shadow," Matthew chuckled. "And here you said you'd come tonight to meet with Sir Digby. We need to have a talk, my boy," he added with mock gravity. "About the Eighth Commandment."

Before he moved away, George bent over Aggie's hand. "Keep him in line," he whispered with a smile.

"Yes, do," Lowell added before he, too was gone.

It wasn't until they were alone that Aggie dared to look at Stewart again. Before she did, she reminded herself to smile, no matter what expression she found staring back at her. "A meeting with Sir Digby. Interesting, that. Something you'd care to talk about?"

Stewart didn't answer. He let his gaze drop from Aggie's face all the way to the tips of her ivory satin shoes, then brought it up again, his perusal so agonizingly slow and careful as to leave no doubt that he was cataloging every inch of her he could see— which was, in this dress, a good many inches—and imagining every inch he could not.

The ball of panic in Aggie's throat slipped and lodged itself firmly somewhere between her heart and her stomach. Her blood turned to fire. Her knees felt weak. She had to remind herself that she was the one who was supposed to be in charge. She was the one who was supposed to be the charmer, not the charmed. The one who was, for all intents and purposes, the temptress, not the tempted.

It might have been far easier to remember if she hadn't suddenly and quite fiercely wanted Stewart

Marsh more than she'd ever wanted anything in all her life.

As genuinely tongue-tied as he usually only pretended to be, Stewart stared at the way the light of the crystal chandelier kindled color in Aggie's hair and washed against her skin. He warned himself it was neither polite nor wise, yet he was powerless to stop himself from following the blush of the light with his gaze. He chased it from where it sparkled in her eyes to where it brushed against her lips. He followed it across the stubborn tilt of her chin and trailed it down her neck. He noted the way it burnished her shoulders, and he couldn't help but appreciate the shadow it kissed in the hollow at the base of her throat. He allowed his gaze to drift further still, and when it came to the place where the smooth swell of her breasts showed above the neckline of her gown, he found he couldn't look any further if he tried.

Had he been thinking more like a rational man and less like a escapee from Bedlam, Stewart might have pulled up his socks and reminded himself that delicious or not, Aggie was as wrong for him as any woman could ever possibly be. He knew it, of course. By now, he should. It was something he'd been reminding himself of ever since the night she'd slipped over Maxwell Barclay's wall and left him with nothing but her hat—and the memory of a glimpse of lacy underpinnings that found its way into his head at the most inopportune times.

He might actually have believed his own advice, or at least pretended to be listening to it, if not for the hint of vulnerability that he saw now and again in Aggie's eyes. And the intelligence, ingenuity, and, perhaps, even talent, that he suspected were lurking behind her posturing. And the fact that when she stood as she was standing now, chin thrust out in defiance and head held high, he could see enough to spark his imagination. Just envisioning the soft, warm shadow between her breasts was enough to make his heart melt and his body feverish for release.

And then, of course, there were the pearls.

It was bad strategy to allow himself even the slightest bit of a smile, yet Stewart could hardly help it. The string of pearls that caressed Aggie's neck might have been a good enough humbug to deceive anyone as blind as a brickbat, but they could hardly fool an expert. And a man who made his living by appropriating valuable things from other people was, after all, something of an expert, if he did say so himself.

Well done or not, he recognized an imitation when he saw one, and in this instance, it was not a particularly well done one. The clasp that nestled at the back of Aggie's neck was metal covered with gold paint and studded with paste diamonds. The pearls that lay in so enviable a place near her breasts were papier-mâché coated with lacquer.

She had gone to some extent to carry off this ruse. He would give her that much. He didn't dare question how she'd managed to gain admittance to Sir Digby's. He didn't want to know. He knew only that she was bound and determined to play her part. Tonight, the part was neither that of burglar, nor maid, nor crusading journalist. It was that of enchantress, surely, and like it or not, Stewart found himself wishing Aggie had come dressed to the nines and looking like a dream not to find Stewart the Shadow, but to find Stewart the man. The realization was enough to tug at his emotions at the same time it pulled at other, even more sensitive, portions of his anatomy.

And enough to warn him that though he may have lost his mind, he'd best be careful not to lose his heart. Not to a woman who wanted nothing more than his head on her trophy wall.

"If Sir Digby finds you here, there'll be hell to pay." He couldn't imagine why he'd care, or why he'd even bother to think about it, but Stewart thought it only fair to warn her.

It was advice that Aggie, apparently, did not take seriously. She gave him a smile so bright it struck like a physical blow, warming Stewart's midsection at the same time it left him breathless.

"I'd hate to cause poor old Sir Digby any distress," she said. She glanced toward the door, an invitation in both her eyes and in the husky murmur of her voice. "Perhaps we'd better leave before he has a chance to take any notice of me."

"Leave? Together?" On his more rational days, Stewart wondered what it would really feel like to be the word-bound and dusty hermit he usually impersonated. Now he knew. It felt like hell. Like his heart and his breathing were working on two distinct timetables. Like his head was filled not with the knowledge he so treasured but with fantasies that surprised even him. Ones that not only featured Aggie but depended on her for their fulfillment.

"Leave. Together." Stewart repeated the words, turning the thought over rather as one might a lit firecracker. He knew it was a dangerous idea even to consider. He was certain it would explode in his face. But it was rather exciting waiting to see just when that might happen, and how much damage it really would do. "I can't . . ." He shook himself out

of the stupor that seemed to have robbed him of his
intellect. "I can't imagine why you'd wish to leave
with me, Miss O'Day. Whatever do we have to talk
about?"

Aggie's laugh was of the kind he could describe
only as silvery. She stepped closer. Not near enough
to look forward or immodest, just near enough for
him to catch the scent of damask roses and the play
of light and shadow against her bosom. "You are a
canny one, you are." Playfully, she tapped his arm
with the folded fan she carried in one hand. She
glanced at him out of the corner of her eye. "We
could do no talking at all," she suggested. "Or . . ."
She moved another step closer, and it took more willpower than Stewart knew he possessed not to snatch
her into his arms. "Or you could tell me why you're
here to see Sir Digby."

She made it sound like the most natural topic of
conversation in the world, and provocative besides.
Her voice wound through him like one of those aph-
rodisiacs the ancients were said to use, clouding his
reason at the same time it turned each sensation that
washed over him into something so achingly physical as to make him afraid he might moan aloud. He
knew what she was saying. He knew what she was
doing. He simply didn't care.

Almost as if it moved without his conscious effort,
he found his hand on her arm. "You're fishing for
information with some very tempting bait," he told
her. This time, he was the one to step nearer. So near
that he could feel the satin sweep of her gown along
the length of his body. He glanced down, ignoring
the dazzling smile that she still somehow managed
to keep firmly in place. Earlier, he'd imagined the
tempting shadow nestled between her breasts. From

this angle, he could see it, and though he was not the least bit surprised, he was unsettled to find it far more tempting than he had ever imagined.

Stewart pulled in a breath to steady himself. "But what will you do if I do tell you something worth writing down? You haven't got your little journal. Unless, that is . . ." He looked up long enough to capture her gaze, then let his own drop just as quickly, back to the swell of her bosom. "Unless you're hiding it in a very interesting place."

Was it his imagination, or did he catch Aggie off guard? It was not a state in which he'd ever thought to find her. Yet there was evidence in the color that suddenly stained her neck and bloomed in her cheeks. Just as there was in the quick, sharp breath she pulled in, the one that made her breasts strain even more against the virginal fabric.

Was she out of her mind? At the same time the smile froze on Aggie's face, her insides completely melted. She must be as mad as May-butter if she thought she could flirt with Stewart and come out unscathed. Otherwise she never would have attempted such a thing. Now her knees were knocking, and her breath was caught behind a tight knot of anticipation in her throat. Her head whirled. Her stomach clenched. Her ears rang from the quiet that suddenly seemed to surround them, shutting out reality, keeping the rest of the world at bay.

She was sure if she looked up into his eyes, he would see that he had unnerved her, so she glanced down instead to where his hand rested on her arm. At the look, Stewart tightened his hold and moved even closer. The warmth of his body brushed against hers. The heat of his gaze scalded her skin.

Aggie closed her eyes against the sensations that

rushed over her. If she had any sense at all, she'd
turn and run and keep on running. She knew that
well enough. Just as she knew that if she put enough
distance between herself and Stewart, she might forget the way his eyes warmed in the light, and the
way his smile wobbled just enough to make it en-
dearing, and the way his touch sent shivers of fire
pouring through her. If she got away, fast and far,
she might regain her senses, she might remind herself there was no future for her, not with this man.
Most important, she might remember that it wasn't
Stewart she was interested in, it was the Shadow.

At least it was supposed to be.

It all might have been far easier if she hadn't
opened her eyes and found Stewart watching her
carefully. In this light, his eyes were the blue of sapphires, as bottomless as the sea. There was a message
in the light that sparked through them, one that
spoke volumes and told her he wanted her as much
as she wanted him. It was enough to take Aggie's
breath away.

And enough to remind her that this was exactly
the reaction she'd hoped to elicit from him. Suddenly
quite pleased with herself and feeling far more cocky
than flustered, Aggie smiled. She'd achieved her mission, or at least this portion of it. She'd accomplished
exactly what she'd set out to do. She'd succeeded at
making Stewart putty in her hands.

It was time to mold him to her liking.

At the same moment Aggie made the decision, the
orchestra started up again. The strains of a waltz
filled the air. Beaming at Stewart, Aggie offered him
her arm.

"Shall we?" she asked.

"Dance?" Stewart looked over at the couples

whirling around the dance floor. He looked back at Aggie as if she had lost her mind. "Dance? With you?"

"Is it such an outrageous suggestion, then?" Aggie tried for a little pout. She knew she'd succeeded when Stewart sighed and cupped her elbow with one hand. He piloted her out to the dance floor, and before he had a chance to change his mind, Aggie put her hand in his and sailed into the dance.

"You're quite a good dancer." It was true, and Aggie didn't mind offering the compliment. In spite of the fact that Stewart's expression made him look more like a man facing a firing squad than one who was enjoying himself, he was capable enough. His dance steps were pure and fluid, the movements of a man comfortable with his body. Because of his height and the length of his legs, he tended to get a bit ahead of her, but he realized it early on and shortened his steps to accommodate Aggie's.

If she had not been so aware of the pulse in his wrist beating against hers as he held her hand, she might actually have relaxed. That was impossible, of course. His other hand was flattened at the small of her back. His body swayed rhythmically only inches from hers.

Relaxing was the last thing on Aggie's mind. She had to remind herself that the first thing was supposed to be gathering information.

She smiled into Stewart's eyes. "Aren't these the sorts of things you aristocratic types are schooled in from a very young age? I would think dancing would be second nature."

"Second nature, perhaps. But that doesn't mean I have to indulge myself. I've made it something of a rule, you see. I never dance."

"Never?" Aggie couldn't help herself. He was so earnest, she had to laugh. "That's ridiculous. Of course you must dance."

Stewart shook his head. "Never. For one thing, I try to avoid these dreary parties. For another . . ." He whirled her around the corner of the room, close to the orchestra and to the Marsh brothers, who were standing nearby watching with what could only be called unabashed interest. Stewart glanced at them over Aggie's head.

"Once you start, you can't stop, you see," he said, returning his gaze to her. "Dancing, that is. It would be one thing if it was just the pretty women who wanted to dance. But it never is. It's matrons with feet of brick and sweet young things who are so busy wondering at the size of your yearly allowance they can't even remember your name. So you see, it isn't very surprising. I have a hard and fast rule. I never dance."

"Yet you agreed to dance with me."

He glanced down at her, his spectacles bright with the swirl of light all around them and the reflected splendor of the other dancers' evening gowns. "I told you, sometimes it's a pretty woman who wants to dance."

It was as much flattery as she'd ever gotten out of him, and as much, she suspected, as she was ever likely to get. It warmed Aggie down to her toes. It also provided her the perfect opening.

"You don't dance. You avoid social functions. Yet here you are."

The words were barely out of her mouth when he took her rather too quickly through the next turn. Aggie kept up, but just barely, and when things settled down again, she caught her breath and pressed on. "Why did you come tonight?" she asked.

A muscle jumped at the base of his jaw, yet he managed a smile. "If you expect me to admit that I'm here to steal the Talbot family treasures, you'll be disappointed. I'm not the sort who tells his private business to the world, my dear. If you think I am, you've got the wrong man."

"Oh, I haven't got the wrong man." Aggie couldn't say why, but she recognized it was one of the few things she'd said that night that was absolutely true. She banished the thought from her head, staying on course. "Besides . . ." She glanced up at Stewart, the look both coy and enticing. "I don't expect you to tell me anything. Not if you don't want to. It's ridiculous to even consider, isn't it? I mean, if nothing else these past weeks, I've learned that much. How could someone like me . . ." She batted her eyelashes. "How ever could someone like me convince a man like you to divulge anything?"

It was meant as a rhetorical question, and the moment it was past her lips, Aggie hoped he realized it. She didn't need to break her concentration by thinking about what he might have suggested. "I don't expect you to tell me anything," she reiterated, doing her best to sound just the slightest bit offended. "It's none of my business if you're here to speak with Sir Digby. Just as it's none of my business that he happened by when we were at the British Museum. I can't imagine what a trusted member of the government would have to discuss with someone like you . . ." She paused only long enough for him to interrupt, and when he didn't, she swept right on and pretended she wasn't discouraged. "I'm sorry if you trust me so little that you think that's why I'm here, but . . ." She heaved a sigh that lifted her breasts against the fabric of her gown and smiled, satisfied, as she felt a shudder pass through Stewart. "I suppose it is all I deserve. I have treated you rather badly."

"And about time you realized it."

Aggie ignored the barb and did her best to give him the look she'd worked for years to perfect: the one that was innocence itself, sweetness and light, flowers in the spring—and just guileless enough to destroy that last of even the most formidable gentleman's good intentions not to speak to the press. "You said so yourself. I've no place to hide my journal. I'm not taking notes. I'm not writing anything down. That's not why I'm here at all."

"Oh?" Stewart brows slid up, then down again just as quickly. He eyed her with suspicion. "Then why are you here?"

It was now or never, Aggie told herself. She turned her smile up a notch and lowered her voice so that it was just soft enough to sound like a secret.

"I'm here to seduce you," she said.

Chapter 9

Whatever reaction Aggie had expected, it wasn't what she got. Stewart tripped over his own feet and nearly knocked Aggie off hers. He righted himself at the last instant, sputtered something that didn't sound the least bit like "excuse me," and hurried off the dance floor.

By the time Aggie recovered enough to follow him out into the foyer, Stewart had already retrieved his top hat and was on his way out the front door.

"Oh, hell!" Aggie muttered under her breath. She might have hurried after him but for the fact that her evening wrap and handbag were, like the gown, the property of Rosie, and she didn't dare return without them. Tapping her foot, she waited for a servant to fetch them for her, and when he did, she snatched them out of his hands, wound the cord that cinched the handbag closed around her arm, and flew out the door after Stewart.

He hadn't gotten in a carriage, but had taken off on foot and by the time Aggie got close, he was nearly to the street. Aggie lifted her skirts and raced after him. She barreled past the impressive iron gates that marked the boundaries of Sir Digby's property just in time to see Stewart turn a corner. As swiftly as she could in the confining dress, she hurried after him, and when she rounded the corner and saw him a good thirty paces ahead, she called his name.

He didn't stop.

Aggie cursed again, louder this time. It was a pleasant night, and there were people strolling about. She ignored the looks they gave her, ignored everything but her quarry. With one final burst of speed, she closed in on Stewart, and by the time he stopped at a corner to wait while a hansom passed, Aggie caught him up.

"There's a fine way . . ." She hauled in lungful after lungful of air, desperate to calm herself, fighting to catch her breath. "There's a fine way to treat a woman who's just divulged a rather sensitive secret."

Stewart didn't answer. He didn't even look at her. A vein bulging rather ferociously at the side of his neck, he stared directly in front of him, his hands curled into fists at his sides.

"I did just admit to something fairly intimate, did I not?" Again, Aggie waited for an answer, and when Stewart didn't provide one, it only made her more determined.

Determined to make him confess all and tell her the secrets of the Shadow? Or determined to elicit at least some sort of response from him?

Even she wasn't sure. Not any longer. She didn't even like to consider the possibility that perhaps she was determined to force him to acknowledge what she'd felt there in the ballroom: that there was something that flashed between them from time to time, some spark that heated the air surrounding them, some hunger as real as it was surely reciprocal.

"It isn't every day I tell a man I want to seduce him," Aggie grumbled, and when she caught the slightest hint of skepticism in the tightening of Stewart's jaw, she stood her ground. "It isn't," she insisted. "And the fact that the man I choose to tell it to chooses to ignore me is . . . is . . ." She fought to find the words that would take her far wide of the perils she could anticipate lurking at the other end of the conversation. She couldn't bring herself to confess that she had been expecting a different reaction altogether. She'd expected curiosity. She'd hoped for interest. She'd not have been surprised at anger. But indifference? Indifference left her feeling as though someone had dumped cold water down her back.

Aggie tossed the thought aside at the same time she rounded on Stewart. She'd be damned if she would leave things to end like this. She'd be damned if she would walk away with her pride bruised and her self-esteem demolished and her story in jeopardy. Damn it, she'd prove yet that he was not insensible to her as a woman.

Setting her jaw, Aggie stepped between Stewart and the street. "This is a damned shabby way to respond to a mighty generous offer," she said. She took a step forward.

Stewart took one back, and though he tried to keep his chin steady and his gaze fixed somewhere above Aggie's head, she couldn't help but notice that his eyes flickered to hers.

It was all the opening she needed.

Aggie took another step forward. Stewart took another back.

Aggie hooked a finger under each of his lapels. "And it can't be every day," she murmured, "that a stuffy scholar such as yourself gets such a generous offer."

A shudder raced through Stewart. He concealed

his response behind an expression that would have turned cabbages to stone. "Aggie," he said, "don't."

"Don't?" Cheered by even that much of a reaction, Aggie laughed. "Don't what? This?" She trailed her fingers to his white bow tie and gave it a playful tug. "Or this?" She moved another step closer.

Stewart backed away from her. "That," he said, looking down at her hands. "And that," he added with a glance to the slim bit of space that separated them. "Don't."

"And why not? Surely you're not afraid of a little thing like me?" Aggie moved even closer. By this time Stewart was trapped. His back to a building, he stood tall and straight, his gaze fixed firmly over her head.

Aggie traced one gloved finger around the front of his collar. "Is that what you're afraid of? Me?" She giggled. "Perhaps you should forget about that Stewart Marsh fellow and just be the Shadow," she told him. "Then you wouldn't need to be afraid of anything."

"There. That proves it, doesn't it?" A hand on each of her shoulders, Stewart did his best to hold Aggie at arm's length, and when she refused to budge an inch he muttered an oath and bent to look her in the eye. "It's not me you want, Aggie. Don't you see? You want some man who doesn't exist, some figment of your imagination. You think I'm that man, but I've told you time and again I'm not. You want brave, not boring. You want reckless, not recluse. I'm not some dashing hero out of your dreams."

"You're a very poor liar." Aggie tapped Stewart's chin with one finger. She kept the finger right there, nearly close enough to trace the shape of his lower lip.

"You don't know what you're doing." Stewart made it sound as if she were torturing him. "Don't, Aggie. You have no idea what you're getting yourself into."

"Do I not?" Aggie managed a laugh, even as a niggling voice inside her head reminded her that he was right. She had never had to resort to such drastic measures with any man. Not to get any story. She had no idea what was ahead.

She leaned closer still. What possessed her to make the next move, Aggie couldn't say. It was impulse, perhaps. Or maybe it was curiosity. Whatever the reason, she slid a finger behind each of Stewart's ears and slipped off his spectacles.

Standing on tiptoe, Aggie stared into eyes that were familiar, yet strangely foreign. They were still the same engaging Marsh blue. They were still clear and steady and as resolute as ever. But the spectacles had done more than simply transform Stewart's face. They had effectively concealed his true personality. Now that they were dangling in Aggie's fingers, the real Stewart was revealed to her in a moment of awareness so crystalline and so cogent, it took her breath away.

There were depths to Stewart's eyes that the spectacles kept well concealed—swirls of color like steel in the glow of the nearby gaslight, determination that was as hard-edged as a sword, clarity of purpose, and shrewdness, and confidence enough for ten men. Somehow the spectacles had served to soften Stewart's countenance. They made him seem stuffy and bookish, academic and boring. Without them, the facade was stripped away and he was revealed for what he truly was. His face looked to be carved from granite, all hard planes and clean lines. There wasn't the slightest trace of mustiness about him. Not the slightest hint of the sheepish, dreary intellectual.

Aggie had never really doubted her sanity or her instincts, but if she had, her fears would have been put firmly to rest. A flood of memories washed over her: the sleek danger of the man, the innate passion, the raw masculinity. For a moment, she could do nothing at all but stare into the face of the Shadow.

She might have gone right on looking if Stewart hadn't gripped her shoulders, pulled her hard against him, and brought his mouth down on hers.

For what seemed an eternity, Aggie was too stunned to do anything but simply stand there. But as each second dissolved into the next, so did her surprise, until it melted completely beneath the heat of Stewart's kiss.

He tasted like expensive champagne and excitement. He smelled of fine, rich soap and limes. His lips sampled Aggie's and teased them. They coaxed hers to relax and when they opened to him, his tongue touched hers.

Aggie made a sound deep in her throat, a noise that might have been a whimper or a purr. She leaned nearer, closing the small space between them, and when her breasts pressed against Stewart's chest, she felt a frisson of excitement travel through him, a twin to the thrill that raced over her skin.

How long the kiss lasted, Aggie couldn't tell. She knew only that it was over too soon. What had begun as a stunning, earth-shattering, knee-weakening surprise ended just as abruptly when Aggie felt a sharp tug on her arm.

"What?" Startled, she pulled away from Stewart, opened her eyes and looked around. She was just in time to see a shabby street urchin run away with her handbag.

Surprised, Stewart took one look at the flush that stained Aggie's cheeks and the dreamy remnants of passion in her eyes and the way her lips were red and swollen from his kiss, and wondered how a man who prided himself on being so academic, so cautious, and so bloody rational could have possibly found himself in a situation that was anything but.

He should have known better than to kiss Aggie. Hell, he should have known better than to let her get within a mile of him. Yet there he was, in public no less, with his fingers splayed over the small of her back and his heart beating double time against hers, and desire so thick inside him that it pounded through him with each breath he took.

The next second, he realized something was wrong. Following Aggie's gaze, he saw the young tough running pell-mell down the street. He also registered the red mark on Aggie's arm caused by the thief wrenching her handbag away. He could never be quite sure exactly what happened next. He only knew that in that moment, what little common sense he had left deserted him completely.

He should have known better than to take off down a dark street in unfamiliar territory. He did know better. At least that's what he told himself. It hardly mattered. Instincts took over and in one motion, Stewart set Aggie aside, chucked his top hat, and dashed after the thief. He closed the distance between them in record time, and in less time still, he grabbed for the man's arm and tugged him to a teeth-chattering halt. The thief was a head shorter than Stewart, but he was younger by a few years and wiry, as were so many who had grown up on the streets and learned to fight before they could walk. His movements were far from graceful, but they were efficient enough, especially for a man who smelled like he slept at the bottom of a bottle of gin. By the time Stewart spun the man around and raised a fist, the young thug already had a knife in his hand.

"Damn!" Stewart muttered under his breath at the same time he dropped the thief's arm and moved out of range of the blade. What he wouldn't give for his trusty Webley now! Not that he would have used it, but it was a damned good intimidator. And right about now, damned good intimidation would serve this rowdy right. Unfortunately, Stewart hadn't been anticipating any need for his pistol that night. It was at home, as were the other tools of his trade, and when he squared off against the thief, feet apart and fists raised, he knew he would have to do without.

"You really aren't serious about using that thing, are you?" he asked, glancing at the knife long enough to gauge its size and assay the damage it might cause. "It would be a damned sight easier if you'd just give the young lady's handbag back."

The thief was too drunk to see a hole in a ladder, but that hardly made Stewart feel any better. It didn't mean the man was any less of a danger. It only meant he was more likely to take stupid chances. He took one then, tossing the blade from hand to hand while he laughed and closed in on Stewart. "Not much of a chance of me givin' back the necessary, guv. She don't need it as much as me, and neither do you by the look of you." Knife raised, he stepped closer. "Don't think the likes of a nob such as you is able to stand up to the likes of me."

"Well, no. I don't suppose I am." Stewart relaxed and pulled his hands to his sides. He let his shoulders sag. Just as he anticipated, it was enough of a feint to catch the thief off guard. He lowered the knife a faction of an inch and in that one second, Stewart launched himself at the man.

The rest of the confrontation was more brawl than fair fight. The thief was a canny street scrapper, and he wasn't the least bit hesitant about pressing any advantage, but Stewart had a few tricks of his own. More than once in the next minutes he was thankful for a houseful of brothers and a father who was enough of a traditionalist to insist that the boys learn to defend themselves.

Stewart circled to his right. The thief moved left.

The thief lunged, a quick thrust that missed the mark by a mile but brought him close enough to allow Stewart a punch that caught him squarely in the jaw. The thief's head snapped back, but he recovered in an instant and swung out blindly. His knife tore into the sleeve of Stewart's jacket.

Behind him, Stewart heard Aggie cry a word of warning. He didn't dare turn his back on the thief. He called to her to stay out of the way, then looked down at the jagged tear that traveled from the elbow of his jacket all the way to the cuff. "Damn!" he said, and this time he didn't even try to conceal his annoyance. "Do you have any idea what I paid for this jacket?"

His lips set in a thin line of displeasure, Stewart closed in on the man and managed another jab, this one to the thief's midsection that doubled him over and left him wide-eyed and panting. After that it was simple enough to finish him off. Another poke, another punch, and the thief's eyes rolled in his head. Before he could recover, Stewart snatched Aggie's handbag from the pocket where the man had stuffed it. He caught the shimmer of Aggie's ivory dress out of the corner of his eye, turned, and tossed the handbag to where she was standing on the sidelines, along with a crowd that had gathered to see what the commotion was all about.

It might have been a successful rout altogether if not for the fact that the thief was young and inexperienced, and he let his anger and the amount of spirits he'd consumed rule him when he should have given up and gone home. With a mighty curse and a face reddened from both embarrassment and fury, the man made one last try. He put his head down, stuck his knife out, and ran at Stewart all out.

Stewart watched him come. He knew what he had to do. He knew exactly when he would have to do it. Years of training, an athlete's sense of balance, and the inherent grace of a jungle cat served him well. He knew the exact moment when he would need to step aside, and when he did, he knew the thief would sail right past.

It was a perfect plan. It might even have worked if at the last second Aggie hadn't thought the fight finished and hurried to Stewart's side. One look at his own position, at Aggie's, and at that of the oncoming thief, and Stewart knew Aggie was in danger.

Still, he waited for the right moment and when it came, he threw himself between Aggie and the thief. He shoved her out of harm's way at the same time he felt the bite of the thief's knife somewhere near his rib cage. Stewart grimaced and cursed, but he kept his feet. In one fluid movement, he stripped the knife out of the thief's hand and before the man regained his balance, Stewart seized his arm, clamped a hand upon his shoulder, lifted and twisted. The next second, the thief was flat on the ground, too stunned to move.

Hands on his knees, Stewart bent at the waist, fighting to catch his breath at the same time he kept an eye on the thief, just in case he was game enough to try again. It wasn't until the man groaned and opened his eyes that Stewart moved to stand over him.

"Go on," he said with a look from the man to the crowd. "Get yourself out of here before the police arrive and cart you off to jail."

"Leave?" Crablike, the man scrambled to his feet. He glanced around at the onlookers and eyed Stewart uncertainly. "You tellin' me to leave, guv?"

"Go on." Stewart was strangely light-headed and too tired to argue the point. "Get out."

The man didn't wait to hear the offer another time. Turning on his heels, he dashed off.

No sooner had he left than Stewart found Aggie at his elbow. Her face was pale, but her cheeks were rosy. Her eyes were luminous with excitement and as round as saucers. She clutched her handbag in both hands. Her evening wrap trailed behind her, half forgotten.

She didn't say a word, but simply stared at Stewart, her lips half parted, her breath coming nearly as hard and fast as his own. Stewart waited for what he very much feared was the inevitable. He hated scenes. Especially scenes in which he was the center of attention. Though he expected a great outpouring of thanks from Aggie, he hoped she wouldn't be too effusive. He was, after all, a modest man. He would have been content, at least for now, with some small show of gratitude. A look of awe. An outburst of admiration. Perhaps even a kiss of thanks for the man who had saved her money and her life.

Very well pleased with himself, Stewart waited to see which it would be. But instead of any of those things, Aggie simply crossed her arms over her chest, tilted her head to one side, and watched as the would-be robber disappeared down one of the dark, narrow snickets that separated one building from another on the other side of the road.

"I see you have a soft spot in your heart for thieves," she said. She didn't sound the least bit impressed. Or grateful. She sounded like a reporter whose nose was atwitch with the smell of a story. She shivered, and damn, if she didn't look like a hound on the scent of game. "But then, that's only to be expected. There's a brotherhood of sorts, I suppose."

"Is that all you can say?" Stewart was the most reasonable of men, yet even he found it hard to stand quiet beneath such an onslaught of bilge. "I just risked my damned life for you, in case you hadn't noticed." His spectacles were still in Aggie's hand, and he reached to snatch them back from her. "In case you . . . ouch!"

Pain shot through Stewart's ribs, and he grabbed his side at the same time Aggie rushed forward to see what was wrong. Her expression suddenly far more concerned than curious, she grasped his elbow in one hand and made to move his jacket aside to take a look. "You're hurt."

Stewart waved her aside. His shirt felt hot and sticky, and beneath it his side throbbed and his ribs ached. "I'm fine," he insisted through gritted teeth. "Never been finer."

Aggie eyed him uncertainly. "Never been more

foolish, you mean. I haven't a stiver in that hand-bag. It was hardly worth getting yourself killed over." She made another move to close in on him. Stewart parried her as easily as he'd sidestepped the thief.

"I don't know what you're talking about," he said, fighting a wave of queasiness. "There was never any chance of me getting killed. Not until you got in the way. I had everything well under control."

"You did, didn't you?" Again, Aggie's eyes lit up. She looked him up and down. "Quite a fine display of battle tactics from a staid and boring scholar. What was that trick you used on him at the end? Where you grabbed his arm and—"

"Jujitsu." Another pain stabbed through him and Stewart winced. "It's something I learned to—"

"To fend off foes who might surprise you at your work." Thoroughly convinced, Aggie grinned. "Yes, of course. I imagine the Shadow must be proficient in all sorts of arcane skills. Picking locks and fighting his way out of any bit of trouble that comes along!" She took a playful jab at Stewart. "Won't that make a grand addition to my story!"

"The Shadow? What's this 'ere about the Shadow?"

"And about a newspaper story?"

"Someone writing this up for the newspapers?"

"The newspapers, you say? Where? Will they talk to me?"

All around them, the buzz of excitement traveled from person to person in the crowd.

Stewart cursed loud and long. It had been a more than lengthy and far too eventful night, and the last thing he needed was for Aggie to turn it into some sort of circus. He needed to quiet her, and he needed to do it soon, before she said too much.

He had few options. And less time even than choices.

Reaching inside his jacket, Stewart touched the warm, sticky patch on his shirt. He drew his hand out again, took one look at the blood that coated his fingers, and did his very best to pretend to faint dead away.

The strategy worked.

Whatever Aggie might have been foolish enough to say, the words left her and she emitted a tiny screech of alarm. She dropped to the pavement beside him, commanded someone to find a policeman, and carefully and ever so gently, pillowed his head in her lap.

This close, he realized Aggie smelled of rose water. Keeping his eyes shut and his body still, Stewart pulled in a long breath. This close, Aggie smelled like roses and felt as soft and as warm as a rose petal in the sun. With each movement she made to settle him more comfortably, her satin gown slid seductively beneath his cheek, and when she leaned over him to wipe his brow with a handkerchief, Stewart felt her breasts brush his arm.

Damn, but she felt like heaven!

In spite of his own best advice to himself, Stewart dared a look from behind his nearly closed eyelids. Much to his delight he discovered that from that angle Aggie looked as good as she felt.

The way she was bent over him afforded Stewart an unobstructed view of the front of Aggie's gown. Her breasts swelled above the plunging neckline. When she moved to nudge his evening jacket aside so she could press her handkerchief to his wound, he had a clear look at skin the color of new cream. It was dotted here and there with freckles, and in spite of the fact that he was injured and supposed to be unconscious as well, Stewart couldn't help but wonder if they would taste as much like cinnamon sugar as they looked. Would her breasts feel as good in his hands as her lips had felt on his? Would her nipples peak when he touched them? Would they tighten when his lips found them?

A better man would have set such thoughts aside right then and there. A better man would have shut his eyes firmly and turned his head away and refused to be tempted.

But then, a better man never would have risked all that he held most valuable for one taste of Aggie's lips. He never would have admitted that whatever the cost, the risk had been worth it and that he'd take it again, willingly and gladly. He would risk all that and more for the chance to touch her with his hands the way his gaze touched her now.

It was a very agreeable fantasy, and he might have gone right on enjoying it if not for the need to maintain his charade. Without even looking, he knew the crowd was closing around them. He could hear people shuffling very close by. After what seemed an appropriate time, he allowed his eyes to flutter open. "What happened?" he asked, his voice sufficiently weak, he hoped, to fool those around him.

Aggie pressed a hand to her lips, her expression so filled with relief at seeing him awake that it made him feel guilty. "You're going to be fine," she said. she removed the handkerchief from his side and frowned down at the wound, then reapplied pressure. "Someone's gone for a policeman. We'll get you home."

"It isn't necessary. Really." Stewart did his best to sit up, but another surge of sickness hit him, and before he knew it, he was flat on his back again, staring up into Aggie's disapproving face.

"Do you always faint at the sight of blood?" she asked.

Stewart grimaced. "Only when it's my own," he admitted. "Not . . . not the stuff of which romantic heroes are made, I'm afraid." He tried for a smile, but it felt weak and tight. Aggie's face blurred in front of his eyes. "I hate to ruin your fun. You're awfully . . . awfully game. Hate to . . . to disappoint you." Stewart closed his eyes against a wave of nausea and a detached sort of light-headedness. He reached for Aggie's arm and pulled her close enough to whisper in her ear. "Sorry to ruin your story." His own words echoed through his head. "But I'm not . . . not that Shadow fellow."

Aggie didn't look convinced. She stared down into his eyes, her own eyes filled with doubt that washed over her, then ebbed away, leaving some other emotion Stewart couldn't name. One so gentle and so filed with tenderness, it made him forget about the pain in his side.

It was the last thing he remembered before darkness closed around him, and he fainted dead away. This time, he didn't have to pretend.

"I don't like it, sir. I don't like it at all."

Stewart watched Trefusis, his butler, pace the library. He was a giant of a man, taller even than Stewart and broader by far, a pug-ugly fellow who moved through the room with all the grace of the proverbial bull in a china shop. He carried a copy of the day's *Chronicle* in one hand, and he slapped it against his thigh, the rhythm in direct counterpoint to his heavy footfalls.

"They're sniffling around like dogs after a bitch." When Trefusis was agitated, his clipped Welsh accent was more prominent than ever. He bit through the words and snarled, "I don't like it at all."

"I know what you mean." Stewart stretched and worked a kink out of his neck. He was not, as a rule, inclined to be idle, nor was he used to being mollycoddled, not by his brothers and certainly not by Trefusis. After a week of being forcibly confined to the house with his feet up and one or more of his brothers hovering about to make sure he neither exerted himself nor aggravated his wound, he'd had enough. He tossed off the blanket Matthew had only an hour earlier draped solicitously across his knees, and he sat up decisively. When Trefusis gave him a look that was half worry, half warning, Stewart waved him off.

"I'm fine," he assured his old friend, and the statement was for the most part true. Despite the fact that his brothers had chosen to act as if he was on death's doorstep, the wound to his side had never been serious. It was a scratch, nothing more, and if it bled a bit more than it should and stung a bit more than he'd expected it to, it was hardly worth worrying about.

"The bandage need changing?" Trefusis's dark brows dropped low over his even darker eyes. "I could nip down to the kitchen and heat some water if—"

"No need." Stewart shook his head. As always, he was grateful for Trefusis's assistance and glad the big Welshman had been there to help him out. Stewart knew it would have been damned inconvenient to be tended to by the expensive Harley Street physician his parents had insisted on sending around. Almost as damned inconvenient as it was to come up with an excuse to explain why he didn't want the physician to have a look at him. Absently, Stewart touched a finger to his chest, a few inches above where the thief's knife had cut into his flesh. There were some things even his family didn't know about him, and the fact that he was the Shadow was the least of them.

It was all the reminder he needed that a week of inactivity was a week in which he should have been planning and preparing and making another try for the crown. There was still a great deal of work to do, still people who stood in the way of his accomplishing his mission.

"Do you think she's dangerous?" It was a question Stewart would not have asked anyone else. But Trefusis was his right-hand man, after all, and he'd told Trefusis all about Aggie.

Well, not *all* about Aggie.

The very thought was enough to make Stewart feel as if his expression might betray him. Holding tight to his emotions, he busied himself by pouring a cup of tea from the tray that had been left on his desk. He handed the first cup to Trefusis and poured himself another.

He'd told Trefusis about the night he'd met Aggie in Barclay's treasure room, right enough, and about seeing her again at the tea party. That much was true, just as it was true that he'd confided in Trefusis when he thought someone was following him about town. When he'd learned who that someone was, he'd shared that information with Trefusis, too, and watched as the Welshman's eyes darkened with concern. When Stewart learned Aggie was a reporter for the rag-mannered *Chronicle*, he'd confided his concern to Trefusis. He had not bothered to add that concerned or not, he couldn't manage to evict Aggie from his dreams. He had not confessed that in spite of his better judgment and what he'd always thought of as a well-honed sense of honor, he'd kissed her.

"Do you think she's dangerous?" This time when Stewart asked the question, he wasn't sure if he was looking for an answer from Trefusis, or from himself.

"Hard to say." Trefusis dropped into a chair, the teacup in one hand, the newspaper in the other. "Her name's not on any of these articles this bleeding newspaper keeps publishing."

"That's what puzzles me." Not for the first time, Stewart thought through the problem. He had read each and every one of the articles in the *Chronicle* carefully. There was no mention of Aggie, no sign of the *A. O'Day* who claimed to know so much and seemed only too willing to tell it to all the world. "She claims to know the truth about me, but it appears she hasn't shared that knowledge with anyone at the newspaper. Does that make any sense?"

Thinking, Trefusis pursed his lips. "Perhaps she wants to keep you to herself?" The moment he spoke the words, his cheeks darkened. "That's not what I meant at all, and you know that well enough, sir. I only meant—"

Stewart laughed. It was one way to ease Trefusis's embarrassment, and at the same time it helped relieve his conscience. "I know exactly what you mean. And you know, I think you're right. She's just the type who would keep the information to herself. Just the type who would want to publish the whole thing with her name atop it."

"Which means?"

Trefusis knew the answer to that question just as well as Stewart did. "Which means," he said, "that she's not about to give up. She's a cagey little thing and as bright as a new penny. The more she interferes, the more chance there is that she'll actually find out something. The longer she noses about—"

"The sooner she'll know something. Yes." Trefusis nodded solemnly. "I was afraid of that."

"Don't look so gloomy!" Stewart drained his cup and set it back on the tray. "There is a cheery side to all this. It means she's forcing my hand, and that means I can finally get out of the house."

Trefusis sat up, his gaze assessing Stewart's ribs, where he knew there was a swathe of bandages. "Are you ready for it?"

"As ready as I'll ever be." Stewart's expression stilled, and he glanced at the shelves of books that lined the library walls from floor to ceiling and at the suit of armor that stood near the door. He touched a hand to his heart. Though it had taken him some time to realize it, he knew now this was one mission he'd prepared for all his life. It was what he'd studied for. What he'd worked for. It was why he was the Shadow.

"It's time to stop mucking about," he told Trefusis. "It's time to get back to work."

　　*At the end of each day, when the golden orb that bright-
ens our exalted English skies withdraws its warm and
cheery brilliance so that those on the other side of the
Earth may share in its munificence, this great and glorious
Country is plunged, as it has ever been, into the inky
arms of Night. The streets of London, so fine and so pleasant beneath the gleaming radiance of the sun, take on*

another character altogether. Gone are the wide thorough-
fares where men from all the four corners of the globe
travel to make their obeisance before the altar of Commerce.
Gone are the pleasant pathways through the parks where
pink-cheeked and dewy-eyed children romp beneath the
watchful eyes of their devoted governesses. Gone are the
bustle of the drays from which the common folk conduct
an honest day's work and the scurry of the omnibuses as
they convey the great mass of humanity from one part of
the city to another.

With nightfall, all is changed. All is in darkness. All in
shade. All in shadow.

Blackness descends. It sits close upon the rooftops and
wraps its tendrils around the chimneys that rise up like
dragon's teeth against the sky. It transforms, as if by
some sinister force of magic, wide thoroughfares to gray
and gaping caverns, and pleasant pathways to black lab-
yrinths. Silence sits close upon the shoulders of the
darkness that hugs the sides of buildings. It caresses
those secret places between, where the shadows are
deeper still. It kisses—

''Oh, hell!'' In the dim light of the gas lamp near
where she stood, Aggie scratched out the last few
lines of her story with her stub of a pencil. She
was writing a newspaper article about a crime, she
reminded herself. Not some flowery romantic
novel. She didn't need to mention kisses and caresses. She didn't even need to think about kisses
and caresses.

She needed to think about her story.

Unfortunately, the advice was more easily given
than followed. If that were not so, she would have
listened to it days ago, and not spent the week since
the party at Sir Digby's filling her head—and her
journal—with ideas that had no place in either.

With a small grunt of disgust, she flipped back
through the pages. Page after page was filled with

her small, neat script. Page after page was blacked
out, the crisscrossed lines as confused and chaotic as
her thoughts.

She should have been writing about larceny, yet
each time she tried, her words drifted from practical
to passionate. She should have been composing
deathless prose about missing treasures, and legend-
ary thieves and justice triumphant. Instead, every
sentence she wrote seemed to bring her back to the
place she'd started, and when she read whatever
she'd just written, she found it filled with words that
teased at her memory. Words such as "kiss." Words
such as "caress." Words heavy with connotations of
the irrational thoughts that had pounded through her
head every day and every night since Stewart kissed
her.

The results were ever the same. No matter how
hard she tried to concentrate on her journalism, she
found herself instead imagining the feel of his lips
against hers, and recalling the taste of his tongue,
and remembering how, when he flattened his hands
against her back and pressed her close, his body fit
perfectly against hers and she felt the undeniable evidence of a desire as strong as her own.

Even now, the very thought caused a blush to heat
Aggie's cheeks. After a week, she knew there was no
use trying to slough the reactions off, just as there
was no use trying to pretend they didn't exist. A
tingling hum of longing had been her constant companion this past week. It vibrated over her skin and
heated her blood. There was no getting rid of it, just
as there was no way she could forget the taste of
Stewart's mouth on hers.

In the past week, Aggie had found her head in the
clouds more often than not. Even Bert had noticed.

While he bedeviled and badgered her about her story, eager to learn more about the Shadow, she found herself daydreaming too much and sighing too often. Still, she couldn't help herself. She sighed again, and glanced across the road toward the lighted windows of the town house where Stewart lived. She should have been picturing him in his guise of the Shadow, she reminded herself. She should have been thinking—and not about his lips or his arms or any other portion of his anatomy. She had to think instead of a way she might catch him in the act of stealing Arthur's Crown and thus assure her place in newspaper history.

That, she'd decided, was the crux of the problem. And the solution, as well.

She couldn't think of Stewart as simply a man. She had to think of him not as the object of her desire but as the foundation stone of her journalistic triumph.

Chastened, if not thoroughly convinced, she waited to see some sign of activity from the house. Much as she had come to expect, nothing happened. No one came or went. No one moved the draperies aside or looked out the windows. If there was any activity at all within the house, it was kept as private as was Stewart's real identity.

By this time, she had stopped worrying about his injuries. After the first few frantic minutes, when she did her best to stanch the bleeding from the wound in his side, help had arrived in the form of a bobby who took things well in control. Stewart had been taken home, and she knew he was well cared for. His wound, though bloody, had never been serious. Only that morning she'd heard from a lady's maid down the road who'd heard from a tweeny across the way who'd heard from Stewart's cook that he was fully recovered.

Aggie had to admit she was relieved. There were other emotions that weren't quite so easy to admit, though, not even to herself. She was not, after all, a shallow creature. Nor was she completely without feeling. But as the days passed and she grew more certain that Stewart was up and on his feet again, there was one thought prominent in her mind: now that he was better, sooner or later he was bound to make another try for the crown.

She hoped it might be sooner rather than later.

Aggie rolled her head from side to side and stretched a twinge out of her shoulders. Dressed as she was in Bert's jacket and newly repaired trousers, she'd been watching the house every night for the last week. She was tired. Tired of feeling her muscles stiffen in the cool night air. Tired of straining her eyes, hoping to see well enough in the darkness so that when Stewart finally left the house, she might follow him. Tired of spending her idle hours thinking thoughts she shouldn't have been thinking about a man she shouldn't have been thinking of.

Better to get her story and get it over and put him out of her mind forever.

As if the very thought conjured his presence, Aggie saw the door across the road swing open. Against the light that flowed from inside, she recognized Stewart's silhouette. He was dressed all in black, and when the door snapped shut behind him, he blended so perfectly with the night that Aggie had to squint to see him. Leaning over as much as she dared, she watched him pause outside the front door and look up and down the street. At the bottom of the wide, shallow steps that led to the door, he turned to his right and started walking. When he was a good twenty paces ahead, she slipped across the road and followed.

Confident in her disguise and in her ability to keep her distance, Aggie moved along behind her quarry. Stewart turned to the right at the next crossroad and walked past the elegant homes that lined the streets. He turned left, then left again, and she followed him past a church with a neatly tended graveyard to the side. After twenty minutes of echoing his every step, she could hardly help her mind drifting. Her gaze glued to Stewart, she noted the agility of his movements, the length of his legs, the breadth of his shoulders. He stopped at a crossroads beneath the thin light of a gas lamp to allow a carriage to pass by, and she couldn't help but notice the confident way he carried himself, the firm line of his jaw, the determined set to the lips that—

"Oh, hell!" Aggie muttered the admonition and reminded herself that Stewart's lips had nothing to do with why she was there and why she was following him.

Or at least they shouldn't.

"Oh, hell!" she muttered again, this time because while she'd been busy thinking about Stewart's lips, he'd rounded a corner and hurried on.

Aggie had to walk fast to try to catch up. She hurried to the corner, rounded it carefully so as not to give herself away. And pulled to a stop.

She was in an alleyway of sorts, the kind of grand horseshoe-shaped street where fashionable town houses stood side by side, as close as kippers in a

can. As far as she could tell, there was no way into
or out of the street except the way she'd come.

And as far as she could tell, the street was empty.
Stewart was nowhere to be seen.

Chapter 10

"If you insist on following people, you really should learn to do it properly."

At the sound of Stewart's voice close to her ear, Aggie jumped and sucked in a sharp breath. She whirled around, and somehow Stewart found himself no more than a hairsbreadth from her, his hands on her waist, his mouth dangerously close to hers.

It wasn't at all what he'd meant to do. What he'd meant to do was teach her a lesson. After all, if a woman fancied herself a crack reporter, she should learn to act like one, and not be so taken by surprise that her face was as pale as alabaster and her eyes were wide with alarm. She should not, by any means, be so unsettled that her lips were parted in such a way that he could see her tongue flick nervously over them, moistening them so they looked slick and delectable and—

"You really are horrible!" With a shrill screech, Aggie propelled herself out of Stewart's arms. She kept herself well out of reach, her arms tight against her sides, her feet shuffling against the pavement in a nervous sort of dance that put the idea into his head that there was more than surprise behind her reaction. If he had been a betting man, Stewart would have wagered that her hasty retreat had less to do with his ambush than it did with the realization that when they stood close to each other, electricity crackled between them, and whether either of them willed it or not, they were drawn, inevitably, ever nearer.

The knowledge should have cheered him, or at least relieved him of the guilt that had spread through his gut like the remnants of a bad meal ever since the night he'd kissed her. Instead, it left Stewart feeling much the same as he'd felt all the last week— as disconcerted as Aggie apparently was and sure that what he'd done, and what he wanted to do, to her was as foolish and as chancy and as wrong a thing as he'd ever thought about.

And he still wanted to do it.

"Imagine, sneaking up on a girl like that!" While Stewart had been busy examining his conscience and finding it woefully deficient, Aggie was still doing her best to keep her distance. She backpedaled her way even farther from his reach. "Do you fancy stopping my heart?"

Whether she meant to or not, Aggie was teaching her own lesson. One that had to do with self-control, or at least with self-denial. It was a lesson Stewart would do well to learn. He stuffed his hands into his pockets. "Do you fancy getting yourself coshed someday when you're following someone not nearly as gentlemanly as me?"

"Gentlemanly?" She stopped just short of emitting a very unladylike snort. "If you're a gentleman, I'm the empress of Australia! Besides . . ." Puzzled, she wrinkled her nose. "How did you even know I was there? And how did you know it was me?"

Lesson or not, Stewart could hardly let the moment pass. He closed the distance between them, glancing over Aggie's shoulder and down as he did. "I didn't know. Not until I came up behind you. Then I knew it had to be you. I'd know that little backside anywhere. There isn't another person in all of England who looks as tasty in men's clothes as you."

She blushed, or at least Stewart thought it was a blush. It was hard to tell in the dark. But it was impossible to miss the way she caught her breath. Or the fact that when he moved even closer, she stood her ground.

"You have a way of flattering a girl." Hesitant or hopeful, Stewart couldn't say which, Aggie's voice fluttered over the words. "No doubt to try and throw me off the scent." She gathered her composure along with her courage and looked up into his eyes. "You're on your way to Barclay's, aren't you?"

Stewart laughed aloud. "Whatever makes you think that?"

Aggie shrugged. "You are headed in that direction."

"And in the direction of a great many other things."

She looked him up and down. "You are dressed rather somberly."

"As are you."

"You're not wearing your spectacles."

Stewart touched a finger to the bridge of his nose. "Damn, and if I didn't forget them at home!"

"You are bound and determined to get hold of the crown," she said.

He raised an eyebrow, being as blasé about the whole thing as he dared. "Am I?"

Aggie grumbled a word she shouldn't have known. Never one to give up easily, she came a step closer, and while Stewart was still wondering how, this time, she might choose to tempt him into divulging more than he should, she flattened a hand against the front of his greatcoat.

His initial reaction was to pull away. He didn't. If this was her way of getting him to talk . . .

His thoughts froze at the same time his insides turned molten. Aggie's hand brushed his chest, her touch as light as butterfly wings. She found the top button of his coat, hooked a finger around it and eased it from its hole. One after the other, she did the same to the other buttons until Stewart's coat hung loose and the cool night air touched him. He stood perfectly still, waiting to see what in heaven's name she might do next. He didn't dare give a name to his hopes or to the ferocity of the emotions that tangled through him. His breath caught up behind a tight knot of anticipation, he waited, and when she slid her hand inside his coat, his heart seemed to stop, then start again with such force that it caused him to suck in a breath that hammered against his ribs.

Obviously, that was precisely the reaction Aggie wanted. She grinned, and her fingers fluttered along the waistband of his trousers. It would have taken a man with more willpower than he ever hoped to possess to be able to contain the instinctive reaction she triggered in him. Balancing on the fine and agonizing line between minding his manners and giving free rein to the fierce cravings that overwhelmed him, Stewart held his breath.

He was still holding it when Aggie patted his pocket.

"You've brought your Webley," she said.

"My Web—" Stewart stopped himself just short of sounding as disappointed as he was suddenly embarrassed. He might have known her intention all along.

He should have known. He cursed himself and his errant imagination and the longings he should have been able to contain at the same moment he decided that two could very well play the same game.

Steeling himself, Stewart looked down into Aggie's upturned face, his eyebrows raised, his eyes glinting with the hint of a suggestion. He might have known he'd meet one of her smiles. If she knew how distracting—and how very provocative—she was at that moment, she didn't show it. Her expression was nothing short of angelic. And all the more tantalizing because of it.

His mouth suddenly dry, his self-discipline tested far beyond its limits, Stewart managed to produce a lopsided grin full of innuendo. "You know," he murmured, "in some cultures, there is great significance to what you're doing. When a woman . . ."

Gad, it was hard to believe so little a thing could drive him to distraction. He steadied himself against a rush of desire that left every inch of his body suddenly not only aware but attuned to each move Aggie made. Her breath rushed in and out against the sensitive skin of his neck, and he shivered. Her hand moved against his pocket and the pistol in it and his knees went weak.

"When a woman touches a man's Webley . . ." he began.

"Yes?" Aggie inched closer. Her hips brushed his. Her voice dropped. "What happens when a woman touches a man's Webley?"

"Well . . . you see . . . in some cultures . . . Polynesian, I think . . ." Stewart couldn't believe his own ears. Or the words that were suddenly pouring out of his mouth. She had him so arse over turkey, he couldn't think straight. Here he was blubbering academic nonsense. "There may, of course, be some connection with the substrata of cultures said to be associated with the seventh-century king Darish, who is said to have established—"

There was no telling how long he might have gone on if Aggie hadn't cupped her hand over his pocket. "That's nothing but gibberish," she said. "It has nothing to do with your Webley." With one finger, she traced the outline of the pistol. Over the butt and across the barrel and over the butt again. "What you meant to say, of course, was that in some cultures, when a woman touches a man's Webley . . ." Drawing out the words, she grazed a finger slowly along the barrel of the pistol. Her voice dropped to a whisper. She inched closer so that her lips were only a heartbeat from Stewart's. "He lets her come with him when he goes to steal Arthur's Crown so that she might watch and write a ripping good story about it."

Stewart couldn't help but smile. He allowed the expression to blossom into a deep-throated laugh, and when he felt rather than saw Aggie's lips lift into an answering smile, he moved close enough for her to feel his words against her mouth. "Not a feather's chance in hell," he said.

Aggie's retreat was nothing less than impressive, even if it was not dignified. With a mumbled word, she bolted away from Stewart and stood staring at him, her fists on her hips. "Why? Why won't you let me come with you when you steal Arthur's Crown? Because you don't trust me?"

Grumbling, Stewart ran one hand through his hair. "Because I'm not—"

"Yes, yes. I know." Aggie glared at him. "You're not the Shadow. You've told me as much before. You weren't the Shadow the night I discovered you in Barclay's treasure room, and you weren't the Shadow the other night, either, when you fought off that young tough who wanted my handbag."

They were on more solid ground again, or at least on as solid a ground as could be reached with Aggie. In any case, Stewart didn't have to worry about the daring brush of her fingers or the tantalizing feel of her lips. That was a relief. Now all he had to worry about was her single-mindedness, but at least that was more manageable than were the emotions that rocketed through him when she got close to him. Or the ideas that tumbled through his head when she touched him. Or the sensations that ravaged him like fire, the ones that started somewhere in the very center of his soul each and every time her lips were near.

Too upended by such thoughts to stand still another minute, Stewart turned on his heel. He stalked out of the horseshoe street and back into the jumble of traffic on the main thoroughfare. He didn't need to turn around to know Aggie had followed him. She fought to keep up, taking two steps to his every one.

"You do owe me some consideration," she said, her voice breathy with the effort of keeping pace with him. "The least you can do is let me have an exclusive story about the Shadow. After all, I did save your life."

"Save my—" Despite telling himself it would be wiser to keep going and never look back, Stewart couldn't help but pull to a stop and stare at her. "You didn't save my life. You never saved my life."

"Of course I did." Aggie sounded so sure of herself, she nearly convinced Stewart. He shook his head, scattering the thought, bringing himself back to his senses. "I had someone call for a bobby. While you were lying there senseless in the street. I had someone get a bobby, and then I went and fetched your brothers."

It was true. She had gone out of her way to find his brothers, and Stewart had forgotten it. Now that she'd reminded him, he felt guilty about not thanking her formally for her assistance. He might have at least sent around a note. But he hadn't. He'd decided to act as if the whole thing hadn't happened. It was the only way he could even begin to forget that he'd kissed her.

He swallowed back the protest he would have liked to make. "Yes, I know," he said. "Much to my endless annoyance, my brothers have yet to tire of talking about it. I can't tell you how many times I've heard how you raced back to Sir Digby's to collect them."

"Once the rozzer arrived and I knew you were in good hands," Aggie reminded him.

"Once the rozzer . . ." He pronounced the inelegant word for "policeman" as if it tasted sour in his mouth. "Once the rozzer arrived and you knew I was in good hands," he conceded. "Matthew has described the scene a dozen times. How you ran into the ballroom, your dress covered in muck and blood—"

"You paid for it!" Aggie's eyes misted. "I am sorry," she said, and her tone of voice left no doubt she was sincere. She rushed through her apology. "I meant to thank you. Really, I did. There you were, hurt and senseless, and you thought about how the dress had been ruined. When you pressed those pound notes into my hand—"

"No more sorry than I am for not thanking you properly. You did fetch my brothers, after all, and while that might not have been the best thing to do, considering the fact that I shall never hear the end of it from them, I—''

''. . . didn't know what I was going to tell Rosie.'' Aggie rambled on, her words lapping over Stewart's bumbled apology. He would be the first to admit he hadn't been paying much attention. He was too busy tripping over his own excuses. But something about the comment brought him up short.

''Rosie?'' he asked. ''Rosie who?''

Aggie's cheeks darkened, and Stewart was caught off guard. He didn't think anything could embarrass her. Yet it was obvious something had. Just as obvious as it was that she didn't like anyone to know she could be vulnerable. Or helpless. She looked away, and when she looked back again her chin was too steady and her gaze too firm.

''It wasn't mine,'' she said. Her voice was as close as the look in her eyes. ''I could never afford a dress such as that, and—''

Stewart didn't want to hear any more, no more than he wanted to see what it cost her to admit to a need he couldn't begin to understand. Before he could think what he was doing or tell himself to stop, he cupped her face in his hand and brushed his thumb across her cheek. ''You should have pretty things,'' he said.

''Yes. Well . . .'' She blinked, setting aside her humiliation. Her voice kindled with indignation. ''That isn't bloody likely. The pretty things, I mean. Not unless I can prove myself as much a journalist as the men who write for the *Chronicle*. Peter Askew is paid more than twice what I am. And he isn't half the writer.'' Another thought struck her, and her eyes lit up. The bare hint of a smile tickled the corners of her mouth. She rubbed her cheek against Stewart's hand. "Now, if I knew something about the Shadow he didn't know . . ."

Stewart didn't give her time to finish. As if her face were on fire, he yanked his hand away and started walking again. "For God's sake, Aggie," he said, "don't do that."

"Don't do what?" Aggie trotted along at his side. "Make you feel guilty?" She grabbed for his hand and held on tight, pulling him to a stop. "Or touch you?"

Stewart looked at their entwined fingers. "Both," he said, and the certainty of the single word seeped through his bones like the chill of a January morning. "Either. They are one and the same. When I touch you, I feel guilty."

"And when I touch you?"

"When you touch me . . ." Stewart drew in a lungful of air and let it out again slowly. His breath puffed around him in the cool night air. Like it or not, he knew Aggie was right. He owed her something. Something for her bravery and her daring. Something for her beauty and her single-mindedness and her intelligence. Even something for the fact that she was too damned sure of herself and far more meddlesome than any woman—reporter or not—should ever be.

Aggie deserved the truth, or at least as much of it as he could give her. "Aggie," he said, "when you touch me, I don't ever want it to stop. I want you to go on touching me. I want you to go on looking at me in that way you do, with your eyes narrowed and your nose scrunched up as if you're thinking very hard, as if you can see beyond what the world sees. I want you to go on saying my name so that when I'm alone, I can close my eyes and still my breathing and hear your voice, and pretend you're there beside me. Damn it, Aggie, sometimes I think if you aren't there, if you don't talk to me and touch me . . . if you don't see the real me . . . sometimes I fear I'll dry up and blow away and disappear."

It was more of a confession than he'd ever intended to make. Aggie knew as much when the first words left Stewart's lips. Still, he didn't stop. He didn't try to soften the meaning of his words, either. He was brutally honest, not sparing either of them, and it was that, more than anything, that made her realize she didn't deserve his admiration or his respect.

Her hand felt cold, even though it was still in his. She listened, stunned and a little self-conscious, remorseful because he was man enough to spill his soul and admit to emotions she had refused to acknowledge. And she? She was a woman who was willing, even eager, to take advantage of his attraction to her, one who was so coldhearted she was willing to trade on something as elemental as the spark that hummed in the air between them.

All for the sake of her story.

The last of Stewart's words fell silent against the curtain of darkness around them. Aggie looked up into his face. His eyes were shadowed and he looked slightly dazed, as if he, too, was stunned by all he'd had the nerve to say. It was that look, more than anything, that brought home the enormity of all that had passed between them. In that one instant, Aggie realized she'd gotten what she'd wanted all along. She'd wanted to be taken into Stewart's confidence. To be privy to his secrets. To take a look inside his heart. And now that she had, she felt something she

had never felt in all her years of prying into other
people's lives. She felt like a trespasser.

Aggie pulled her hand out of Stewart's. "It's late,"
she said, and as if to reinforce the thought, the bell
of a nearby church rang the hour. She barely glanced
in his direction before she started back the way
they'd come. "I'd better get home."

"That's the long way back. If you'll come this way
with me . . ."

It wasn't so much the words that stopped her as
it was the thin glimmer of hope that shimmered in
his voice. She gave him a questioning look.

"You want me to walk with you?"

"Well, 'want,' of course, is a word with a good
many connotations. I might mean—" Stewart
stopped short, listening to his own stuffy reply echo
back at him from the surrounding buildings. He
drew in a breath and if she hadn't known better, she
might have suspected it was to bolster his resolve.
"Yes," he said quite simply. "Yes, I'd like it very
much if we could walk together. If we could forget,
just for the rest of the evening, that you're a reporter
and I am . . ." With the movement of one well-
shaped hand, he waved away the rest of whatever
he might have said. "We could just walk. And talk,"
he said. "Though considering the fact that you're
dressed like a boy . . ." He looked her up and down.
His eyes lit up, and an answering warmth circled
Aggie's heart. "I hope you'll understand if I don't
offer you my arm."

"Of course!" As charmed by the invitation as she
was by the way he'd offered it, she laughed and fell
into step beside him. They talked of trivial things—
the weather, the latest news from abroad. They
talked about their families, and Stewart mentioned

that he owned an estate in Wales that he sometimes visited, and he described it so vividly and with such relish, Aggie was sure it was a place he loved. They talked about the celebration that was being prepared to commemorate the Queen's Diamond Jubilee, and Aggie confessed that she couldn't wait to see the fireworks extravaganza she'd heard was being planned to mark the occasion.

It wasn't until they'd walked for nearly half an hour that Aggie realized they were in front of Maxwell Barclay's home.

"I knew it!" Aggie could barely control her outburst of triumph or the barrage of questions that crowded her mind. She drew to a stop outside the iron gates that were closed across the drive. "You were headed here. Just as I suspected." Feeling more than a little pleased with herself, she turned to pin Stewart with a look. "I knew—"

An expression of disappointment clouded Stewart's face, and Aggie's excitement evaporated along with her questions. She bit down on her lower lip, forcing herself to keep silent.

Stewart was right. Just this once, she could forget that she was a reporter burning for a story. It was the least she could do to repay his honesty and his kindness.

"What I mean, of course, is that this is just what I suspected." Aggie forced a laugh. "I suspected this would be a fine evening for a stroll and I was absolutely right. It will be warm soon, don't you think?"

Stewart was hardly listening. Suddenly as alert as he had been relaxed only moments before, he narrowed his eyes and peered intently through the darkness that enveloped the house.

Aggie looked that way, too. For the longest time,

she saw nothing at all. Nothing but the inky shadows and the shapes of the trees that stood upon the lawn, like black paper silhouettes.

And then she saw something move. It wasn't much, just a ripple in the shadows, but it caused a tingling to start along the back of her neck, the first stirrings of excitement.

"It's nothing," she told herself. She knew Stewart wasn't listening. His head cocked, he leaned forward, and she had the same impression of him that she'd had that first night she stumbled upon him in Barclay's treasure room. Of a man with the instincts and power of a jungle cat. One poised to strike. "It's an animal," Aggie mumbled. "Or simply a trick of the light."

But it wasn't. The next second, the shadow moved closer to the house, close enough to a lighted window that they could make it out more clearly. There was no mistaking the fact that it was a man.

"A servant," Aggie speculated.

"Perhaps." Stewart tried the gate. It was locked.

"Or it could be Barclay himself."

"Barclay has gone to Brighton for the weekend." Stewart didn't bother to explain how he knew this interesting bit of information, and Aggie didn't have a chance to question him about it. He tugged at the gate and finding it secure, he grumbled. Fists on his hips, he stepped back and took stock of the brick wall on either side of the drive. "He's taken most of his staff with him," he said, gauging the height of the wall, then nodding to himself. "He left the butler, of course. But the man's a drunkard and no doubt is fast asleep by now. There's a footman who sleeps around back and a housekeeper who—"

This was too much to accept in silence. When

Stewart made a move toward the wall, Aggie plucked at his sleeve. "How do you know all that?" she asked. "About where Barclay's gone for the weekend? And his butler? And the footman? And—"

A smile relieved the worried expression on Stewart's face. "Why, I read the *Chronicle*," he said. He turned and in one movement as fluid as the shadows that surrounded them, he hoisted himself to the top of the wall. "You really should keep up with the news in your own paper, Aggie. Your friend Peter Askew published a story about Barclay this morning." He glanced down at her, his expression suddenly grim. "Stay here," he said and disappeared over the wall.

Aggie didn't follow immediately, but only because it took her a while to find a place where a sturdy-looking tree grew close enough to the wall to climb. By the time she scrabbled up the tree, hopped down from the wall, pulled herself to her feet, and dusted off the seat of her trousers, she could see Stewart already nearing the house.

There was no sign of the other man, and for a moment Aggie felt relief. If there was no intruder, there was no need for Stewart to go investigating. And if there was no need for Stewart to investigate, there would be little chance that he would be discovered, or worse yet, captured.

The thought didn't simply surprise her, it positively upended her. She stopped in the center of the lawn, wondering how she'd arrived at so different a place from the one she'd started for. She'd started by wanting to expose the Shadow's identity to the world. Now here she was, worried that Stewart might be caught.

The thought no sooner occurred to her than she

saw Stewart near an open back window. He didn't look surprised to see her. With a shake of his head that might have been interpreted as either exasperation or displeasure, he put one finger to his lips and motioned toward the open window with a tip of his head.

Aggie knew what he meant. He'd seen the other man slip inside, and he intended to follow.

Her heart crashing against her ribs, her breath tight in her throat, Aggie fell in step behind him. They were in what looked to be the morning room. The door at the far end of the room was open and as quietly as the night, Stewart slipped through it and out into the passageway. Afraid to make a sound, Aggie followed slowly, and by the time she caught him up, he was already on his way upstairs to the treasure room.

At the top of the stairs, they saw that the door to Barclay's display room was open. There was a light burning inside.

Carefully, Stewart inched down the hallway. He paused outside the open door, motioning Aggie to keep behind him. When he peeked inside the room, then glanced back at Aggie with a question in his eyes, she took a look for herself.

What she saw was a heavyset, middle-aged fellow who was winded from the simple exertion of crossing the lawn. In the thin beam of the single lamp he'd lit, his bald head was slick with perspiration. His nose was red and bulbous. He had an unlit cigar clamped between his teeth.

He was taking a crowbar to the mahogany chest where Arthur's Crown was kept.

Aggie could never say what possessed her to cry out. It was certainly not the fact that he was about to destroy what was no doubt an expensive piece of furniture. As a matter of fact, she might have done the same had she thought of it herself. But when she saw him, she could think only one thing: he was going to get a look at the crown before she did.

"Peter Askew! How dare you resort to underhanded means to try and get a story!"

Aggie's voice rang clear through the silence. It was enough of a shock to cause Askew to drop the crowbar. It hit the floor with a *clang* loud enough to raise the dead.

Stewart grabbed for her and signaled silence, but Aggie hardly cared. Outraged, she marched into the room.

"Of all the devious, dishonorable, despicable things . . ."

Askew whirled around. His mouth dropped open and his cigar hit the floor. "You!" He choked on his surprise. "And don't tell me you didn't have the same idea, missy. What else would the likes of you be doing here in the middle of the night? Hoping for a story of your own, no doubt."

"Hoping? Hah! As if I'd resort to such means." Wrapping her indignation around her like a cloak, Aggie lifted her chin. Out of the corner of her eye she saw Stewart. She knew he was trying to pull her back into the relative safety of the darkness outside the doorway. She knew he was gesturing to her to stay calm, to stay quiet, to get out. She simply didn't care.

The thought that Peter Askew might see the crown, and thus write a story about it before she did, robbed Aggie of all sense of what was prudent.

Askew knew it, of course. He chuckled. "Sorry you didn't think of it first?"

"Sorry?" Aggie couldn't invest the word with enough sarcasm. "I hardly think I would need to go so far as to—"

Her statement was cut short by a call from belowstairs.

"Who is that? Who's up there?"

Aggie froze. Stewart dropped his head into his hands. Askew mumbled an oath.

"Me?" Aggie wasn't about to be outdone by an out-and-outer with as little talent as he had hair. "I'll give you what for, Askew. And as far as—"

"Who is it? Who's that I hear up there? We're coming up!"

Aggie might have gone right on arguing with Askew except for two things. One was the commanding feel of Stewart's hand on her arm. The other was the shrill blast of a police whistle.

"Now you've done it!" Askew took off through the doorway, though where he hoped to get to in that direction was a mystery to Aggie. She hardly had time to care. At the same time every light in the house came on, Stewart seized her hand and ran for the French doors and the balcony that lay beyond.

The next minutes were a blur. They raced across the lawn, but even before they got as far as the wall over which they'd climbed, Aggie heard footsteps behind them. From the sound of it, there was more than one person after them, and something told her it wasn't simply a cadre of servants.

Someone issued a sharp command, another whistle sounded, and Aggie knew with sinking certainty that the police had been lying in wait for the Shadow to make another try for the crown.

Fear seized her, and she would have stopped then and there and hunched into a ball in the deepest shadows if Stewart hadn't been beside her, keeping a tight hold on her hand. Moving faster and faster, he dragged her along to the wall, and when they got there he didn't wait for her to scramble to the top. He clasped his arms around her so fast and so tight that the air whooshed out of her lungs. Before she knew it, he had lifted her off her feet, put her on top of the wall, and jumped up beside her.

There was a policeman not three feet behind them.

Through the dark, Aggie saw the man's raised face. She heard him call a warning to his mates, and even as they hopped off the wall and onto the pavement beyond, the iron gate flew open and a phalanx of uniformed policemen emerged.

Where Askew had got to didn't seem to matter. The police officers spotted Aggie and Stewart and took off running toward them.

"Damn!" Still holding tight to Aggie's hand, Stewart darted into the road, weaving in and out of a line of hansom cabs to get to the other side. The police were right behind.

Stewart stopped only long enough to look into Aggie's eyes. "Can you keep going?" he asked. She couldn't. She couldn't catch her breath. Or hear anything except her heart hammering in her ears. She couldn't feel anything at all but the pain in her legs, her muscles cramping, screaming that it was time for her to stop running.

Aggie wanted to say *no*. She wanted to tell him she had to stop and to hell with whatever it was the police would do with her. But one look at Stewart's expression, and she knew she could not say that. She knew if she told him she didn't have the strength to go on, he would push her on ahead and stay back himself to buy her time.

Aggie nodded. "Yes." Her voice was shallow. Her breath came fast. "Yes. Let's go."

It was all the assurance Stewart needed. He hurtled along the street, hanging on to Aggie. With the police close on their heels, they darted into alleyways and charged through gardens. They raced along the outskirts of what looked to be a hospital and bolted through an open-air market where the stalls were shut up for the night.

Step by step, they gained ground. Aggie didn't dare look back to see how far away their pursuers were. She only knew that suddenly she couldn't hear their footsteps or the rough sounds of their breathing anymore.

Still, Stewart didn't stop. They shot through a tiny park with a sparkling fountain at the center of it, scattering the pigeons sleeping there, and it wasn't until Aggie caught sight of Stewart's house that she realized their escape had not been as impetuous as she'd thought.

The front door looked very far away.

At the same time she had the thought, Aggie saw two policemen move to block their path. A strangled sound rose from her throat. Stewart paid her no mind. There was a garden to one side of his house, and while Aggie prayed that there might be a gate that would let them inside to safety, Stewart made his way at top speed along the border of boxwood hedges that were higher even than his head.

"No gate." Aggie's worst fear charged through her, and the words rushed from her mouth. "No gate . . . can't get . . . in."

"Never mind that." Stewart was just as breathless as she was. He pulled to a stop next to what looked to be a living wall of hedges and wrapped an arm around her waist. "Hold on," he said.

He touched a hand to a certain spot in the hedges and the next thing Aggie knew, the boxwoods seemed to open around them, then close just as quickly to swallow them up. She found herself in a pitch-dark garden with a stone path at her feet, rosebushes to either side of her, and Stewart's arm still around her waist. Not three feet away, on the other side of the boxwoods, she heard the police call out.

"Where the bloody hell—!" One of the policemen must have stopped directly outside the concealed door. His voice was so close, Aggie was sure she could reach through the hedges and touch him. "Where did they go?"

Another policeman answered, but by then Aggie wasn't even listening. Relief washed over her, and that, along with the exhaustion that instantly swept over every part of her body, made her knees weak. She sagged against Stewart and felt his arms tighten around her waist. She might have stood that way forever if he hadn't urged her on.

Without a sound, he led her through the garden and around to the back of the house. As soon as they got there, a door snapped open. A middle-aged man of great height and girth, whom Aggie recognized as Stewart's butler, stepped back to let them inside. He seemed neither surprised to see them nor in any special hurry. Once the door was closed, he turned up the gas jet on the wall, and Aggie saw that they were in the kitchen. There was a sturdy oak table set in the center of the room with four chairs around it. In the center of the table sat a steaming teapot and a plate of shortbread. Now that she'd stopped running,

Aggie's legs felt like rubber. She sank into the nearest chair and gasped for breath.

"Thank you, Trefusis."

As perfectly at ease as his servant was, Stewart nodded to the man. He slipped out of his coat and handed it to his butler. "Be a good fellow and fetch a cab, will you, Trefusis? Miss O'Day and I will take our tea and then I shall escort her home."

"Yes, sir." Trefusis brushed at Stewart's coat with one gloved hand. "And if that's all, sir . . ." The butler's voice held the clipped, musical notes of Welsh. "After that, sir, I shall get to bed. There's a great deal to do tomorrow and—"

His words were cut short by the harsh sound of the front bell.

"Damn!" The word came simultaneously. From Aggie, Stewart, and Trefusis. They exchanged looks, but before either Aggie or Stewart could say a word, Trefusis had everything under control.

"It is sure to be the police," he said, as casually as if he were announcing a morning's visitor. With movements far more fastidious than might have been expected from a man who looked like a prizefighter and was as big as a bull, he set Stewart's coat down on a chair near the stove. There was a tall, narrow cupboard nearby, and Trefusis opened it, reached inside, and retrieved a newly starched white shirt.

The bell rang again.

Trefusis unfolded the shirt, shook it, and held it out to Stewart. "I would think you might want to receive them in the library, sir."

Stewart was apparently anticipating Trefusis's every move. Before Trefusis was done, he stripped off his dark jacket, turned his back on Aggie and slipped his black sweater over his head. When Trefusis came up behind him, he jabbed his arms into the shirt.

"I'll take Miss O'Day up with me," he told Trefusis. He didn't wait for Aggie to agree or disagree. He pulled her up from the chair where she sat struggling to find her voice and calm her heartbeat and escorted her through the kitchen and into the front hallway.

The doorbell rang again.

"She can stay in my room until the police leave," Stewart told Trefusis, and while the butler went to answer the bell, Stewart urged Aggie up the stairs.

By the time they heard the front door open and voices sound through the foyer, they were in a long passageway outside a row of closed doors.

Stewart paused before one of them. He opened the door and hustled Aggie inside. Before she could protest or ask what he was going to do, and what she could do to help, he closed the door in her face.

With one problem out of the way, Stewart turned his thoughts to the other, the one that was, for the moment, far more pressing. Belowstairs, he could hear Trefusis explaining that it was very late and that Lord Stewart was probably not in the mood to receive visitors.

"Good man," Stewart mumbled. He finished fastening the pearl studs on the front of his shirt and hurried into the library. He'd left his spectacles on the desk, and now he slipped them on and took a quick look around. As usual, the place had a time-worn, snug look about it that made it Stewart's favorite room. It smelled of incense and sealing wax and the ancient leather-bound books that lined the walls floor to ceiling. As was his custom every evening, Trefusis had laid a fire, and it blazed brightly in the grate. Its dancing light touched the stacks of books on the desk, the slightly shabby chair in front of the fire, and the collection of bric-a-brac and oddities arranged throughout the room.

"All as it should be," Stewart told himself. He pulled a book off the pile on the desk, sat in the chair in front of the fire, and opened the book on his lap.

It fell open to a familiar tract, one that discussed the treasures of King Arthur.

Chuckling at the irony of it all, Stewart drew in a deep breath, closed his eyes for a moment to focus his energies, and ran a hand over his hair to smooth it into place.

Just then, Trefusis tapped on the door and announced that the police wished to speak to him.

Chapter 11

It was obvious from the start that the policeman who was sent inside to question Stewart was nervous. Stewart supposed he didn't blame the man. It was odd enough for a man of a policeman's class to be inside a home as grand as his. It was positively overwhelming for the poor man to be addressing the master of the house, one who had "Lord" in front of his name besides.

Sergeant Reggie Bumpers, a man with a broad face and a disappearing hairline, turned his hat in nervous hands. "So you see, your lordship, what I'm saying, your lordship, is . . ." The policeman shifted his weight from foot to foot as he stood on the carpet Stewart had brought back from a journey to Persia. "What I mean, of course, your lordship, is no one means to bother you, your lordship, sir, seeing as how it's late and all and such, but . . ." Bumpers kept his gaze firmly on the toes of his boots. He cleared his throat, and Stewart wished the poor man wasn't on duty so that he might offer him a whisky. Bumpers sorely needed one, and now that Stewart thought about it, he could do with a drink himself. It had been an eventful evening.

"There was some . . ." Bumpers hemmed and hawed, searching for the right word. "Some suspicious activity, you might say, sir. Outside the house just now."

Acting surprised, Stewart sat a little straighter in his chair. He thought he might set the book he was reading aside on the table next to him, but at the last moment he noticed a tear at the knee of his trousers. He had no doubt it had happened when he'd scaled Barclay's wall. He adjusted the book to cover the rip in the fabric. "Suspicious activity?" He looked over to the door, where his butler was stationed. "Do you know anything about this, Trefusis?"

"No, sir." Trefusis was as good as any at keeping his thoughts to himself. His face completely without expression, he looked straight ahead.

"No. Well, I certainly don't, either." Stewart looked back to Bumpers. "I really am sorry, but it doesn't appear that I can help—"

His words were cut short by the ringing of the front bell.

Stewart and Trefusis exchanged a look, and without a word, the butler left to answer the door. He was back in less than two minutes, and while his expression was as calm as ever, his eyes betrayed a worry Stewart had never seen in them before.

"Reinforcements," Trefusis mumbled, right before he stepped aside to allow another man into the room.

"Evening, Lord Stewart." Unlike Bumpers, Inspector Stanley Greenfield didn't seem the least intimidated by the surroundings or by the company. He glanced around the room, his gaze assessing and curious, and when he was satisfied he'd seen everything there was to see, he turned his attention to Stewart. As if it was an afterthought, he removed his brown bowler hat and tossed it on a nearby table. "You won't mind if I ask you a few questions."

It wasn't a request. Stewart noticed that straight off. He pushed his spectacles up on his nose and assumed the slightly confused expression so many people expected from the eccentric Lord Stewart Marsh.

"Questions?" Stewart settled the book on his lap to cover the tear in his trousers more completely. "Of course you may," he said. "Although as I've told your sergeant—"

"You've told him you were here all night?" Greenfield pulled a notebook from his pocket and flipped it open. He did a turn around the room, glancing at the bookshelves, noting the titles. "You've been reading? All night?"

"Reading?" Stewart ran a finger down the page of the book his lap. "Yes. Reading. Studying, really. I am something of a scholar, you see, Inspector, and I—"

"And you haven't been out at all?"

Stewart sighed. It was a sound he'd perfected over the years, the sound of a man who grew weary when forced to discuss the inconsequential problems of the everyday world. A man who was anxious to get back to his books. And his solitude. "Of course I haven't been out," he said. "And I can't help wondering why you care. Has there been some problem, Inspector?"

"Problem? Yes. Indeed there has." Greenfield completed his perusal of the books nearest to Stewart and came to stand in front of him. "A burglary," he said. "Or at least an attempted burglary."

Stewart looked up at the detective, taking his measure. "And this concerns me . . . ?"

"This concerns you, sir, because my men followed the burglars—there were two of them, you see—and we followed them all the way from the scene of the attempted crime, to . . ." Greenfield paused, heightening the drama. "To here."

"Good Gad!" Stewart took off his spectacles and wiped them on a handkerchief he fished out of his pocket. "Did you hear that, Trefusis?" He placed the spectacles back on his nose. "Here! Here?" His eyes widening with alarm, he looked around. "Here?"

It was on the tip of Greenfield's tongue to tell him to quit playing the fool. Stewart could see as much. Fortunately, the man had enough sense to keep his temper and his opinions to himself. He offered a brittle smile. "Well, actually, sir," he said, "not here, exactly. We followed the culprits as far as your garden."

Pretending relief, Stewart exhaled. "Well, really, Inspector, I must thank you, then, for this visit. You've certainly done the right thing. Letting me know that some villain has used my garden as a byroad. Of course, you are free to search it, though you may find it easier to wait until first light."

"We don't want to search the garden." Greenfield had the eyes of a ferret, close set and deep as pitch. He pulled a pencil from his pocket, touched the tip of it to his tongue, and paused with it poised just above the pages of his notebook. "We think the fellows came into the house."

"Well . . . I . . . But that's . . ." Stewart did his best to sound astonished. "It's impossible!" he said. He removed his spectacles again, cleaned them, and put them back on. "Trefusis and I are the only ones here tonight. Cook is gone for the day, and the other servants are out for the night, at some fireworks show at the Crystal Palace. I assure you, Inspector, it has been as quiet as a tomb. Just the way I like it. Surely Trefusis or I would have noticed if—"

"Unless it was you."

Stewart allowed Greenfield's words to fall like lead in the silence. Long enough for the inspector to think he'd got the best of the situation. When Greenfield rocked back on his heels, Stewart barked out a laugh.

He scrubbed a thumb below the wire frame of his spectacles, wiping a tear. "You're daft! Trefusis? A burglar?"

Greenfield didn't smile. He didn't spare a glance for Trefusis. He gazed firmly at whatever it was he was scribbling into his little notebook and said, "Your trousers are torn."

Stewart slid the book from his knee. "Why, so they are. Really, Trefusis!" He glanced at his servant, silently praying the man would see the look he sent his way and know what it meant. It wasn't time to panic. Not yet anyway.

"I really must apologize." Stewart rose to his feet, looking down at the tear while hoping Greenfield hadn't noticed that his knee was scraped and bleeding. "I don't usually receive visitors in this sorry state. My valet will hear about this in the morning."

"The burglar climbed a wall," Greenfield said.

"Really? How amazing to think that someone might actually go to such effort." Stewart gave the inspector a level look. "Was it a high wall?"

"High enough that a man might tear his trousers," the detective replied. "And skin his knee besides."

Stewart smiled. He had to give Greenfield credit. The man lived up to his reputation. He was as cold as cucumbers and as cagey as they came. The trick, of course, was to convince him he was also wrong.

Still wondering how he was going to do it and what he was going to say when he opened his mouth, Stewart cleared his throat, ready to speak.

He never had a chance. Before he knew it, the library door bounced open.

Every man in the room turned to look at the doorway, and to a man, each and every mouth fell open.

Aggie stood on the threshold, half in and half out of the room. Outside, the passageway was lit only by a row of gaslights upon the wall. As it was late, they were turned low, and the odd yellow light added a faint glow that shimmered in the air around her and turned her hair the deep red of a garnet.

She looked sleepy and disheveled and so positively delectable that Stewart caught his breath—right before his blood went cold, his eyes went wide, and a feeling twisted through his gut that told him beyond the shadow of a doubt that something was happening. Something he didn't know about. Something he didn't understand. Something he was sure he was going to regret.

He might have spoken up. He should have. He should have jumped in with both feet and explained away the incident with a carefree wave of his hand. He should have used that supposedly famous wit of his to come up with something clever. Or something profound. Or at least something clichéd.

Instead, all he did was stare.

When last he'd seen Aggie, her hair was stuffed up under her hat. Now it was mussed and loose, a glorious cascade of curls that caressed her shoulders and spilled over her breasts. When last he'd seen her, she was wearing a man's trousers and a black jacket and a sweater as dark as the night. And now . . .

Stewart swallowed hard and hoped the sound wasn't enough to let the rest of the men in the room know that he was teetering on the fine edge between asking her what the hell she was doing and scooping her into his arms.

Aggie was dressed—or "undressed" might have been a better word—in one of Stewart's own white linen nightshirts. As if she'd done them up too quickly, the tortoiseshell buttons along the front of the nightshirt were fastened all wrong. The resulting effect might have been artless, but it was also so alluring, even Inspector Greenfield couldn't help but stare.

The nightshirt swept the floor on Aggie's right and was hiked above her bare toes on the left. The right side of the neckline drooped over her shoulder just enough to expose a rather delicious looking expanse of freckled skin. And to leave no doubt in any of their minds that she was wearing absolutely nothing underneath.

Aggie's cheeks were pink, and while Stewart knew her heightened color came from the exertion of their headlong escape, it was obvious that Bumpers and Greenfield had other ideas. No doubt, that was just what Aggie intended. Her lips were the color of cherries and just puffy enough to make it look as if she'd been kissed very thoroughly and very recently. Her eyes flickered with an enticing combination of passion and sleepiness.

Bumpers turned beet red.

Greenfield went as still as a stone.

Aggie was enough of a judge of people to realize the reaction she'd produced in them all without ever taking her eyes off Stewart. Like a cat with its whiskers in cream, she grinned, and that one look told him all he needed to know. Suddenly he knew exactly what she had in mind.

Stewart went as hot as if he had a bellyful of wasps

and salamanders, then just as quickly, cold. It was as if his wildest fantasies had been hung out like wash for the world to see. He batted away the thought and the mixture of discomfort and exhilaration that filled him at it, and did the only thing he could do. He allowed Aggie to take control of the situation. Stewart removed his spectacles and cleaned them on his handkerchief, giving Aggie his silent consent.

It was just what she was waiting for.

As if they were alone, as if he were the only person in the world who mattered, Aggie kept her gaze full on Stewart.

"Stewart, you bad boy, you must really come back to bed. I'm lonely." She pouted prettily and sauntered into the room, standing close enough to Stewart for him to feel the press of her breasts against his chest. For one disconcerting moment, he felt the world tip and had to close his eyes against the wave of desire that swept over him. If he had thought the finest thing he might ever have experienced was the feel of Aggie in his arms when she was dressed up to the nines in a borrowed ball gown, he had certainly been mistaken. Standing so close, with only a thin layer of linen separating him from her bare flesh was a sensation both exquisite and agonizing, and it was only with the most hard-fought exercise of self-control that Stewart was able to appear unaffected by it.

Aiming an apologetic smile over Aggie's head toward Inspector Greenfield, Stewart put a hand on her shoulder and gently turned her so that she could see they were not alone.

He had to give her credit. If she was half the journalist she was the actress, she wouldn't need to worry about earning her living writing trash for a newspaper such as the *Chronicle*. The world would be beating a path to her door. No mistake about that.

She blushed even more prettily than she pouted. With one hand, she caressed Stewart's where it lay against her shoulder. "Your friends will simply have to excuse you, darling," she said, turning back to him. With a look, she dared him to dispute the intimate way she'd cooed the last word. "It really was bad of you not to tell them you were busy. I've been all alone for a full five minutes. I'm cold." Enough of a shiver ran over her shoulders to make the nightshirt droop even more. Aggie leaned nearer, her voice a little growl just loud enough for everyone to hear. "Come keep me warm."   •

Stewart wasn't sure if the feeling that began at his toes and snaked all the way through his body was embarrassment or out-and-out desire. He rather suspected it was a combination of both. Fighting to push the desire aside, he swallowed around the embarrassment and gave Aggie as indulgent a look as he could muster.

"You're going to have to wait a while longer, darling," he said, the sobriquet as tight in his throat as it had been pure heat coming from hers. "These gentlemen are from the police. They've come to question me about a burglary."

"Really?" The picture of excitement, Aggie bit her lower lip and whirled to face Greenfield and Bumpers. "How very exciting!" The inspector was standing nearest to her, and she gave him a naughty little smile. "If there's anything at all you want to know about Stewart, you might ask me. I know everything about the man, including—"

"Yes. Well." Greenfield scratched under his nose. Fighting to keep his gaze from wandering to Aggie and all the delicious parts of her that were all too evident beneath the fine linen, he locked his gaze on Stewart and kept it there. "I think we've found the answer to our question as to where you've been all evening," he said, and he looked no more pleased than he sounded. He allowed his gaze to flicker to the tear in Stewart's trousers. "I could have sworn—"

Aggie laughed. Bless her, she'd seen the rip in the fabric, too, and as if she could read Greenfield's mind, she knew exactly how to counter his suspicions. She leaned nearer to him, and as if she were revealing a very special secret, she lowered her voice. "I do hope you'll understand. Lord Stewart and I . . . well . . ." She giggled. "We do tend to get a bit vigorous at times."

It was enough to make Bumpers redden all the way from his shirt collar to what was left of his hair. Enough to make even Trefusis choke out a cough.

Enough to let Greenfield know he'd met his match.

He reached for his hat and signaled to Bumpers that they were done for the night. With a word of apology that sounded no more sincere than the expression on his face looked, he followed Bumpers out of the room.

Still fighting to control a chuckle, Trefusis offered Aggie a bow as eloquent as a pat on the back. "I will show the police out," he said, moving to the door. "And then, I am going to bed. I might suggest, sir . . ." He stepped into the hallway and closed the door behind him but not before he nodded his approval of Aggie and gave Stewart a wink. "I might suggest, sir, that you do the same."

The door closed behind Trefusis, and silence filled the room. Just as quickly, the rush of triumph Aggie had felt at besting the police dissolved, evaporated, and finally disappeared like a bit of ice left out in the noonday sun.

She couldn't think why. It was, after all, as masterful a plan as any she'd ever conceived. And she had carried it out to perfection. Just as she'd anticipated, the police might be ready to face down criminals of every ilk. They might stand fast in the face of thieves. They might be brave when dealing with bandits. But policemen—even policemen as crafty as the renowned Inspector Greenfield—were, after all, only men. And like all men, they were defenseless when it came to women.

That being true, there was no reason Aggie shouldn't be feeling as proud as old Cole's dog. No reason she shouldn't be bursting with the kind of heady intoxication that always buzzed through her when she schemed her way into a rattling good assignment from Wallingstamp, or manipulated her way into some meeting or another where no reporters were allowed, or used the Smile to cajole an especially reticent source into parting with the information she wanted.

And yet she didn't.

She didn't feel proud. Or exhilarated. Or even as pleased as Punch.

Suddenly, Aggie didn't feel anything except foolish and awkward and terribly self-conscious. They were unusual emotions for her, and she wasn't sure what to do about them. She only knew that now that her audience was gone and she was alone with Stewart, she felt embarrassed, and more ill at ease than she ever had in her life.

Wrapping her arms around herself, Aggie moved closer to the fire. She was cold and the heat felt good. Besides, it put some distance between her and the disturbing looks Stewart was giving her. Even with her back to him, she knew he was still looking at her the way he'd been looking at her since she entered the room, with a curious mixture of amazement and . . .

And what?

There was no word Aggie knew that could define the kind of emotion that had sparked in Stewart's blue eyes the instant he'd seen her standing on the threshold in nothing but his nightshirt. No description, not even from a writer with so much talent, for the sensations that sizzled in the air between them like the lightning that sometimes cut through a hot summer sky.

The vibrations intensified each time she and Stewart met, and tonight they buzzed in the air like a swarm of bees. They had tingled along her skin when she'd first heard Greenfield's voice as he came up the stairs with Trefusis and she formulated her plan. They'd shivered through her while she dug through the wardrobe in Stewart's bedroom looking for the appropriate attire in which to carry out her charade. Like electricity, they'd hummed through her the moment she'd stepped into the open doorway and watched Stewart watching her. They'd upended her enough that she nearly hadn't found the courage to walk into the room.

The same sensations shivered their way over her body even now, prickling along her skin, generating a curious tightness in her breasts and a delicious heat deep at her center.

"You didn't have to do that." Stewart's voice was as intimate as a caress. As real as a physical touch, Aggie felt it stroke her skin.

"No." She could hardly help but agree. Shrugging

off the warmth carried by his words, she hoisted the nightshirt up on her shoulder and turned to face him. "But it worked a charm, didn't it? And taught that pompous fool a lesson."

"And your reputation?"

"My reputation?" Aggie had to laugh, though when she thought about it, she realized there was no amusement in the sound. She rubbed her hands up and down her arms. "You always thought me devious. Not above doing anything for the sake of a story." She shrugged away the feeling that he'd been right about her all along. "I suppose all I've done is live up to my reputation. And your opinion of me."

"No." Stewart shook his head. He moved a step closer and the air warmed considerably. "That isn't why you did it. Not for your story. If you were worried about your story—"

"If I was worried about my story I would have marched right in and announced to that smarmy peeler that you were the Shadow. Is that what you were going to say?" She smiled. "Perhaps I didn't want to see you carted away. Not yet. Not until I have a look at that crown and all the proof I need that you're who I think you are."

"Perhaps that isn't it at all." Stewart removed his spectacles and stepped around the chair that separated them. His gaze slid from the top of Aggie's head to her arms, crossed over her breasts, and when he raised his eyes to hers again, they shimmered with the light of the fire. "Perhaps you had something else in mind," he said.

"Perhaps I did." It was impossible to keep still when he was looking at her that way. Impossible to stay calm when her skin was on fire and every breath she took caught in her throat behind a knot of anticipation. Every ounce of her wanted him to kiss her, every breath, and every drop of blood that pounded through her veins, and every part of her heart and her soul. Every bit of advice whispered by her brain told her it was ill-advised, and every inch of her body told her not to listen to her own advice.

As uncomfortable with the thoughts as she was with the fact that each second Stewart kept his gaze riveted on hers, her knees felt weaker and her heart beat stronger, Aggie retreated to the other side of the room and found herself behind Stewart's desk. She had a choice: she could face up to her own feelings and look Stewart in the eye, or she could make herself look busy.

Still feeling foolish and vulnerable, she took the coward's way out. There were two books open on the desktop, and one of them caught her eye. She bent closer for a better look.

The book was obviously old. The leather cover was tattered. The pages were yellowed, and it was apparent that they had been hand-lettered. The script was intricate. The letters twirled and whirled across the page in a convoluted pattern. The language—

Aggie squinted at the strange writing.

Not Latin, she thought, though she couldn't be sure. And not Greek, either, if she had to guess. But it was neither the elaborate hand nor the curious language that caught her attention. It was the illustration on one corner of the page.

At first glance, Aggie thought it must be a coat of arms. But closer inspection showed her it was something else altogether, a seal of sorts, rendered in purple. The drawing showed a shield with an elaborate border decorated with the kind of whorls that distinguished the writing on the page. Across the bottom of the shield, words were written in the same fantastic language as the text. The shield was held in the talons of a dragon. In the center of the whole thing was a crown.

It didn't look at all like the kind of crown kings wore in children's fairy stories. It wasn't pointed like a tiara. It wasn't heavy with jewels. This crown was a simple band that would circle its wearer's brow. It was impossible to say what the thing was made of, Aggie told herself. After all, she was looking only at a rendering in purple ink. Yet she could have sworn the crown was forged of solid gold. There were three jewels at the front of it, one large and two small, and she had no doubt they were diamonds.

Her reporter's instincts stirred, along with her natural curiosity. Forgetting her embarrassment, she looked at Stewart and found him watching her carefully.

As if he were reading her mind, he glanced toward the book. "It is the symbol of the Knights of Avalon," he said.

"Knights of—?" She ran her finger over the illustration. The paper was old and very soft. "Why does that sound familiar?"

Stewart strolled over to the desk. She thought him more at ease now than he had been since she'd made her grand entrance into the room, but on second look, she knew she was wrong. None of the intensity had gone out of his eyes, only now his gaze wasn't fixed on Aggie. As if he could see far beyond its ancient pages, he looked down to the symbol of the Knights of Avalon.

"According to the old legends, King Arthur was seriously wounded at the Battle of Camlann. That was sometime around 542 A.D." He glanced up at

her, and for a second she saw the gleam of the
scholar in his eyes. He tossed his spectacles down on
the desk. "He was taken to the Isle of Avalon," he
told her. "Some say it was for burial. Others . . ."
He twitched his shoulders. "Others say he was
healed and he waits there still. Like Mallory, they
think him *rex quondam rexque futurus*, the once and
future king."

"And you think?"

"I think there are as many versions of the story as
there are scholars who study it."

"And the Knights?"

Stewart turned to face the fire. From where she
stood, Aggie could see his silhouette against the orange glow. His chin was firm, his eyes steady. He
watched the flames leap and dance, and his eyes narrowed, as if he was wrestling with some great
decision.

Afraid to let the moment go, afraid to pursue it to
its inevitable end, she crossed the room to stand next
to him. Hesitantly, she reached out and touched his
shoulder. "What are you thinking?"

For a moment, Aggie thought he'd forgotten she
was there. Then she saw the color of his eyes darken
from clear blue to sapphire, and she knew he hadn't
forgotten. He couldn't. No matter how hard he tried.

"The Knights of Avalon are part of the legend,
too," he told her. "The old stories say they await
Arthur's return. They have their stronghold on a
place called Ynys Enlli, Bardsey Island. It's off the
coast of Wales. That's where, at least according to
the legend, they guard Arthur's treasures."

"Treasures?" The very word caused a tingle to race
up Aggie's spine. "Like his crown?"

Stewart nodded. "Like his crown. And then someone like Maxwell Barclay comes along and—"

"Are you saying the crown is real? That it actually
belonged to King Arthur?" The idea was so preposterous, Aggie could barely put it into words. She
wasn't surprised when Stewart shook his head.

"The crown Barclay has? There's no telling, of
course. No one's seen it yet. But it doesn't sound as
if it could possibly be authentic. Arthur's Crown
would be more like . . ." He looked toward the book
opened on the desk. "More like the crown pictured
there. All this talk of gold and jewels, well, it isn't
much more than a way to get people excited so
they'll pay their money to see the thing once Barclay
puts it on display the weekend of the queen's Jubilee.
And as far as that curse . . ." Stewart mumbled a
curse of his own.

Aggie clutched her hands together at her waist.
There was something in the way Stewart responded
to the very mention of the curse that made her feel
repentant. "I thought the more fantastic I could make
the thing sound, the more likely it would be that
people would want to read about it," she confessed.

Stewart stared at her in wonder. "Then I was right,
just as I suspected all along! You—"

"I invented the curse." Aggie nodded. She scrambled to redeem herself. "Curses sell newspapers, and
my stories haven't hurt a soul. I daresay Barclay's as
thrilled as can be. Because of my curse, everyone's
talking about his crown. By the time he's ready to
put it on display, they'll be in queue for blocks just
to see it."

"Oh, Aggie . . ." Stewart turned to her. He looked
ready to speak, then changed his mind.

"Do you think they'll be angry with me?" Aggie

asked. "These Knights of Avalon fellows? If they're in charge of seeing that Arthur's treasures are kept safe—"

"The Knights are part of the tradition," he said, glancing away. "A bit of legend, nothing more. They were supposed to be a very secret society. Very exclusive, don't you know. A sort of leftover from the Knights of the Round Table. But, well . . . it all sounds as unlikely as your sea monster in the Thames. Scholars agree that they are nothing more than a bit of folklore invented by some ancient people who needed assurance that their king hadn't deserted them. Fairy tales. No more real than the stories of Avalon itself." Stewart looked back at her. "Aggie, I—" He swallowed hard, fighting with his words and his emotions. "I would ask you—"

"What?" Aggie couldn't help herself. There was something in Stewart's voice that drew her nearer. As quickly as it had come, her embarrassment disintegrated, annihilated by the sudden spark that heated his eyes. She ran her tongue across her lips and kept her arms at her sides and when Stewart's gaze strayed to the outline of her nipples beneath the linen nightshirt, revealed by the firelight, she shivered. "What do you want to ask me?"

For a moment, Stewart's gaze flickered over her head, back to the desk and the book with the curious seal of the Knights of Avalon. He brought it back to her, to her eyes, and her lips, and the tumble of curls that skimmed her breasts. "I want to ask you . . ." His gaze traveled from the top of Aggie's head to the tips of her bare toes and up again. It stopped at her hips and the place where the swell of her breasts showed beneath the fine linen. It brushed the row of poorly fastened buttons and touched the hollow at the base of her throat.

Stewart gave her a lopsided smile. "There's so much I want to tell you," he said. "So much I want to ask you. But mostly, Aggie, I want to ask if I can kiss you again."

A swell of excitement surged through Aggie and gave her the most ridiculous urge to giggle. She suppressed it as best she could, though there was little she could do about keeping a tremor of very real interest from her voice. She tossed her head and gave him a coy look. "Can I come with you when you go to steal Arthur's Crown?" she asked.

"No." Stewart closed the distance between them. "I'm not going to steal Arthur's Crown," he insisted. "But I am going to kiss you."

"We'll both regret it."

"I have no doubt of that." Stewart's smile faded bit by bit, and when it was gone, the only emotion left on his face was longing. He tunneled his fingers through her hair, then linked them at the back of her neck and pulled her close. "Would you stop me if I tried?"

Aggie thought she might answer. She thought she might say no. She thought she might tell him that she was far beyond the point where she could deny him anything. But even those few words refused to make their way past the longing that filled her. She found she couldn't do anything but keep her gaze on Stewart and hope he saw the answer in her eyes.

He did. A smile flickered over his face, softening the lines of worry between his eyes. He inched nearer and cupped Aggie's chin in one hand.

As if his touch were magic, her eyes fluttered closed, and when he bent down and grazed her lips with his, she leaned toward him. There was a certain sweet hesitancy in his kiss that tugged at her heart, a bashfulness that reminded her of the Stewart Marsh the world knew, the reserved scholar, the shy gentleman. It was all well and good, she supposed, for it was as much a part of what made Stewart the man he was as was his ability to thwart a robber with a single blow or his affinity for upper-story windows and other peoples' jewels.

But it wasn't that Stewart Marsh she wanted.

When he finally settled his mouth over hers, Aggie made up her mind. It was time to show him exactly what she had in mind. She linked her fingers at the back of his neck and squirmed just enough in his arms for him to feel the press of her body against hers. As she'd hoped, it was all the encouragement he needed.

With a burst like that which comes from a photographer's flashpan, the reserved scholar was gone. Aggie didn't need to open her eyes to know she was with the Shadow. She could feel his presence in the air. She could taste it in the kiss that got more urgent by the second.

Stewart's mouth closed over hers. He parted her lips with his tongue. He pressed her close, and when Aggie groaned her approval, he tugged the nightshirt over her hips.

Aggie hardly felt the scrape of air against her naked flesh. Stewart stroked her hips. He traced the shape of her buttocks, and when she gasped and murmured her pleasure, he slid his hand between her legs.

"I've been waiting for this moment for a long time." Stewart's voice was harsh against her ear, his impatience as desperate as her own. He covered her neck with kisses and backstepped her to a table that stood against the wall. He scoured his arm across the tabletop, scattering the things that had been displayed there, and lifted her up to sit on it. His mouth slid to her neck and then to the hollow at the base of her throat while he unfastened the buttons on the front of his trousers and eased her legs open.

Desire built like liquid fire in Aggie, burning all the way through to the tiny thread of panic that snaked through her insides. She didn't want to appear foolish. She didn't want to look inexperienced or naive, too anxious or too balky or too unsophisticated altogether, and so she squeezed her eyes shut and held her breath and waited for the inevitable.

It was a full minute before she realized Stewart hadn't moved.

She opened one eye, then the other, and found him looking at her with an expression so tender, it brought tears to her eyes.

He moved back a step, skimming his hands down the outside of her thighs. "Aggie, have you ever done this before?" he asked.

It was on the tip of her tongue to lie. It was, after all, embarrassing to admit that a woman who pretended to have such power over men had never, herself, been in such an intimate situation with a man before. She bit her lower lip. "Not exactly, I—"

"Damn!" Stewart looked up at the ceiling, gathering his self-control. "You might have told me, I never would have . . ." He took her hand in his and tugged her to her feet and smoothed the nightshirt down over her hips. "I'm sorry, Aggie," he said.

"Are you?" Aggie tipped her head, trying to get a better look at his face, hoping to gauge his reaction. "I'm not."

"Really?" Stewart brightened. He glanced toward the door. "A woman shouldn't . . . I mean, not the first time . . . not in a damned library. It isn't exactly romantic, is it?" He laughed and Aggie did, too, and her heart squeezed with affection and something more.

Stewart planted a kiss on the top of her head. "Come on," he said, tugging her toward the door. "Let's go do this properly."

Chapter 12

How any man in his right mind could have second thoughts about taking Aggie into his bed was a mystery to Stewart.

She was as beautiful as any woman he'd ever seen. As delicious as any he'd ever tasted. She was everything he'd dreamed of these past weeks. And more. She was willing, even eager, for him to make love to her, and if her response to his impulsive behavior in the library meant anything, she was adventurous enough that any encounter with her might prove not only satisfying but invigorating as well.

The thought was not without merit, and possibilities, and as if to reinforce each and every one of them, the first thing he saw when he led Aggie into his bedroom was the garments she'd tossed onto his bed. Her trousers, jackets, and sweater lay in a jumble across the blankets. Atop it all, stark white against the night-black clothing, lay her scanties. The lace-edged corset and bloomers were supremely feminine and eminently titillating, and for a moment, Stewart could do no more than stare at them while a sizzle of desire throbbed inside him at the very thought of what their presence meant.

He automatically tightened his hold on Aggie's hand, but he could find neither the nerve nor the lack of principles to take the next step and gather her into his arms.

Having a conscience was damned inconvenient, he decided. Especially at a time like this.

He could smell the scent of rose water on Aggie's skin and hear the quick, impatient breaths that told him that though he might be having second thoughts, she had none at all. In the thin light of the gas jets on either side of the chest of drawers across the room, he could see the flush that stained her skin, and the way her breasts pressed against the fabric of the nightshirt.

Stewart closed his eyes against the havoc the sight wreaked on his heartbeat and his self-control. He wondered again that any man could be foolish enough to even think of passing up the opportunity to lose himself in a night's lovemaking with a woman such as Aggie.

Yet he hesitated.

It wasn't as if he didn't want to make love to her. He wanted that well enough. Wanted it more than he wanted his next breath. It was simply that he knew what it would cost both of them. And he wasn't sure it was fair to ask her to pay such a price.

As if she sensed his indecision, Aggie trailed one finger up the length of his arm. "You were saying . . ."

Roused from his thoughts, Stewart jumped. "Saying?" He sounded, even to himself, more like the timorous scholar than ever. Embarrassed and apologetic, he gave Aggie as much of a smile as he could manage. It came and went quickly, like the sharp stab of anxiety he felt when he looked into her eyes. "I was saying . . . in the library . . . I was saying . . ."

His fumbled explanation was interrupted by Aggie's light laugh. "You were saying that we were going to do this properly." Her eyes alight, her voice warm with anticipation, she advanced on him, close enough for him to feel the brush of her breasts on his arm. "I may not have much experience, but I do believe the way we tried it in the library was more proper than this. Standing here staring at each other and talking in half sentences. Well . . ." She glanced around the room. "If you need a table . . ."

The reminder of his impetuous conduct in the library made Stewart laugh. "No table," he said. "We'll save the table for next time."

But even as he said it, he knew it was a lie. There would be no next time. There couldn't be. Whatever they had, whatever pleasure they might share, whatever contentment they might find in each other's arms, it had to end here. Tonight.

The very thought was enough to remind him that he was a fool. Not for wanting to make love to Aggie. But for hesitating, even for a minute. Before he could let his conscience and his damned sense of honor get the best of him, Stewart pulled Aggie into his arms. Before he could talk himself out of it, he kissed her.

And once his mouth was on hers and one hand was holding her close while the other grappled with the buttons on the nightshirt, he didn't care a fig about his conscience or about the consequences. She tasted as sweet as she smelled, and the flavor of her was enough to drive away his doubts. He slipped his hand inside the nightshirt to caress her bare breasts, and the very feel of her skin against his dissolved his worries.

In the morning, he might think himself the biggest lunatic ever to walk the earth. Tonight, that didn't matter.

Anxious for a taste of her, eager to see the delights

only hinted at beneath the thin linen, Stewart pulled back just enough to unfasten the rest of the buttons. He watched, fascinated, as the last button slid free, and he held his breath while he parted the fabric.

Aggie's breasts were ample, as round and as firm and as beautiful as he had dreamed they would be. Like the touch of an artist's brush, the light of the gas jets stroked them with golden color. He cupped one and brushed his thumb across her nipple, and she shivered and closed her eyes. When she murmured her approval, he bent and trailed his tongue along the path his thumb had followed.

Aggie arched closer, encouraging and eager. Her hands traveled up his chest and along his shoulders. Her fingers splayed through his hair. They toyed with the studs on the front of his shirt.

Like the vibrations set off at the touch of a tuning fork, Stewart tingled with anticipation. He eased the nightshirt over Aggie's shoulders. He watched it skim over her breasts and slip over her hips. He watched it pool on the floor around her, and when he stepped back to admire her, he knew that just for this night, he'd made the right decision.

Every bit of her was as beautiful as he'd imagined. Every curl of carroty hair, and every inch of bare skin, and every curve of her hips and her breasts and her incredibly shapely backside.

He hadn't realized he was staring until he heard Aggie clear her throat. Her eyes bright with pleasure, she traced a finger down the front of his shirt, all the way to the waistband of his trousers. "You said we were going to do this properly, remember?"

"Oh, we're doing it properly, all right." Stewart could hardly help the honest sigh of approval that escaped him when he slid his gaze from the top of

Aggie's head to the tips of her toes and back again. Shaking his head in wonder, he marveled that any woman could be so perfect. That any woman so perfect could also be as eager to please him as he was to pleasure her.

He fitted his hands against Aggie's hips and caressed her backside. "It doesn't get any more proper than this," he said.

"I think you're quite wrong." There wasn't the least bit of criticism in Aggie's words or in the saucy look she gave him. Her gaze on his even while his roamed over her, she unfastened the studs along the front of his shirt. One by one, she loosened each one from its place and tossed it out of the way and as Stewart's shirt fell open, she pressed a line of kisses down his chest.

"Correct me if I'm wrong—though I never am, you know." She looked up at him at the same time she pulled the tails of his shirt out of his trousers. "But I do believe to do this properly, you must be as undressed as I am." She dragged the shirt down his shoulders and tugged it off his arms, and Stewart smiled. With as much enthusiasm as she'd ever attacked any story, she went to work on removing his trousers and his smile turned into a grin of out-and-out delight.

Too late, Stewart remembered the small purple tattoo over his heart. A feeling like a splash of ice water in the face assaulted him. He went still and rigid. Grateful that Aggie was concentrating on other portions of his anatomy, he twisted out of her arms and turned away.

For what seemed too long a moment, the sound of her uneven breathing washed against the noise of his own rough breaths and the rushing of the blood in his head. He wanted to curse, but the words wouldn't come. Besides, there were no words that would blunt all of what Aggie must be feeling.

The sound of a strangled sob of surprise escaped her, and it stabbed Stewart's heart like a well-placed knife.

"Have I done something wrong?" Her words were tight, her voice as cold as it had been brimming with warmth only moments earlier.

Stewart shook his head. He couldn't stand to think she might be unhappy. No more than he could stand the chill that invaded him, body and soul, now that he was away from her warming touch.

"Of course not," he told her. "We said we were going to do this properly, didn't we?" Careful to keep his words light and his back to her, he crossed the room and turned down the lamps. "There." He turned and searched through the darkness for her, and when his eyes finally adjusted to the lack of light, he caught the shimmer of her skin and the mahogany fall of hair cascading over her shoulders. "Just as I promised. That's the proper way to do this, you see. With all the lights down."

It was a lie. He knew it even as he discarded the rest of his clothing and tossed it on a chair in the corner. He knew it as he crossed the room. Knew it as he folded Aggie into his embrace.

The proper way to make love to Aggie was with every lamp blazing, with music playing and her laughter like church bells ringing through the air. He wanted to light every lamp in the room, to watch every nuance of emotion in her eyes, every smile that crossed her face. He wanted to see the way her breasts reddened when he suckled them and the way her lips parted when she moaned.

He didn't want to make love to Aggie in the dark.

But there was the matter of the tiny purple dragon on his chest.

Stewart pushed the thought to the back of his mind at the same time he led Aggie to his bed. She sat on the edge of the bed while he removed the clothing she'd stacked there and when he was done, he sat down beside her.

"The proper way to do this," he told her, "is to start with a kiss."

Aggie leaned her head against his shoulder. Her hair felt like silk against his bare skin. Her hand trailed over his thighs. "We've already done that," she said with an exaggerated sigh. "But if you insist."

Before Stewart could react, Aggie knelt on the bed next to him. She took his cheeks between both her hands and pulled his face up to hers, and even before her lips were on his, he felt the intimate thrust of her tongue. She kissed him long and hard, and by the time she was done Stewart didn't know or care about the lack of light, or the chance that she might see the telltale tattoo. He didn't care about anything at all except the world within the circle of Aggie's arms.

Consumed by desire, he nuzzled her breasts and kissed every delicious inch of her, and when he was certain neither one of them could stand to wait a moment longer, he pressed her back against the pillows.

"Aggie." Her name escaped him on the end of a sigh, close against the hollow at the base of her throat where he brushed a kiss. "You see, Aggie, this is the proper way. Slow." He trailed his tongue over her collarbone and down to her ribs. "And leisurely." He kissed his way back up to her earlobe. "And without a table in sight!"

"And in the dark!" Aggie laughed. The sound of it was like water rushing over pebbles. It bubbled through Stewart, fresh and cool and exhilarating. Aggie looked up into his eyes. "How appropriate," she said, and she smiled. "Here we are in the dark again, just as we were when we first met, in Maxwell Barclay's treasure room."

He should have let it end at that. He should have stopped her words with a kiss, stopped his own doubts with the silken feel of her body welcoming his. He wished he could have, but, damn, there was his conscience again, pricking away at him, even in this most private moment.

"Aggie . . ." Stewart caressed her cheek and looked deep into her eyes, and it was only after he saw the smile fade from her lips that he dared to continue. "Aggie," he said, "listen to me. Believe me now if you ever can. Aggie, I'm not the Shadow."

It was one more lie. One more on top of all the others. And Stewart didn't care. He saw her smile and nod, and then she raised herself up enough to capture his lips with hers and his mind went blank and he gave himself to the sensations that engulfed him.

Stewart lowered his body onto hers and lost himself in her, and for a few incredible hours he forgot all about the lies.

There was no doubt in Aggie's mind that she was an intelligent woman.

There was no question that an intelligent woman should have been able to find a thousand reasons why what had happened between her and Stewart in the small hours of the night was neither wise nor proper.

But though she sincerely believed it was not possible to lose her intelligence along with her virginity, and though she tried her best to demonstrate that intelligence by thinking of at least one of those reasons, Aggie came up short.

By exactly one thousand.

Closing her eyes against the sliver of sunlight that peeked through the slim opening between the drapes, she stretched beneath the rumpled blankets. Stewart was already up and out of the room, but the sheets still held the scent of him. She breathed in the heady aroma and glided her hand over the pillow still bowled with the shape of his head. She reached out to touch the blankets that, the last she'd seen them, had been twisted around his legs. They were still warm with the heat of him, and Aggie scooted over and snuggled into them, letting the warmth soak her body. It fired her senses and ignited any number of memories, each and every one of which left her breathless and eager for Stewart to return.

"Intelligence be damned!" she announced to no one in particular and the world in general. She tossed back the blankets, splashed water over her face from the pitcher on the chest of drawers, and found her clothes. A plan already fully formed in her mind, she dressed hurriedly and tugged a comb through her hair. She would simply go in search of Stewart, she decided. She would convince him to come back to bed. And once he did . . .

Aggie glanced at the bed, at the jumbled blankets and the sheets that had nearly been pulled off the mattress in the enthusiasm of their lovemaking. She grinned.

Once Stewart accompanied her back to the bedroom, she would prove to him and to herself that she was just as intelligent as ever. She would show him that an intelligent woman knew what she wanted. She went in pursuit of it. And got it every time.

That thought singing through her blood like the effervescent bubbles in a glass of champagne, Aggie was ready to open the bedroom door and head belowstairs to find Stewart when she heard voices floating up the stairway from the foyer.

"Lord Stewart is in the library."

There was no mistaking the voice. It belonged to Trefusis, Stewart's butler.

For a second, she found herself uncommonly piqued and more than a little disappointed. She'd hoped to have Stewart to herself this morning, and the thought of having to wait until he was done with whatever business occupied him left her feeling impatient and cross.

But then she heard the voice that replied to Trefusis's polite greeting. "I know where the library is. I'll show myself up, why don't I."

She recognized the voice instantly. Stewart's early-morning visitor was Sir Digby Talbot.

Aggie's displeasure disappeared in a rush of full-fledged curiosity. She bent her ear to the door, and when she heard one set of footsteps pass and head on toward the library at the other end of the passageway, she opened the door a crack and peeked outside.

She could see Sir Digby dressed in his old-fashioned frock coat. He must have given his hat to Trefusis at the door, but he hadn't surrendered his silver-tipped walking stick. He stopped outside the open doorway and leaned on his stick. Looking inside the library, he shook his head.

"You look like hell, young man. When was the last time you slept?"

From inside the library, Aggie heard Stewart bark out a laugh. "Good morning, Sir Digby. I hadn't thought to see you quite so early. Has Trefusis offered you coffee?"

Sir Digby advanced into the room. Fortunately for Aggie, he didn't close the door behind him. "He offered it," Sir Digby said. "I refused. No time for the niceties. There's much to be done before the Queen's Jubilee and not much time to do it. We've got a damned elaborate parade to organize, and trouble with the fireworks show that is supposed to accompany it." He heaved a sigh. "I hope you have better news for me."

Though she could no longer see him, Aggie imagined that Sir Digby must have seated himself in one of the chairs near Stewart's desk. His voice was muffled, as if he was turned away from the door. She could picture Stewart behind the desk, shuffling through the books open there.

He didn't answer right away, and Aggie took the opportunity to inch out of the bedroom and slip down the passageway, closer to the library door. Her back to the wall outside the doorway, she heard the sound of footfalls on the carpet and pictured Stewart coming around to the front of the desk.

"I hate to add to your troubles," he said. Stewart's voice was level, and Aggie wondered if he looked any more disappointed than he sounded.

He must have. In response, Sir Digby grumbled a word that might have been an oath. "Don't tell me you don't have it."

"I thought I might," Stewart said and though he was apparently delivering bad news, he sounded neither apologetic nor humbled. "I had planned to retrieve the thing last night, but . . . well . . . things got a little complicated."

"Complicated?" Years of diplomatic experience had obviously served Sir Digby well. He spoke the word completely without emotion but still managed to pack it with criticism. "Young man," he said, "I don't pay you to run into complications."

Pay?

The single word spun through Aggie's head like a whirlwind, churning up memories and old suspicions, fanning the reporter's intuitions that had nearly been consumed by the fires that had ignited in Stewart's bed. Her instincts took over, and before she even realized what she was doing, she reached into her pocket, grabbed her journal and her pencil, and began to write.

"Unavoidable, really." Stewart must have had a pot of coffee brought up for himself earlier. Aggie heard the clink of a cup against a saucer. "I wasn't the only one to visit Barclay's last night. There was a reporter there. From the *Chronicle*."

"Not that damned O'Day woman." Sir Digby grunted his disgust, a sound that made Aggie's hackles rise. "Can't understand it. Can't understand it at all. Why anyone would let a woman—"

"No. It wasn't Aggie." Was it her imagination, or did Stewart's voice warm when he spoke her name? Aggie liked to think so. Still, she didn't let the tickle of awareness that skipped up her spine stop her from transcribing every word the men exchanged. "It was a man. Can't remember his name. He wasn't as quiet as he should have been."

"Did they arrest him?"

"You might ask if they arrested me." Aggie didn't need to see Stewart's face to know he smiled. She could picture the one-sided, cynical grin. "No. On both accounts," he said. "But it wasn't for lack of trying. That Greenfield fellow is a damned nuisance."

"In other words, you don't have the crown."

The simple statement hit Aggie with all the force of a well-thrown punch to the stomach. It chased away whatever heat still lingered from Stewart's touch and left her chilled to the bone and gasping for breath. Even though her pencil was poised over the page, she could barely make herself write the words. She stared down at her journal, its pages blurred suddenly by the tears that sprang to her eyes.

"No. No crown." She was jarred out of her shock by Stewart's voice. "Not yet, at any rate."

A chair creaked, and Aggie knew Sir Digby had risen to take his leave. It was time for her to scurry back to the bedroom and close the door. As wise as the maneuver may have been, she couldn't make herself accomplish it. Her legs felt like lead. Still, her pencil flew across the page, keeping up with the conversation.

"You'll have it to me before the Jubilee?" Sir Digby's voice drew nearer.

Not sure what she expected Stewart to say, Aggie held her ground and her breath.

"If I'm not distracted again," he promised.

"Distracted?" Sir Digby grumbled, and Aggie heard the sound of his footsteps nearing the door. "I don't pay you to get distracted. I pay you—and may I remind you, I pay you very handsomely, indeed—because you are the most skilled thief in all the empire. We need that crown, Stewart, my boy. Her Majesty needs it. Before the twenty-first of June."

"I am, of course, aware of that." Stewart's voice grew closer, and Aggie knew he must be walking Sir Digby to the door. "You'll have Arthur's Crown soon enough. I intend to get the damned thing tomorrow night."

"Tomorrow?" Sir Digby didn't sound as if he thought it a good idea. "We've been keeping an eye on Barclay. You know that well enough. He'll be fishing in Scotland this weekend. The house will be empty. Why not wait until—"

"Tomorrow," Stewart said again, more firmly this time. "Greenfield will be expecting me to make another try when the house is empty. No doubt he'd be there waiting for me. No. That won't do. I'll get the crown tomorrow night. When Barclay is at home. And all the servants are on duty. And there's little chance that I shall trip over someone in the treasure room. I'll get the crown this time. You have my word on it."

"Your word?" Sir Digby's voice was tight and decisive. "Or the word of the Shadow?"

Stewart's voice chilled. "We are one and the same, are we not? My word's good, Sir Digby. As good as my honor. Whether I'm Stewart Marsh the scholar or Stewart Marsh the Shadow."

"It better be." Sir Digby's voice was nearer than ever. Knowing she had little time to conceal herself, Aggie rushed back to the bedroom and closed the door. She heard Sir Digby take his leave and, opening the door a fraction of an inch, she watched him go belowstairs.

She couldn't have said how long she stood there.

She knew only that the longer she waited, the more confused she felt.

There was some relief, she supposed, in knowing what was surely the most delicious secret in the empire: the Shadow was not, apparently, what he seemed. He was not an unprincipled rogue, a thief with no honor and a great deal of nerve.

Stewart's thievery was somehow tied not only to Sir Digby but to the queen herself.

It was incredible. Marvelous. A turn of events so unexpected, it surely should have been enough to shore up Aggie's spirits. But try as she might to rejoice in the news, she found herself instead staring at the bed. She closed her eyes and saw herself in the silky darkness, looking up into Stewart's eyes, listening to the sound of his voice.

"Aggie, I'm not the Shadow."

There was a time she would have challenged the statement. A time when she would have laughed it off and kept up a barrage of questions aimed at getting to the heart of Stewart's secret identity. But last night she hadn't cared if what he said was true or not. She hadn't cared about anything outside the circle of his arms and the feel of his mouth on her skin and the heat that built inside her and shattered, finally, like a million stars shimmering all around.

"Aggie, I'm not the Shadow."

Aggie opened her eyes and blinked against the glaring light of day.

"But you are," she whispered. "Just as I suspected all along." She moved across the room, and before she could stop, or remind herself that what she was about to do would only reinforce the opinion he had of her as an eavesdropper and a rumormonger of the worst sort, she yanked open the door and made her way to the library.

She stopped at the threshold. Stewart was busy behind his desk and he didn't notice her. It was just as well. At least for the moment. It gave her time to compose herself, to still the instinctive fierce beating of her heart and the heat that spread through her at the very sight of him. It gave her time, too, to study him, to compare all she remembered from the night before with what she saw now in the harsh light of day.

As if he'd dressed as quickly this morning as he had undressed the night before, Stewart's shirtsleeves were rolled above his elbows, and his hair flopped over his forehead. His expression was far grimmer than the white-hot looks he'd given her so short a time before. His mouth was pulled into a thin line. A muscle jumped at the base of his jaw.

He shuffled quickly through a stack of papers on his desk but obviously didn't find whatever it was he was looking for. He cast each paper aside with barely a glance, and when he was done sorting through the entire pile, he grumbled a curse and stepped back. It was only then that he noticed Aggie.

In the time it took her to pull in a sharp breath, Stewart's eyes lit up and one corner of his mouth tipped into a smile. The look was just self-conscious enough to tell her he remembered each and every moment of their intimacy as well as she did, and just cocksure enough to let her know he didn't regret a bit of it.

His gaze wandered over Aggie, from her hair— barely tamed and still tangled around her shoulders—to the trousers and sweater she'd thrown on in such a hurry, to the journal and pencil in her hands. He stopped there, frozen, and when he finally raised his eyes to hers again, his smile had vanished and his expression was unreadable.

The heat of his smile had been nearly enough to incinerate each and every one of the accusations Aggie had come to hurl at him. The icy expression that followed so quickly in its wake brought everything back in a rush that started out as cold as Stewart's expression and turned to the heat of anger straightaway. Aggie stepped into the library and closed the door behind her. "You lied to me," she said.

Stewart made no attempt to address the charge. For an instant his gaze flickered back to her journal. "Do you always listen at keyholes?" he asked.

Aggie forced a smile and tried to pretend the words hadn't struck like a slap. "What luck! For once, I didn't have to. Sir Digby was good enough to leave the door open."

"Which you, of course, construed to be an invitation to listen in on a conversation that was clearly none of your business."

There was no use denying what was true, so Aggie didn't even try. Besides, she had no intention of letting him avoid the issue. Not this time. The fact that she'd listened in on his conversation with Sir Digby was not the issue. What was, was the fact that he'd taken advantage of her when she was at her most vulnerable, that he'd taken the trust he'd so tenderly built all through the night and twisted it inside out.

"You lied to me," she said again.

Stewart pulled in a breath, then let it out slowly. "Yes," he said quite simply. "I did."

Aggie took another few steps into the room. There was a knot somewhere around her heart, and she pressed her journal against it. "You might have told me the truth. You might have said you were working with the government."

"It isn't as easy as that." Stewart pushed the hair off his forehead. "Besides, after all these weeks . . . after Barclay's treasure room . . . and you following me about . . . you didn't actually believe me, did you?"

"Last night? When you looked into my eyes? When you lay with your heart beating against mine? When you whispered the words so close to my lips? When you so expertly convinced me that all you wanted was to make me happy, to show me how wondrous an encounter could be between a man and a woman who desired each other, and respected each other, and—"

Aggie's voice broke with emotion. She covered the telltale sound with a harsh laugh and hid the fact that her hands were trembling by turning away from Stewart and crossing the room. A bookshelf covered the wall from ceiling to floor, and Aggie did her best to calm herself by focusing on the tattered leather bindings and the odd titles written in strange languages she could not begin to decipher. It was only after she was sure she could face him without betraying her emotions, that she turned to Stewart again.

"No," she said. "I never believed any of that. How could I after all the proof I've amassed? I wanted to believe it, I think, but . . ." It was as close as she was willing to come to telling him he'd broken her heart.

As uncomfortable with the fact as she was with the emotions it sparked in her, Aggie shrugged away the pain of her own words. "A woman will believe anything in certain situations. I'm sure you know that well enough. It is, no doubt, why you chose that particular moment to try and convince me."

"Aggie, I—" Stewart took a step toward her, then stopped himself. He leaned forward, his palms flat against the desktop. There was no remorse on his face, just as there was none in his voice, and she knew it was because he wouldn't allow it. There was nothing he could do, though, about his eyes. They sparked with a color that reminded Aggie of the hottest flame in the heart of a fire. "Aggie, I thought it best if we—"

"If we lied to one another?" Aggie couldn't help herself. She had to stop him. She couldn't bear to listen to whatever he might say. His explanation might make her feel better—about him, about all that had happened the night before—and she didn't want that. She wanted to endure the full measure of her misery. She was too numb to feel anything else.

"Yes, I can see how that might be best for both of us." She wasn't good at sarcasm, not when her voice shook with the same emotions that churned her insides. It took more resolve than she knew she possessed to keep the acid from seeping back into her voice. "If you expected me to be pleased that you're working for the government—"

"What I expected was that you'd stay where you were and not poke your nose into things that didn't concern you."

His words were like stones, and they hurt. Aggie braced herself against them, but she refused to let him see what he'd done. With enormous self-control, she clenched her jaw until it hurt, flipped open her journal, and poised her pencil over the pages. "How long have you been working for the government?" she asked.

"What is this? A damned interview?" Stewart stalked around the desk and came to stand in front of her. "You don't expect me to—"

"I expect you to cooperate," she shot back. "If not . . ." She flipped the journal so that it snapped shut and turned, headed for the door. "If not, it hardly matters. I'll see you here tomorrow. I expect you'll want to wait until nightfall?"

"Aggie. No!" Stewart's hand clamped down on her arm, holding her in place. "Don't even think it. You're not coming with me."

"Really?" Aggie glanced at him over her shoulder. She tried not to be affected by the blue of his eyes, or the feel of his hand on her arm. She tried not to remember that so short a time ago, they had been even closer than this, that they had shared themselves freely and eagerly with each other, taking and giving pleasure as only lovers can.

She yanked her arm to her side and went to the door. "It would have been simpler if you hadn't said anything at all, don't you think?" she asked. She opened the door, stepped into the passageway, and started for the stairs. "You might have left the lie unspoken between us. You might have thought of anything else at a time like that."

"I might have. I didn't."

She heard Stewart's voice from inside the room, but she didn't turn to look at him. She couldn't bear it. No more than she could the realization that in her secret heart of hearts, all she wanted was for him to race after her. And take her into his arms. And kiss away her doubts. She didn't wait to see if he would. She couldn't endure the tension of waiting, or the pain when she realized he wasn't going to do anything at all.

Aggie pounded down the wide circular stairway. It wasn't until she was halfway down that Stewart appeared on the landing. He clutched the banister, his knuckles white.

"You know I won't allow you to come with me," he said. His voice was silky soft, but it echoed in the high-ceilinged entryway, sleek and sure and as hard-edged as a steel blade.

Aggie stopped and turned to look up at him. "Won't allow it? You really have no choice. I'm coming, Stewart, and I'm going to write about every minute of our little adventure."

Stewart slapped the banister in frustration and hurried down the stairs. It was clear from the start that the last thing on his mind was consoling her, or kissing away her doubts. He pulled himself to a stop on the step above Aggie and glared down at her. "You heard Sir Digby. You know this is important to Her Majesty's government. You can't jeopardize all we're working to accomplish for the sake of one of your absurd stories."

She hated it when he was right. Especially when he was right in the same breath he criticized her writing talents. Aggie swallowed down the anger that threatened to escape in a shriek. She lowered her voice until it was as dangerously quiet as his. "I don't understand what's going on. At least not yet, but I will give you this much. There is, apparently, some connection between all this and Her Majesty's Diamond Jubilee. Far be it from me to compromise so solemn an occasion. And far be it from you to let it be compromised. A deal is in order, don't you think?"

She didn't wait for him to answer. Though he towered over her, she lifted her chin so that she was looking into his eyes. "Let me come with you. Let me write about the exploits of the Shadow from the perspective of someone who is right there at his side. In return, I promise not to reveal your identity. And if there is some secret connected with Her Majesty's involvement with all this—"

"There is."

"Very well." Aggie nodded. "I swear I won't reveal that either. Not if I can get around it and have my story as well."

Stewart pulled himself up to his full, considerable height. "And if I don't agree?" he asked.

Aggie tossed her head. She turned and sauntered to the bottom of the stairs, and it was only after she got there that she bothered to stop and look back at him. "If you don't agree, I'll be at the offices of the *Chronicle* within the hour, and I'll publish everything I know. I will tell tales and name names."

Stewart's voice was rough with disbelief. "You wouldn't."

Aggie held her place. It wasn't easy. There was blue lightning in Stewart's eyes and a bite to his words that made her feel more like an intruder than the woman to whom he'd made love all night long.

"Are you willing to take that chance?" she asked, and before he could answer, she spun away and headed for the door. She saw Trefusis out of the corner of her eye, but she didn't wait for him to step up. She yanked open the door and marched out of the house and before the door shut behind her, she called back to Stewart, "I shall see you here tomorrow night."

She found the irony in the situation instantly, and while she didn't appreciate the black humor, she could hardly fail to acknowledge it. All she'd ever wanted was a story sensational enough to make her journalistic fame and fortune. She wanted to know the true identity of the man the world called the Shadow. She wanted to follow in his footsteps, to watch him at his work, to be there at his side when he carried away the most celebrated prize in all the empire.

She'd gotten what she wanted all along. She should have been crowing in triumph.

But if that was true, why did she feel a hollow place where her heart used to be?

Chapter 13

"Can you trust him?"

Aggie didn't have to ask who Bert was talking about. She stared straight ahead out the front of the hansom cab they'd hired to take them to Mayfair, and a picture of Stewart formed in her mind. He was a damned hard fellow to pin down, and so were her memories. He was the rogue one second, then the scholar, then the confidant of Sir Digby Talbot and instrument of Her Majesty's government. He was the stern-faced man on the stairway who had challenged her right to accompany him when he went to steal the crown, the man who'd warned her that the Queen's Jubilee celebration would somehow be threatened if she revealed all she knew. He was the sweet, gentle man who'd carefully and deliciously introduced her to the fine art of lovemaking. The man who had looked into her heart and touched her soul. The one who had stared into her eyes and told her he was not the Shadow.

The memory was still too agonizing, and Aggie twitched it away. Could she trust Stewart Marsh? "Not as far as I can throw him," she told her brother.

Bert seemed neither surprised by the revelation nor shocked by it. But he did look confused. He scratched a hand through his hair. "Then explain to me why you're going with him tonight. If you can't trust him, you don't know what he might have in mind. He could be meaning to take you to some out-of-the-way place and cosh you, or have someone else waiting there to do it. He might be thinking of setting a trap of his own, and having the police there waiting for you."

"No. I don't think so." Aggie had been through the same questions herself a dozen times or more. "He wants the crown too badly for that. And he wants to buy my silence. He knows the only thing that will make me happy now is to let me go along. Besides, you're with me." She patted Bert's hand affectionately. "And before we ever start out this evening, I'll make sure he knows you have a copy of my journal. And if anything happens to me—"

"I'll see that it's published." Bert nodded, pleased at his place in the plan. "What I don't understand is what his brothers—"

He never had time to finish. The cab pulled to a stop in front of the private and quite exclusive Apsley Men's Club, and Aggie straightened her straw boater, tugged her skirt and jacket neatly in place and signaled her brother that it was time to get down to business. While she paid the jarvey, Bert went to work on the scheme they had concocted that was designed to get her past the front door to the expressly male enclave.

When Bert stepped out of the cab and fell to the pavement in a surprisingly realistic-looking fit of apoplexy, Aggie screamed for help. When Aggie screamed for help, the doorman who guarded the front entrance of the club came running. And when the doorman came running and bent over the apparently ill Bert, Aggie ducked inside the Apsley.

The place was as quiet as a tomb and as regal as any palace. Not that Aggie had ever been inside a palace, but she imagined that a palace would have looked like the building spread out before her. The walls were paneled with dark wood, the lights were turned low, the carpets were so thick her boots didn't make a sound. There wasn't a soul about, but off to her left she heard a low rumble of male voices in what looked to be a cardroom. To her right, she could see another room where a dozen or so men sat in high-backed leather chairs, reading their newspapers and sipping their afternoon whiskey and sodas in peace.

As quickly and quietly as she could, Aggie hurried toward the staircase. She didn't have much time. Someone was bound to notice her sooner or later. Before sooner could happen, she headed up the stairs toward the private room where, according to the reporter who wrote about Society news for the *Chronicle*, all but one of the Marsh brothers met every afternoon to take tea together.

She had slipped into the room and closed the door behind her before any of Stewart's brothers bothered to look up.

Matthew was the first to notice her. "I say! You're not the fellow who's supposed to be bringing more sandwiches."

"Not a man at all, if I'm not very much mistaken." George rose a second before all the others and made her a showy bow.

"It's Miss O'Day!" Edward moved forward. He glanced at the door, as if asking how in the world Aggie had made her way through a building where women were strictly forbidden, but apparently deciding he'd rather not know, he didn't pursue the subject. "Is Stewart here with you?" he asked.

"No." Aggie drew in a deep breath. She looked from Charles to Edward, and from Edward to Matthew, and from Matthew to George and Lowell, and reminded herself that she had a plan and she'd promised herself she would stick to it, no matter what. "He didn't come. He couldn't. He was detained, so he sent me."

"Well, we're certainly pleased to see you again." It was Charles who took charge, of course. He pulled out a chair and invited Aggie to join them at table, and when she was seated, they all sat down again. "Truth be known, Miss O'Day, we've just been speculating about you."

"And about your relationship to Stewart, of course." George added.

"It isn't that he's a damp squib, mind you—" Matthew began.

"But he does tend to be a bit reticent," Lowell finished for him.

"And after seeing how well you two got along at Sir Digby's gala—" Charles said.

"We naturally wondered about his intentions," Lowell finished for him.

"Not that we are prying," Matthew interjected, before Aggie had time to take offense. "It's simply that we are quite fond of the boy, naturally, and after meeting you . . . well, I think it fair to say that we are fond of you as well." He looked around the table at his brothers, who nodded their agreement.

"After all, you came and got us when Stewart was injured," Lowell reminded her.

"And you did dance so well together!" Matthew's sigh was echoed all around. "So, naturally, the sub-

ject was bound to arise sooner or later. And we wondered—"

"As is only natural," George reminded her.

". . . what Stewart's intentions—"

"Though they are surely honorable," Edward
interjected.

". . . might be," Matthew finished.

Aggie clutched her hands together on her lap and
stared at Stewart's brothers. They were an overwhelming lot, and for a moment she could do no
more than blink at them in stunned silence, unsure
of how to proceed.

"But surely, we are not being fair." It was Edward
who rescued her. Sensing her bewilderment, he
poured a cup of tea and set it before her. "Miss
O'Day has come here for a reason. We must let her
get a word in edgewise and tell us what that reason is."

"Thank you." Aggie looked around at the brothers.
"It is rather difficult to explain," she said, "as it is
quite complicated."

"Take your time," Matthew urged. He passed a
plate of biscuits in her direction.

"Thank you. No." Aggie left the biscuits un-
touched. "You see," she said, easing into her plan,
"it all has to do with Maxwell Barclay."

"Barclay!" Lowell was out of his seat in an instant.
His face went red. His hands curled into fists. "We
ought to bring suit!"

"Or at least have the man drawn and quartered!"
Laughing, Edward leaned back in his chair. "You'll
have to excuse Lowell," he said. "He's still a bit
upset over that unpleasantness at Barclay's dinner
party."

"But Miss O'Day wasn't there," Matthew reminded them all. "She doesn't know what happened."

"Actually, I do." Aggie couldn't bear to have the situation explained to her, not when she knew more about it than they did. "Stewart told me all about it. He told me he and Barclay are rivals of sorts and—"

"Rivals!" Lowell pounded the table. "The man's a lunatic! Seems to have it in his head that Stewart actually had something to do with that madness up in the treasure room."

"And we know it isn't true." Charles pronounced the words with certainty. "We were all there. We saw that Shadow fellow. He was a scrawny little thing. Certainly not Stewart."

"And yet Barclay's got that Inspector Greenfield sniffing about." George was outraged at the very thought. His eyes went cold. His back went stiff. He shivered. "Imagine. A policeman! Involved with our family!"

"It must be very difficult for you." Aggie did her best to pull them back to the matter at hand. It wasn't easy. She sensed that given half the chance, the Marshes would merrily take her along on whatever flights of fancy occupied their minds. She heard a door slam somewhere downstairs and the sounds of voices raised, and she knew she didn't have time to accompany them.

"Stewart and Barclay are rivals," she said and she hoped not one of them noticed that she crossed her fingers against the lie. "Which is why Stewart is planning a sort of practical joke."

"Just like him," Matthew chuckled. "Used to love to play tricks on us when he was a boy. Why, one time—"

"Yes. I'm sure." The sounds from belowstairs grew

louder, male voices, and they didn't sound happy. Aggie rose out of her chair. "He'd like your help."

"I say! What a marvelous lark!" Matthew leaped out of his chair, ready to assist. "We'll join our dear brother in battle against the foe!"

"Well, it's nothing that dramatic, I'm afraid. But if you could visit Barclay this evening, distract him, so to speak—" Footsteps pounded up the stairway, and the door to the room opened. Bert was outside in the passageway. He ducked into the room and slammed the door behind him.

"They're onto us, Aggie," he told her, just as the door flew open again.

As if they'd been schooled in the maneuver, the Marshes charged into the fray. While George and Lowell came up on the right of the red-faced doorman, who pointed at Bert and yelled something about trespassing, Charles and Matthew circled the man from the left. Like dancers executing the steps of some very complicated figure, they moved bit by bit away from the doorway, and the man had no choice, he had to move with them. When the doorway was clear, Edward ushered Aggie and Bert out and pointed them toward a back stairway.

"We'll see you later this evening," he told Aggie, right before he turned and headed back into the room, toward the sounds of what looked to turn into a full-scale ruckus.

"Are you ready?"

At the sound of Stewart's voice, Aggie stopped work on the story that was slowly but surely taking shape within the pages of her journal. If she had been writing about the scene instead of living it, she might have said her hand *stilled* over the pages. Or perhaps even that it *was poised* over her work. But reality, she was finding out, was very much different from the world she created with her words.

There wasn't the least bit of stillness in her. Her heart thrummed and her hands shook. There was an odd, queasy feeling inside her. It made her sorry she had been fool enough to listen to her brother. Though she hadn't been the least bit hungry since her confrontation with Stewart the day before, Bert had convinced her to eat a little something before she left the house. Much to her discomfort, she was finding that bangers and mash did not sit well on a stomach already full up of regret, remorse, and misery.

And as for poise . . .

Without bothering to acknowledge Stewart's presence, Aggie slapped her journal shut and stuffed both it and her pencil into the pocket of her black coat. She had arrived early for their rendezvous, and Trefusis had escorted her to the library. There, she'd passed the time writing what would surely prove to be her finest journalistic triumph: the final installment of her story about the Shadow.

She rose from her chair and reached for Bert's fedora, and after she'd shoved it on and made sure her hair was tucked beneath it, she forced herself to meet Stewart's eyes. Her gaze was as steady as his and she congratulated herself.

Only she knew that what appeared to be poise was actually numbness. She could look at Stewart levelly because she couldn't feel anything past her heartache. She could walk beside him to the door, and wait as he opened it for her, and accompany him down the stairs and out through the kitchen garden because all the while she wasn't thinking about what they'd meant to each other. Or what she'd thought they meant to each other. Or where it all might have led.

In the hours between her departure from Stewart's after their night of lovemaking and her return to accompany him to steal the crown, she'd decided she couldn't think of any of those things.

She couldn't think of the way he moved alongside her, athletic and as smooth as the darkness that surrounded them. Or the way, dressed completely in black, he prowled the night as silently as the shadows from which he'd taken his name. She couldn't look at him out of the corner of her eye and notice the hands that were as skilled at bringing pleasure as they were adept at thievery. Or the mouth that had not always been drawn into such a thin, hard line. She couldn't stand too close as they waited for a hansom cab to pass so they might cross the road. The night was cool, and she knew she'd find herself invariably thinking about the warmth of Stewart's touch and the heat of his body.

It was all too painful, and she'd be damned if she'd let him see how much she was hurting, so she decided not to think of anything at all.

Anything except her story.

It was fitting, she supposed.

Her story was all she had left.

Keeping well to the shadows, Stewart pulled to a stop across the road from Maxwell Barclay's mansion. He didn't need to look to know that Aggie stopped next to him. He could feel her there as surely as he could feel his own heartbeat. In a moment of insight that made a mockery of him, he realized that wasn't at all unusual. They were one and the same,

Aggie and his heartbeat, both as necessary to his existence as his next breath.

The thought sat uneasily with him, and he twitched his shoulders inside his black greatcoat, as if the movement could jostle the thought from his mind. It was no use and he knew it. He would have no more success than he'd had trying to rid himself of the guilt that had taken up seemingly permanent residence in the vacancy left by the conscience, the honor, and the principles that had deserted him the moment he took Aggie into his arms. As uncomfortable with the thoughts as he was aroused by the memories, Stewart crossed his arms over his chest and instinctively put another step's distance between Aggie and himself.

There was little satisfaction in the thought that he needed Aggie as much as he needed air, and none at all in the realization that for once his razor-edged reasoning brought him no comfort. Aggie might be essential to his being, but she was playing hell with his peace of mind.

Stewart didn't realize he'd grumbled his annoyance until he heard his own voice rumble back at him from the stillness that surrounded them. Aggie didn't respond. She didn't even acknowledge that she'd heard him, and as far as Stewart was concerned, it was just as well. At this stage in their relationship, small talk would have been nothing less than pathetic, as pitiful as the apologies he had practiced since he'd first seen her there on the threshold of his library and heard the pain of betrayal in her voice.

"You lied to me."

Stewart closed his eyes against the memory. What

difference would apologies make when what she said was true? He had lied. Knowingly. Willingly.

He'd lied because he had to, and there was no way he could explain or hope she would understand. He'd lied because he was too much of a man not to want to make love to Aggie and not enough of one to stop himself from possessing her. He'd lied to Aggie the way he'd lied to his family, to Sir Digby, even to the queen, because years before, he'd pledged himself to a cause he'd thought more sacred even than his own honor.

He'd never questioned the decision or felt any remorse about it. He had never imagined there could be anything he could want more than to keep his integrity and defend those principles to which he'd vowed his allegiance. Until now.

And now, it was too late.

"This is all your fault, you know." Stewart hadn't meant to speak, and he certainly hadn't meant to try to console himself at Aggie's expense. Yet there was something about the dark that invited confidences, something about the thoughts eating away at what he'd always believed to be a firm resolve that made him realize he was not fully to blame for the first-class cock-up they found themselves in.

As he might have expected, Aggie did not take the statement at face value. For the first time that evening, he saw that her icy composure was neither as icy nor as composed as he'd thought it to be. There was fire beneath the frigid demeanor, surely, and anger just behind the thin veil of her self-control. Automatically, her chin went up and her fists went to her hips. "My fault!"

Stewart found himself uncommonly pleased by the reaction. All things considered, he would rather fight then feel sorry for himself. "Your fault." In deference to the hour, and the fact that they were supposed to be inconspicuous, he kept his voice down. "If it wasn't for you and that damned curse of yours—"

"What more do you want from me?" Aggie glared up at him. Her face was nearly lost in shadows, but he could well imagine her expression. Defiant. Combative. Astute enough to have figured out nearly all the puzzle and inexperienced enough to have neglected this one very important piece. "I've already admitted I invented the curse."

"Ah, yes. You invented it." For the first time, Stewart acknowledged that he was no more dispassionate than Aggie was. There was an edge of sarcasm in his voice that surprised even him. He reined it in, or at least he tried. He very much feared that he sounded the same way his brothers accused him of sounding when he was lecturing on a subject of particular interest to him but to no one else. "Did you stop for a minute to think what you were doing, Aggie? Or did you merely write the first thing that came into your head?"

Aggie's shoulders straightened defiantly. "I am not a hack, if that is what you're suggesting. And I am certainly not like one of those writers who sit down and simply let every word in their heads flow down upon their papers without ever stopping. I write. And I rewrite. And I take a good deal of time to—"

"Tell me what the curse says again, why don't you?"

Try as he might to keep his voice level, Stewart knew he sounded smug and superior. It would serve him right if Aggie didn't answer him at all. She did, though, and he suspected it was only because she was particularly proud of her absurd curse. She recited the words with just enough intensity to make them sound as dramatic and mysterious as she apparently thought them to be.

"'All hail the monarch of the Britons who possesses this crown,'" she intoned. "'Woe be to whoever does dare to defile it. Death and destruction shall follow its path. And glorious praise to the rightful sovereign who is its owner.'" She waited for Stewart to respond, and when he didn't, her shoulders drooped and she let go a sigh of annoyance. "It is a fine curse," she told him.

"As fine as any," Stewart agreed, and it was true. In his studies of the arcane, he'd come across some genuine curses that didn't have half as much starch. "But, Aggie . . ." He told himself it was the last thing he wanted to do, the last thing he should do, but he couldn't help his reaction. He reached out and touched Aggie's sleeve.

As if she'd been shot through with electricity, she jumped. Though he didn't need the reminder, it was enough to make it clear that he couldn't let his instincts get the better of his reason again. He stuffed his hands into the pockets of his coat. "Aggie, have you thought of the ramifications of your curse?"

Aggie laughed. "The ramifications . . ." She pronounced the word as if it was too big for her mouth. "The ramifications are that I've single-handedly increased the circulation of the *Chronicle*. Folks can't hardly wait to read about the crown. Not because it's some moldy old treasure, but because there's magic involved. And wizardry. There's nothing that gets the attention of a crowd like the mention of the supernatural. Ol' Wallingstamp may not have realized yet what I've done for his newspaper, but he will, sooner or later." She warmed to the subject, or at least she might have had they been able to erase the last twenty-four hours. Now, Stewart suspected that Aggie's chatter had less to do with exhilaration than it did with covering up her nervousness and the awkwardness of standing in the dark with a man who'd so recently seen her without a stitch on and with her inhibitions flung off along with her clothing.

"Wait until Wallingstamp gets hold of this final installment," Aggie said, patting the pocket where she'd stored her journal. She sounded so enthusiastic, Stewart wondered if she was trying to convince him or herself. "Cor, but it'll make him sit up and take notice. I can't tell I was right with you, of course. When you pinch the crown, I mean. Greenfield would be all over me like a bee in a rose garden. And I suppose, as much as I'd like to, I can't reveal that you are not as much of a scoundrel as everyone thinks, but rather that you're working with Sir Digby and the government. But I can tell your methods, step by step. I can talk about how you go about the thing. But don't worry. I've given my word. I will say that though I know you stole the crown I never saw your face. It's more than you deserve." She stopped long enough to be sure the words had hit their mark. "But it's the least I can do. Seeing as how you're a spy, or whatever it is you are."

Stewart ignored the last part of her ramblings. It was not something he wanted to address. Not now. He shook his head. "Increasing the circulation of the *Chronicle* can hardly be considered a ramification of your curse," he said. "It's merely a result."

Aggie harrumphed her disregard. "You're quibbling, surely, though I can't imagine why. It may be very well for scholars to sit around and discuss the difference between ramifications and results, but—"

"Aggie!" Frustration bubbled through Stewart. Frustration at not being able to explain everything he wanted to explain. Frustration at not being able to tell the entire truth. He settled instead for the piece of it he could tell and hoped it would be enough. It wouldn't exonerate him. Nothing could do that. But at least when Aggie thought of him in years to come as some distant memory out of a more distant past, it would not be with complete contempt.

"You haven't listened to the words of your own damned curse!" Stewart raked his fingers through his hair at the same time he fought to control his voice. "You haven't even considered that there are people who might take advantage of things such as this, people who might use your curse for their own purposes."

"People?" There must have been something about the way he said the word that caused a shiver to scurry up Aggie's back. She jigged her shoulders and stared up at him. "What people?"

Stewart chose his words carefully. "If you bothered to read your own newspaper . . ." Not carefully enough. He was sounding like a bombastic bore again. He pulled in the words along with a lungful of cool night air. "There are anarchists at work on the European continent," he said. "Surely you've heard. The czar in Russia is already feeling threatened, and he isn't the only one. Our government . . ." A carriage went by, and he instinctively stepped further into the shadows and lowered his voice.

"Our government is concerned that those same anarchists may be looking for a foothold here. Your curse affords them the perfect opportunity."

He had to give Aggie credit. She had listened in silence. But this was obviously too much for her to believe. He saw her press a hand to her chest, as if she was trying her best to contain a burst of laughter. "My curse! Anarchists!" Her voice bubbled with amusement. "You're mad. Even madder than I thought."

He wasn't about to argue that point with her. "Your curse," he pointed out instead, "says that only the rightful monarch can own the crown. Think about it, Aggie. The rightful monarch doesn't own the crown." He turned and looked at the mansion across the road, and Aggie looked that way too. "Maxwell Barclay does."

For a moment, he thought he'd convinced her. But then he saw her face split into a grin. When Stewart didn't return the smile, Aggie's faded bit by bit. "That's ridiculous!" she said, but there was less conviction in her voice than there had been only a short time before. "You can't possibly believe—"

"It doesn't matter what I believe. It doesn't matter whether the crown ever really belonged to King Arthur or even if, as so many scholars assume, there never was a King Arthur. What matters is what you said earlier. You've got everyone excited about the crown. You've got everyone talking about the curse. You may have single-handedly increased newspaper circulation, but you've also made everyone think that the crown can belong only to the rightful monarch. And as our good queen does not own the crown . . ."

It wasn't necessary for him to say any more. Stewart realized that straightaway. Even in the thin light, he saw Aggie go pale. "Are you telling me there are people who want to overthrow the government? People who would take advantage of my curse to—" She put a hand to her lips, too afraid to even speak the words.

She didn't need Stewart to answer. She was far too intelligent for that. She put the last bit of the puzzle in place just as he'd known she would. "So Sir Digby has asked you to steal the crown? So that Barclay doesn't own it any longer?"

"That's right. Everyone will know the Shadow has stolen the crown. You and the *Chronicle* will make sure of that. And then . . ." Like a magician putting the finishing touches on an especially skillful trick, he held out his hands, palms up. "The crown will simply disappear. No one's supposed to know it, of course, but it will be given to the queen quietly later this week, on the day of her Jubilee. Thereafter it will be kept by the government. They haven't said where yet, but I suspect they will lock it away in the Tower. Or keep it in some secret place at Windsor.

"Whatever they decide to do," Stewart continued, "there will no longer be a question of Barclay owning the crown. Or of what right the queen has to the throne if she doesn't own the crown. The crown will simply be gone. Out of sight and—it is my most fervent prayer—out of mind. Gone and forgotten, as it has been these thirteen hundred years since Arthur sat on his throne. It isn't the perfect solution," he admitted when it looked as if she had already seen the holes in the logic of the plan.

"It would have been far better to convince Barclay to present the crown to the queen at her Jubilee. To make a public spectacle out of the fact that the crown is in the possession of the rightful monarch again."

"But you've tried."

"Sir Digby has tried," Stewart corrected her. "He wasn't successful. Barclay says the crown belongs to him and he'll do whatever he likes with it. What that means, of course, is that he wants to display the thing and make a fortune doing it. And that means more opportunities for those who oppose the monarchy to try to make the most of your little curse. Right now, the best we can hope for is that once the Shadow disappears into the night with the damn thing, people will simply forget that the crown—and the curse—ever existed."

He suspected there were a dozen questions Aggie wanted to ask, just as he was sure they would be questions he wouldn't want to answer. He was grateful when a carriage rumbled down the road and turned into Barclay's drive, distracting them. A servant arrived at the gate to welcome the visitors, and once the man's head was bent toward the carriage door and his attention focused elsewhere, Stewart grabbed Aggie's arm and tugged her across the road. They watched the servant let the carriage pass and waited until he trotted off toward the house behind it. Stewart hadn't been anticipating guests, but now that he thought on it, he decided it might be beneficial. The more activity there was in the house, the less likely it would be that anyone would notice two intruders.

Stewart leaped onto the brick wall that surrounded Barclay's property and offered Aggie a hand up. She was talking even before she settled herself at the top of the wall. "So the Shadow is a government agent. You work directly for Sir Digby?"

Of all the questions she might have asked, leave it to Aggie to find the one Stewart was least inclined to answer. He skirted the issue as well as he was able.

"I'm not as noble as all that," he told her. That much at least was true. "I work for whoever pays me." He jumped down onto Barclay's lawn and waited for Aggie to do the same. "This time, it happens to be Sir Digby. I owe him something of a debt, I suppose. He was the one who first noticed I had a peculiar aptitude for making other people's property disappear. He convinced me to put my talents to good use. We've worked together before." He sidled along the wall, one hand on Aggie's arm to help her along. "There are governments and patriots all over the world who object to having their national treasures plundered by archaeologists and adventurers. If they are willing to pay the Shadow to return those things to the places they belong, so much the better."

By the time they scurried across the lawn and settled themselves in the deeper shadows beneath an ancient oak tree, the front door of Barclay's home had swung open. Light spilled onto the lawn and the carriage that had pulled up to the front of the house. Curious, Stewart watched Barclay's guests descend. There were five of them. All men. And something about them was strangely familiar.

His eyes narrowed, Stewart watched the men approach the door. When the light fell on their faces, he mumbled his surprise. "It's Charles! Charles and Matthew." He shifted his gaze to the others, who still waited to give over their hats and walking sticks to Barclay's butler. "And Lowell and George and Edward. What the hell are my brothers doing here?"

"You didn't think I was going to take the chance of getting caught, did you?" At his side, Aggie sniffed. It was a small sound filled with disdain. "I knew you wouldn't think of a diversionary tactic, so I did. Your brothers have promised to keep Barclay busy. Whist, I think, or some such game. I'm sure they'll think of something. And I suppose we can trust Matthew to keep the servants running back and forth to the kitchen so that they can't possibly think of anything else."

"Aggie . . ." This time Stewart didn't listen to the voice that reminded him to keep his hands to himself. He took a firm hold of Aggie's arms and bent to look into her eyes. "Are you telling me you had something to do with this? That you told my brothers—"

"Don't worry, I didn't reveal your secret identity, or the fact that you are working with Sir Digby." Aggie watched the last of the Marsh brothers enter the house. The door closed behind them with a click. "I simply told them we needed their assistance." She turned her attention back to Stewart, her expression steady. "They didn't seem at all surprised, and they were only too willing to cooperate. Said it would be grand fun to keep Barclay occupied while you did whatever it was you wanted to do."

"Did they? Did they really?" Stewart's blood turned to fire, then to ice. The same ice he felt in his gut. He tried to think through all that was happening and came up woefully short of any solution. The only thing he could reason his way through to was the fact that Aggie had complicated things beyond reason.

And the only thing he could do about it was the one thing he'd known he had to do all along.

"Come on," he said. He turned and headed toward the house and a window in the conservatory that he knew had a broken lock. "Let's get that damned crown."

Chapter 14

Thanks to the Marsh brothers' unexpected arrival, Raleigh House was thrown into what might have been called, if Aggie had been writing the scene, an unmitigated uproar. A fire needed to be laid in the parlor where their surprised host would entertain. Refreshments needed to be prepared and served. Just as Aggie had anticipated, it was enough of a distraction to keep the army of servants who manned the place busy and quite blessedly out of the way. The back stairway was dark and deserted, and Aggie and Stewart ascended all the way to the third floor without meeting another soul.

The least Stewart might have done was compliment her on her brilliance. He didn't. He didn't say anything at all. Every muscle tensed, every sense alert, he made his way down the passageway toward Barclay's treasure room. Outside the door, he signaled her for silence. "We were lucky last time, but we won't be again. There's sure to be a man on the balcony," he whispered. "A private detective. We're going to have to be very careful and very quiet and—"

"Here, what are you doing up there?"

From outside the house, Aggie heard a voice calling. She breathed a sigh of relief. Bert was right on time.

"Who's that? Who's down there?" Another voice answered her brother's, and from the balcony they heard the sounds of scrambling. "Who's down there in the garden?"

Stewart's eyes narrowed. He tipped his head, straining to hear. "What the—"

Aggie couldn't help but smile. "You didn't think I was going to go through all this trouble and take the chance of getting nabbed by that split, did you?" She shook her head, honestly amazed at Stewart's naïveté. "Please tell me you weren't just going to walk in there with that man out on the balcony. That would have been lunacy."

"I was going to be quiet. And very, very careful." Stewart spoke from between clenched teeth. "There was no way that fellow out on the balcony would have—"

"Nonsense!" Aggie discarded his explanation with a toss of her head. "There's no such thing as very, very careful," she told him and at the same time she knew it was true. She had tried to be careful, too, careful with her heart. It hadn't worked, and she'd promised herself it was the last time she would take such a chance. She grabbed Stewart's sleeve when he made a move toward the door. "No, wait! Bert will take care of things soon enough."

Stewart didn't bother to ask what she had in mind. Together, they listened to the detective.

"What are you doing down there?" the detective called, and when he apparently didn't get an answer, they heard him again. "You stay away from them windows, lad. You get away from Mr. Barclay's house. Did you hear me? Eh? All right, then, my fellow, I'm coming down there."

Satisfied, Aggie listened as the detective clambered

over the balcony with a grunt, followed by the equally satisfying sounds of what was apparently a spirited foot chase.

"Now," she said, nudging Stewart toward the door to the treasure room. "Bert's a fast runner, but he can only keep it up so long. We don't have a great deal of time."

For once, Stewart apparently agreed with her. Moving swiftly but quietly, he glided into the treasure room and took a quick look around. "No other detectives," he mumbled. "And no signs of a trap." He hurried over to the mahogany wardrobe, lit his dark lantern, and got down to work.

Staying close enough to watch and far enough away to keep out of trouble, Aggie settled against the arm of the sofa. She didn't realize how nervous she was until she pulled her journal out of her pocket. Her fingers shook, and her pencil skipped over the page. She calmed herself with a deep breath, poised her pencil, and watched the Shadow at work.

Quicker than hell would scorch a feather, the Shadow had the shiny brass lock of the wardrobe open. Just as quickly and ever so quietly, he went to work on the combination safe, his dark head bent over his work. His fingers were skilled and sure. His timing was impeccable. He was surely as adept at thievery as he was at—

Aggie scratched that last line through with a long pencil scrawl. The last thing the readers of the *Chronicle* needed to know was that the Shadow was as adept at thievery as he was at making love. It was the last thing she needed to think about as well, and just to prove it to herself, she crossed through the words again, blotting them out of existence. Her heartbeat had sped up at the very thought, and she willed herself to calm down. It was not as easy forcing herself to get back to work. It was much more tempting to keep an eye on Stewart.

Watching him work, Aggie found herself feeling as much one with him as she had when they lay in bed together, wrapped in each other's arms. This was his private world, and now that she'd shared it with him, she also shared a dangerous secret. The realization was like a drug. It coursed through her bloodstream, reawakening feelings she'd tried to keep at bay since she'd overheard Stewart's meeting with Sir Digby.

Aggie dashed away the thought along with the single tear that coursed down her cheek. She gulped down the swell of emotion in her throat and forced herself back to work.

> While far belowstairs voices rose to remind him he was not alone in the house, the Shadow kept his mind completely on his work. When the lock finally gave a decided click that announced he'd conquered its combination, he didn't stop to bask in the accomplishment or even to enjoy the moment. He opened the door of the safe and reached inside.

Aggie hurried through the last words, tucked her journal away, and headed toward the safe. She got there just in time to see Stewart turn away from it empty-handed.

"Where's the crown?" Aggie looked past Stewart to the safe. Now that the door was open and the light of his dark lantern gleamed full on it, she could see inside it clearly. It was empty.

"Stewart?" Aggie looked into his eyes. "Stewart, where's the crown?"

"Not here." His voice was flat. His expression,

empty. The look in his eyes was desolate. It didn't stay that way for long. "Damn!" His eyes glinting with determination, he grabbed the dark lantern and arced its light around the room. "He knew we were coming, damn it. We warned him with our last visit. He's moved the crown."

"Moved it where?" Aggie followed the path of Stewart's light. It was just as simple to follow his thoughts. Barclay would never get rid of the crown. It was far too valuable. It had to be there in the house, there with his other treasures.

While Stewart examined the display cases on the far side of the room, Aggie hurried to the ones close to her. The last time she'd seen the cases, their glass fronts had been smashed, but Barclay was apparently a fastidious man. The cases had been repaired, and the glass gleamed. As quickly as she could, Aggie took note of the treasures inside. She knew there wasn't much time. Already, she could hear Bert's voice again as he called out to the detective, who was apparently still in pursuit. They must have made a full circle around the house, and as the voices trailed away, she knew they'd started on another. But she also knew they couldn't keep up the pace for long.

Peering into the treasure cases through the darkness, Aggie saw sculptures and gilded masks, carvings and books, vases and rings and necklaces the likes of which she could never have imagined. There was a statue of an Eastern god with many arms and legs, and a tiny painting of a woman with hair bright enough to glow white. There were beads of silver and a cross that looked to be carved of solid marble and—

"The crown!" Aggie's strangled exclamation brought

Stewart running. In the darkest corner of one of the display cases his light glanced off a tall, pointed crown. Gold gleamed back at them, and a shiver raced up Aggie's spine.

Stewart threw open the door to the case, allowing Aggie a better look. The crown was everything she'd pictured it would be, and as she watched Stewart reach inside the case to retrieve it, she caught her breath. Even in the thin light of his lantern, it gleamed, an enormous crown of gold and jewels that was as beautiful as any she'd seen in storybooks. The jewels that encrusted the crown caught the light and sent it back to her in a million flickers of red and blue and icy white.

Before she even knew what she was doing, Aggie reached out a hand and reverently touched a finger to the crown. "It's beautiful."

Stewart answered with a harsh laugh. "It's a fraud," he said. "A sham of poorly painted metal and paste jewels." He made to toss the crown back into the display case, then stopped and hefted it carefully in his hands. "Unless—"

Stewart flipped the crown over and examined its underside. What he was looking for, Aggie couldn't imagine, but he apparently found it. With a muffled cry of triumph, he wedged his fingers beneath the brightly painted metal and pulled. The crown gave way easily enough. Bit by bit he pulled the crown apart and when he was done, he turned it right side up again and shook it.

Something hit the carpet. From what little Aggie could see in the darkness, she knew it was something smaller and plainer than the crown, but before she could get a better look or ask what it was, Stewart scooped the object up off the floor and tucked it into his greatcoat.

It was just as well that he did. At that very moment, they heard voices and footsteps coming up the stairs.

"You must see my treasures," they heard Maxwell Barclay say. "It is, after all, the least I can do since you've been kind enough to visit me like this."

"Really not necessary." Aggie recognized Charles's voice.

"Not one of the things we're really interested in, you see," she heard Matthew say.

Stewart didn't wait to hear more. Moving as quickly as he had when he entered the room, he returned the fraudulent crown to the display case and snapped it shut. He grabbed Aggie's arm and led her toward the French doors, and just as the doors to the treasure room opened and Maxwell Barclay snapped on the electric lights, they jumped over the side of the balcony.

That damned crown, as Stewart called it, was not at all as fabulous as the false crown in which it had been hidden and not at all what Aggie expected it to be.

She leaned back in his chair and looked at the crown, which sat squarely in the center of Stewart's desk. Had she seen such an object displayed in a museum, she would have walked by it without a second look. Had she stumbled upon it in a pawnbroker's shop, she might have generously thought it curious. She suspected she also would have thought that no matter the cost, the thing was overpriced. Obviously, Barclay realized the public would, by and large, agree with her. That's why he'd hidden the real crown inside a crown that looked like a real king's crown should look. The false crown was glorious. And the real one? Aggie sighed.

Arthur's Crown looked amazingly similar to the crown pictured in the book she'd seen in Stewart's library, the one that showed the symbol of the fabled Knights of Avalon and the fantastic purple dragon that guarded Arthur's hoard. It was a circlet of gold no more than an inch wide and just big enough, it seemed, to fit around the brow of an adult male. The gold was not as glittering as she'd promised her readers it was in the series of articles she'd written and hoped to see published soon. It was dull and heavy-looking, and even if she hadn't been told it was old, she would have guessed as much. Had she given Stewart the chance, he would no doubt have embarked upon a discourse about the goldsmithing processes of their Celtic ancestors. He would have talked about impurities and imperfections, crude instruments and poor conservation techniques.

She was wise enough not to give him the chance, and wiser still not to let any of those things influence her opinion.

There were three stones in the crown, just as there were in the drawing in Stewart's book. Although Aggie was no expert, especially when it came to stones that were coarsely cut and poorly set, she suspected they were diamonds. They were as unremarkable, though, as window glass, and after the dazzling picture she'd built up in her head and in her journal, she found herself seething with dissatisfaction.

She propped her elbows on the desk and cupped her chin in her hands. "Are you certain you've stolen the right thing?"

Since they'd come into the room a few minutes

earlier, Stewart had been busy rearranging the books on one of the shelves along the far wall. Aggie couldn't imagine why. They looked much the same now as they had before he'd begun mucking with them, just a shelf of ancient, tattered books. His hand on a particularly large volume covered in red leather, he stopped and looked over his shoulder at her. "Disappointed?" he asked.

Aggie tilted her head, trying to see the crown from another perspective, hoping it would look better. It didn't. She pulled a face. "No wonder Barclay created the false crown. Who would pay money to see this old thing?"

"Ah, but you're forgetting the curse!" Whatever he'd been doing, Stewart was finished. With an air of finality, he brushed his hands together and turned to her. "What was it you said about magic and wizardry? Yes, the false crown was beautiful, but Barclay didn't know he didn't even need it. He thought he needed a way to entice people to see the crown. But once you created your curse people would have flocked from all over the country for a look at the thing anyway. Just to see if they could get close to a cursed crown and live to tell the story."

He didn't need to remind her about her part in the business, especially not with that much relish. Aggie sat back. As she'd done since they arrived at Stewart's, she tried to keep her gaze on the crown and not on him. She didn't need to see the sleek figure he cut in his black burgling clothes. She didn't need to remind herself that she'd watched him carefully as he worked in Barclay's treasure room and what she saw—and all she felt—astonished her.

In spite of her own best advice to herself, Aggie felt her cheeks grow hot. She forced away the emotions that threatened to betray her and dared to glance up at Stewart.

Perched on the arm of one of the chairs in front of the fire, he was watching her carefully. The realization was enough to make Aggie panic. She stood so quickly that she upended the chair. After she'd righted it and settled it back where it belonged, she headed for the door.

"I suppose I should say it's been grand, but—" As if her air supply had been cut off, Aggie's words stopped short when Stewart moved in front of her, blocking the door.

He offered one of the smiles that tugged at the left side of his mouth and made his eyes crinkle at the edges. It wasn't as lighthearted as usual, and neither was his voice. "I suppose we should say a lot of things."

"I suppose we should." Aggie held her arms tight at her sides. It was clear that their business was over, and now that it was, it was clear that they would never have to endure each other's company again. The thought should have been spread relief clear through her. Instead, it only wound an imprudent and uncontrollable thread of desire tighter. She found herself breathing hard.

Eager to get control of the reaction, Aggie did her best to be her old flippant self. It had taken years to perfect her image as a coquette. It was a shame now, that when she needed those skills so badly, they deserted her instantly. She thought back to all the women she'd admired, the ones she'd watched and tried so desperately to emulate. The ones who could twist a man's willpower around their fingers like so much thread, or reduce him to a quivering mass of longing with so little as a look, or a touch, or a silvery laugh. They were women who were adored but who knew better than to adore, women who had trapped many men but were never foolish enough to get trapped themselves. The kind of woman Aggie had always thought herself to be.

"I suppose I should thank you." She managed a light note to her voice that did not match the heaviness in her heart. "There had to be someone, after all. Someone . . . the first one . . . I mean, if I could choose the first man I . . ."

"I'm glad it was me, too." Stewart's smile thinned. He moved a step closer and put a hand on her sleeve. "Look, Aggie, I—"

It was all he had a chance to say. From belowstairs, the front bell rang, and even before it was possible for Trefusis to get to the door, a bellow of voices invaded the foyer. Aggie recognized them at the same time Stewart mumbled, "My brothers. I'll need to deal with them, I suppose. But first—"

He looked down into Aggie's eyes, and she thought he was going to say something more. Until he glanced over her shoulder and saw the crown.

His eyes darkened with an emotion that might have been regret. Then he moved briskly around Aggie and to the desk. At the same time he picked up the crown and headed to the other side of the room with it, Aggie went to the door.

In the passageway just outside, she stopped and turned. She wasn't sure why. Perhaps she hoped there might be something left for them to say to each other. Perhaps she simply wanted to prove to herself there wasn't.

She watched as Stewart strode to the shelves where he'd rearranged the books earlier. He drew down the large book with the red leather cover and flipped it open, and Aggie saw that the book wasn't a book at all.

It was hollowed out, the space inside just big enough for the crown.

His hands around it as reverently as if he actually believed it might have been the crown of a might-have-been king, Stewart settled the crown into its hiding place and slipped the book back on the shelf. He pulled his spectacles out of his pocket and put them on, then went back to the desk and busied himself with some papers. He never once looked toward the door.

Aggie told herself it was just as well. They had fulfilled their bargain. He had the crown he would present to the queen, and she had her story. From this moment on, she was invisible to Stewart, no more than a memory from a past he would rather forget.

She supposed it was as fitting a good-bye as either of them deserved.

Chapter 15

It was all Aggie's fault.

Stewart stalked across the library, glancing at the familiar objects displayed on shelves and tables, cataloging which were the most valuable, which the most expendable. Deciding which would have to be sacrificed.

Not the Aztec ceremonial mask, he concluded. He lifted it from its place on the wall and handed it to Trefusis, who was following in Stewart's wake, his arms already full. And certainly not the Egyptian papyrus. Stewart handed that to Trefusis as well. He might take a chance with the small statue of the goddess Aphrodite that stood on one corner of his desk. He stopped and regarded the thing, then gave her a pat as if in apology for what he knew she would have to endure.

"Marble will only need a good cleaning by the end of it all." Trefusis put into words exactly what Stewart was thinking. "She'll make it, sir."

Stewart didn't bother to reply. He took one more look around the room. He knew from the start that he didn't have the heart or the appetite to destroy the collected wisdom of hundreds of years, so along with Trefusis, he'd spent the better part of the day removing and packing the books, then carting them to safe storage. They'd been replaced on the shelves by an odd collection that Trefusis had managed to purchase that morning at the bookstalls in Portobello Market. The books were similar in size to those they had taken away. Some even had the same sorts of tattered leather bindings. But they were decidedly inferior volumes, not Stewart's precious books at all. They looked unnatural on the shelves, like uninvited guests, strangers in a room full of what should have been old and dear friends.

In spite of the fact that he knew he was doing only what needed to be done, Stewart's mood plummeted from merely sour to downright venomous. "It's all her fault," he mumbled.

"Is it, sir?" Trefusis had the good grace not to ask whom he was talking about.

"If she hadn't involved my brothers . . ." There was no use going over it again. Stewart had played and replayed the scene a hundred times in his mind. But the words still hammered in his brain, and he couldn't help himself. He had to let them out. "Once they knew I'd been at Barclay's, I couldn't very well lie to Sir Digby, could I? He was bound to find out I'd finally gotten hold of the crown. Why couldn't she mind her own business?"

Trefusis cleared his throat. It seemed the only diplomatic way to respond to the question.

"I know. I know." Stewart ran a finger along the closest bookshelf, following the path of the charges Trefusis had finished laying. "She didn't mind her own business because it is completely and totally impossible for Aggie to mind her own business. If she would have minded her own business in the first place . . ." He didn't bother to finish, but not because he didn't want Trefusis to know what a fool he'd been. Trefusis knew it well enough. So did his brothers, if the way they'd acted the night before meant anything. Each time Aggie's name was mentioned—and they'd made sure to mention it often enough—they winked at one another and made not-so-veiled references, and teased him like schoolboys. Stewart supposed he couldn't blame them. It seemed that of all of them—Trefusis and his brothers and probably even Sir Digby—Stewart himself was the last to figure out exactly how he felt about Aggie.

He took a deep breath, then let it out slowly, ridding himself of the thought. It was too late for regrets and far past the hope of second chances.

The hollowed-out book covered with red leather that he'd had made expressly to store Arthur's Crown was on his desk, and he picked it up and slipped it into place on the shelf. He paused with his hand on the binding for a moment, then turned to Trefusis. "Shall we get on with it?" he asked.

"Right enough, sir." Trefusis deposited his armful of treasures in the last of the boxes waiting to be carted away. "I've got it all arranged with Lady Mallright across the way, sir." He tipped his head in the direction of the window and the house directly across from Stewart's. "She's been after you for a month of Sundays, that one has, sir. Anxious as can be to get you to dinner. Seems she has a niece she's wanting you to meet."

Stewart didn't bother to speak the first words that came to his mind. He rolled his eyes toward the ceiling instead and pulled back his shoulders, like a man about to face a firing squad. "Very well," he said. "Dinner with Lady Mallright it is." He knew every detail of the plan he and Trefusis had so carefully coordinated, but he asked again, just to be sure everything was in place. "What time are the charges set to go off?"

"Ten minutes after nine exactly, sir."

Stewart didn't doubt his butler's accuracy for a moment. Trefusis was an expert when it came to explosives. It was one of the reasons Stewart valued his services so highly. Trefusis didn't take chances, and he didn't make mistakes. "And the rest of the staff?" he asked.

"Maid's day out," Trefusis informed him. "I told her you wouldn't be needing her at all, so she's staying with her mum for the night over to the other side of Southwark Park. Cook's gone visiting as well. She was a bit put out that you'd choose Lady Mallright's table over her roast mutton, but I told her you'd make it up to her."

Stewart nodded. "And you?"

Much to Stewart's surprise, the big Welshman reddened to the roots of his coal-colored hair. He didn't meet Stewart's eyes. "Lady's maid over at Lady Mallright's, Sally Hawkins by name. She's asked me around to the kitchen for tea," he said. He shifted from one foot to the other. "I thought it best if we were in the same place, sir, and—"

"Yes. Of course." There was no use embarrassing Trefusis. Stewart changed the subject. "Sir Digby received my message?"

"Delivered it myself." Trefusis smiled, obviously relieved not to have to explain any further about Sally Hawkins. "Said he'd be here just as you asked. Fifteen minutes after nine, and knowing Sir Digby, he'll be on the dot. By the time he gets here, the place should be blazin'."

"Good." Stewart lifted the last box into his arms and went to the door. He took one final look at the library, at his favorite chair and the carpet he'd gone to such lengths to haul all the way from Persia. At the statue of Aphrodite that he hoped to see again in one piece and the hollowed-out book covered in red leather. The one that had once contained Arthur's Crown.

He didn't bother to spare a glance for the table he'd so nearly used in place of the bed where he'd finally made love to Aggie. There was no use regretting what couldn't be changed and no chance of making himself feel better, just as there was no use telling himself again what he'd told himself a thousand times since he let Aggie walk out of his life: sometimes in order to save a county's heritage and the legacy of a king, you had to sacrifice the one thing in the world you loved the most.

Not twenty-four hours earlier, Aggie had sworn she'd never go near Stewart's house again as long as she lived. At the time, she meant every word of that promise.

But that was before she'd found Inspector Stanley Greenfield waiting for her at the offices of the *Chronicle* when she arrived for work that morning. Before he'd just happened to come by her house after dinner that evening.

Years of newspaper work had taught Aggie to be fast on her feet and faster with her tongue. When Greenfield told her he suspected who she was the moment he saw her wander into Stewart's library clad only in a nightshirt, she pretended to be flattered at the scope of her reputation. When he informed her that Arthur's Crown was missing and waited to see what her reaction might be, she pretended to be surprised and grateful to have the information before any of the other reporters did. When he questioned her about Stewart, she informed him they'd had a lover's spat the very night Greenfield had come upon them together. She hadn't seen Lord Stewart Marsh since, she notified the inspector with an imperious sniff. With any luck, she would never see him again.

There was truth enough in what she'd said to Greenfield, though in what part of it, even she wasn't sure. She didn't want even to think about it. Not now, when the last bit of evening twilight cast its purple shadows along the street where Stewart lived.

She didn't dare go to the front door.

She stopped at the crossroads a hundred yards from Stewart's home and glanced back over her shoulder. As far as she could tell, no one had followed her, but she couldn't be certain. There was nothing to be gained and a great deal that might be lost if the blokes from Scotland Yard knew she was on her way to talk to Stewart. She went around the long way instead, to the street that ran parallel to Stewart's and stopped in front of the home directly behind his. A long look at his house revealed that it was dark, which seemed odd at this hour, but she decided it was just as well. With nighttime fast closing around her and the house in shadows, it would be impossible for anyone to see her, even if they'd followed.

Aggie closed her dark jacket over her white blouse, ducked through the hedges that bordered the garden, and wound her way through Stewart's garden. At the kitchen door she stopped and knocked softly.

There was no answer.

She tried again and waited what seemed an eternity for some sort of response.

When there was none, Aggie let go a ragged breath

and sagged against the door. Of all the scenarios she'd played out in her mind, this was not one of them. She'd imagined Stewart poring over his dusty books and Stewart being perturbed at the interruption and Stewart coming to the door to toss her into the street. She'd imagined Stewart refusing to see her altogether. She'd even imagined Trefusis carrying a message from his master, one that was cryptically apologetic (in deference to his butler's sensibilities), one that offered an invitation to come up to the library to talk, and a thin ray of hope.

As she had done a hundred times since she'd envisioned the scene, Aggie banished it. There was no use bedeviling her mind, or her body, with thoughts of things that were clearly out of her reach. Her resolve firmly back in place, she raised her hand to knock on the kitchen door one more time.

She never had a chance. From out in the street, she heard the clatter of a cab. Horses whinnied and Aggie's heartbeat jumped. It was surely Stewart, she told herself; she would give him a minute to get into the house before she knocked again.

"I'll try the front door."

But it wasn't Stewart. The moment she heard a man speak, she recognized Inspector Greenfield's voice. Aggie bent her head, straining to hear the rest of what he said.

"You wait here. If we don't get an answer up front, we'll signal to the fellows going around the back and have them try there."

She didn't wait to hear any more. Instinct told her to try the doorknob, and she was convinced that it was only pure luck that made it turn in her hand. . She opened the door, slipped into Stewart's kitchen, and snapped the door closed behind her. The key was in the lock, and just to be certain the police wouldn't be as lucky as she had been, she turned it.

Except for a gas jet burning low against one wall, the kitchen was dark. Black shadows filled the corners and the space beneath the table. Aggie flattened herself against the same wall that contained the room's only windows and listened as the front bell rang and rang again. There were no answering footsteps, just as there had been none to her knocks, and a moment later someone thumped on the back door.

Even though Aggie had realized the police would be sure to try the back, her breath caught on a gasp of surprise. She pressed a hand to her heart.

The police knocked a second time. And a third. When they got no answer, she heard them grumble their displeasure and head toward the front of the house. A minute later, she heard the sounds of the cabman calling to his horse and the cab pulling away.

Relieved, Aggie slumped against the wall. She waited a few minutes for her heartbeat to slow and when it had, she breathed deeply and looked around the room.

At the first, she'd thought the house might be dark and quiet simply because Stewart knew the coppers were sure to come around and he was avoiding them. But the more she listened, the more she strained to sense at least some sign of life within the house, the more certain she was that she was alone.

"Queer as Dick's hatband," Aggie told herself, and her own voice echoed back at her from the stillness.

She knew she had waited long enough. The police were surely gone, and even if they left someone behind to watch the house, it was probably safe to leave the way she'd come. But by the time she told herself as much, she was already heading out of the kitchen

through the baize door. She told herself the same
thing again as she stopped at the bottom of the winding stairway that led to the first floor, and again as
she paused outside Stewart's library long enough to
scrape her damp palms against her dark skirt.

In the quiet that enveloped the house, Aggie's
heartbeat thudded in her ears, and when a clock
somewhere chimed the nine o'clock hour, she
jumped. At the same time she scolded herself for
being so nervous, she looked over her shoulder.
There was no one there, of course. There was no one
in the house except her.

A tiny thread of triumph displaced Aggie's jitters.
"Alone," she told herself, and a slow smile spread
across her face. She opened the door to Stewart's
library and stepped across the threshold. "Alone.
With one more chance to get a gander at Arthur's
Crown."

Aggie hurried into the room. There were no lights
left burning, and she didn't bother to turn up the gas
jets. If the rozzers had left someone to watch the
house, there was no use advertising her presence.
She had her dark lantern with her, and she lit it and
shone the beam into the darkness.

Something was different.

Aggie squinted into the gloom trying to get a better look at the room. She remembered every inch of
it, or at least she thought she did. But things looked
different. Out of place. Wrong.

Curious, she angled her light along the far wall.
Directly across from where she stood, the bookshelves looked the same as ever. They were packed
with time-scarred volumes, the color of their leather
bindings muted with age. She swung her light the
other way. The draperies were open, and she aimed

the beam toward the floor. In its thin light, she could see Stewart's desk, piled as it always was with stacks of papers and mounds of books.

"Gammon and pickles," she mumbled. She tried to shrug off the effects of her own overactive imagination and failed miserably. Though everything looked the way it was supposed to look, something didn't feel right.

Aggie squeezed her eyes shut and willed herself to relax. She knew that to her left, the wall was taken up mostly by bookshelves. But along their perimeter Stewart displayed an odd collection of objects that included strange heathen masks and even a framed page from an illuminated medieval manuscript. Just to prove to herself she was overreacting, she swung her light that way.

The wall was bare.

And Aggie's uneasiness blossomed into curiosity.

She moved through the room for a closer look. The fireplace mantel that had so lately contained an assortment of ancient artifacts was crammed now with old bottles, tobacco tins, and bits of wood that looked as if they'd been dredged up from the bottom of the Thames. The bookshelves nearest to where she stood that had been filled with volumes with Latin titles she could never hope to read, now clearly proclaimed among their number *Mrs. Gray's Cooking School, Birds of the British Isles,* and *A Traveler's Companion to the Interesting and Unusual Sights of Australia.*

"Cor, and if that ain't odd." Aggie shook her head, hoping to clear it and order her thoughts. She stepped away from the bookshelves and sat back against the arm of the nearest chair. It wasn't until then that she remembered Arthur's Crown.

Hurrying across the room, Aggie shone her light

along the bookshelf where she'd seen Stewart slip the hollowed-out volume with the red leather cover. She found the book easily enough, but it was too large for her to carry in one hand. She set down her lantern and pulled the book off the shelf.

It was lighter than she'd thought it would be.

Aggie's ears rang from the silence. Her blood buzzed with anticipation. Even before she flipped the book open, she knew it would be empty, still, she stood for a long time staring at the hollow space where she'd seen Stewart place the crown.

In an instant, a hundred possibilities presented themselves: the crown had been stolen again; it had been removed and taken somewhere else; Sir Digby had come to collect it, and even now it was hidden away deep in the recesses of the Tower.

She would never know, she supposed, and not knowing made the mystery even more tantalizing. Thinking it through, Aggie did a turn around the room.

"It's possible the thing's here somewhere," she told herself. She poked at the cushions of the sofa and peered into the fireplace, and when she didn't find anything there, she went to look through Stewart's desk. Because the draperies were open, the light was a little better there. "But not good enough," Aggie grumbled. "If I had more light—"

No sooner had she voiced the wish than Aggie heard a series of pops like the noise made by a child's Christmas crackers. There was a flash and a smell like sulphur, and all four walls of the room burst into flame.

Lady Mallright's dining room faced the front of the house, which, as far as Stewart could tell, was fitting punishment. Not only would he get to spend the evening thinking about his home going up in flames, he'd get to watch a good deal of it as well. He supposed it was no more or no less than he deserved. He consoled himself by counting out the chimes as the tall case clock in the corner struck nine and with a sip of champagne that, though the other guests had declared it superb, tasted like vinegar in his mouth.

"We will be standing right up front, of course. To watch the parade. And when the queen drives past . . ." As she had done throughout dinner, Lady Mallright's niece, who was seated to Stewart's left, droned on and on. Her name was Esmeralda, and she was no more than eighteen. She had the large, square teeth of a mule and a jaw to match, and what she was yammering about, Stewart really couldn't say. Though he had done his best to be polite, to pay attention, and to make at least as much conversation as was expected of the eccentric Marsh brother, he found it harder than ever. In spite of Esmeralda's best efforts to charm him, his gaze was drawn constantly to the house across the road, even while his thoughts were elsewhere.

He didn't like to think where that elsewhere was.

Stewart whisked off his spectacles and cleaned them with his handkerchief. He tried to concentrate. He tried to make himself say something to Esmeralda. He tried to rally an expression she might interpret, by some leap of faith, as interest. But each time he looked at the poor, plain girl with her dun-colored hair, her sallow complexion, and her watery blue eyes, he saw instead eyes like emeralds and cheeks dotted with freckles and hair the color of flame.

And when he thought about flame, he only felt worse and more inclined to be even more sullen than he had been all evening.

"It's all right, dear." From deep in the heart of his reverie, Stewart heard Lady Mallright clucking at her niece. "Lord Stewart is a scholar, you know. And scholars are often preoccupied."

"Not too preoccupied to offer a toast to my hostess." Stewart pulled himself from the brink of impropriety by slipping his spectacles back on and lifting his glass toward Lady Mallright. He offered her a toast and a smile that felt tight and unnatural, but was apparently real-looking enough to satisfy the ladies. Lady Mallright blushed like a schoolgirl, and Esmeralda reddened rather unattractively and smiled enough for Stewart to see there was a cavernous gap between her two front teeth.

The footman handed around fruit and cheese, but Stewart declined. He had no stomach for pears and cheddar, and he wondered how he'd come up with this harebrained plan in the first place and why he'd let Trefusis agree to it when the man should have known better and told him outright that he was a lunatic. He would have been far better off spending the night at the opera, or visiting Charles at his country home, or being anyplace else but here where he could gaze out the window and think about all he had and all he was about to lose.

And all he'd already lost.

This time, not even a sip of champagne would serve to wash away the bitter taste in Stewart's mouth. When Lady Mallright finally pushed back from the table, he was only too happy to stand with the other gentlemen. Just as he did, he saw a flash from across the road.

As one, the other guests turned toward the window. Though he knew exactly what he would see, Stewart looked that way too. Just as he expected, he saw the first burst of the charges Trefusis had so skillfully laid. Just as he'd imagined, he saw the explosion of flame that licked the bookshelves and caught the draperies in an instant. Just as he'd known it would, the fire burned hot and bright and fast, and just as it did, he saw Aggie standing in the front window of his library, her lips parted in a silent scream, her body outlined in orange flame.

"Get Trefusis!" Stewart was already to the door of the dining room when he barked out the order, and when no one moved fast enough to satisfy him, he bellowed at them again. "In the kitchen, damn it! Tell him to come. Fast!"

He didn't wait to see if they would follow his order. He didn't wait for Trefusis, either. He raced out of Lady Mallright's house. He had deliberately left the back door to his own home unlocked so that he and Trefusis could easily gain access to the house and, as much as possible, keep the fire from spreading from the library to the other rooms. The thing had seemed simple enough in the planning: they would pretend surprise, hurry across the street, trot to the back of the house. And by the time they got there and gained entrance, everything in the library was sure to be destroyed.

But Stewart never counted on the seconds it took to cross the road as being interminable. He never supposed the distance from the front gate to the back of the house could be so far. By the time he got to the back door, he was breathing hard. In spite of the sweat that beaded on his brow and trickled down the back of his collar, he felt as cold as death. He expected the doorknob to turn easily in his hand, the door to fall open against his weight, and when it didn't, he froze. Out of the corner of his eye he saw Trefusis round the house.

"She's locked it," he said. He pounded the door with his fist. "She's locked it and she's inside."

Trefusis didn't need to hear any more. He put his shoulder to the door and ran at it. It didn't give way the first time, or the second, and Stewart swore and went around to the kitchen windows. There were three, and none was especially wide. Still, he knew he had no choice. He bent his head and went at one of them and before he knew it, he was lying on the kitchen floor with shards of glass all around him, his evening jacket torn to shreds and a pain in his shoulder that was quickly turning hot and sticky.

He bounded to his feet and unlocked the kitchen door. He was on his way to the library even before Trefusis got inside.

The smoke had been part of the plan, and at the time Trefusis had suggested he might be able to arrange it, it had seemed brilliant. The smokier the fire, the harder it would be for the fire brigade to gain access to the first floor; and the harder it was for the fire brigade to gain access to the first floor, the less likely it would be that they might salvage anything.

But what had seemed brilliant was now bedeviling. The smoke caught at the back of Stewart's throat and stung his eyes. It rolled down the stairway, blacker even than the gathering night, and pooled around his feet. By the time he was halfway up the stairs, it hugged his knees and billowed up to his chest. It was thick and acrid, and he coughed and ripped off his spectacles to rub his eyes. As he took the steps two at a time, he stripped off his evening jacket, folded it, and held it over his mouth.

The smoke was even thicker at the top of the stairs and in spite of the fact that he knew the house as well as he knew himself, Stewart had to pause to get his bearings. Smoke covered the floor, undulating as if it were alive. Even the walls seemed to have lost their shape. They were real and solid one second, hidden beneath a blanket of smoke the next. Already he could feel the heat that emanated from the library. It flickered in the air all around him, and when he put one hand on the wall to help guide him to the door, the wall was hot to his touch.

At the library door, he took as much of a deep breath as he could manage, held it in his lungs, and plunged into what looked like the heart of hell.

Just as he had known they would, the old books provided the perfect kindling for the fire. They had never been well cared for, and their pages were brittle, their bindings dry. They snapped and popped along the walls and, one after another, they burst into flame. The fire had already caught the draperies and now it licked the ceiling. Flaming debris rained down on Stewart. He brushed aside a piece of burning paper that landed on his shoulder and ducked when a shower of sparks erupted overhead. It was a world of gray swirling smoke and blinding flame, and it was impossible to see anything. Still, Stewart made his way to the desk by the window, the last place he'd seen Aggie.

He called her name and got no response. His arms

out, he felt all around and met with nothing but gritty smoke and flame. He might never have found Aggie at all if he hadn't tripped over her feet.

"Aggie?" Stewart knelt on the carpet and peered down into Aggie's face. Her eyes were closed, her face was rimmed with soot. He didn't dare take the time to check for a pulse. Just as the corner of the Persian carpet where she lay caught fire, he scooped her into his arms. When he turned to try and find his way back to the door, he found Trefusis right behind him.

"Here." Trefusis shouted over the sounds of crackling flame and the clanging of the fire brigade out on the street. He had a stack of wet towels with him, and he draped one over Aggie's face and another over Stewart's head. The smoke was now impossibly thick, but Trefusis had anticipated as much. Before he'd come into the room, he'd tied a rope to the knob of the door across the passageway. Following his lead, Stewart felt his way to the door. Out in the passageway, the air was cooler but just as poisonous. Stewart tried to take a breath, but it wouldn't come. He coughed and gagged, and he might have lost his grip on Aggie if he hadn't felt Trefusis sling one strong arm around him. Trefusis led the way to the stairway and out the front door.

Outside, the street was alive with members of the fire brigade scurrying to save what they could of the house. The neighbors had gathered to watch. They stood in tight knots, pointing and jabbering, and when Stewart stumbled out onto the pavement, he saw Esmeralda clap her hands and jump up and down. Lady Mallright fainted on the spot, as if it were her house smoldering around her. Out of the corner of his eye, Stewart saw Sir Digby Talbot's carriage further along the road.

He ignored them all and hurried across the road. At a spot in front of Lady Mallright's where the grass was soft and lush, he laid Aggie down and knelt beside her. Almost afraid of what he might see, he gently removed the wet cloth from her face.

She was very still.

"Aggie?" Stewart's voice was heavy and rough. He coughed, and when someone offered a hand to help, he pushed it aside. Under the layer of soot that coated her cheeks, Aggie looked too pale. Gently he wiped the wet towel over her forehead. He brushed her cheeks with it and touched it to her lips. "Aggie, can you hear me? Aggie, it's me, Stewart. Open your eyes, Aggie. Please, open your eyes."

Like a drowning person rising to the surface one last time, she came around with a gasp that shuddered through her and a cough that seemed to be torn from her lungs.

"Aggie! You're all right!" Stewart's voice was choked with more than smoke. He held her close against his chest and breathed in the caustic smoke that clung to her hair and her skin and he couldn't help himself. He laughed.

Even though all he accomplished was to smear the layer of grime on her face, Stewart wiped it again, and when someone thrust a cup of water in front of him, he lifted Aggie in his arms and held it to her lips. He made sure she took a drink, and when she had, he hugged her close and looked into her eyes. Her gaze was soft and unfocused. It moved over him slowly, and when it finally settled on his face, she managed a weak smile.

"Stewart." Aggie lifted a hand to his cheek. Her

voice was as rough as his, choked with smoke and emotion. "You came for me. You didn't let me go."

"No. I didn't let you go." He smoothed a hand over her hair. "I swear, Aggie, I'll never let you go again."

Chapter 16

A ggie dreamed about a purple dragon.

Her eyes fluttered open, then closed again, and in the clouded moments between wakefulness and sleep, she realized her chest felt as if there were rocks piled on it, and her eyes burned, and her head pounded. From what seemed a very long way off, she heard the dull sounds of people yelling and a fire brigade with its clanging bell. Yet she didn't turn her head to see what was happening. She didn't rub her eyes, and she didn't dare try to take a deep breath. She didn't want to take the chance that she might break the spell and the dragon might disappear.

He was a vicious-looking fellow, but Aggie wasn't afraid. She let her gaze drift from the top of his scaly head all the way to his tail. He was holding a shield in his talons, and in the center of the shield was a crown.

Arthur's Crown.

Like the biting breath that wracked her body and tore through her lungs, memory flooded back to Aggie. She coughed, bolted upright, and found herself in Stewart's arms.

"Aggie?" He crushed her to his chest, then looked into her eyes. It was dark, but there was a glow of orange light from somewhere behind her, and in it

Aggie saw Stewart's eyes go misty. As if to belie the very notion, he tossed back his head and laughed. His face was coated with what looked to be a layer of coal dust and his teeth looked very white. As if two cats had used it as a battlefield, his hair stood on end. A patch of it just above his left ear was gone completely. The ends seemed to have been burned away.

"Aggie, you're alive!" He hugged her close again, and Aggie felt the scrape of grit beneath her cheek. Stewart's shirt was in shreds, his chest and shoulders were nearly bare. His skin was covered with the same soot as his face. "I wasn't sure. I didn't know. When I found you, I—"

Still caught in Stewart's arms, Aggie looked over her shoulder. Across the road from where they sat in a patch of soft lawn, flames shot out of the front windows of his home. She closed her eyes against the sight, then moved back just enough to look up into Stewart's face. "You came? In there? For me?"

Stewart answered with a kiss. His face was gritty next to hers. His lips were as soot-coated as his chest. His mouth tasted smoky. It was the sweetest kiss Aggie could ever remember.

"I'm not going to let you get away from me again." Stewart gathered the tatters of his shirt around him, but not before Aggie caught the hint of purple beneath the smudge of soot on his shoulder. She thought to ask about it, to ask him if he knew about the dragon she'd seen in her dream, but he didn't give her the chance.

He put both of his hands on her shoulders and looked into her eyes, his own eyes bright with the reflected light of the fire. Words tumbled out of him, along with a dizzying mix of kisses and laughter. "I was a fool, Aggie. A bloody fool. I let you walk away and I shouldn't have. I knew I cared about you. You know that's true, don't you? But I never realized . . ." He pulled in a breath and looked at the burning house, and for an instant, the excitement faded from his expression. When he looked at Aggie again, his face was solemn, his eyes the color of the heart of the flame.

"It wasn't until I saw you in that window and realized you were in danger that I understood how much I love you, Aggie. Damn me for a fool, but I do!"

Aggie's heart squeezed, but in a curious turn of events that she could attribute only to the excitement of the fire and the fact that her lungs were still choked with smoke, words failed her for the first time in her life. She said all she needed to say just as Stewart had earlier, with a kiss, one that might have lasted a good long while if Stewart hadn't pulled away. He knelt in the grass and pulled Aggie up so that she was kneeling face-to-face with him and when she was, he took both her hands in his.

"Marry me, Aggie," he said.

"I—" Aggie drew one hand away and pressed it to her forehead, hoping to clear her thoughts. It was all coming so fast—the fire and Stewart's rescue and his declaration of love. "Marry?" Though the word squeaked out as a question, Aggie suspected that Stewart knew her answer from the smile that inched up her face. She held it in check as long as she could and tried her best to talk some sense into the both of them. "But your family won't approve. I'm not blue-blooded like the rest of you."

"My brothers adore you, and so do I." He kissed

the tip of her nose. "The rest of them will feel the same once they get to know you."

"But I'm a newspaper reporter!" Aggie didn't bother to add that she was a newspaper reporter of the sort Stewart most despised. The sort who shamelessly embellished stories and invented them just as brazenly when they weren't interesting enough to embellish. She wasn't sure she wanted him to remember that part. If he did, he might withdraw his proposal, and if he did that, she wasn't certain she'd be able to draw another breath. The prospect of marrying Stewart was too exciting, the emotion that swelled in her throat and heated her blood, too real. Still, she could not help but remind him that he was taking a step that would cause him no end of problems. "Your colleagues will think you've lost your mind," she told him.

He kissed the top of her head. "I have."

"But you're the Shadow and—"

"Damn the Shadow!" Stewart took her in his arms. "I've got the only treasure I'll ever want or need," he said. "Right here." He brushed a hand across her back. "We'll have to have five groomsmen, I'm afraid. It will make for a rather cumbersome wedding party, but you understand, don't you. The five of them are—"

"Six," Aggie corrected him. "There will have to be six groomsmen. There is Bert, after all."

"Of course." Stewart chuckled. "And after that, what would you like? A house in the country? A dozen children? Your own damned newspaper?"

"All of those, I think." Aggie closed her eyes and rested her cheek against Stewart's shoulder. Happiness settled in her heart. "I wouldn't dream of refusing," she told him and before the words were ever fully formed, he brought his mouth down on hers again. The kiss was as filled with passion as it was with promise, and when it was—too soon—over, she sighed, content. There was a great deal she needed to say, a great deal he needed to explain, but they would have time for that now. All the time in the world. They would put their differences behind them. She knew that now. They wouldn't allow anyone, or anything, to pull them apart again.

"It's Sir Digby, sir."

From somewhere far outside the bliss that enveloped her, Aggie heard the sound of a voice and a polite, apologetic cough. She looked up to find Trefusis standing at Stewart's elbow. He looked no better than Stewart did. The big Welshman's face was smudged and blackened. One of his pant legs was missing at the knee. There was a gash along the bridge of his nose and another on his cheek. He hardly seemed to notice. Looking as unperturbed as if he were doing nothing more remarkable than handing around cakes at afternoon tea, he glanced down at what was left of Stewart's shirt and his eyebrows rose ever so slightly. With a nod and a rather meaningful look at Stewart's shoulder, he held out an evening jacket.

Stewart nodded his understanding and slipped on the coat, then got to his feet and helped Aggie to hers.

"Sir Digby, sir," Trefusis said. He indicated a carriage pulled to a stop far enough down the road to be out of the way and safe from the danger of the fire. "He wishes to speak with you."

"Of course." Stewart straightened his jacket and ran a hand through his hair. "He's come about the crown, of course."

"The crown?" Aggie made a grab for Stewart's sleeve, but he was already on his way to Sir Digby. Her legs felt as if they'd been weighted down with stones, and her head spun from both the aftermath of the fire and Stewart's proposal, but she followed along as quickly as she could. She had to. After the terror of the last minutes and the stark realization that had she died, she would have forever been denied Stewart's kisses, she couldn't bear to let him out of her sight. It wasn't easy keeping pace with him. The street was choked with people and horses and fire hoses that zigzagged across the pavement like fat white snakes.

She wound her way through the crowd of men struggling to control the fire and the crowd of onlookers that had gathered to see what the excitement was all about. She maneuvered her way around a collection of fire brigade vehicles and horses and was within sight of Sir Digby's carriage when a figure stepped in front of her, blocking her path.

"Greenfield!" Aggie did her best to contain her surprise and her annoyance. She looked past Greenfield to Stewart, already deep in conversation with Sir Digby. "You've got a brass neck, Greenfield. Sniffing about at a time like this when you should be leaving people in peace."

"Sniffing about for what, though?" The light of the fire full on his face, Greenfield shook his head. "Doesn't seem like there will be much left to find when the fire's out." He turned his attention to Aggie. "Is that why he set the fire, do you think? To destroy the evidence?"

It was on the tip of Aggie's tongue to tell him that Stewart couldn't have destroyed the crown. The crown wasn't in the library. The book where it had been so cleverly hidden was empty. As empty as the walls were of their displays and the mantel of its treasures.

The memory caused a shiver to scuttle over Aggie's spine. She wrapped her arms around herself and sidestepped the inspector. "Looks like you're through here, Greenfield," she told him. She didn't wait to hear his reply. She hurried over to the carriage.

No doubt Stewart was breaking the news to Sir Digby even now, telling the old man that they would never be able to present the crown to the queen. Poor Stewart. After all he'd been through to recover the crown. After he'd risked himself and his reputation. How awful for him to think that the fire had consumed the crown.

"But it didn't." Aggie whispered the words to herself as she closed in on the carriage, and her spirits brightened. The crown wasn't there, but Stewart apparently didn't know that. How relieved he'd be when she told him the news, and how happy. It was the least—and the best—thing she could think to do for the man she loved.

She got near enough just in time to hear Stewart. "It was there, right enough," he told Sir Digby. "The crown was hidden in a hollowed-out book."

The old man sat in his carriage. The window was down and like a portrait on a wall, his face was framed in it, his skin as white as chalk. Sir Digby gave Stewart a thin-lipped look. "You're sure?"

"Sure as a man can be about something as important as the future of his country and the reputation of his queen." Sarcasm did not become a man begrimed with soot, and one look from Sir Digby told Stewart as much.

The old statesman frowned. "Of course, we've accomplished our purpose either way, and for that, I suppose I owe you some thanks, and just in time it seems. The Jubilee celebration is tomorrow. We wanted to keep Barclay from displaying the crown, and we have achieved that much. Still . . ." He glanced back at the house. The flames had finally subsided, and his eyes sparkled with the fading light. "It's a shame. I would have liked to see the thing. Shame it's destroyed."

"But it's not!" Aggie hurried forward. She was no more sure now about what had happened to Arthur's Crown than she had been when she found the hollow book empty. But she knew Stewart's passion for ancient relics. She knew that wherever the crown was, he would be overjoyed to know it hadn't perished in the heart of the flames. Whoever had taken it, she knew he would do his best to steal it away again. Whatever had happened, she knew she could trust him to do the right thing, to risk himself for queen and country as he had so valiantly done in the past.

She wound an arm through his and smiled. "I saw the book, Stewart. When I came to the house to speak to you. I saw the book where you'd hidden the crown and—"

"And it was one of the first things to catch." Stewart interrupted so quickly that Aggie barely had a chance to take in everything he said. "I know." He stroked her hand. "As I told you earlier, Sir Digby . . ." He turned to the old statesman. "I saw the remains of the book myself. Right before I scooped Miss O'Day up off the floor and carried her to safety. The cover was nearly burnt away, but there was no mistaking it. All that was left of the crown was an unsightly lump of melted gold, and inferior gold at that. By the time the fire has burned its course . . ." He sighed. "I daresay we won't find even that much of it left."

"But you're wrong!" Aggie uncoiled her arm from Stewart's and faced him square on. "It was like the pictures on the wall and the gewgaws on the mantelpiece. Missing."

"Yes, indeed." Stewart gave her a smile, and although the night was pleasant and the fire warmed the air even further, his look was suddenly wintry. He turned his back on Aggie. "After a fire like that," he said to Sir Digby, "everything is missing. Everything's destroyed. There isn't a thing that could have survived it. I'd hoped, of course." He patted the side of the carriage as if to send Sir Digby on his way. "But as I said, Sir Digby, I saw the crown, or at least all that remained of it. We've no need to worry any more about Arthur's Crown or the curse or even about Inspector Greenfield. Maxwell Barclay will never display the thing, and neither will anyone else."

Stewart nodded, and on his signal the carriage pulled away. But when he made to lead Aggie back toward the house, she faltered, lost in a jumble of thoughts.

"Stewart?" Aggie's confusion rang through the simple question, and he turned to her.

His back was to the fire and she couldn't see his face well. Aggie cursed herself and her luck. There was something about Stewart when he stood in the shadows that was more formidable than it should have been. Something about the silhouette he made against the last dying flames that sent a chill up her back. She ran a tongue over her lips and grimaced at the taste and the feel of grit.

"Stewart, you weren't listening. I told you. The crown couldn't have been destroyed. You couldn't have seen it destroyed, not when you came to rescue me. It was already gone, you see. It's the strangest thing, I know, but I swear it's God's honest truth. You may think you saw the thing melted, but that's impossible. A trick of the light, perhaps. Or the smoke in your eyes. I came to see you. To tell you Greenfield was poking his nose about where it had no business, and when you weren't home . . . well, I decided I'd have another look at the crown. But the book was already empty. So were the walls, and the mantelpiece, and the books on your bookshelves weren't the books that had been there before—"

As if they'd been slashed with a knife, Aggie's words cut off abruptly. A thought careened through her head, a thought so absurd that she batted it aside as quickly as she was able and did her best to get back to the matter at hand. "The walls were bare," she said, "which is queer enough, but no queerer than—"

Again, the thought assailed her, and again, she tried to cast it away, but she had even less success in doing so than she'd had the first time. Like the smoke clearing from around Stewart's house, the truth of the matter presented itself, bit by bit, until it was so blatant that she couldn't fail to recognize it.

"The walls were bare. The mantelpiece was empty. Your books were gone." She blinked back the sudden burning in her eyes that had nothing to do with the smoke, and swallowed around the knot of emotion that made her throat feel more constricted than ever. When she spoke, her voice was small and tight. "You lied to Sir Digby," she said.

If the light had been better, she might have been

able to see the expression that crossed Stewart's face. As it was, she had to content herself with supposing it to be indulgent, and even understanding. The kind of expression a man would turn on the woman he loved when she was talking nonsense.

Yet there was nothing understanding or the least bit indulgent about the way he stood before her. His feet were apart. His arms were tight against his sides. His head was high and steady, and his voice was as cold as the look he'd given her when she dared to challenge him in front of Sir Digby. "Don't be ridiculous," he said, and there was no doubt that the last thing he thought she was being was ridiculous. "After all I went through to get the bloody crown, why would I lie to Sir Digby about losing it?"

"You might." Like a chasm, the idea sprawled before Aggie, dark and dangerous. She curled her fingers into her palms and held herself steady. It was the only thing that kept her from falling headlong into the abyss. "You might. If you wanted to keep the crown for yourself."

"Is that what you think?" It may have been a trick of her imagination, or perhaps it was wishful thinking, but Aggie thought Stewart's voice choked on the words. "Aggie . . ." He took a step forward, but it seemed he knew better than to come too near. "Aggie, I just asked you to marry me. Have you forgotten that?"

"Forgotten?" Aggie laughed. It seemed the only appropriate response to a question so absurd. "I haven't forgotten." She closed her eyes, holding tight to her emotions and all that was left of the feelings that had flooded her when she and Stewart knelt together in the grass. "I'll never forget," she told him. "But I'll never forget what I found when I got here, either. And what I found was that the house had been cleaned out. I don't want to believe you're the one who did it, Stewart. I want to believe what you told me. With all my heart, I want to believe you. Just as I wanted to believe you that night when you lay with me and told me you weren't the Shadow. But if you didn't remove all the books in the place and replace them, who did? And if you say you saw the crown melted and destroyed, and I know it wasn't there . . ."

She let the rest of the accusation fade into the night, like the last of the smoke that swirled into the sky and was lost in the stars.

"Please tell me what's going on." This time, Aggie couldn't help herself. Her voice broke and she sniffed back tears. "You say you want to marry me, and you know I would say yes, but if you can't trust me—"

"If that's what you think . . ." Like a man dismissing an acquaintance he found unworthy of his presence, Stewart gave her a quick, stiff bow. "I can't change your mind. I thought things could be different between us."

"I thought you'd stopped lying."

"Then it seems we've both made a mistake."

"Mistake" was hardly the word for it, but Aggie refused to get into that now. Like the water the fire brigade was pouring on Stewart's house, anger rushed over her, filling all the places that only a few minutes earlier had brimmed with happiness.

"I swear it's my last mistake," she said. He didn't answer. He didn't rush forward to try and explain. He didn't take her into his arms and kiss away her doubts, and it was that more than anything that convinced Aggie they had, finally and inescapably, come to the place where she supposed they'd been headed since the night they'd first met. He still wanted the crown more than he wanted anything. Even her.

And if that was true, it stood to reason that the only thing she could count on was the only thing that had mattered to her back then: her story.

Holding her chin up and refusing to let him see the tears that shone in her eyes, Aggie marched past Stewart.

"There's no use going to the police," he called to her. "The evidence is gone. There's nothing you can say to Greenfield that will make any difference."

Aggie kept walking. "I'm not going to Greenfield," she said. When she was well beyond his reach, she spun to face him. "I'm going to the *Chronicle*," she told him. "And this time I'm going to tell everything I know. This time I'm going to tell the world."

Outside the office of Horace Wallingstamp, publisher of the *London Daily Enquirer and Illustrated News Chronicle*, Aggie smoothed her best jacket into place and whisked a hand over her hair.

It had taken her the better part of the night to get the smell of smoke out of her hair and off her skin, and now, just to be sure she'd succeeded, she sniffed delicately. What the Pears soap hadn't accomplished, it seemed a change of clothing, a large dose of rose water, and a brisk walk through the crisp morning air to the offices of the *Chronicle* had. The atmosphere around her was as sweet as springtime. There wasn't a trace left of last night's adventure.

At least none that anyone could see or smell.

Uncomfortable with the thought, Aggie paced in front of Wallingstamp's closed door, firmly ignoring Bill Bickles and listening to the muffled sounds of voices from within. Though she had arrived for her meeting right on time, Wallingstamp was busy with another of the reporters. From what she could hear, things were not going well, at least for the other reporter. She heard a mumbled comment, and Wallingstamp's bellowed reply. She heard a halfhearted rebuttal, and Wallingstamp's roar.

A second later, Peter Askew scuttled out of Wallingstamp's office. Ever since he'd been arrested and held very briefly after the debacle at Barclay's, Askew was a humbled man. With barely a nod at Aggie, he headed out the door.

"O'Day?" Wallingstamp sounded no more calm than he had during his interview with Askew. He bawled Aggie's name without bothering to look and see if she was there. "O'Day? You wanted a meeting? Well, by God, you've got five minutes, so if you're there, get the hell in here and tell me what you want."

Fingering the journal in her pocket for courage, Aggie straightened her shoulders and headed into the publisher's office. She consoled herself with the fact that by the time she walked out again, Wallingstamp would be fawning over her like a puppy. Everything she needed to establish herself as the preeminent journalist in the empire was contained in her little book, and it wouldn't take Wallingstamp long to realize as much. She had worked furiously through the night to finish her story, and now that she had, she knew she had every word she needed. Every date. Every fact. Every damning bit of evidence that would expose the Shadow. She would single-handedly do what no one else in the empire could. She would expose Stewart Marsh as a charlatan and a fraud. She would reveal that he had lied, even to Sir Digby and the queen. She would bring him to justice, and in the process, she would send the *Chronicle*'s circulation soaring into the stratosphere.

Aggie paused just inside the doorway and gave her boss a careful look. Whatever he had been discussing with Askew, it had obviously not been pleasant. Wallingstamp's chubby cheeks were as red as apples. His brow was rimmed with sweat. He stabbed the stub of a cigarette out on his desk and swept the ashes onto the floor.

"Don't you know it's the day of the Queen's Jubilee? Good God, woman, can you imagine how busy we are? You ought to be out there with Askew and the rest of 'em, gatherin' material for stories. Not sending me notes at the crack of dawn, demandin' a meeting. Tellin' me you've got something so interesting it'll change my life."

Aggie drew her journal out of her pocket and held it in both hands.

"Well?" Never one to be patient, Wallingstamp was especially on edge. The Jubilee was the most monumental event the empire had ever witnessed, and the fact that Aggie had not given the day a second thought only underscored how distracted she'd let herself become.

Wallingstamp, however, had not been the least bit distracted. It was obvious that he considered his role in reporting the celebration to the masses not only important but crucial. He flipped through a stack of papers on his desk, lit another cigarette, and gave Aggie a glare of epic proportions.

"You're wasting my time, O'Day. And your own, too, if you're not out there in the crowd. Who knows what kind of stories you'll find out there today? The streets are teeming with humanity. There are bound to be mothers with lost children, husbands watchin'

the parade with women who aren't their wives,
wives who've kept back from the grocery money so
they could take the train into town to watch the
whole thing. The stuff of real human drama." Wallingstamp bounded out of the chair behind his desk
and went to the window. It was coated with the
grime of too many cigarettes, and it overlooked the
brick wall of the building next door, but he made to
look out of it anyway.

"Have you got anything like that for me, O'Day?"
he asked. "Anything like a kitten stuck up in a tree
over the parade route, or a woman havin' her baby
just as the queen rides past, or—"

"I've got the Shadow. And this time, I've got
proof." The words were out of Aggie's mouth in one
rush, but though she'd thought finally saying them
would leave her feeling lighthearted, she felt more
burden than relief. She closed her eyes to compose
herself, but when she did, all she saw was Stewart's
face, and when she opened them again, all she felt
was emptiness at thinking that he was gone from
her life.

The very thought made Aggie's stomach jump. She
clutched her journal tighter, as if it was her anchor
to the world, and only found herself feeling more
qualmish than ever.

"What's that you say?" Wallingstamp's question
brought her tumbling back to earth. He spun to face
her, looking all agog. Just as Aggie always pictured
he would when she told him what she'd accomplished. Only, when she'd imagined the scene, she
had felt as light as air in it, as merry as a mouse in
malt. And now that she was living it, she felt as
miserable as a rat in a tar barrel.

Wallingstamp jerked forward as if he'd been shot.

His red-rimmed eyes widened. "You say you've got the Shadow?" He eyed the journal in Aggie's hands, and his tongue darted over his lips. "In there?"

Something about the way he looked at her little book made Aggie clutch it tighter. "Not in here, of course." She laughed, the sound halfhearted. She pulled the journal back, well out of Wallingstamp's reach, and clutched it to her chest. She couldn't say what possessed her to lie. She'd never intended to. She'd intended to trumpet her triumph to the world. But something about the gleam in the publisher's eyes made her feel suddenly protective of the information. And incredibly enough, of the Shadow. "What I mean, of course," Aggie said, "is that I have a . . . well, a fellow who's willing to talk and he's a sort of . . . an informant. He knows the Shadow and I've checked, of course, and it's true and—"

"You're certain?" Wallingstamp's voice was dubious, as was his expression, poised between wanting to believe and being afraid of where believing might lead. "This time you have proof?"

"The crown is stolen, as I'm sure you'll find out soon enough. That is surely proof."

"Stolen?" Wallingstamp's beefy face split into a grin. "You swear it, O'Day?"

It might have been simply her voice that deserted her. Or perhaps it was her courage. Whatever the cause, all Aggie could do was nod.

"Huzzah!" Wallingstamp whooped and did a little jog. He was surprisingly light on his feet for a man who was so heavy, and he twirled and smiled and gave Aggie a quick hug.

"Do you know what this means?" It was a rhetorical question and even if Aggie didn't know as much, he didn't give her a chance to answer it. He waved one ink-stained hand in the air above his head as if he could see the bold print there. " 'Shadow unmasked,' " he intoned dramatically and though she was sorely tempted to tell him the headline lacked the drama and passion a story such as hers deserved, she said nothing at all. She couldn't. Her words were blocked by the ice that seemed to have filled her head to toe. She stared at Wallingstamp.

"Headlines in all the editions. Drawings and diagrams. I suppose he's the one who pinched Arthur's Crown, eh?" He elbowed her good-naturedly. He rubbed his hands together. "Delicious! That's what this will be for our numbers. Delicious! I can see the fellow in the dock now. Right there in front of a judge and jury. You'll have a front row seat, of course. If this works for our good, I'll guarantee you an exclusive on the story. I'll see to it that you're right up front, watching the whole thing, so's you can see that devil's eyes when they sentence him to twenty years at hard labor. Maybe even get you a pass to visit him in his cell. That's the ticket. Yes. Yes! The reporter and the villain she brought to ruin! You've done it, O'Day!" He thumped her on the back. "No doubt about it. You'll cause trouble for that bastard!"

The picture was all too clear in her head, and Aggie swallowed hard. She told herself she had known all along it would come to this. For all he'd done, the Shadow deserved harsh punishment. He had misrepresented himself. He had pretended to uphold the queen's honor when all he wanted was to keep Arthur's Crown for himself. He deserved to be made to pay for his crimes. For once, Horace Wallingstamp was as right as right could be. What Stewart had done, and what Aggie was prepared to tell about it, would get Stewart into trouble.

Terrible trouble.

Unless she tried to stop him.

Like one of those storms that is said to strike in places where it's hot and tropical, the idea slammed into Aggie out of nowhere. It picked her up and carried her along like a hurricane wind and before she'd even thought about where it might take her, she was headed out of the publisher's office.

From the corner of her eye, she saw Wallingstamp's face go pale and his mouth drop open.

"I've . . . I've made a mistake. A real mistake this time." Just to be safe, Aggie tucked the journal back into her pocket. She hurried through the outer office and was almost out the door when she heard Wallingstamp sputtering behind her like a faulty steam valve.

"But you swore. O'Day, you gave me your word!"

"I did." Aggie stopped at the door, but only long enough to look back and give Wallingstamp as much of an apologetic look as she could manage when she wasn't feeling the least bit apologetic at all. "But I was wrong. I don't have an informant. I don't know a bloody thing about the Shadow. I've . . . I've got to go."

Wallingstamp followed after her, a dog on the scent of the meatiest bone in London. Through the building and out onto the pavement. "But what about the story? You promised me, O'Day. You got my hopes up as high as a kite."

Aggie didn't answer. Even this early, the streets were crowded. People were heading toward the route the queen's royal procession would take. She wound her way around groups of festive parade-goers and was already turning a corner when she heard Wallingstamp bellow after her.

"Play these games, will you, O'Day? Well, don't bother comin' back. Not ever. Not until you're ready to serve me that bastard's head on a platter!"

By the time Aggie got near Stewart's, London was alive with the sights and sounds of the Jubilee festivities. Streets were festooned with bright displays of flowers. Lights were lit in every window, and bands played from every corner. The procession was scheduled to start promptly at noon, but from back in the direction of the parade route, she heard the sharp explosion of fireworks and imagined that some of the rockets were being tested.

The elegant neighborhood where Stewart's house had once stood whole was as deserted as the rest of the city was crowded. Though the acrid smell of smoke still hung in the air, there was no sign of the frantic activity of the night before. Houses were closed up. The street was quiet. She imagined most of the city's residents had headed out to watch the parade or to attend the church service to honor the queen at Saint Paul's. She hadn't thought that perhaps Stewart might be one of their number, but as she neared the charred remains of his home, her footsteps slowed.

What if he wasn't here?

Aggie refused to consider such a thought. Or to panic before she knew she had need to. When she saw a man in the street in front of the house bent over a mountain of what looked to be scorched furniture and other household items, her heartbeat quickened along with her pace.

It wasn't until she was within ten feet of the house

that the man stood and turned to face her. It was Trefusis. The butler's wounds had been skillfully bandaged, and aside from a bruise that extended from his nose across his right cheek, he looked none the worse for wear. His jacket off, his shirtsleeves rolled above his elbows, he poked through the furniture, no doubt to see what might be salvaged.

"Where is he?" Aggie didn't bother with formalities, or with explaining why she needed to talk to Stewart. Somehow, she knew Trefusis would understand, even though he might not agree. Right about then, she didn't care if he agreed or not. "Stewart. Where is he?" She hauled in a breath and realized she hadn't stopped moving since she'd left the offices of the *Chronicle*. She'd made record time, and her lungs, still weak from the smoke, reminded her of every second of it. "It's important."

It seemed that Trefusis was no more in the mood for formalities than she was. Lifting a small table that looked to have escaped the most serious ravages of the flames, he carried it over to where he'd stacked some other things worth saving. He spared hardly a look for Aggie. "Gone," he said.

It was as simple as that.

Gone.

Simple, perhaps. But not acceptable.

"Gone where?"

Trefusis set down the table and brushed his hands together, his gaze fixed firmly on some point over the top of her head. "Gone," he said.

"Damn!" Aggie spun away. She wasn't sure if she was angry at Trefusis for being so uncooperative, or Stewart for being so elusive, or herself for caring so much. She knew only that she couldn't let it rest at that. Not on that one word.

She turned and found Trefusis back at the pile of furniture. "You have to tell me," she said, as she hurried over to him. She was convinced she could talk some sense into him if only she could make him pay attention. If only she could make him understand. "I've got to talk to him and—"

Aggie's gaze fastened onto a purple tattoo on Trefusis's burly forearm, and her words caught on a gasp of surprise.

The picture was familiar. A dragon, holding a shield in its talons. A shield that bore a picture of Arthur's Crown. The same dragon she'd seen the night before when she woke and found herself with her head against Stewart's shoulder.

Like the wind that had dissipated the smoke the night before, realization washed over Aggie. She knew exactly where Stewart was.

Chapter 17

By the time the boat left Aberdaron, Stewart was feeling about as cheery as the weather. In spite of the fact that it was the middle of June and all the tourist guides promised that the north of Wales was sunny and even temperate at this time of year, a dense fog had descended on the fishing village overnight. It still clung to the sides of the whitewashed houses like lamb's wool and hung over the waters of Bardsey Sound so gray and so low that it was hard to tell where the sky ended and the sea began.

He had been lucky to secure a large boat for the four-mile trip. Though it was nearly impossible to see the water, there was no mistaking its swell. Luckily, far before the first light, Stewart had left the inn where he'd spent a sleepless night. He was a competent sailor, if not an experienced one. He'd been on the boat long enough to join the captain of the vessel, an old and trusted friend, for coffee, and to enjoy the fresh bread the captain's wife had sent along, and to find his sea legs.

Automatically, he adjusted his stance enough to accommodate a rolling wave and watched as the one and only train that visited the village each day pulled away from the station. Just thinking about its passengers spending all of the cold, misty night on the journey from Pwllheli and before that, from Caernarfon, was almost enough to make him forget his own troubles.

Almost.

His arms braced against the boat rail, he watched the town of Aberdaron disappear into the mist, and he let his thoughts drift along with the fog that surrounded him. After all this time of wanting the crown, after all the effort he'd gone through to get it back, he should have been feeling nothing less than relief. Yet all he felt was a vague uncertainty that gnawed at his insides and clawed at his composure.

To possess one treasure had he given up another, perhaps greater, one?

Stewart had no doubt of that. The challenge had never been between the Shadow and the police. Or between Stewart Marsh and Sir Digby Talbot. The contest had been one of Stewart against himself. The person he loved the most in all the world against the ideal he held in the most esteem. Another man would have chosen Aggie, and perhaps, just perhaps, that other man might have been right. But Stewart had chosen as he'd known all along he would have to choose. He'd chosen his honor, his integrity, his vow to serve an ideal that was as old as the mountains and a king whose fame and memory belonged to both the past and the future.

Was it the right choice? Stewart honestly didn't know. He would never regret serving the cause to which he'd pledged himself, but regret . . .

Stewart sighed.

"Regret" was not an adequate word for what he'd felt when he watched Aggie walk away.

As if even his own mind was intent on making a mockery of him, he saw a flash from the corner of his eye, a streak of carroty color that split the unrelenting fog like sunshine. He turned away from it, grumbling to himself, refusing to give in to the tricks of his own yearnings.

"Stewart?"

The voice that called his name was not a cruel trick. Or at least Stewart didn't think so. It was real, as real as anything could be in a world where the clouds lay so close upon the earth. He knew what—and who—he wanted to see when he turned around. He reminded himself that it was impossible and scolded himself for being prone to fancies and warned himself that he was sure to be disappointed, but he turned nonetheless.

And found Aggie not ten feet away.

Stewart had told himself so many times that he would never see her again, he was almost beginning to believe it. Apparently he'd been good at deluding himself. A swell of emotion surged through him, and instinctively, he moved away from the rail and toward Aggie.

Until he remembered that she'd promised to publish a story so sensational it would eclipse even the news about the Queen's Jubilee.

The chill that pervaded the air penetrated Stewart's greatcoat and wrapped around his heart. "What the hell are you doing here?" he asked.

Aggie's cheeks were pale. Her hair was tied back from her face and hung down her back, a cascade of color wildly out of keeping with her dark jacket and skirt and the swirl of gray around them. The smudges of color under her eyes reminded Stewart of the sea. There was a metal handrail outside the square wooden structure that served as the captain's cabin, and Aggie held on to it for dear life, shuffling her feet and adjusting her stance with each roll and every wave so that it looked as if she was doing a sort of dance. Her hands were so tight around the railing that her knuckles were white. Still, she managed a sort of half smile. "I'm a stowaway."

She turned the smile up a notch and waited for Stewart to respond, and when he didn't, she let go of her death grip on the rail and ventured a few steps closer. "I had to come," she said. "I had to talk to you."

"More interviews?" What Stewart really wanted to do was take Aggie into his arms and kiss her until her head spun, but that was impossible. He did his best to remind her, and himself. "I thought you had it all. Everything you needed to make yourself famous and me infamous."

"I do. I do have it all." Her back to the cabin, Aggie slid closer. She reached into the pocket of her jacket and pulled out her journal. "It's all right here. And it wasn't until I was about to give it to Wallingstamp yesterday that I realized exactly what I had to do with it."

Without another word, Aggie shuffled across the deck toward the railing. She reached back and chucked the journal over the side.

Instinctively, Stewart reached forward to try and snatch the book out of the air. He missed and together, they watched the journal bob up and down on the crest of a wave.

As if nudged by an invisible hand, the journal flipped open and Aggie saw her own words as if they were written on the water: "In the Footsteps of the Shadow." She watched for a moment longer, wondering why she didn't feel worse to see the work of so many months disappear into the seafoam. But she didn't, and when she turned to face Stewart, she laughed at the look of utter astonishment on his face. "I should have done that a good long while ago," she said.

"But your story!" His brows low over his eyes, Stewart looked at the slate-colored water and flashing whitecaps. When he turned back to Aggie, the beginnings of a smile tugged at his lips. "You've drowned your story."

A wave rolled beneath them and the boat bucked. Aggie screeched in surprise and skidded across the deck, but even as she did, she knew she wasn't in danger. Stewart's arms went around her and he held her close.

"Aggie . . ." He looked down into her eyes, his own eyes sparking with the color at the heart of a sapphire. "Aggie, are you saying . . ."

"I'm saying there are some things more important than a story. I've come to learn that."

Stewart laughed. Just as quickly the sound faded, muffled against the fog. "It's not that easy. You still don't know everything."

"Don't I?" It was Aggie's turn to laugh. On the long railroad journey from London, she had put together all she'd discovered on her own with what she'd been able to cajole out of Trefusis. She had a whole picture now, one that made sense of everything, and she didn't bother to ask Stewart if she was right. She knew it. In her head and in her heart.

She stood on tiptoe and kissed his chin. "I know you lied to Sir Digby, but then, I knew that the night of the fire, didn't I? Not that it matters much. He got his way. Her Majesty no longer has to worry about the crown. And if I'm not very much mistaken, you got your way, too."

Stewart slipped his arms around Aggie's waist. "Sir Digby is a fine fellow. He'll never know the crown survived."

"And Maxwell Barclay?" Aggie asked.

"Barclay had no right to the crown in the first place. He didn't find it on an archaeological expedition as he claims. He stole it. He bribed a man to get hold of the crown. One of my men and—" Stewart swallowed the rest of what he had to say, but where before he'd always walked the fine line between what Aggie knew now was the truth and his honor, this time he didn't hesitate. He was not going to make another mistake and lose Aggie again. "There's more," he said. "If only you'll understand."

"I already understand." Aggie let her hands drift up to Stewart's shoulders. His coat was open, and she slipped a hand inside and flattened it against his chest. "I think if I were to look, I would see a purple dragon. Right here. Near your heart."

Stewart sucked in an unsteady breath and caught her hand in his. He twined his fingers through hers and pulled her nearer. "It was up to me to get the crown back," he explained. "And it would have been simple enough if you hadn't invented that damned silly curse. Then when you involved my brothers . . ." He lifted Aggie's hand and kissed each of her fingers, one after the other.

"Before you involved my brothers, it still would have been relatively simple. I would have told Sir Digby I'd never had a proper chance at it. But once my brothers knew I'd been to Barclay's, Sir Digby was bound to find out. I had no choice but to deceive him."

"And me?" Aggie frowned. It was not an easy expression to bring to pass, not when happiness rolled through her like the waves that rocked the boat. "Why did you deceive me?"

"I didn't want to," he said. The truth of his statement shone in his eyes. "I would have given anything if I hadn't had to. But . . ." He glanced out over the churning water in the direction they were headed. "There are things here older and wiser and stronger than either of us, Aggie. A king whose memory must be preserved. *Rex quondam rexque futurus.* When I pledged myself to serve his memory and guard his treasures, I also took a vow of secrecy. I swore I would do everything I could to champion his honor. As much as I wanted to tell you . . ." He looked at her again, his eyes as warm as the smile that lit his face. "I love you, Aggie. It's all that really matters. Now that you know the truth."

"You'll still be the Shadow, won't you?" It was an important question. Aggie realized it, even if Stewart did laugh. "I'd miss the excitement," she admitted. "And if I ever wanted to write something, you know, one of those incredibly romantic novels about—"

Stewart didn't give her the chance to finish. He kissed her so long and so hard it took her breath away.

When he finally pulled away, he was smiling. "I will still be the Shadow," he said. "There are plenty of treasures that need protecting, and besides, someone has to finance this place."

As he spoke, the boat slowed and the sounds of activity floated to them on the air. Aggie looked up to see that the fog was gone. The sky was the color of a robin's egg. The sea was as smooth as glass. Ahead of them lay Bardsey Island, a place of bold rocks and gentle green hills where the treasures of

King Arthur were said to be protected for all time to come by the Knights of Avalon.

On the dock, a handful of men waved and Stewart signaled back to them. There was a dark portmanteau on the deck beneath a wooden bench and Stewart opened it and lifted out Arthur's Crown. He held it in the air for the men to see, and a cheer went up. Aggie applauded, too, right before she caught her breath.

The sun shone full on the crown. It burnished the gold until it was blinding and glittered against the diamonds so that they looked like stars.

"It is a treasure," Aggie sighed.

"A treasure, yes. But not my most valuable treasure." Stewart pulled her close and kissed her, and again she heard a cheer from the men on the island. The boat scraped against the dock and Stewart wrapped an arm around Aggie's shoulders. "I have a house here on the island," he whispered in her ear. "If you'd like to see for yourself about that dragon . . ."

Aggie leaned back in the circle of Stewart's arms. She tipped her face to the sun that shone as brilliantly as the diamonds in King Arthur's Crown and smiled.

The golden orb that brightens the majestic skies over this great and glorious land heated her face and mixed with the distinct and quite extraordinary warmth that tangled around her heart. It was a fine, bright light, a light so striking and so clear as to reveal the path that had once been murky and was now true and straight and certain. It was a light that chased the shadows, one that showed the Truth in all its splendor: she was not meant to follow in the footsteps of the Shadow, but at his side. And in his arms. And in his heart. It was much the best place to be.

Dear Reader,

Diamonds and Desire follows *Devil's Diamond* and *Diamond Rain* as the third book in my series honoring Queen Victoria's Diamond Jubilee. The celebration took place in June 1897 and commemorated Victoria's sixty years on the throne.

Diamonds and Desire is a celebration, too, a celebration of true love, exciting adventure, and those wonderful eccentricities that made the characters in this book so much fun to create.

As I'm sure you'll agree, Aggie O'Day is a woman ahead of her time. She's a reporter for a sensational tabloid, a writer who creates fiction far more often than she reports fact. I have to confess, some of the most difficult writing I've ever done was Aggie's "In the Footsteps of the Shadow" story. The Victorians loved melodrama, and newspapers such as the one I created for Aggie were only too happy to give it to them. With Aggie's writing, I think I've used up my store of adjectives! I know I've depleted whatever purple prose might have been lurking in my computer.

Aggie is a special woman and she needed a special hero. Enter Lord Stewart Marsh. As Aggie learns soon enough, there's a lot more to Stewart than meets the eye. He's a man with a mission, and he's as single-minded and as brave and as charming as every hero should be. But Stewart is first and foremost a scholar, a man who values knowledge over beauty, truth over fiction, and ancient books over the pleasures of the world—at least until Aggie comes along. Together, Stewart and Aggie fight to save a treasure and discover that their love is a treasure all its own.

It was especially enjoyable for me to include the legend of King Arthur in this story. For as long as I can remember, I've been fascinated with Arthurian fact and fiction. From the Broadway musical *Camelot* to the archaeological digs at Cadbury in England, I am constantly intrigued. It's great to have a hero who shares my interest in the Once and Future King.

With every book I write, there are always people to thank: my readers who continue to let me know how much they enjoy my stories and the romance of Victorian England, my writing friends who teach me so much and help me as I work with my characters and my plot, my nonwriting friends who listen and offer support. As always, a big thanks to David, Anne, and David, too, the folks who understand when the dust bunnies grow to dust dinosaurs!